Countess of Stars

KIMBERLY CATES

CHAPTER 1

Twenty years was a long time to wait for the sword to fall, but Lucien Harcourt, 6th Viscount Everdene, could feel the cold blade of retribution against his neck.

The brigantine, *Aurora*, was sailing into London Harbor at long last.

He'd received the message soon after he arrived at his office near Whitehall that morning, a hasty note scrawled in his brother, Simon's, hand. From that moment, his world narrowed to the next hours and whatever waited on the other side.

He stared down at his desk, scarce seeing the sea of correspondence and notes on upcoming legislation. The missive seemed to have a life of its own. In the background, the sound of his best friend's voice had become a blur. Rhys Arkwright had arrived, God knew how long ago, and hadn't stopped talking since.

A sharp rap on his desk startled Lucien, and he looked up to see Arkwright's knuckles drumming the polished wood.

"Damnation, Luce," his friend complained. "Are you even listening?"

Lucien rubbed his temple. "I didn't sleep well."

"Do you ever? Your mind is like one of those infernal locomotives that are tearing across the countryside. I'm just never sure if it's careening into the future or ready to plunge off a bridge."

Arkwright shoved his hand through thick waves of tawny hair.

"You are dashed disconcerting to us mere mortals. When we don't sleep, we look like we've been dragged behind a coach—but you don't even loosen your cravat. You could at least have the decency to look a trifle disheveled."

"I am never disheveled." Lucien knew his dark hair had not a strand out of place. His perfectly tailored coat was as pristine as when his valet had helped him into it that morning. Everything in its place, no surprises...

"You've not attended a social engagement all week. The ladies are in full rebellion."

Arkwright shoved a newspaper across the desk and Lucien looked down at the cartoon displayed there. Cruikshank was at it again, his latest offering a caricature that was unmistakably Lucien walking the plank while crocodiles in wedding veils snapped all around him. The print read: *The Elusive Viscount E...*

Once, Lucien had been amused by the sobriquet with which the famed cartoonist had christened him. But the cartoons had taken on a nastier edge of late, and his patience with it all had palled.

"I can't imagine why the chits are so damned determined."

Arkwright shrugged. "You've made it clear you never intend to marry, and men aren't the only ones who like the chase. You're the tiger in Blake's poem, burning bright. The ladies long to 'twist the sinews of your heart.' But when they try to pet you, they realize just how dangerous you are."

Lucien's lip curled in disgust. "If I'm the dangerous one, why are all the women depicted as crocodiles?"

"Last night you didn't even show up at the club," Arkwright pressed him. "No potential bride would have troubled you there."

Which was why he'd all but lived at White's since he'd first come to London, partaking of its daily fare of cards, brandy, billiards, and conversation. The business of the kingdom was conducted there, and at political dinners in the homes of members of Parliament.

Once, he'd felt a surge of excitement, being sought after for the power of the Harcourt name, then, once he'd proved his own worth, for his sharp intellect and abilities.

But since his brother's renovation of the village at New Everdene, Tory landlords saw Lucien as a traitor to his class while the progressive Whigs were suspicious of his motives. Lucien couldn't blame them. His father, the Earl of Ravenscroft, was as ruthless a landlord as anyone had ever seen. Even now, confined to his secluded estate at Bitterne Tower, the old man was like Vesuvius looming over Pompeii.

"I decided to go to the fencing club instead," Lucien said. At least there he could see where an attack was coming from. The past two years had been a series of ambushes by shadows who disappeared into the dark.

He'd come home from the fencing salon with sweat dried on his skin, his arms and shoulders aching, so exhausted he'd thought he could sleep. He should have known better. Nights were too quiet. That was when the ghosts came. But they weren't ghosts, he told himself grimly. In truth, they never had been.

And now, they were coming home…

There was a flurry outside the office and it took all Lucien's will to keep his face impassive as the door burst open, revealing the tall form of his brother, Captain Simon Harcourt. Simon beamed with excitement, unrecognizable from the battle-scarred cavalry captain who had returned to England four years ago.

"Mother is waiting in the coach. They will be disembarking within the hour!"

Lucien rose, every muscle in his body tight.

"Who are 'they?'" Arkwright asked.

"My sisters," Lucien said, his voice precise enough to cut diamonds.

"Sisters?" Arkwright laughed. "You don't have any sisters. I've known you since we were at Eton and you've never once mentioned them. Where have you been keeping them? In a dungeon somewhere?"

Lucien met his gaze in silence.

Arkwright looked from Lucien to Simon and back again. "Jesus, Luce," he said uncertainly. "It was a joke."

But Lucien was already walking out the door.

It was time for the sword to fall. He only hoped the blade was sharp.

LUCIEN SAT STILL AS STONE ACROSS FROM HIS BROTHER AND MOTHER as his luxurious coach jolted over the cobblestoned roads. Simon could scarce contain his excitement, his body twitchy as one of the race horses he bred, his hair tousled and cravat askew. Their mother, Lorena Harcourt, Countess of Ravenscroft, leaned against her younger son, her gloved hands trembling where she clutched them in her lap.

Today would provide the last puzzle piece in the mystery that had begun to unravel two years ago when a carriage accident had nearly cost the Earl of Ravenscroft his life, drawing Simon back to the estate he hated. That act of fate had thrown the Harcourt family into a spiral that had ended in the revelation of secrets buried for twenty years, and a marriage of almost-unbelievable happiness for Lucien's brother. Lucien was still uncertain which of these events had infuriated their father the most.

What he did know was this: The impending reunion would mean healing for Simon and their mother.

For Lucien, it was shattered glass, cutting deep.

The instant the coach shuddered to a stop, Simon flung open the door, leaping out before a footman could attend them. He reached up and swung their mother down as if she were a young girl instead of a grandmother past her fiftieth year. Her gown of cornflower blue swayed like a bell.

"There it is, Mama," Simon exclaimed, wrapping an arm around the countess and pointing to the forest of ships that thronged the harbor. "I can see the Italian flag from here!"

Lucien waited for a footman to lower the step then alighted from the equipage.

The countess turned to Lucien. "The wait is almost over." Her hand moved toward him, then she let it fall to her side. She had been missing from their lives until three years ago. But even since their reunion, his mother hesitated before she touched him.

He put distance between them, sparing them both the sudden awkwardness. "We'd best hurry before they ferry passengers ashore," Lucien said. "I'll lead the way."

It was no effort to forge a path through the crowd. People from the lowliest dock worker to the high born gave him wide berth, motivated by equal parts awe and fear.

"Know who that is, ducky?" he heard a skinny sailor say to a doxy. "That toff all the fine ladies keep tryin' to snare."

Lucien leveled the pair a glare.

The doxy went goggle-eyed and they scurried off into the crowd.

When the Harcourts neared the brigantine, Lucien squinted into the sunlight. It was all a blur, people leaning over the ship's rail, searching for familiar faces. Women held gloved hands to their bonnets, gowns of every color rippling in the wind. Men stood like sentinels, sheltering them from the wind off the Thames as they waited for sailors to help them into the wherries that would bring them ashore. A drop of sweat trickled down Lucien's spine.

Could Cassandra see him from wherever she stood at the rail? Could Jane? All he knew was that his sisters were somewhere in that crowd.

Simon broke into his thoughts. "I wonder what they'll look like. I keep picturing Jane with jam on her chin, and Cass hiding that ratty blanket of hers from father. Do you remember, Luce?"

God yes, he remembered. She'd been clutching what remained of that blanket the night their world had fallen apart.

The image tightened around Lucien's chest like a vise until it was hard to breathe. His father's voice echoed in his head.

What do you imagine will happen when your sisters return? A heartwarming reunion? I don't suppose I will be included.

No.

Family…the tie that binds…Or chains you can't kick free.

His father's ugly laughter haunted Lucien as Simon spoke. "Look!" his brother enthused. "They're helping passengers onto the wherries to row them ashore!"

"So many lost years." Their mother's voice quavered. "I haven't seen the girls since they were in the schoolroom. I feared…prayed…" She clung tighter to Simon's arm, tears shimmering on her cheeks. Lucien's jaw ached.

The mocking voice echoed again in his head. *You think your sisters will welcome you with open arms? After what you did?*

A touch, tentative as butterfly wings, brushed Lucien's arm. He looked down to see his mother's gloved hand. She smiled up at him, something hopeful, vulnerable in the curve of her mouth. "I can't believe we'll all be together again."

The vise twisted tighter, crushing his chest.

I can't. Lucien thought. *I can't be here...can't do this...*

He pulled away from his mother's touch, scrambling for some reason, any reason, to get away. When he glimpsed a familiar figure disappearing into the customs house, he seized his chance.

"That is Sir Fred Whitby just returned from France." Lucien was already stepping away from Simon and their mother. "It's imperative I speak to him without delay."

His mother tipped her head to the side, bewildered.

Simon flushed. "What the devil?"

"You heard what I said. It's imperative—" *that I get away from here, away from this. I can't breathe...*Somehow he kept his voice level. "Simon, take mother and the girls in my coach and head to Everdene while I tend to business here. I need to discern what is happening on the continent. There are barricades once more in Paris, uprisings in Italy and Germany."

"I—I don't understand why you're bringing this up this now," his mother stammered. "That's still all far away."

"We've already had rioters in Trafalgar Square and flooding down Pall Mall, breaking windows. How much closer do you want riots to get?"

"You can deal with that tomorrow," Simon insisted. "Jesus, Luce. This is your *family*. You haven't seen them for twenty damned years."

Damned...Did his brother know just how apt that description was?

"I will come to Everdene Hall once Parliament lets out. I will see Jane and Cassandra then."

Simon grabbed his arm. "How the blazes are we supposed to explain..."

"It's been twenty years," Lucien said. "A few more weeks will hardly make a difference."

He caught a glimpse of his mother's gentle face beneath the brim of her bonnet, life's hardships etched deep. Their gazes met. Held.

Her lovely eyes filled with a deep knowing. His mother said gently, "Simon, let him go."

Simon's hand fell away, and Lucien felt a knife twisting in the hollowed-out shell where his heart used to be. Was some part of his mother relieved to be rid of him? Could he blame her?

She knew better than anyone who he really was.

The one who had betrayed them all twenty years ago.

CHAPTER 2

The little hellions were at it again. Grace Elliot stood in the doorway to the study observing her three younger brothers, Ethan holding an ink pot, Bennet's jacket decorated with a large smudge over his little belly, while Avery, at twelve, wielded a quill with fierce concentration, drawing a curly mustache on one of the rather alarming peacocks on their stepmama's beloved French silk wallpaper.

"It's the third mustache this week," a deep, familiar voice whispered to Grace. She turned to smile at Martin Pevensey the beloved butler who had served the Elliot family since before she was born. He wore his usual inscrutable expression but couldn't quite hide the twinkle in his eye.

Grace tucked a strand of brown hair behind her ear and sighed. "I know I should put a stop to their mischief, but one can hardly blame them. The peacocks are vastly in need of improvement."

Grace still felt a sick twist in her stomach every time she entered the hallway that had delighted her as a child. The lovely mural of mythical creatures and pastoral settings her mother had commissioned in the entryway had been blotted out by swaths of wallpaper flaunting a flock of garish peacocks. Papa and his new 'bride' had brought them back from their honeymoon on the continent. The trip had been cut short when revolution broke out in

Paris and Italy, but it seemed the newlyweds had carried the insurrection home.

Grace's brothers were in revolt.

The trio of nursery-room pirates had been turning The Willows upside down since their new stepmother had arrived at the Elliot country seat. Not that Grace could blame the boys for acting up, all things considered. The garish peacocks that had covered the once-tasteful mural that their mother had painted were just one of the changes confronted. Lord Vernon Elliot had eloped less than a year after his first wife's death, the precipitous union sending shock waves all the way to London. And no one had been more stunned than his only daughter.

After three years of her mother's illness and a too-brief period of mourning, this sudden flurry of activity felt like being roughly shaken awake and finding oneself still trapped in a bad dream. All five of the Elliot children were reeling. The childless widow who had wed their father had come from a quiet household. She hadn't expected boys popping out at her from behind drapes to catch their sixty-year-old father kissing his new wife with the ardor of a green lad, his cheeks flushed, silvery hair tumbling across his brow, gold-rimmed spectacles askew.

"He's acting like a beau in his first season," nineteen-year-old Will had complained when he'd arrived from Oxford for the holiday. "Mama would never act so foolish."

No, Grace thought with a fresh pang of grief. Their mother would have told them of hearing the great emancipator, William Wilberforce, speak and how she'd helped gather petitions that had overturned the slave trade. She had even named her eldest son in honor of the great man and urged her children to fight for justice, too.

The new Lady Elliot had no interest in the world beyond her doorstep. Her one desire was to make Papa *comfortable* as she so often insisted.

"Comfortable?" Will grumbled uncharitably after one such declaration. "Then stop changing everything."

Grace had to agree. Helen spent her days remaking The Willows to her liking, flinging up wallpaper, painting the rooms and rearranging furniture. Meanwhile, the Elliot boys had mastered the art of hiding bric-a-brac and returning furniture to its rightful place in the middle of the night—with Will's help, Grace suspected. When questioned, the culprits regarded their father and stepmother with the innocence of newborn lambs.

Maybe we have a ghost.

Yes. They certainly did.

Perhaps it was just as well the new Lady Elliot had locked the east parlor up tighter than the Royal Treasury since she had decided to hold her luncheon in that sunny room.

"I must say, the mustache is rather dashing." Pevensey's comment shook her from her musings.

Despite his efforts at levity, Grace couldn't muster a smile. "I'll be so glad when this luncheon is over, Pevensey. It's hard, watching her get out my mother's finest things. Even using the silver tea set the Benevolent Society engraved specially for her."

"No one could ever take your mother's place, Lady Grace. Or your own. All the servants say so."

Her eyes burned at the tenderness in his words, and she wished he could gather her in his arms as he had when she was little and sprained her ankle. But she was a woman of five and twenty, and had been mistress of the house during her mother's illness. Everyone was looking to her to make things right. She heard the unmistakable sound of Helen's voice and the click of heels descending the stairs.

The boys looked up in horror, saw Grace, then dashed past her into the study with a pleading glance.

She looked from the freshly inked mustache to Pevensey. "The table," she hissed, gesturing to the demilune that sat a few feet from the freshly decorated peacock. Pevensey leapt into action, dragging the table beneath it, while Grace snatched a tall flower arrangement from a pillar in a niche and set the flowers where the spray of gladiolas and lilies obscured the mustachioed bird.

Funeral flowers, she thought.

With one last conspiratorial glance, Pevensey walked one way, while Grace raced, breathless into the study, flinging herself into a chair and scooping up a newspaper. She hid behind it, focusing on the caricature on the front page of the daily as if, by will alone, she could make her stepmother walk past the study.

The Elusive Viscount E—who will snap him up first?

She'd been following the series of caricatures depicting her childhood neighbor since Cruikshank began it, and the thought of the arrogant, aloof Lucien Harcourt being chased by crocodile brides was the most diverting yet.

However, at the moment, her own vexation was at hand. Helen blew into the room like a sprigged muslin hurricane. "Oh, Grace!"

With an inward groan, Grace peeked over the top of her newspaper.

Corkscrew curls of faded blonde framed her stepmother's once pretty face. Age had softened the jawline and pressed fine wrinkles here and there that rice powder and rouge could not conceal. Her eyes were the gray of an overcast sky. Plump hands clutched at the blue velvet ribbon on which a brass key hung against a bosom like the prow of a ship.

"I've been searching all over for you!"

"Well, you've found me." The newspaper rustled as Grace set it aside.

Helen paused, regarding the publication as if it were a rat. "How can you bear reading that dreadful thing? I can't see why you'd wish to pollute your mind with matters that are so unwomanly."

"It's something Mama and I liked to do together," Grace said. "Mama always said it was absurd for women not to know what was happening in the world around them when their husbands, brothers and sons would be the ones sent off to war."

Tears glistened in Helen's eyes as they so often did when someone extoled the first Lady Elliot's virtues. Which, Grace had to confess, was often.

"Tell me, what is troubling you so?" Grace asked more gently.

"Oh, Grace! Such a calamity I don't know what to do!" Lady Helen twisted the ribbon until she was in danger of strangling herself. "Nanny has run off to the barber to have her tooth pulled."

No wonder her brothers had been up to no good, Grace thought. Helen was fortunate it wasn't worse.

"I hope Nanny is able to get some relief," Grace said. She pictured the round face of Nanny Bea as it had been of late, the sunny smile that graced the Elliot nursery tight with pain.

"Yes, yes, but *such* an ill-fated time! I spent all yesterday getting everything arranged quite perfectly for my luncheon in the east parlor and now Nanny has left the boys to run wild and my guests are due to arrive in an hour!" Her lower lip trembled. "Wilberforce refuses to aid me in my time of need. He insists he has another engagement."

No doubt he does since *you* insist on calling him by his full name, Grace thought wryly. He'd told Helen a dozen times to call him Will. There had been increasing strain since Will had come to visit from Oxford, and Grace was beginning to think it would be a relief when her brother headed to London to spend the rest of his holiday with friends.

"I would ask the maids to mind your brothers," Helen rushed on, "but I had such charming new uniforms made for them. You must think I'm a silly goose, fluttering around here like a new bride but I never wish to give dear Vernon cause to regret wedding me."

The fact that this bride was well past her fifth decade, and had been a wife of thirty years before the whirlwind courtship had brought her to The Willows, made this fuss feel a trifle ridiculous. Still, there was a desperate eagerness in Helen's actions that sparked Grace's sympathy as much as they irritated her.

"These ladies are most helpful with maternal advice," Helen said, fiddling with the key at her breast. "Especially Mrs. Kemble."

Neither Grace, nor her mother had had any patience for that pinched, judgmental woman, but from the moment Helen had met the vicar's wife, Ianthe Kemble had appointed herself the second Lady Elliot's bosom friend. She was the last person anyone should listen to when it came to children. The woman loved nothing more than finding fault with any spark of spirit or humor.

"Mrs. Kemble says if I take a firm hand, the boys will accept me in time," Helen continued. "Why, Bennet is so young, I'll be the only mama he remembers."

Was it possible that Bennet, who shared mama's smile, would forget how wonderful, how fierce and intelligent and wise Barbara Elliot had been? How much Mama had loved him?

Not while Grace drew breath.

She looked past Helen just in time to see the drapes moving in a most unnatural way, the shiny toe of a boy's boot peeking beneath the fringed hem.

Was Ethan still holding the inkpot? *Dear God, don't let him spill it.*

Grace rose and walked toward the door, to draw Helen's gaze away from her brothers.

"I'll be happy to take the boys for the afternoon," Grace offered, linking her arm with Helen's and drawing her out into the hallway. "I promised them an outing to the lake, and this is a perfect opportunity." Grace heard a muffled exclamation from behind her and prayed the boys would curb their enthusiasm until she drew Helen out of earshot.

"Oh, would you, Grace?" Helen beamed. "You are an absolute angel!"

No. She'd managed the perfect escape. This way she would not be expected to spend the afternoon smiling while curious neighbors gushed over the peacock wallpaper. Hopefully, none would get close enough to see the birds' new facial hair. Grace parted from Helen and was on her way upstairs to change into her oldest gown when she all but crashed into Will. Lean and lanky, he looked every bit the young thoroughbred, dressed for riding.

"So, you're abandoning ship?" she teased.

"I won't cancel my plans for another of Helen's crises!" Will declared, a mulish set to his jaw. "She's turned the whole house topsy-turvy for the past week and if I hear one more mention of her nerves, I vow my head will explode. Mama was sick for three years, and she didn't fuss half so much."

No, Mama hadn't said a word about her pain where Will or the other boys or even their father could hear...but there had been nights while Grace slept on the cot beside her bed when even laudanum hadn't helped. They'd held each other and wept.

"I *am* sorry to leave you to Helen's machinations, Gracie," Will said, tapping his riding crop on his gloved hand, "but it's every man for himself. There is some niece of Lady So-and-So that Helen wants me to meet, and I know what that means. If she has her way, she'll marry the two of us off and pack the wee lads off to school so she and the pater can dally in every room in the house." He shuddered.

Was he right? Words Helen had spoken when Papa had first brought her to The Willows echoed in Grace's mind. *I have always dreamed of being part of a large family.*

Helen had seemed sincere at the time, but an imaginary family and a real one were very different things. Flesh and blood boys seldom wore halos. If only Helen had not pushed quite so hard, or taken the boys' resistance to change personally. If only...she had been a little more like Mama.

"At least I'll be off to London with my mates in a few weeks," Will said. "But you'll be stuck here."

Grace rubbed her temple, weary, the future stretching out before her looking rather bleak. It was easy enough for Will to go on his way—as he should! But for her, it was far less simple.

"Promise you'll never leave us like Mama did..."

Six-year-old Bennet's words haunted Grace.

She drew a deep breath and looked out the window where the sun glistened over green fields. She would make today the best that she could for the brothers she loved. Seek out fresh air and fun in a place filled with happy memories, and maybe for just a little while they could forget their 'home' would never be the same.

———

THERE WAS NO QUESTION THE BOYS HAD BEEN PLOTTING MISCHIEF today, Grace thought as she watched her brothers firing mudpies at the forts they'd each built on the lake's shore out of branches and stones. She smiled from her cozy spot on a blanket beneath a tree, her heart swelling with love and a fierce protectiveness.

Bicorne hats folded out of the morning's newspaper perched jauntily on their heads. Small trowels and string trailed from over-stuffed pockets. Favorite toy soldiers were mounted on the battlements, or manning an armada of boats constructed of twigs tied together with twine, the wee ships enclosed in a harbor made of stones.

The lads were wound tighter than clockwork, racing about at an almost frenetic pace. Avery had that hard edge to his smile that Grace had learned to be wary of. Ethan wore a secretive look and Bennet wouldn't quite meet her eyes.

Thank heavens she had carted them far away from their step-mother's guests, and temptation. Here they could shout and wrestle and squabble with no one to tell them to hush, or objectionable peacocks to deface, no chairs where their mother had once sat occupied by someone else.

Grace felt a surge of freedom as well. She adored the simple dress her mother had always insisted she wear for such family outings, one of the few gowns that hadn't been dyed black for mourning. It had grown looser since she'd lost weight over the years of worry and change. She sucked in a deep breath, reveling in the fact she could even leave off her corset. But her respite was nearing an end.

The boys were getting tired. Their voices had that thread of querulousness she'd come to recognize. She was thinking of packing up the basket and warning them they'd soon go home, when Bennet came over and snuggled against her. He was a grubby mess, smelling of sweat and lake water and boy.

"Have you had a lovely day, sprig?" Grace asked.

"Except when Avery and Ethan said The Victory would lose our battle."

She smiled. Lord Admiral Nelson had definitely taken a beating over the past year. Bennet had even painted the tin soldier's coat navy blue, and the admiral practically lived in the boy's pocket. "I'm sure Nelson put up a gallant fight. Just think of the Battle of Trafalgar."

But it seemed Bennet was no longer thinking of the admiral's noble deeds. His mouth was a soft frown, and she saw his throat convulse. Was he having some twinge of guilt over whatever mischief he'd planned with his brothers? Or had the two older boys hurt his feelings somehow?

She looped an arm around his little body, felt the delicate bones of his shoulders. "What is troubling you, sweeting?"

Bennet paused for a moment. "Grace, did Mama look like me?"

The words were a sudden, surreptitious blow, but Grace kept her voice even. "What, love?"

He looked up at her with sad, solemn eyes. "That's what Nanny said, but I don't remember."

"You have Mama's eyes, and her smile. Your hair is a bit darker, like Papa's. But your nose is all your own." She touched the tip of his nose with her finger. "You know how you like to hum songs when you have a problem to solve? Mama did that, too. Sometimes, she'd creep to the nursery and stand in the hallway, just so she could hear you."

"I miss—" Bennet began, his words cut off by a sudden splash and a cacophony of shouts from the lake shore. She saw sticks floating in the water, Ethan and Avery shoving each other, red faced, angry.

"Avery! You just made it worse!" Ethan accused. "We'll never reach it now!"

"It's not my fault! The wind caught it." Avery shoved Ethan back and grabbed another stick, hurling it into the water, the waves it made nudging what looked like a small pale smudge further out on the lake.

"Boys! Whatever are you squabbling about?"

Ethan pointed to the object that was drifting ever farther toward the lake's center. "Avery stole the rocks from the harbor," Ethan shouted, "and Admiral Nelson floated away."

Bennet scrambled from her lap, wailing.

Grace peered out across the shining water. The boat was already a good ways from shore. Worse, Bennet's beloved toy was on board. Any second it could capsize, the lead soldier plunging to the lake's bottom.

"He's sinking!" Tears streaked Bennet's cheeks. "Grace, help!"

God, how many times had she seen that look—her brothers pleading with her to make things right. Things she couldn't fix for them, no matter how desperately she wished she could. But with this, at least she had a chance.

She hastily unfastened her frock, stripped to her chemise, then dove in, the cold water driving breath from her body. The boys gathered, frantic, on the shore, waving their arms as she struck out, swimming, keeping her eye on the floundering boat.

"He's drowning!" Ethan yelled.

"Save him! Save him!" Bennet shrieked, frantic. The tiny craft wavered, disappeared.

Taking a deep breath, she dove beneath the surface, praying she was not too late.

CHAPTER 3

*L*ucien had always craved the peace the first hours in the country offered, away from the crush of people, the thick coal smoke, the constant demands on his time, purse, and the decisions to be made.

But there was no respite to be had today.

Leaving his coach behind, he rode his favorite Turkoman gelding along paths he hadn't taken since boyhood. Even a condemned man was allowed solitude to make peace with his fate before he mounted the gallows, he told himself as he crested the hill. But when he saw the lake below, his whole body stiffened.

Children, he thought, grinding his teeth. Why did it have to be children today of all days? He could hear their shouts, glimpse hats made of folded newspaper as boys raced about in chaotic glory flinging something at each other, dodging, reminding him of his childhood, his sisters and brother…

He turned the horse away from memories hot as an iron brand, but before he could urge Atlas into a canter, the lakeside shrieks changed. Piercing, raw, with a hysterical note that sent chills down Lucien's spine.

"Help! Help!"

He wheeled Atlas back toward the lake, seeing three small boys clustered on the shore, one sobbing as someone near the lake's center thrashed wildly. Lucien glimpsed a flash of white face and arm. "Bennet! It's got me..." a feminine voice cried just before her dark head disappeared under the water.

Lucien swore and spurred his horse toward the lake at a run.

TRIUMPHANT, GRACE WAVED LORD ADMIRAL NELSON ABOVE THE water so Bennet could see his beloved toy before she dove beneath the surface again, indulging in a few moments of freedom. The glide of the water against her skin as she swam was a blissful release, all of her cares seeming to slip away in this glorious, weightless world. She could hear muffled sounds—the boys shouting, a splash that no doubt meant one of them had fallen in. With a hard kick she propelled herself upward, the lakeshore a blur through streaming water and a tangle of sodden hair. One. Two. Three. All boys safe on the shore. She grinned, made a show of splashing in the game they loved. "It's got me! Pulling me down!" She plunged under again, saw something churning toward her. What on earth? She instinctively started to kick away, but a strong arm shot out amidst a flurry of turbulence and clamped around her waist. Grace gasped in surprise, sucking in lungful of water. Her captor pulled her against a hard-muscled body, yanking her upwards. Her head broke the surface and she emerged coughing, sputtering. She glimpsed the harsh planes of a masculine face. She kicked harder, fighting to get free.

"Let go—" she tried to choke out, but his fingers only dug deeper into her waist.

"Quit flailing," a rough voice ordered just as the toy soldier in Grace's hand collided with the man's face. She heard a grunt of pain, but instead of loosening his hold, he held on, crushing her against him until she could scarce breathe. When he started towing her toward shore, she realized he thought he was saving her.

She'd be lucky if he didn't drown her instead!

Cheeks hot with embarrassment, she pushed one more time at his chest, but it was hopeless. When she could finally touch the lake bottom, she scrambled to get her feet underneath her, explain she was fine but couldn't catch her breath. As he dragged her up out of the water, her legs tangled with his. She stumbled and he caught her, tight in his arms. Her breasts flattened against the hard wall of his chest. The heat from his body burned through the barely-there covering of her chemise. Awareness jolted through her.

She pulled away and he finally let her stagger back a step. But her bare feet slipped in the mud, and she started to tumble backwards. He grabbed her arms with strong hands, steadying her.

Despite being half-blinded by her tangled hair, she knew where her 'rescuer's' gaze was fixed. The sodden muslin sheathing her body was all but transparent, clinging to her chill-hardened nipples. The man released her, but the damage had already been done. Every inch of her was visible. She hastened over to the cast-off frock that was pooled on the ground. Dropping the metal soldier, she scooped up the fabric, clutching it in front of her in a belated effort to hide behind her discarded clothing.

Fortunately, the boys didn't note her discomfiture. The little rogues were doubled over, laughing.

Grit from the churned-up water still blurred her vision as she turned back toward her 'rescuer.' His face was obscured behind one large hand as his fingertips explored the line of blood welling on his cheekbone.

Apparently, Lord Admiral Nelson's sword had found its mark. Thank God it hadn't been a little higher, or the man might have been missing an eye.

Sick with embarrassment, Grace fixed her gaze on the fabric bunched at her chest. "We were just -just playing a game. I'm so sorry for the misunderstanding."

He cut her off, his voice iron hard. "There was no *misunderstanding*. These lads were screaming for help. They said you were drowning." He gestured to the boys who huddled together beside their stockpiles of mud-pies.

"Actually The HMS Victory came apart, and, it was Lord Admiral Nelson who was drowning," she tried to explain. "I was being pulled under by our sea monster."

Oh, God. She sounded like a madwoman. Stiffening her spine, she craned her neck back and took her first full look at her rescuer. Ebony hair, eyes like blue flame, a blade-straight nose and lips curled in a scowl that could turn people into stone.

Oh, no. Not him. Anyone but him!

"L-Lord Everdene." Her voice came out in something resembling a squeak.

He stared in disbelief. She had never seen Lucien Harcourt shocked. Hadn't known he could be. But the expression on his face might have made her laugh—had she not been perishing from humiliation because he'd been staring at her breasts.

"I know you!" He pointed an accusing finger at her, and it was as if every misstep she'd ever made was writ plainly on her face. "Lady *Grace*."

The emphasis on her name felt like a slap. The boys in her childhood had often taunted her about it. She'd been awkward as a new filly, all elbows and spindly legs. Doubtless, Lord Everdene remembered just how pointy those elbows were. When the local dancing master had held fetes for his students, he'd always paired her with him. The result: Everdene had viewed her with cold disdain. She'd trod on his toes—on purpose.

But this was no irritated boy standing before her. Lucien Harcourt had grown into a formidable man. He stood, stripped to his shirtsleeves, the fabric of his soaked shirt clinging to every rippling muscle, his horseman's thighs encased in buckskin, his stockinged feet squishing in the mud. A lily pad drooped over one iron-stiff shoulder.

"At least your memory is intact." she said, trying to drag the tattered remnants of her dignity around her along with her dress. "Not only am I Lady Grace, I can swim perfectly well. My brothers and I were only playing a game. This was all a mistake."

"It was no *mistake*." He wheeled on the boys, his glare piercing. "You three tricked me on purpose. You watched me take off my boots." He looked at gleaming Hessians that now lay in a heap, caving in one wall of Ethan's fortress. "You boys had every chance to warn me off." The viscount took a menacing step forward.

Only then did Grace notice the clump of mud in Avery's hand. She started to shout a warning, but it was too late.

Avery flung the mudpie.

Grace watched in horror as it flew through the air, catching Harcourt on the right side of his jaw with a sodden smack. Ethan and Bennet followed their captain's lead, scooping up handfuls of mud as Lord Everdene stalked toward them.

"Stop! Ethan! Bennet! No!" Grace cried out as the missiles hurtled toward the viscount, striking him in the chest and thigh with alarming accuracy.

She dove between the boys and the man who looked ready to murder them with his bare hands. "This was just a case of boyish mischief," she pleaded. "Surely you indulged in some pranks yourself." She swallowed hard. Had he? At the moment he looked as if he'd never smiled in his whole life. "Or—or your own brother did so…" She was babbling, but he really was quite alarming.

She flattened her palm against Lord Everdene's chest, could feel his heart hammering, his muscles shifting. "I give you my word the boys will be made to see the error of their ways," she vowed. "I promise I will…"

"Flog us?" Bennet suggested, trying to be helpful. "Tie us to the yardarm?"

Ethan nodded. "That's what Lord Admiral Nelson would do."

"Enough, boys!" Grace cried, eyeing Lord Everdene warily.

With a fierce control more terrifying that simple outrage, the viscount stripped the soaked cravat from his neck, then used it to wipe the mud and blotches of blood from the wound on his face. His blue eyes seared lightning hot.

"I truly am sorry, my lord," Grace stammered. "We were just having an outing and my brothers got carried away with their game as children do. They had no idea who you were. I'm so sorry for the inconvenience."

"Inconvenience." He enunciated the word, sharpening each syllable as if it were a knife. "I have a vital meeting to attend at Everdene Hall and my horse has run off. Perfect. This is just perfect."

Grace swallowed hard. "If you come with us to The Willows, I'm sure we could loan you a horse."

"You have done quite enough."

Bennet and Ethan shrank back as Lord Everdene retrieved his boots, shaking off the dirt, then stuffing his sodden, stocking-clad foot into each one. As he yanked the Hessians into place, they made a wet, slurpy sound so like a bodily function that Avery actually snickered. Grace shot him a quelling glare.

"I *am* sorry, my lord. Boys, apologize right now."

There was a murmur that might have been an apology—or the first salvo in a war.

Lord Everdene snatched his very expensive coat from the ground, and with a parting glare, stalked off.

Grace stared at him until he disappeared from view, then she buried her face in her hands. After a moment, she spun around to face the three culprits who appeared far from contrite.

"Whatever possessed you to do such a thing? Fling mud at Viscount Everdene, no less?"

"He was shouting at you," Avery declared with a pugnacious tilt to his chin. "And he had mean eyes."

True enough. The look on the viscount's face could have matched that of any dragon.

She turned her glare onto the younger two. "Bennet and Ethan? What were *you* thinking?"

"Avery did it." Ethan looked at his brother and little Bennet nodded.

Exasperation welled up in her. "If Avery flung himself out of the tower window, would you boys do it, too?"

"Yes," Avery said, unrepentant. "But they'd try to jump farther and land harder."

"Gather up your things," she said. "We're going home."

She could only hope that her stepmother's luncheon had gone flawlessly. At least her brothers' talent for mayhem had been loosed far from The Willows. Perhaps Helen had been wise to lock the parlor's door.

A HARD EXPRESSION CROSSED AVERY'S FACE AS GRACE HERDED THE boys toward the servant's entrance, and she thanked God she'd gotten the lot of them out of the house before the guests arrived. If they were in luck, the luncheon might be over and Helen might have retired to her room to bask in her social triumph. She paused and looked around. There were no carriages visible.

Now, if she could only could get the wee rogues up the stairs before Helen saw them. She was desperate to turn them over to one of the maids to be bathed and dressed and hopefully barricaded in the nursery while she went to her bedchamber, sank into a hot tub and tried to scrub this day from her skin and her memory.

Not that she'd be able to forget the scene at the lake with Viscount Everdene. It felt as though Lucien Harcourt had imprinted himself on her body. Even now she could feel his chest, the racing of his heart against her breasts, his long, strong legs propelling them through the water as she sputtered, and desperately tried to break free, to explain…

What her stepmother would have to say about this little escapade, Grace could only imagine. Heaven help her if anyone else found out, she thought as the boys started squabbling beside her.

She turned to them, making sure she had their full attention, then put her finger to her lips. "We need to be very quiet, so no one hears us go in."

Bennet furrowed his little brow. "But Papa says we mustn't sneak." The other two nodded in agreement.

Now they find their conscience? She closed her eyes for a moment, took a calming breath, then chose her words carefully. "Just this once. Everyone has been so busy with Helen's luncheon we don't want to disturb them."

Avery shouldered his way in front of his brothers and Ethan shoved him. "Oww! You stepped on my boot!" he squawked.

Avery shoved back. "I did not!"

Grace sucked in a breath, thinking they were done for, desperate to calm the storm. "We're going to sneak into the house, as if we're spies carrying secret missives to the nursery. If we fail, Wellington will lose the battle of Waterloo."

Their eyes lit up. Bennet looked down at his toy soldier. Avery and Ethan put their fingers to their lips. Grace gave a silent sigh of relief then peered into the hallway. Seeing it was clear, she signaled for the boys to follow her in. Maids and footmen raced about, so harried they barely noticed the muddy, sodden crew making their way to the back stairs. But as Grace and the boys rounded a corner, they nearly collided with Pevensey, the butler more rattled than she had ever seen him.

"Lady Grace, young sirs." Pevensey scanned the lot of them.

Grace felt as if she were suddenly six years old and caught stealing jam tarts. She gave an apologetic smile.

Unperturbed, Pevensey directed them to the back stairs. "I will have baths sent up the moment the maids are able. And, Master Bennet, I took the liberty of placing your toad in a bucket in the scullery," the butler told the boy with tender solemnity. "It is, perhaps, a better home than a sugar bowl." The elderly retainer's eyes hid a twinkle.

"Toad?" Grace said, looking at Bennet.

"Poor Trevor!" he moaned. "I forgot all about him!"

"You what?" she queried, telling herself it couldn't be all that bad. Helen had kept the parlor key on the ribbon around her neck. There was no way the boys could have made mischief.

"I put him there for safekeeping when he crawled out of my pocket."

A growing sense of dread filled her. "*Which* sugar bowl?"

"Boys!" came their father's dooming command, reverberating from somewhere down the corridor. "Present yourselves. Immediately!"

Bennet cowered behind Ethan who huddled near Avery. It was Avery who alarmed Grace. He didn't look nearly surprised enough for comfort.

She followed the trio to the east parlor.

Helen was gathered in Papa's arms in the midst of the chamber she'd arranged so carefully. Broken china was being carried out on trays. Footmen tried to set fallen chairs upright. Flowers spilled from vases, like fallen soldiers after a battle.

Grace's stomach hollowed out. "The door was locked," she said more to herself than the other five Elliots. "I saw the key on a ribbon around Helen's neck."

"Tell your sister what happened," Papa boomed.

Not that she needed much illumination. Between toads in sugar bowls, the carnage of china and the absence of guests, she could well imagine.

Ethan looked up at her, always first to confess. "It was Avery's idea," he blurted.

Avery jabbed his elbow into his brother's ribs, but Ethan went on. "A maid left the window open to air the room and Avery boosted Bennet in."

So Bennet had dragged himself, belly first over the windowsill, Grace thought. No wonder he'd smudged the front of his jacket.

Helen dissolved into tears at the boys' confession.

Dismayed, Bennet ran over to Helen, flinging his muddy little arms around her and buried his face in her cream-colored skirts.

Obviously encouraged by the impact of his revelations, Ethan burst out, "And that's not all. Avery threw *mud* at a *viscount!*"

Helen's jaw dropped, her face paling. "Oh, no…"

Grace, feeling a stab of terror that Ethan would comment on her state of undress during the mud-pie altercation, broke in hastily. "Lord Everdene happened upon us at the lake and there was —was some confusion…" An image flashed into her mind, Lucien Harcourt's body, his

soaked shirt clinging to every muscle, a dusting of dark hair visible through the thin fabric, ending in a shadowy ribbon that arrowed down to the waistband of his riding breeches.

Grace hadn't expected to feel such a visceral reaction to the sight, but she and Lucien Harcourt might as well have been naked on that lake shore, two thin layers of linen between them, her breasts unbound, nipples puckered tight from cold.

"Everdene?" her father's voice jolted her from the memory, his face stricken.

Helen wailed. "You let them throw mud at the Earl of Raven- scroft's son? How could you let this happen, Grace? I'll be ruined for all society here! I must go to Everdene Hall."

"No!" Grace exclaimed in horror. If Helen discovered that Lucien Harcourt had seen Grace in her chemise, it would be the stuff of nightmares. The new Lady Elliot would merrily turn Grace into one more crocodile bride snapping at the Elusive Viscount's heels. "I'll make it right myself. I promise."

She pictured Lucien Harcourt, standing on shore, blood trick- ling from the small cut on his sharp cheekbone, the planes of his face so severe, even she had been a little bit afraid.

There was no help for it now. She would go to Lucien Harcourt herself. She would have to face the tiger in its den.

CHAPTER 4

*N*ever, in his wildest imaginings, did Lucien conceive he'd arrive at Everdene Hall atop a cart full of cabbages. He sat on the hard bench seat beside a farmer who smelled strongly of garlic and sweat, watching the rumps of weary shire horses as they plodded along.

He supposed he should be grateful the man had picked him up at all, since he looked like some unwary traveler who had been set upon by brigands. As it was, one stern glance had put an end to any questions the farmer might have ventured about his identity. The last thing Lucien needed was for word to spread that the fastidious Viscount Everdene had been seen in such a condition. He could just picture Cruikshank's next cartoon.

The wet stockings in his boots had rubbed his heels raw, his sodden breeches chafed, and the indignity of the entire situation felt like pouring whiskey over a wound.

Grace Elliot.

The expression on her face when she'd recognized him might have been amusing in any other situation. Those large, green eyes rounded with horror, her nose, sprinkled with cinnamon freckles. And that berry-red mouth falling open. Even as a child, she had been a calamity waiting to happen. If possible, the years had only made her behavior worse. And now she had accomplices. No rookery in the Seven Dials could have given rise to a more devilish gang.

The two smaller lads had taken steps back in the face of Lucien's outrage, but the eldest had met his most blistering glare with sheer defiance. And Lady Grace…she'd sprung between them like a lioness, shoulders squared, hand splayed on his chest.

He'd felt the wildness in that touch, something primitive, infuriating and irresistible that made him want…what? To haul her against him again, feel that unexpected heat.

Of all the distractions he didn't need right now…or perhaps it was exactly what he *did* need as the cart neared the drive that led up the hill to Everdene Hall. To think of anything but the reunion with his sisters.

The cart rolled to a halt at the foot of the tree-lined lane, the farmer nodding to his passenger. "Whatever business ye have at the manor, Captain Harcourt will take care of ye. A war hero, he is, and the best of men. Built a village finer than any ye've ever seen."

One Lucien was still trying to pay for during a time when too many English landowners were barely keeping their estates afloat.

"Aye," the farmer continued. "It'd be best for everyone in this borough if he was to be the earl, 'stead of that brother o' his. Viscount Starch-In-His-Smallclothes."

The muscles in Lucien's face tightened. Obviously, the farmer had no idea who he was speaking to. Lucien leapt to the ground, his boots giving an inelegant squishing sound. He pulled a sovereign from his rumpled coat's pocket, narrowing his eyes. "In the interest of quelling rumors," he said, placing the gold coin in the farmer's callused hand, "I don't require starch in my smallclothes. Only in my cravats."

The man's Adam's apple bobbed as he looked from the coin to Lucien. "Yer—yer pardon, yer lordship," he managed. "I didn't—it's just what other people say…Me wife is always warnin' me I shouldn't run off my mouth t' strangers."

"A wise woman."

"Aye. May Gor' bless ye with such a fine wife one day. I can drive ye the rest o' the way up to the house, yer lordship. I'd be honored."

Lucien glanced at the cabbages, then shuddered inwardly at the thought of being seen in such proximity. "I'll walk."

Hopefully, he could slip through a rear entrance without anyone being the wiser. Hooking one finger in the collar of his coat, he slung the crumpled garment over one shoulder then strode up the lane, the farmer's jabbered apologies following him until the sloshing of his boots and the pounding headache behind his eyes drowned out all sound.

Over the years, he'd been forced to visit the estate more often than anyone in his family, conducting business affairs long before Simon had built his stable here. During all that time, Lucien had refused to acknowledge the tightening in his gut whenever he first glimpsed the red brick towers and creamy gold columns of the Tudor era county seat. Echoes of sins past…

But today's arrival was different. He ground his teeth as he saw two horsemen in front of the sweeping stairs that led to the grand front door. Simon sat astride his cavalry mount, Brutus, while Simon's best friend and partner in the stables, Jamie MacLeod, rode a golden mare. Lucien's own winded gelding stood nearby, a village lad holding its reins.

A cluster of women looked on. Lucien didn't need to draw nearer to know who they were.

Simon's wife, Penelope, their small son, Christopher, called Kit, in her arms, and two other women, something achingly familiar about their golden curls. His sisters. One of them pointed down the lane.

Simon's gaze lit on Lucien and he froze, then swung down from the saddle, passing the reins to the village lad. It was the longest walk of Lucien's life, striding toward them, the dried mud on his body cracking, sticking cloth to his body. He reeked of lake water and fish.

Lucien's jaw knotted as everyone stared at him.

He'd been bracing for this meeting with his sisters like a man anticipating the surgeon's knife. When last he'd seen them, Cassandra had been fifteen, Jane twelve. They had been girls. Now they were women. Cassandra had grown, tall, the fine bones of her face reminding him of a cat, her eyes tip-tilted and keen. An edge sharpened her beauty, as if to remind the world that she had claws sheathed beneath velvet.

Jane was her opposite, delicate and ethereal in a petal-pink frock. She stood just a little behind Cassandra, regarding him with the wide, wary eyes of a shy, woodland creature.

Simon's voice jolted him out of his thoughts. "Luce…We were just about to go out looking for you," he said. "What the devil happened? Tripp found Atlas running loose and brought him here."

What could Lucien say? *I dove into a lake to save a woman who didn't need saving? I was duped by three boys bent on deviltry? I made a fool of myself and ended up with a nearly nude woman in my arms? And, by the way, did you know that that scrawny Grace Elliot has the most lush breasts I've ever felt?*

He cleared his throat, trying to banish that last thought from his mind. "A minor mishap," he said with a wave of his hand. "Don't mind it." He did his best to attempt a somewhat cordial look toward his sisters. "Cassandra, Jane, perhaps we could postpone our greetings until I'm properly attired. This is hardly the way I intended our first meeting to go."

Cassandra looked from the top of his damp hair to his sodden boots. "I don't know. I rather like it. Considering how long I've been waiting to see you again, brother, it seems somewhat fitting, don't you think? After all, we left Everdene precipitously, and, if I recall…we didn't get to properly say goodbye."

The spark of satisfaction in her smile stung.

"We did not," he said, sketching his sisters a bow, only then aware of another figure in the shadows.

Cassandra beckoned the woman forward. "Paola, this is the brother I told you about. Lucien, my maid, Paola Vincenci. She has been kind enough to accompany me through all of my adventures."

The hot suns of Italy had turned the woman's complexion olive, her hair thick and black. Her nose was a trifle hawk-like, but what struck him most was the silken patch that covered her left eye, the ribbon that held it in place scarlet. Her remaining eye narrowed until it glittered like a sliver of jet.

"I am in your debt for seeing my sisters safely to England," he told the woman, then turned to his family. "I will see you all at dinner."

"Perfect," Cassandra said. "That will give us the opportunity to discuss guests for the dinner our dear Simon's wife is being gracious enough to host for us on Friday."

Penelope's cheeks flushed as she looked at Lucien. "I thought it would be nice to have some old acquaintances to welcome Cassandra and Jane home, if you've no objection."

"Everdene Hall is yours in all but name now. I urge you to do as you wish." They'd had a rocky beginning to their relationship when Simon first courted her, complete with threats Lucien had issued to Simon's future wife in an effort to keep family secrets hidden. Things were better between them, but there was still a distance he could not quite bridge. If the estate hadn't been entailed, Lucien would have signed it over to his brother in a heartbeat. Payment for grief caused.

Penelope regarded Lucien's cheek with a worried expression, the babe in her arms tugging at the bodice of her gown. "There is a cut on your face."

"I'm fine," Lucien answered more sharply than he intended. The babe started to cry and Lucien felt like a right bastard. He resisted the urge to reach out, touch his nephew's small back. Lucien's hand was filthy. Better to let people who knew how to soothe a child comfort him. Eight-month-old Kit had plenty of those.

Thank God, a voice buried deep in him whispered.

He turned and walked through the front door, one wave of his hand sending servants running to heat bath water and bring him brandy. Then leave him alone.

THE HOUSE GREW EERILY QUIET AS GRACE PUT HER BROTHERS TO BED. The staff was exhausted from preparing for the luncheon and the drama afterwards. The boys, scrubbed until they were pink-skinned from their baths, snuggled into their beds, their hair soft and silky against their pillows, their nightshirts smelling fresh from the wash.

They looked like little cherubs, Bennet's arm clutched around a stuffed horse, Admiral Nelson on the bedside table to stand guard against any nightmare that might creep in. Grace could only hope the toad was still confined in a bucket somewhere.

"Grace?" Bennet caught her hand as she bent down to kiss his forehead, his voice so soft, tentative.

"What is it, sweeting?"

She heard his breath hitch. "Promise you won't leave us 'cause we're wicked."

Her heart squeezed. How many times had her littlest brother begged her for just such a promise? "You aren't wicked," she soothed. "You're just full of high spirits. You must make amends for what happened today like an honorable gentleman, but I know that you will. And there is nothing you could ever do that would make me stop loving you."

"Mama left us." Bennet's brow furrowed. "Promise you'll never leave us like mama did."

She wanted to promise him the world, anything to drive back that haunted curve to his mouth, a grief no child should bear. And yet, she measured her words with care. "Sometimes things happen we can't control. Mama was sick. She didn't want to leave you. I promise I'll stay as close as I can, and I'll always be with you in my heart."

She sat beside him, his small, warm hand in hers until his breath softened, steadied, his fingers relaxing in sleep. Gently, she tucked the coverlet up to his chin and brushed a kiss across his brow.

Drawing a deep breath, she went down to the dining room to face her father and Helen. As she entered the room, she saw her father at the table, only two places set, just as it had been before Helen had come along. She felt a twinge of wistfulness.

"Helen is not joining us?" Grace asked as she slid into her chair.

"No." There was something unnerving about that single word. She braced herself, sensing they were on unsteady ground, a new tension showing in her father's brown eyes.

Grace sipped watered wine from a crystal goblet. "Papa, I know the boys made a mess of things. I promise, I will take the situation in hand."

He gazed at her tenderly, a little sadly. "My dearest girl, you have carried far too much responsibility on your young shoulders for too long. You have been invaluable to me and to your brothers during your precious mama's illness, and our grief after her passing, something for which I will be eternally grateful. But I have not been entirely fair to you."

"Not at all! I—"

He cut her off with a wave of his hand. "Helen has helped me to see that harsh truth. You were in the midst of your first season when your mother became ill. I'll never forget your delight, the two of you planning beautiful gowns, chattering about balls and beaus for half the night through."

Grace's eyes misted. How many times had she sifted through memories of those magical days. Visiting modiste's shops, receiving nosegays and invitations. That heart-pounding moment when the dance partner she longed for approached from across the room. She could see herself garbed in a rose-pink gown, feel Mama's hand brush back a curl that tumbled across her brow. *Oh, my beautiful girl. Look at you! You are perfect.*

Her mother had been the only one to think so.

She tucked the memory away.

"All of us changed our plans once we knew Mama hadn't much time left," Grace said. "The little boys didn't go off to school."

Papa shook his head. "That is not the same. Were it not for us, you would have married Neville Freyne and likely be a mother by now."

She had a vague memory of an earnest face, waves of golden hair, the cool slide of a ring on her finger. "Papa, please don't blame yourself. I wouldn't change it."

"Perhaps not, my dear, but I would. In your mother's absence, everyone here at The Willows has looked to you for guidance. The servants. Your brothers. They continue to do so. It is unfair to you and…," he hesitated, "to Helen, as my wife."

Grace couldn't quell the resentment that sparked in her chest.

"It is time for you to go back out into the world," her father said. "I've discussed it with Helen, and you will go to London for the season. You shall have a whole new wardrobe, enter the social whirl as you should have done. Most importantly, Helen has a young man in mind for you to meet, a cousin she thinks would suit you. He owns an estate near Inverness."

Her gaze sprang up to meet her father's. "In Scotland? But that's so very far away."

"It is. But I've heard it's lovely there."

A wave of bitterness washed over her. Will's warning before the ill-fated trip to the lake echoed in her ear.

If Helen has her way, she'll marry the two of us off and send the wee boys away to school...

She recalled the clasp of Bennet's hand, his pleading gaze as he begged for her promise. She stared at her father, feeling betrayed.

Was it true what Will had predicted? Would their father send his children away from the home they'd always known? Be relieved when they were gone?

*I have to think of something to stop this...*Grace thought, her heart squeezing. *Mama, what can I do?*

CHAPTER 5

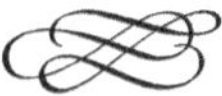

Are you certain you won't come with us?

Simon's urgings from earlier that morning haunted Lucien as he wandered the echoing emptiness of Everdene Hall.

We can make room in the coach.

That might be true for almost anyone else, Lucien thought. But if he had joined the other Harcourts on their visit to their old nurse, the luxurious space would have filled with suffocating tension. The walls closing in as they had whenever he entered the room where his family gathered.

No. It was better that he remained behind to deal with the one complication only he could resolve: What the devil to do about their father, the Earl of Ravenscroft.

Thus far, the earl seemed ignorant of his daughters' return.

But, at some point, he would hear the news, even exiled as he was to the isolated estate of Bitterne Tower. And when he did…

Lucien stalked to the window and peered into the distance at the empty space where a collection of thatched roofs and a church spire had once been visible from the manor house—the village that had been razed at their father's command. Thanks to Simon and Penelope, a New Everdene had been built elsewhere to house the displaced tenants. But Lucien had often caught his sister Jane staring in horror at the place where the old village once stood, evidence of the earl's willingness to lay waste to lives upon a whim, just as he had shattered his children's world twenty-odd years ago.

Lucien twisted the signet ring on his finger, the Harcourt motto pressed beneath his thumb. *While I am vigilant, I am safe.* He'd failed to keep his sisters safe years ago. He would not fail them now.

He needed to attend the small party Simon's wife, Penelope, had planned with just a few trusted guests to welcome Cassandra and Jane home and acclimate them to their new surroundings. If he left for Bitterne Tower as soon as it was over, surely that would be soon enough to warn the earl away?

Lucien was startled from his thoughts by the sound of a coach coming up the drive. A sudden jolt shot through him, as if, just by thinking of his father, he could summon the devil. But the coach was unfamiliar. One more annoying interruption. He was turning to instruct the servants that he was not to be disturbed when he saw a flash of heart-shaped face and rosewood colored hair framed by the coach window.

Lady Grace.

He didn't want to feel that kick of recognition in his chest or feel himself drawn to the door as if by an invisible thread. And, yet, that is exactly what happened.

By the time he stepped outside, Lady Grace had handed something to the footman and leapt lightly to the ground.

Today, she wore a blue and white striped day dress with soft, bell-like sleeves and a straw bonnet trimmed with silk buttercups. Wind tugged at curls that peeped out beneath the brim, the tendrils a changeable mix of brown, auburn and a hint of deep gold. A locket dangled from the blue velvet ribbon about her throat, the delicate oval cradled in the hollow between winged collar bones. The glint of sunlight on gold drew his gaze down to where full breasts filled her bodice. Suddenly he pictured her as he'd seen her last—soaking wet, her chemise clinging to her body, outlining every curve.

After their encounter at the lake, he knew the shape and feel of those breasts far better than any man save her husband should.

"Viscount Everdene," she said, dipping into a curtsey, not a hint of shyness or uncertainty in her face. One had to admire her courage.

"Lady Grace." Lucien bowed stiffly. "To what do I own this unexpected pleasure? After our encounter by the lakeshore, I hardly expected you to appear on my doorstep."

A dimple flashed in her cheek. "Actually, I am only here as a chaperone." She rapped on the side of the coach and three small boys edged out. Garbed in suits of solemn black, they clumped together.

"Avery, Ethan, and Bennet are the ones who have come to see you," she said, gesturing to each lad in turn. They might have been facing a tribunal, their faces as sober as it was possible to be when one was plagued with a button nose and cowlick.

Avery took a round tin from the Elliot's footman and stepped forward. The cloth covering it rustled slightly. "My lord, we're here to apologize for throwing mud at you, and to bring you this. It's to show how very sorry we are."

The two youngest Elliots looked appropriately repentant. The eldest—Avery—did not. There was a subtle tilt to his head that made Lucien question his sincerity.

Lucien took the peace offering and peeked beneath the cloth as if expecting to find a rat trap. Instead, he found what appeared to be a rather lumpy pastry.

"Grace says this is penitent pie," Ethan added. "Full of berries Grace made us pick for hours!"

"You needn't worry, my lord," Bennet assured him. "Grace watched us every minute. Even if we wanted to put pebbles in it, we couldn't have."

The reassurance should have been more comforting than it actually was. "Thank you," he said, then muttered sotto voce, "I think."

"Grace, did we apologize well enough to see the horses?" Bennet asked hopefully, then turned a pleading gaze to Lucien. "She said if we were very sorry, we could visit the horses. I brought this, just in case." Bennet dug into his coat pocket and produced a lump of sugar with bits of lint clinging to it. He held it out to Lucien with a sticky hand.

"I hope you don't mind," Grace said. "We saw a groom working one of your beautiful horses when we drove up. The boys were entranced."

The trainer in question was Simon's friend and partner, Jamie McLeod, no doubt. After years in the army and being a prisoner of war, the Scotsman had no more use for company than Lucien did. He never spoke of what happened between his capture and his stunning return from the dead. It remained a mystery. Those years left him with little patience for anything, save the exotic horses he and Simon were determined to breed in England.

Lucien handed the pie to the footman. "Take this to the kitchen with strict orders that no one is allowed to cut into it but me." This caused Bennet to grin as if given some sort of culinary accolade. The truth: Lucien wasn't risking someone breaking a tooth—despite the assurances he'd received. He turned back to the lads and gave them the stern look that had sent members of the opposition into full retreat. "Do I have your word as gentlemen that there will be no more flinging of mud, or waylaying travelers?"

"Yes, my lord," the boys chorused.

"Then you may go to the paddock if your sister allows it. Do not make noise or startle the horse," he warned sternly.

With a chorus of whoops, the three bolted off.

"So much for not making noise," he observed with a grimace.

Grace sighed and toyed with the ribbon streamer on her bonnet. "You'd think they'd be exhausted. I made the wee rogues pick the berries themselves, and they groaned the entire time because I would not allow them to eat their harvest."

A tender, wistful expression softened her face. Lucien took it in, the peach color on her high cheekbones, the freckles dusting her nose. She'd eschewed gloves, he noticed, and there was a purple stain on one knuckle. Berry juice from the pie, he deduced. He had an absurd impulse to raise that hand to his mouth and suck the juice off.

He shook himself inwardly. He wasn't the kind of man who went about licking young ladies' hands willy-nilly. Not even those of his former mistress. What the blazes was wrong with him? Taking stern hold of such impulses, he withdrew his handkerchief and offered it to her. "Lady Grace, something seems to have spilled on your hand."

She looked down. "Oh, bother! The piecrust was leaking on the way here. The jolting of the carriage, you see. I was holding the pan and didn't want to spoil my gloves, so I stripped them off."

She dabbed at the mark ineffectually with the linen square, then turned her face away, to hide what she was doing. But Lucien still glimpsed her raising that stain to her lips, her small, pink tongue dampening it before she wiped the juice away.

His throat went dry. He searched for a way to change the subject before the front of his breeches became an embarrassment. To his great relief, Grace turned toward the stables.

"I'd best keep an eye on my brothers so they don't get into any more mischief," she said. "I'd hate to see one of them climb up on those remarkable horses you and your brother raise. Perhaps you could keep me company until I can tear them away? Unless, of course, you're too busy."

He was. Busy. Always. He made sure of it. He certainly didn't have time to be chasing after a pack of rambunctious boys who threw mud pies at those unfortunate enough to cross their paths. One shuddered to imagine what they might find to launch at him in the mews.

"I could say I will accompany you to put a damper on any wild schemes," he said, and they fell into step together. "But..."

"My lord?" she said, looking over at him.

"The truth is, you pique my curiosity. After our disastrous encounter at the lake, most ladies of my acquaintance would either hide any time they saw me or cry ruin."

"Ruin?" She laughed, and he felt a strange sensation, as if he'd just taken that first drink of superior brandy. He wanted more. "You could hardly ruin me with my three brothers looking on!" she said. "As for hiding...Mama taught me to always face mistakes instead of pretending they don't exist."

"I attended several dinners with your late mother when I first came to London. Not only did Lady Elliot have one of the finest minds I've yet encountered, she was happy to tell members of parliament they were making mistakes."

She stopped for a moment, toying with a small gold locket at her throat. "Mama never shied away from speaking her mind when it came to important causes. I only wish others would follow her example." Her smile grew wistful. "How I miss her."

Lucien drew back a step, the ache in those words chafing him.

"As for mistakes, her theory was that everyone makes them," Grace said, unaware of his discomfort. "It's what you do afterward that matters."

The words hung between them. Lucien did not know what to say.

"To that end," she continued, "I made certain my brothers understood the error of their ways. After all, you *did* believe I was drowning and dove in to save me. It was very gallant of you, really. Had the situation been different, I would have owed you my life."

"To be fair, you were thrashing about as if you were in distress."

"That was the sea monster's fault."

Lucien shook his head, thinking he'd misheard. "Sea monster?"

"It's a game we play. Loch Ness has one," she quipped. "Why not our lake?"

"Perhaps Loch Ness has one because Scots are a trifle mad."

Lines appeared between her winged brows at his words and he wondered if she disliked Scots. When they reached the paddock fence, she looked at her brothers, the shadow deepening in her eyes. He felt an unexpected urge to banish it. "You must admit, one hardly expects a lady of noble birth to be creating such a scene," he said.

"I suppose that is true. I've been told that my behavior was beyond reproach until my mother died. After that..." She swallowed hard. "I would do anything to make my brothers smile. The best way to get them to romp about again is to join them. In the beginning, I did so for them. But as time passed, I found taking part in their antics delightful, freeing after so long in a sick room."

Lucien raised one brow. "You find ice cold lake water delightful?"

"No. But I adore my brothers' laughter. So much better than the silence of mourning." She paused, staring out across the field at the horse and trainer. "Perhaps you have heard that my father remarried?"

"I had heard something of it," he replied. Rather precipitately after his first wife's death, from all accounts.

"The elopement was quite...unexpected."

Lucien could hear so much unspoken in her hesitation. "Has the adjustment been challenging, to have a new person in charge of the household?"

"Our stepmother is a widow who never had children of her own. Since her arrival, the boys have gotten a bit out of hand. Our encounter at the lake was only the first of the day's events."

"I shudder at the possibilities. What, pray tell, was their grand finale?"

She spun out the tale, the luncheon with the vicar's wife, the open window, 'ghosts' moving furniture.

Lucien didn't want to be amused, but her words painted the picture so vividly it reminded him of Simon many years ago. For once, in ways that didn't cause pain.

When she finished, he gave a sympathetic nod. "One can always depend on family to throw things into chaos."

"Oh, undoubtedly. But also, to love you, even when you are putting toads in sugar bowls and flinging mudpies. Perhaps *especially* when you are flinging mudpies."

His brows drew together as he tried to sift through what she'd implied. "Did you say toads in a sugar bowl?"

"I did."

He couldn't help but smile at the thought.

"There, now!" She clapped her hands, startling him. "I've won my wager with Avery."

"What wager is that?"

"You *do* smile! It's just a bit like a shooting star."

Lucien shook himself inwardly at the absurd comparison. "Shooting star?"

"It's rare, and you have to be watching to see it or *snap*, it will be gone. I am quite an expert on the subject as it happens. Shooting stars, not your smiles. It began when mother was ill, and we spent many a long night peering out the window. When we imagined what might come after life, we weren't satisfied with harps and angels, and decided if the heavens were to be her next residence, we should become familiar with it. We began studying astronomy with the boys. We even chose the star that she would wait upon, so they could see it winking and know she was still watching over them."

He was charmed in spite of himself. He looked across at the three boys and added more gently. "Your brothers are fortunate to have you. My mother has always loved stars as well," Lucien said. "She has a room we call the Sky Chamber, painted blue, with gilt stars on the ceiling."

Servants had accidentally put his father there after the carriage accident that had nearly cost him his life, that location setting in motion events that had turned the world of Everdene, its tenants, and the Harcourt family on end.

Only he knew why those servants had placed his unconscious father in that chamber. And damned if Lucien would enlighten anyone.

"I remember that room from when I was a child," Grace exclaimed. "The stars were arranged in constellations, weren't they? I wanted to paint some on the nursery ceiling for my brothers, but my father would not allow it."

A slight breeze wafted her scent toward him, sunshine and meadow grass. Natural, real, warm.

"I'm afraid I'm quite chattering on," she said. "It's been a very long time since I've spoken to anyone save my family."

Lucien followed her gaze to the paddock where the three Elliot rapscallions clustered.

McLeod sat astride the mare, Titania, the horse's rare golden coat shimmering like liquid metal. Dainty round hooves seemed barely to touch the ground as she changed leads, her neck arched, cream mane flowing. Avery and Ethan stood on the bottom rung of the gate, transfixed, while Bennet balanced on the top, every muscle in his small body seeming to strain toward the horse.

"I know my brothers seem incorrigible, but I believe boys—like horses—need a deft hand to civilize them, without breaking their spirits." She smiled at her brothers, so warmly it made Lucien's chest feel tight. He wanted her to smile at him that way. "Wait until you have a son, my lord."

"I have no intention of doing so." The words slipped out, sharp edged.

"But you're a viscount. You will need to provide an heir."

"My brother is busy filling the Harcourt cradle."

Green eyes regarded him askance. "So, you are expecting your brother to do your sums?"

"Pardon me?"

"Avery used to do that with Ethan until I caught him. He'd bribe Ethan to do his maths so he could run out to play." She levelled Lucien a teasing look that gave him a glimpse into the elder sister she was. "It's called cheating."

Lucien's shoulders stiffened. "Compromises need to be made in certain situations," he said crisply. "My family is nothing like yours."

"Not many families are. At least as we were before." A soft sigh stirred the lace at her breast. "It is painful when families change. But then, you know that as well as I. It was no small thing when your sisters left."

You have no idea, Lucien thought grimly.

"I wrote to Jane, but she never answered," Grace said.

"She and Cassandra were sent to aunts in Italy. They are recently returned to Everdene."

Grace's eyes sparkled. "Jane and Cassandra here! Oh, I would so love to see them again!"

"They have gone to Galen's Well for the day, the place where my mother resides, but my brother's wife is having a house party over this weekend. Dinner on Friday night then hunting Saturday morning if the weather holds. Perhaps you would care to join us?"

He made it sound casual, and yet he wanted Grace to be there. Wanted it with a fierceness that was inexplicable. "Your brother is invited as well," he added to dispel the uncomfortable sense of intimacy between them.

She slanted a merry glance up at him through thick black lashes. "Avery, Ethan or Bennet?"

He arched one brow. "I'd prefer the only Elliot brother who hasn't doused me in mud."

"Why, I think you made a jest, my lord." Her smile lit up her whole face. He experienced a pull of desire deep in his chest. Suddenly he felt as if he were back on the lake shore, the swells of her breasts against his chest.

"I think calling me 'my lord' is becoming absurd," he said. "Call me Lucien."

Where had that come from? Nobody called him Lucien except his family. But then, *she* had. The Grace of his childhood, merely copying the informality of his siblings.

"You may use my name as well—" She looked at him a trifle sternly. "As long as you don't use that taunting inflection that always made me want to slap you."

"You should have done it." He grimaced.

She smiled, her lips teasing, tempting. "I would love to join your house party for the weekend," she said. A dimple peeked out and he felt an urge that astonished him.

What would she do if he claimed those berry-sweet lips? It would be madness to do so. Yet, he couldn't help but think what the weekend house party would bring. Friday, she would be just down the hall from his bedchamber.

A mistake waiting to happen.

CHAPTER 6

"*I* wish you would not go."

Irritation flickered in Grace at the sound of her father's words and she looked up from the valise Will was loading into the carriage.

"Papa, it is decided."

IIis brow creased and he peered over the rims of his spectacles. "You could plead a headache or some female complaint."

Helen *tsked* and placed a hand on his arm. "Haven't we been urging Grace to go out in society? Now she has secured an invitation to a most exclusive party my friends will all envy. We can hardly deny her this chance."

"But the Harcourts are known for some havey-cavey doings," Papa hedged, twisting a button on his waistcoat and pulling it askew. "The countess vanished for decades, then suddenly reappeared. I cannot help but be concerned."

"Captain Harcourt is a war hero and raises some of the finest horses in England," Will insisted, chafing like a Thoroughbred waiting for the starting gun. "His wife is a trifle odd, meddling in architecture and his brother, the viscount is less than amiable, but the Harcourt sisters are earl's daughters! They will go about in the best society."

Papa flushed. "That earl—"

"Lord Ravenscroft is a recluse on some distant estate," Helen soothed, straightening the mussed waistcoat. "Besides, Wilberforce will attend the house party with Grace. If there is any questionable behavior, he can fetch Grace home straightaway."

"Papa, I am going and that is the end of it," Grace said, straining to have patience. "The Harcourt sisters and I were great friends before things went awry between you parents. Whatever you argued about was a long time ago. Surely, Jane, Cassandra and I should not be punished for it."

Before her father could argue further, Bennet tugged on Grace's skirt. "You *will* be home to check under the bed for monsters tonight, won't you?" The expression in his large green eyes hurt her heart. It was the first time she would be gone overnight since their mother took so ill.

She cupped Bennet's cheek. "No, little man. You might ask Stepmama to do it."

Avery made a scoffing sound.

"For shame, boys!" Helen scolded. "You great big lads mustn't be selfish. You can't expect Grace to be tied to the nursery forever! She needs to have a husband and babies of her own."

"She doesn't want them," Ethan said stoutly.

Avery's chin tipped at a pugnacious angle. "She has *us*."

"I will be back to tuck you in on Saturday night." Grace reassured them, but she fidgeted with the strings of her reticule. True, she had her brothers, but did she want babes of her own? A husband?

She had dreamed of having her own family once. Sometimes she lay awake, imagining what it might have been like to share Neville Freyne's bed. But now, it was Lucien Harcourt's face that flashed in her mind.

"Grace?" Bennet's piping voice drifted up to her. She shoved such absurd imaginings from her mind as her littlest brother beckoned her to lean down. Cupping his palm around his mouth, he whispered in her ear, "Do you think your reticule is big enough to bring me cake?"

Grace grinned. "I am sure of it."

"Promise?"

"I promise. Now, you mustn't fret." She ruffled each boy's hair in turn then bestowed a kiss on her father's cheek. "*Any* of you," she admonished sternly. "I will be back before you know it."

Steeling herself against the cluster of long faces, she let Will hand her into the coach. He climbed in after her, sprawling against the squabs as the coachman set the horses in motion.

"Father looked ready to lock you in a tower until Helen intervened," Will said, his lanky body taking up as much of the space as possible. "Makes you wonder what all the fuss was about long ago, doesn't it? As to the Harcourts, I mean. Mysterious disappearances. That strange business of a perfectly good village being torn down." He waggled his eyebrows. "Perhaps we can find out what really happened."

"Please, Will, don't pry. And for heaven's sake, *move over!*" She tugged a fold of her skirt from beneath his leg.

"Don't you wonder what happened?" he asked as she smoothed the crumpled fabric. "One moment the countess is every tenant's dream of the perfect mistress, the next, the whole family disappears from the county. I tried to wring information out of the pater, but he's a sphynx, except for harping that I am to watch over you. I told him there is no reason to worry. That dashing Captain Harcourt is already wed, and the viscount is far too stern for your taste. Might as well be made of stone."

She thought of the feel of Lucien Harcourt's body against hers. Sinew and muscle, elegant bones and strong hands. Definitely not stone. A shiver went through her at the memory of those moments at the lake.

Yet, as intense as that experience had been, it was the next time she'd seen him that haunted her. The way his dark hair had been precisely in place, the lines of weariness—wariness—in his severe face. The unexpected jolt in her chest when he smiled.

"Think how you feel when everyone starts asking about Papa and Helen," Grace pleaded.

That actually seemed to affect Will. He scowled. Plenty of people had plied them with questions about their father's courtship, speculating that the affair had been going on even before 'dearest Barbara' had died. *The marriage was very sudden, was it not? Barbara was ill for such a long time. Even the best of men have needs...*

Grace's stomach knotted, and she shoved that question away,

focusing on the party to come. Lucien Harcourt, Viscount Everdene, was not 'the best of men' by anyone's account. He was a hard-edged, ruthless nobleman, with a physique all too tempting—combined with the aphrodisiac of power, an irresistible mixture to many women.

And Grace wanted to see him again.

LUCIEN WAS *NOT* WATCHING FOR GRACE ELLIOT'S ARRIVAL. HE WAS merely taking in the fresh air and talking to his brother about horses while the household prepared for the party he dreaded to the marrow of his bones. Two dozen guests would be attending, including Penelope's loquacious sisters, Fanny and Kitty Waverly, Rhys Arkwright and a few assorted neighbors Lucien would rather not see. And now his mother had been detained in Galen's Well. Some business with the hospital she was patroness of. Not that he could complain about the party since Penelope was serving as hostess and he had not provided the estate with a viscountess.

No, he'd not been waiting for Grace Elliot, but as he and Simon returned from the stables, there she was in the Everdene garden. She looked like springtime in an airy white muslin frock, trimmed with green ribbon, her silk-covered bonnet exactly the color of her eyes.

When she saw him, she dipped in a curtsy. "My lord, it is good to see you again." She smiled, that damned dimple peeping out. "Did you enjoy the pie?"

"Very much," he replied, trying to forget that he'd thought of her with each bite.

"I have just been taking in your lovely garden while my brother Will is getting settled in his room. The brother who *doesn't* throw mudpies, as you requested."

Lucien sent Simon a quelling glance before he could ask questions.

Grace continued blithely. "You may prefer the mud-throwing ones once Will starts pestering you about horses."

"I highly doubt it," Lucien said, then gestured to Simon. "Lady Grace Elliot, you may remember my brother, Captain Harcourt."

"Of course, I remember you!" She clasped her hands in delight. "I'm glad I can finally congratulate you both for what you have accomplished with New Everdene. My mother would have been so impressed with the model village Lord Everdene has built here on the estate."

"It is wonderful, isn't it?" Simon enthused.

"My brother and his wife are the force behind New Everdene," Lucien interjected quickly.

"Then they are to be congratulated. But it is your estate, is it not? You must have approved the project."

"Must I have?" Lucien gave Simon an arch look. He was not about to regale her of the real story of the village and the consequences that followed, consequences that had nearly severed his bond with his brother forever.

"We have more ideas for improvements." Simon's eyes held that enthusiasm for such projects that Lucien had learned to be wary of.

Lucien's lips thinned, as always, the one who had to make practical sense. "Improvements will have to wait. All estates are struggling."

"Of course, they are," Grace said, her eyes warm with empathy. "It's no wonder, between crop failures and political unrest. In Ireland, it's worst of all, with the potato blight. I keep hoping parliament will help them weather the disaster. The people are starving but there are shiploads of grain leaving Irish ports every day."

Lucien had made enemies pressing for just such relief.

Grace tilted her head. "My lord, you are looking at me strangely. Has a bird landed on my bonnet?"

No. It was what lay beneath that bonnet that intrigued him. Not her pretty face, not even those berry red lips, but her mind. "You surprise me, my lady. I was not aware young ladies such as yourself were aware of challenges in agriculture or political matters."

"Then, perhaps you are not speaking to the right ladies," she said, squaring her shoulders. "Not all women waste time chattering about fashion and gossip when important matters need attending to." She shook out her skirts with a militant air. "Now, if you gentlemen will excuse me, I'll retire to my room and send my brother to see your horses. He's been talking of nothing else."

She curtseyed again, then disappeared into the house. Lucien twisted the signet ring on his finger. Suddenly, the impending evening didn't seem quite so bleak.

THE PARTY HAD BEEN A MISTAKE. THERE WERE TOO DAMNED MANY people. Lucien watched his sisters from his place across the room.

He'd done his best to draw the men away. With every gruff masculine greeting, Jane shrank deeper into the corner of the peach-and-cream striped settee as if she longed to disappear entirely. Cassandra mounted guard at her side, the fierce expression on her face sending the women edging away. Even Penelope had vanished to answer a summons from the nursery.

And Lady Grace—she was nowhere to be seen. He was considering sending a servant upstairs to knock on her door when she swept into the room, looking more than a little exasperated. Her curls were a bit mussed, her cheeks flushed. He went to her at once, surprised to feel some of his tension ease.

"You're late," he said.

"I am sorry for the delay, my lord," Grace said, tucking a wayward tendril behind her ear. "My brother insisted he would come to my room and escort me down. Apparently, he forgot."

She leveled a wry glance at the youth who was engaged in a heated discussion with Arkwright over some bare-knuckle fighter he'd seen. Lucien would have been happy to climb into the ring with The Crusher himself to escape his present circumstance.

Lucien frowned. "I do hope your father has arranged for a capable bear-leader to keep your brother out of trouble when he comes to London. The way he instigates arguments, it will be pistols at dawn before a week's out."

"I hope father engages someone wise to watch over Will, too."

Before he's fleeced at some gaming hell or falls prey to some doxy, Lucien added silently. After years of trying to stop Simon's reckless antics, Lucien knew the possibilities were endless.

Grace scanned the room, observing the clusters of uncomfortable guests and Lucien's sisters, wary and withdrawn. "Where is your sister-in-law?" she whispered.

"Penelope? The nursery. Apparently, the child is wailing and has a fever. Teeth are involved."

She gave him a chiding look. "If you had sharp teeth cutting through your tender gums, you'd expect whiskey or laudanum. The comfort of his mother's arms is little enough for a babe to ask. Let us see what we can do to salvage the evening."

He felt a surge of relief at her words and guided her toward his sisters. "May I present Lady Grace Elliot," he began.

"We need no introductions," Grace exclaimed, eyes shining. "Welcome home, Cassandra. And Jane." Grace went to his shy younger sister and reached out her hands. "Oh, my dear! How I have missed you!"

For a heartbeat, Jane hesitated, staring down at Grace's upturned palms, then carefully joined hands with her childhood friend. Lucien watched in astonishment as Jane smiled, a smile more like that of the little sister he remembered than he'd yet seen. Envy jabbed him. What would it be like to bestow affection on his sister so freely? To have Jane welcome it?

"Grace…" Jane said softly. "You are the person I—I most wanted to see in England. Besides Mama and Simon."

Did Grace notice she'd not included him? Lucien wondered.

"I'm glad to see you as well," Grace confided. "I confess, I was a bit nervous about this party. I feel very strange being out in society after so long."

"*You* have not socialized?" Cassandra demanded.

"Not for three years, since my mother became ill."

Lucien watched his sisters' faces. He could see what Grace was doing—building bridges between them, putting them at ease. Gratitude made his throat feel thick.

Even Cassandra softened a bit. "I heard of Lady Elliot's passing. I am very sorry."

"Thank you. I attempted to go to several parties when she first got sick, but I spent the whole time worrying about her. Between that and the ceaseless questions about her health, it was too jarring."

"Yes," Jane said barely above a whisper. "It seems very…noisy here." She glanced around, as if the slightest movement might bring some calamity down on her.

It hurt Lucien to see it, made him want to shield her, be the barrier between her and the rest of the company as he might have when they were small.

But damned if Grace hadn't already maneuvered herself so that the curious strangers were no longer in Jane's line of vision. Clever woman, Lucien thought with admiration.

"I cannot wait for us to have a comfortable chat like we used to," Grace said. "Remember the lovely times we had driving your pony cart? And that time our mothers took us to the linen drapers in London and we went to Gunter's for ices."

Lucien saw Jane's eyes brighten. "You were never able to eat yours. Those awful apprentices flung a kitten into a fountain and you splashed in to save it. Your mother didn't scold even though your frock was ruined."

"The ungrateful beast scratched you terribly," Cassandra cut in.

"It is hard to tell who is friend or foe when you're drowning and afraid." Grace slanted a glance at Lucien.

Something in those words impelled him to sketch a bow and join Simon, Arkwright and the other men as they talked about races Everdene horses had won and the latest news of revolution on the continent. Still, Lucien couldn't take his eyes off of Grace Elliot.

Even once Penelope returned to her duties as hostess—a patch of something he feared was drool on her crumpled bodice—Grace remained the warm center to which others in the room were drawn. Arkwright seemed charmed, as well.

Lucien's eyes narrowed as he saw his friend lean near her, heard her laughing.

"Poor Everdene got stuck with me as a roommate at Eton," Arkwright said, pulling a face. "He couldn't shake me, though God knows, he tried. I've been eager to meet the woman who got Viscount Everdene to actually issue an invitation. He *did* invite you? Personally, I mean. Or is it a scurrilous rumor he devised just to taunt me?"

"Yes," Grace said, with a laugh. "His lordship invited me."

"How did that miracle come about?" Arkwright asked. Lucien disliked the purely masculine appreciation in his friend's eyes. "You *are* uncommonly pretty, but he's had diamonds of the first water hurling themselves at him for ages. The notion of Everdene inviting a lady to a party is so uncharacteristic, I almost summoned a physician when I heard."

Lucien barely stopped himself from doing the unthinkable and tugging at his own cravat.

"His sisters were my friends when we were children," Grace explained.

"Ah, so you and Everdene—"

"Were decidedly not," she supplied, her dimple appearing. "I tromped on his toes during dance lessons. Mostly on purpose."

Arkwright shot Lucien an obnoxious grin. "I understand the urge completely. Perhaps we can get one of the ladies to play the piano forte so you can demonstrate."

"I'll play!" Penelope's youngest sister, Kitty, cried rushing to the piano.

Of course, the chit would play, Lucien thought. Like most women, she never missed a chance to display her talent. The problem would be getting her to *stop*.

"Do you know a country dance so we can all join in?" Grace asked Kitty. When the girl nodded, Grace turned to Lucien's sisters. "Come, Jane and Cassandra! Remember what fun we used to have dancing?"

"A capital idea!" someone else exclaimed. As others began to pair up, Arkwright led Grace to the open space on the floor.

Suddenly, Lucien found himself striding over to where Grace and his friend stood. "Since this demonstration is to display our past encounters, Lady Grace, I will be your partner," he said.

"Really, Everdene—" Arkwright started to tease, then stopped, with a strange expression. After a moment, he stepped away and bowed. "As you wish." Arkwright went to ask Jane to dance, but not before Lucien caught the hint of a smirk on his friend's face. Lucien would remember that the next time they crossed swords at the fencing academy.

As the dancers gathered, Grace looked up at him, and he noticed a small emerald twinkling in the tender lobe of her ear.

"I do hope your boots are sturdy, my lord," she teased.

"At least they aren't doused in mud." Lucien glanced down toward his gleaming footwear, but his gaze snagged on the vee of her bodice. A cluster of pink rosebuds was pinned to the lace between her breasts. The scent wafted up to him, warmed by her skin. He took his place with Grace at the head of the set of dancers, a primitive thrumming in his blood.

The first notes rippled out a spritely tune and they began the familiar steps. As a girl, Grace had been awkward, or perhaps his own impatience with the lessons had made her so. Now, she was light as thistledown, her face suffused with pleasure, as if she were savoring a confit after being deprived for far too long. He met with her and separated, whirling in the figures they had practiced years before. Every time they joined hands, he felt an urge to pull her closer than necessary. When she linked arms with Arkwright further down the line, Lucien counted the minutes until she returned to him.

The chilly aura that had plagued the room began to thaw as the music cast its spell. Even his sisters seemed more at ease with no one trying to make awkward conversation. Skirts whirled in bright colors. Fanny Waverly made a misstep, then recovered and laughed. When the dance ended, she pulled her skirts to one side to display a torn flounce.

"Let's go to the retiring room," Grace offered. "I have a great deal of experience pinning up troublesome hems." The other women followed her, the men seeking refreshments. Lucien drew apart from the rest of the company, peering out into the darkness.

He should have guessed Arkwright would follow him.

"I trust," his friend said, "that you didn't take offense at my bit of flirtation earlier? Everyone was so grim I was only trying to lighten the mood. It was never my intention to poach on your preserves."

"Don't be a blockhead. There is no preserve to poach."

"In any case, Lady Grace is lovely. I remember her now from her first season. She got engaged to some fellow or other. The Honorable Neville Freyne, I think."

"Engaged?" Lucien echoed, his mood souring once again. "What happened?"

"Their betrothal fell through. I'm not sure who jilted whom."

A rustle of gowns and soft feminine voices sounded in the corridor, nearing the doorway.

"Freyne just returned to England after spending time in the

colonies, I think," Arkwright said under his breath as the ladies flowed into the room. "Something about factories and investments…"

Fanny Waverly's enthusiastic voice broke through Lucien's disordered thoughts. "I would give anything to study art in Italy, Cassandra! Did you see the great masters?"

"Yes, in spite of the nuns."

"Nuns?" someone echoed.

"Convents usually have them," Cassandra said. "That is where we lived in Italy. But I wasn't about to be cloistered. I would climb over the wall and run away to the museums. My friend Paola would meet me there with my paints and sketchbooks so I could make copies of my favorites."

Paola, Lucien thought. The maid with the eyepatch.

"How deliciously romantic!" Kitty Waverly exclaimed.

"Until you get murdered wandering the streets alone," Lucien muttered under his breath.

Fanny clasped her hands to her breast. "I'd give anything to go to Italy for art lessons."

"I intend to continue my work here," Cassandra told her. "Penelope has helped me make a studio out of a room with good light. There are easels and paints and fresh canvas—everything an artist could ask for."

Penelope looked at Lucien as if to say *just as you ordered*.

"My completed canvases arrived yesterday from Florence."

"Perhaps we can hang some of your work in the gallery or entry hall to make this feel more like your home." Penelope said warmly.

"That would be *perfect*," she said.

Cassandra's lips curled in an unsettling way, but Lucien's focus was on Grace. "Shall we continue with another dance?" Lucien said. "A waltz."

———

A WALTZ.

Grace startled at the low command in Lucien's voice.

As Kitty returned to the piano, he strode toward Grace and

bowed, his blue eyes fixed on her in a way that made her feel like she had been tippling punch.

If that was the way he looked when asking for a dance, it was no wonder every woman in London was flinging themselves at his feet.

An exquisitely tailored coat of black superfine fit him to perfection. His waistcoat of claret silk gleamed, his snowy-white cravat crisp beneath his square jaw. She felt the urge to thread her fingers through his hair, muss it, just a little, to prove he was not quite so perfect as he seemed.

She stepped into his arms and their surroundings faded. He splayed his right hand on the curve of her back, the warmth of his hard palm penetrating the thin fabric of her gown. Kitty played the first strains of something by Schubert, and Lucien took hold of Grace's hand, drew her close. So close she could feel his breath feather against her cheek as they began to whirl about the floor.

"My lord, you surprise me in your choice of dance," she managed to tease, her heart hammering. "If I recall, you loathed waltzing when we had lessons."

Something intense fired in his eyes as he peered down at her, and she felt it all the way to her toes.

Those bone-meltingly sensual lips parted, but before he could speak, the sounds of harried voices could be heard above the strains of music—some kind of disturbance sounded in the entryway. The sound of agitated servants grew so loud Kitty struck a discordant note and fell silent. The guests stumbled to a halt and exchanged confused looks. "A late arrival?" someone guessed.

Lord Everdene's hand dug into her waist so tight she knew it would leave a mark. His shoulder tensed beneath her fingertips like iron cords as the music faltered and he jolted to a stop. For a heartbeat, the handsome planes of the viscount's face turned stark, vulnerable. In the next breath his countenance was stone. The door burst open, a man of about sixty entering the room.

Jane shrank back. Cassandra raced to her side.

The Earl of Ravenscroft strode toward his daughters, his face suffused with unholy pleasure.

CHAPTER 7

$\mathcal{E}$ven as a child Grace had disliked the earl. Ravenscroft had loomed over every occasion, crowding people, his booming voice obliterating what anyone else had to say. In the ensuing years he'd become a rather frail old man, but he'd obviously not lost his taste for making a grand entrance.

Lord Everdene dropped his hand from Grace's waist and moved toward his father. "What are you doing here?" His words seared through the room like lightning.

"An acquaintance informed me that my daughters had arrived at Everdene Hall and there was a party being given in their honor. My invitation must have gone astray."

Simon moved beside Lucien, blocking the earl's path.

All night, Lucien had looked severe, never truly at ease. But, now, as he faced the earl, his whole body exuded something almost frightening.

Someone had to break the awful spell that gripped the room. Grace approached the earl and dipped into a curtsey. "Good evening, my lord. I fear you will not recognize me without a doll in my arms. I am Grace Elliot from The Willows."

She'd hoped to defuse the situation, but her words seemed to heighten the tension. The earl's eyes took on a shrewd glitter. "That interfering Lady Barbara Elliot's chit. I've no desire to renew our acquaintance."

His gaze fixed on his daughters like the point of a blade. "Cassandra. Jane. Come greet your father as obedient daughters should."

Simon's teeth set and he moved as if he wanted to grab the old man by the collar. But Lucien put a hand on his brother's arm, nodding to the other people gathered around.

"This *family reunion* should be conducted in private," Lucien said with a tight smile. "If our guests will excuse us."

Cassandra cut in. "Perhaps the company would like to visit my studio before we Harcourts retire. Now that father is here, I am even more eager to display my paintings—see if he thinks the art lessons he supplied were worth the expense." She turned that cat-eyed stare on the earl. "I painted one in particular with you in mind."

The earl's nostrils flared in disdain. "By all means, let us see my daughter's *works of art*. And then I might finally meet my grandson."

He hadn't met his own grandchild? Grace tried to comprehend it. The child was eight months old.

"Impossible," Simon ground out the word.

What was happening here? Grace felt as if she'd walked in midway during a very disturbing play. Jane was trembling. Grace went to slip her arm around her waist. Lucien shot her a glance so grateful it shook Grace to the core.

The crowd flowed up the stairs, following Cassandra, the earl between his grim-faced sons. At the door to the studio, Cassandra held up a hand.

"Wait here until I light the lamps. The first impression is always the most important." She slipped into the room and partially closed the door. Grace stole a look at the earl and his children. She remembered her own father over the years. Papa was not perfect, but she'd never once doubted he loved her or the boys. Or that Papa loved her mother, in spite of what gossips might say. The earl's sons regarded him as if he was their enemy. One daughter was so frightened by his presence she was trembling. The other...

Clinks and rustling sounded inside the studio, then light began to glow. At last, Cassandra bade them enter. The room was lined with canvases in various stages of completion.

Cassandra Harcourt was gifted. That was Grace's first impression even before Penelope's art-loving sister, Fanny, began to exclaim. There was passion in the brushstrokes, power.

But it was the canvas on the easel in the room's center that arrested Grace's attention. Cassandra had clustered branches of candles around the painting, as if encircling it in flame, the image so powerful it took Grace's breath away.

A half-naked dark-haired man sprawled on his back, while two women held him down. His mouth gaped wide in a silent scream as one woman wrenched his head back to expose his throat, while the other prepared to slash it with a knife.

"The original is far better than my copy," Cassandra said. "But the subject pleased me."

"What is it called and who painted it?" Fanny asked, mesmerized.

"*Judith Slaying Holefernes.* It was painted by a woman. Artemisia Gentileschi."

"You've done a remarkable job," Grace said staring in fascination. "My mother and I read about Artemisia. She was the first woman admitted to the *Accademia di Arte del Disegno* in Florence."

Cassandra arched her brows in approval. "Very good, Lady Grace. But Artemesia's skill wasn't the thing her contemporaries remembered most about her. She was raped by her father's apprentice, Agostino Tassi, and the court tortured her with thumbscrews to try to get her to recant her accusation."

"How awful." Grace shuddered, curling her own fingers into her palm.

Cassandra's gaze fixed on the earl, her last words chilling Grace to the bone.

"Her father watched."

THE BRUTAL IMAGE COMBINED WITH CASSANDRA'S WORDS HIT LUCIEN like a fist. From the instant his father had burst through the door, he'd wanted to drag the earl out of Everdene Hall and send him to hell or Bitterne Tower. Now, more than ever. But that was impossible with the guests looking on—which was how the scheming earl had planned it. The last thing Jane and Cassandra needed was another cruel attack by their father.

Lucien took Simon's arm, saying under his breath, "I'll deal with father. Keep Jane and Cassandra and everyone else the hell away from him."

Simon nodded and Lucien stepped to the earl's side.

"My lord, I need to speak to you on an urgent matter regarding the estate," Lucien announced. "Alone." Cassandra started to argue, but Lucien's pointed glance at Jane stopped her.

"We can talk after dinner," the earl insisted.

"No. You and I will conduct our business while the others retreat to the dining room."

He thought the old man might defy him. Their eyes locked and he realized that if the earl made a scene he would remove him by force if he had to.

The moment seemed to teeter on a razor's edge until Grace broke the fraught silence. "The smells wafting from the kitchen are divine!" she said, starting to herd the other guests toward the doorway with Simon and Penelope's help. "I am sure we are all growing hungry after so much dancing."

At the doorway, she paused and glanced back at Lucien. He shot her another grateful look then retired with his father to the study. Once inside, he closed the door and locked it.

"Still determined to play my jailer, are you?" The earl took the chair behind the large desk where Lucien conducted the business of the estate. Another calculated maneuver—seizing the seat of power.

"What are you doing here?" Lucien demanded.

"I am an old man," the earl said with deceptive innocence. "Is it so strange that I want to see my daughters before I die? I am their father. *Your* father."

"You gave up your rights when you sent Cassandra and Jane away twenty years ago. You've done enough damage."

"What about your own part in this little drama? Your mother and Simon may be weak enough to forgive you, and Jane...she would cry for a bee that died after it stung her. But Cassandra...ah, now, she is a different matter. She knew how to hold a grudge from the time she was born. And she resented you even before you gave her such good reason to. She would have made a formidable political ally out of Thornsby if she'd wed him as I planned. But no. Your mother had to meddle."

"Cassandra wasn't even fifteen yet."

"The girl had steel in her spine for all that. You know as the others never will that ruthlessness is required if a man is to lead."

"Which is why I'll do whatever is necessary to keep my sisters safe." Lucien struggled to keep from clenching his fists. "I am summoning your coach and you are leaving Everdene Hall before the others finish dining."

"You would send your father out onto the open road in the middle of the night? How will you feel if I am killed by brigands or the coach plunges off the road?"

"You should have thought about that before you came here. I won't have you sleeping under the same roof as Jane and Cassandra."

"A little late for you to play the great protector, is it not?"

The old man's verbal riposte drew blood, but damned if Lucien would let him see it. He forced his voice to remain cold, calm. "We had an agreement that I would be responsible for the Harcourt estates and you would remain at Bitterne Tower."

"Yes, yes." The earl waved one heavily beringed hand. "If I refused to comply, you would reveal my machinations to the ton and drown the Harcourt titles in scandal. But the title will be damaged anyway. There are rumors you have made certain comments regarding the Irish question that are most disturbing for a landlord and peer of the realm. My former allies in parliament consider you a traitor to your class. You are making dangerous enemies."

"Are you one of them?"

"Your sister might be. It was not just my head she was imagining on that platter. The last year she was at Everdene Hall your mother even moved you to separate rooms to put an end to your fighting."

Yes, they had squabbled. Cass had been furious that he was taking father's side in their parents' conflicts.

Now he knew she'd been right.

"My issue with you is that you've not provided an heir."

"Simon has a son."

"One he won't even let me see! Simon and that wife of his are no more capable of raising a peer of the realm than they are of flying. You know full well that a future Earl of Ravenscroft must be raised from the cradle to bring honor to his name. By the time you were five years old you'd learned to respond to my directions with alacrity. Do you remember?"

God, Lucien wished he could wash himself clean of the memory. That strange, heady sensation his father had fostered in him, that Lucien was marked by fate…special in the eyes of the world…and in the eyes of his demanding father.

"Until the title is secured to my satisfaction, I will continue my interest in everything that affects the Harcourt name." The earl's gaze bored into his. "Marry, get your wife with child, and my interest in your sisters will wane. Until then, I will do as I see fit."

Of course, Lucien couldn't sleep. The infernal night had dragged on forever. He had all but physically loaded his father back into the coach, then stood outside in the darkness, until it disappeared down the drive, outriders with lanterns leading the way.

Once the last spark of light winked out, he'd ironed the turbulent emotions from his face and returned to his guests. He'd intended to suggest the party end early, but the company was already dispersing as if the earl carried some malignant fever. Anyone who lived near Everdene Hall made excuses and fled home, while those staying the night had hastened behind closed doors.

Even his family had retreated to their rooms, his last glimpse of his sisters: Cassandra with an arm wrapped around Jane as they disappeared up the stairs. He couldn't blame them. His father's aura hung in the air like a miasmic poison. When he'd climbed the stairs to his own chamber hours later, Jane's bedroom door stood open, the soft green bedcurtains caught back by gold cords, her coverlets smooth. Light shone through the crack at the bottom of Cassandra's bedchamber door. He paused, aware of faint murmurs, and was glad Jane would stay with Cassandra tonight.

His brother's door was closed as well, but he could hear the rise and fall of Simon's low voice and his wife answering. Lucien felt a jab of envy that his brother had someone to talk to about their father's unexpected appearance, about their sisters, about anything that troubled him. Simon would always have Penelope's wise counsel and the comfort of the love that shone in her eyes. But then, Simon was the sort of man to inspire that sort of love. Not that Lucien wanted such intimacy for himself. But tonight, as he entered his solitary room, the silence was deafening. His father's warning to Lucien echoed, dark and dire.

It was not only my *head Cassandra was imagining in that painting.* Lucien could see it every time he closed his eyes—Cassandra's rendering of *Judith Slaying Holefernes*, the expression on her face. Her words. *Her father watched...*

What had happened to his sister? Would she ever tell him? Could he bear to know?

Lucien stripped to his drawers, roughly scrubbing his face and chest at the washstand, then concentrated on the most difficult problems of the estate, hoping they might distract him. It was no use. When the clock struck two, his restlessness could not be contained any longer. He drew on his banyan, retrieved a silver candlestick from the bedside table, then stepped into the corridor. Even the servants were long in their beds, the house silent, the way he usually liked it.

Yet, as he made his way downstairs he realized that someone else was stirring. A sash from what might be a lady's wrapper lay on the bottom step. He picked up the silk ribbon, and the feminine scent of jasmine teased his nose. Experience on the marriage mart had taught him that he should head in the opposite direction, but he paused, listening. Had one of his sisters come downstairs? Or Penelope, after a tiring night with her teething son?

A faint light shone from the kitchen, stealthy sounds drifting out. He set his candlestick on a table and moved silently to peer into the vast, echoing room. A lone candle cast light upon polished copper pots dangling from hooks and crockery that marched along shelves. A vast wooden table in the center of the room held baskets of berries waiting to be made into jam tarts and the neatly covered remnants of last night's repast.

A woman stood at the table's edge, intent on some mysterious task. He knew in a heartbeat it was Grace. She was angled away from him, her wrapper flowing loose without the ribbon sash he'd found, her feet bare on the cold slate floor. Rich curls tumbled free, veiling all but the curve of one cheek, her skin a soft peachy glow.

Lucien knew entering a room where he'd be alone with her in the middle of the night was a spectacularly bad idea. Situations like this could force a man to the altar faster than you could spell 'compromising position.' But instead of retreating somewhere—anywhere—where he couldn't fall into the matrimonial snare, the 'Elusive Viscount E' drew closer.

What the devil was she doing? She might have been stealing the silver, she looked so guilty. But after a moment, he realized that she'd peeled the cloth covering a tray aside and was tucking three of the dainty pink-frosted cakes it held into a clean handkerchief. After all the grim happenings of this dinner party, somehow discovering Grace Elliot absconding with cakes unscrewed some of the tension that tied him in knots. Lucien tried hard not to smile, but he couldn't help it.

He held up the sash in his hand. "Missing something, Lady Grace?"

Choking back a shriek, she wheeled toward him, the tray starting to skid off the table, tipping precariously. She spun back toward the tray, trying to avert disaster, but the weight of her hand hit the tray's unmoored edge, catapulting the cakes through the air. He heard the soft thud as they struck her.

She shoved the tray back onto the table, the clatter so loud he could only hope it didn't rouse some overly vigilant servant. For a long moment, Grace stood with her back toward him, peering down at the mess. She looked smaller somehow, more vulnerable. "*Why* is it that every time I'm near you I make a total mess of things?" she complained.

"It *is* becoming something of a habit. But at least I know where your brothers inherited their penchant for trouble." Lucien set the silk sash on a chair, then curved his hand over her shoulder and gently turned her to face him. Hot spots of color blazed in her cheeks, flecks of sugar adding sparkles among her dusting of freckles. The cakes had made icing prints on the thin white lawn of her nightgown. Pink frosting clung to her collar bone, and Lucien had an absurd urge to taste it. He shoved the thought away. "You perceive me agog with curiosity. What drove a well-bred young lady such as yourself to kitchen thievery?"

She was staring, but not at his face. Her eyes fixed on the deep vee where the brocade of his banyan exposed a wedge of skin. "I—I meant to ask Penelope for permission," she faltered, "but then the earl came, and your family seemed so upset, it completely slipped my mind. By the time I remembered, everyone was abed. You see, Bennet asked me to bring back cakes. This is the first night I've spent away from him since our mother got sick, and...well...I promised."

Lucien reached up to the wooden rack overhead and pulled down one of the cloths that were drying there. Night air cooled his bare chest as the banyan gaped wider. Fetching a jug of water, he dampened a corner of the towel. She stood, frozen, as he started to clean the icing off of her skin. First, the elegant bow of her collar bone, then upper swell of her breast. He dabbed, then dipped the towel into the water, and returned to begin again.

Her pulse fluttered wild in the hollow of her throat as his knuckles brushed the velvety warmth of her skin. He felt his cock stir. How long had it been since he'd been in a room with a woman in dishabille? Too damned long. And it sure as hell hadn't been with a gently bred lady like Grace Elliot.

He had no business touching her, but he couldn't help himself. There was something about her that made such forbidden intimacies irresistible.

She spoke, her voice a little breathless. "I am not certain what happened tonight, but I am sorry for it," she said. "I know you wanted this to be a happy occasion."

He made a sound that might have been assent or irony. Just having it not blow up like a mortar shell would have been enough.

He waited for an avid spark of curiosity to show in her face, braced himself for inevitable questions. There were none, only a quiet empathy that unnerved him.

"I was thinking," she hesitated, then plunged on. "Doing something familiar might help to ease the strangeness of being in England after so long away for Cassandra and Jane. Perhaps you could all come to The Willows and spend the day. It is lovely this time of year. We could picnic on the lawn as we did when we were children."

His hand went still, the backs of his fingers lightly pressed against her slender throat. He could feel the throb of her pulse. He peered down at her, a crease forming between his brows.

"You are very kind," he said.

A fetching blush colored her cheeks. "I've missed them."

"I have, too." The confession surprised him, but it was true. He missed the sisters he'd known, little girls…who didn't hate him.

Lucien banished the image that haunted him, concentrating on Grace instead. "I'm aware of all you did tonight to help my sisters feel at ease and smooth over awkwardness with the guests. I've seldom seen anyone manage a challenging social situation more seamlessly than you did. It will be no small asset to a husband." The slightest lift of his tone made the last a question.

He knew damned well what he was doing. Probing, because of Arkwright's revelation about her broken betrothal.

Those thick lashes dipped lower, veiling her eyes. She took the cloth from him and busied herself cleaning the front of her night-gown. It clung to her now, in damp patches, the soft peach of skin showing through.

"I learned how to manage such situations by watching my mother, believing one day I would have the kind of partnership my parents had."

With the Honorable Neville Freyne? An intense dislike for the man stiffened Lucien's shoulders.

"Once Mama fell sick, I thought looking after Papa and the boys would be my life."

Lucien's eyes narrowed. "Is that what you wanted for yourself? To remain a dutiful daughter, sitting at your widowed father's knee?"

What a waste that would be, Lucien mused as he peered down into her animated face. All of that laughter, cleverness and courage hidden away in life as a spinster.

"I suppose I've been too preoccupied to consider what I want. It is high time I puzzle it out." There was something about the way she lifted her chin just a fraction. Something brave.

Lucien didn't need any time to discern what *he* wanted. He'd felt every curve of her body on the lakeshore, but that was pure chance. This pull he experienced now was different. A choice? No, a *need*. He couldn't take his eyes off of the smudge of icing near her lower lip.

Could a man taste her sweetness? He'd be a fool to try. He'd regret it forever if he did not.

He threaded his fingers back through the silky fall of her unbound hair, tipped her face up, and lowered his mouth to her cheek. Her breath caught as he trailed kisses down to the bit of icing, tasting it. Tasting *her*. She gasped, and he caught the alluring sound with his mouth, exploring the plush velvet of her lips. Flames licked through him as he traced the seam of her lips with his tongue and she opened, letting him inside, the contact almost too potent, too intense. He gathered her in his arms, molding her body to his, and she kissed him back, her fingertips easing up around his nape to draw him closer. Her palm cupped his neck, brushing the sensitive strands of his hair, her touch devastatingly feminine and eager. The points of her nipples puckered, hard against his chest, only the thin lawn between them. A throbbing began in Lucien, low, primitive and unexpected. So damned dangerous.

After a long, searching moment, he drew away. "You taste like vanilla and sugar and cream," he murmured, tracing a fingertip over her bottom lip. "So damned sweet."

Grace stared up at him, wide-eyed. "It's the cake."

He laughed for the first time in God knew how long, and her face turned scarlet.

"I'd better go," she stammered. "Before..."

Before someone discovered them? Before he kissed her again? Before he lifted her onto the table and did what his body was clamoring to do?

She spun away, but he caught her arm, gathered up the handkerchief with its purloined cakes.

"Don't forget these," he said, pressing the bundle into her hands. She snatched it up and fled.

He watched her, her wrapper streaming out behind her, her feet bare, dainty and doubtless so cold he wanted to warm them in his hands. Her words echoed through him.

No, Lucien thought. It wasn't the cake he'd tasted in that kiss. Grace Elliot tasted like something else entirely. Something he could never have.

Redemption.

GRACE PRESSED A HAND TO HER BURNING CHEEK AND FLED UP THE stairs, groaning in despair.

It's the cake...?

What kind of absurd thing was that to say after Lucien Harcourt had kissed her until her toes curled, and every inch of her skin seemed afire? There were a hundred things she could have said to him. *You taste like sin. You kiss like the devil himself. Why, thank you very much for showing me what I'd have sacrificed if I'd remained cloistered at The Willows.* Now, she sounded like an absolute ninny. She'd been embarrassed by their encounter at the lake, but that had been her brother's mischief. This disaster was her own making. How would she ever face him again?

She darted into her room and shut the door a trifle too hard, the sound seeming like a gunshot. She leaned her back against the portal. What if she'd awakened someone? What if someone discovered.... A chill whisked through her nightgown, and she looked down at the open front of her wrapper, suddenly aware she hadn't taken the sash Lucien had set aside in the kitchen. Evidence of her nighttime escapade.

For a moment, she thought of retrieving it, but she didn't dare go downstairs again in this condition. No one would know it was hers, would they? And the sash would be the last of the kitchen staff's concern when they saw the mess she'd left behind.

Lucien had left behind, she amended. *He* was the one who had startled her. Creeping up behind her in the middle of the night, stealthy as a tiger, scaring the life out of her! Kissing her until she couldn't string three coherent words together. Her heart raced as she remembered every sensation.

It wasn't as if she'd never been kissed. Certainly she and Neville had done so after their betrothal, but those were the tentative fumblings of inexperienced youth. A trifle too eager, a bit awkward. Lucien had kissed her with the skill of a man who knew all the secrets of awakening a woman's body. How to set every nerve ablaze...

And she'd fired off the most ridiculous reply ever, her night-gown smeared with icing as he pressed the handkerchief filled with cakes into her hand. How would she ever face him again? She would have to, she thought. She'd invited the Harcourts to The Willows.

Oh, God, what was she thinking? Her cheeks burned with a mixture of embarrassment and excitement as she remembered those moments in the kitchen.

The truth? Deep down she wanted to repeat the night's escapade...

"YOU CAN COME OUT NOW. THE LAST OF THE GUESTS ARE GONE."

Lucien looked up at the sound of Arkwright's voice, his friend strolling, uninvited, into the study.

"Seriously, Luce, failing to bid them goodbye is a bit surly even for you."

"It seemed the best course after last night."

"Your father—"

"No. The encounter in question happened in the kitchen after the clock struck two. Lady Grace and I—"

"What the devil?" Arkwright gaped at Lucien as if he'd swallowed a rock. "You were in the kitchen with Lady Grace? In the middle of the night? Alone?"

"Isn't that what I just said?"

Arkwright ground his fingers into his temples. "Jesus, Luce! I've been pulling you out of marital traps like that for years."

"It wasn't a marital trap." A smile played about Lucien's lips. "She was bent on thievery."

"Thievery?"

"Lady Grace was stealing cake." Lucien chuckled.

Arkwright stared. "Wait—did you just laugh?"

"My God, if you could have seen her face. She flipped a tray of them when I startled her."

The memory of her was still fresh in his mind. He could picture every line and curve, the precise arch of her brow, the thick lashes. Flecks of sugar spangling her cheekbones. He was not a man given to flights of fancy—*any* fancy, truth be told—but she'd seemed like the women in tales Nanny Rowley had told in the nursery long ago, a fairy queen, tempting mortal men beyond reason.

Lucien shook himself inwardly, dispelling the absurd comparison. Remembering instead the warmth of Grace's lips, the way she'd gasped just a little when he kissed her.

By any measure of the ton's rules, he'd compromised Grace Elliot. In Everdene Hall's kitchen and at the lakeside when he'd held her in his arms, her lush body covered in nothing but a sheer, wet chemise. "She invited all of us to a day of picnicking at The Willows Thursday next," he added.

"That sounds…pleasurable?" Arkwright ventured, regarding him warily.

"I won't be attending." Lucien's jaw knotted. "I'm going to Bitterne Tower to see what the devil is going on with my father and warn him to stay the hell away from my sisters."

Yes, he resolved, picturing Grace's slender form, her eager lips, her eyes glowing with empathy. There was only one thing to do about a woman who tempted him to such recklessness.

Stay the hell away.

CHAPTER 9

"I thought you had business to attend to?" Rhys Arkwright called out merrily from the archery range that had been set up a safe distance from the cluster of gaily colored tents on the Elliot lawn.

Lucien strode toward him, barely avoiding Grace's brothers as they pelted toward archery butts to retrieve their arrows from the straw bales.

Simon regarded Lucien as if explosives might be involved, understandable since Lucien had just returned from seeing their father. "What are you doing here?" his brother asked.

"He's looking for cake, no doubt." Arkwright quipped. "He's seemed to take a fancy to it of late."

Lucien leveled a deadly glare at his friend, but Arkwright only winked—the insufferable bastard.

"Cake?" Simon's brow furrowed and he turned to Lucien. "What's he on about?"

"Clearly, he's started drinking too early." Lucien straightened his cravat as he scanned his surroundings. A cadre of servants garbed in Elliot livery moved about the tents—while Cassandra's grim Italian maid with her black silk eyepatch stood beneath a tree, watching the proceedings.

Penelope and Cassandra were speaking to an older woman in a

cream silk bonnet who clasped her hands in delight when she noted his approach, while Lord Elliot exuded grim displeasure.

But the one person Lucien wished most to see was nowhere to be found. Perhaps Grace had drawn his sister Jane off somewhere quieter.

"Did something go wrong with Father?" Simon pressed him.

"Our meeting went as expected." Lucien masked the resentment that gnawed inside him. After discovering the full extent of the Earl's perfidy two years ago, Simon had shut their father out of his life and never looked back. But necessity demanded Lucien and his father make business decisions regarding the earldom's estates, forced conversations that gradually dulled the cutting edges of past sins. The exchange with Cassandra and Jane at Everdene Hall had sharpened the blade again.

"Everdene," Lord Elliot said stiffly.

"My business took less time than expected," Lucien explained. "I do hope my arrival does not prove an inconvenience."

The woman in the cream bonnet bustled up and took Lord Elliot's arm, her plump face beaming. "On the contrary! You are very welcome, my lord!"

So this was the stepmother who had upended Grace's life, Lucien thought, regarding her with an appraising eye. "You must be Lady Elliot." He sketched her a bow. "Viscount Everdene, at your service. Best wishes regarding your recent marriage."

"We understood you would not be joining us," Lord Elliot said between clenched teeth.

Cassandra walked toward them. "Where is Jane?" Lucien asked.

Cassandra shook out her skirts. "Jane joined mother in Galen's Well for a bit of respite," she said, her eyes locked on him. "Too much time in company troubles her."

My company in particular, Lucien thought with a twinge.

At that moment Grace swept from beneath an awning and bustled toward him, a vision in buttercup yellow. The sleeves of her gown ended in a bell shape just below her elbows, a fichu of fine white lawn was pinned at her throat with a brooch. Her hair was caught up in a loose chignon, and Lucien wondered how many pins he would have to pull from those shining tresses to make them tumble free down her back, the way they had in the kitchen at Everdene Hall.

"Welcome to The Willows!" Grace exclaimed, as the wee pirates surrounded her, one wielding a cricket bat, looking ready to defend her. "Captain Harcourt said you were off to London."

"Far better to avoid cities for now." Lady Elliot gave a delicate shudder. "We've heard the most alarming reports about unrest there. My dearest Lord Elliot and I had to cut our honeymoon in Paris short for safety's sake. The rabble were throwing up barricades and rioting in the streets. One hears the most alarming things about what is happening up north and in London. Is it true mobs even marched up Pall Mall and St. James's, breaking windows at the gentlemen's clubs?"

"Yes. I'm afraid it is," Lucien admitted.

"I was at Whites when the riot broke out," Arkwright supplied. "For once, Everdene wasn't there."

Lucien had been arguing with a cadre of Tory lawmakers about how to deal with the public's growing dissatisfaction, urging them to provide pure water and better drainage in poorer areas, insisting better health for one meant better health for all. He'd have had better luck dealing with a riotous mob.

"Someone tried to shoot the queen herself!" Lady Elliot exclaimed, fluttering her hand in front of her breast.

"It was pure luck her attacker forgot to put a bullet in his gun," Penelope interjected.

"I am sorry the man gave the queen a fright," Grace said, "but we must look to the reasons behind the unrest. People are hungry, and not all landlords are as forward-thinking and caring in regards to their tenants as the Harcourts are."

Her father cleared his throat. "Perhaps we should turn our attention to more pleasant subjects, my dear," he said, looping his arm around his bride.

But Lady Elliot would not be so easily deterred. "I can only say I'm grateful that there are men like Lord Everdene who will crush this anarchy. Especially when we need to prepare for Grace's return to society." She turned to Penelope. "Will you be going to London for the season?" she asked.

Penelope looked as if Lady Elliot were suggesting a visit to the tooth drawer. "Heavens, no."

"Lord Everdene, *you* will be there, of course," the new Lady Elliot continued, undaunted. "And pursued by all of those desperate women, no doubt." Her lips curled in what passed for a teasing smile. "Yes, my lord. Your wicked fame as the Elusive Viscount E has reached us even here in the country. You know, our own Grace will be making her grand re-entry into society. She has been so good, these past years, caring for her dear Mama and Papa and brothers. But now, I am here, and determined she shall enjoy herself."

Lucien felt a prickle of annoyance as he remembered Grace's confession at Everdene Hall. God knew, she deserved to be released from years of seeing to her family's needs. She deserved trips to the theater, waltzing at balls, all the diversions London could offer. But he suspected Lady Elliot's real motive was to wrest control of the household away from Grace, and it left a bad taste in his mouth. "Have you enquired as to what Lady Grace would prefer?" he inquired.

"What young miss doesn't love a London season? I've never been blessed with a daughter," Lady Elliot continued. "My late husband and I...well, it was not to be. I intend to enjoy every minute of mothering this dear girl." She laid a hand on Grace, and Lucien saw Grace give an uncomfortable smile. "We've gowns to buy and dressmakers to visit. If Mrs. Harcourt can suggest any modistes the ladies of the ton are favoring I would be grateful."

Since Penelope had been a governess before she and Simon met, she'd hardly been frequenting shops Lady Helen might consider.

Simon laughed. "If it was a shop filled with books on architecture, my wife would be waiting with bated breath. She has served as my brother's hostess when necessary, but she'd prefer to be in the study with architectural drawings spread across the desk."

"Architectural drawings?" Lady Elliot looked as if Penelope had just sprouted a Doric column from her head. "How...singular." She turned to Lucien. "Your lordship, I hope we can count on you to see that our Grace's dance card is full. She has been away from London so long, she'll be short of acquaintances."

Grace's cheeks turned scarlet, but before she could speak, her father cut in.

"I am sure Lord Everdene has no time for such frivolous matters." Lord Elliot's brusque tone made his wife's eyes go wide, and startled Grace as well. "His lordship is a very busy man. I am astonished he made time to come here today."

"Of course," his wife said, "but perhaps Lord Everdene could make time for—"

"My dear, Grace will have no problem finding willing partners. In fact," Elliot pushed on, totally unaware of his daughter's reddening face, "I have received news that the Honorable Neville Freyne is returning from the Americas to take over his father's business concerns."

The fiancé who had jilted her?

Grace curled her fingers into her palms, then gave a brittle smile. "I'm sure his family will be very glad to see him."

Something akin to jealousy stung Lucien. Would *Grace* be pleased to see the bounder as well? He turned to Lady Elliot. "I will be happy to claim the first dance at any event Lady Grace and I attend," he said. "But first, perhaps, we should enjoy this beautiful day in the country. A little archery, perhaps?"

"A splendid idea," Grace said.

The relief on her face made Lucien want to deal old Lord Elliot and his meddlesome wife a cutting remark. Another time, he promised. He'd not embarrass Grace further now.

With enthusiastic whoops, the three youngest Elliots absconded with Arkwright, all but dragging Rhys to the range set up with miniature bows and larger targets while Grace led their elders to a table where a set of larger equipment lay.

Cassandra went first, followed by Penelope, then Grace, who selected a bow made of yew and a quiver of arrows. Stepping up to the mark, she nocked the arrow and raised the bow into position. She blew a wayward tendril of hair from her brow, and Lucien felt an almost irresistible urge to sweep it back with his fingertips, remembering the velvety warmth of her skin. Instead, he watched as she drew back the bowstring and narrowed one eye. She let the arrow fly, the point striking dead-center in the straw target.

The onlookers clapped in approval.

Lucien smiled. "You always were a keen shot."

Arkwright hastened over to praise her, the small boys trailing in his wake, damn him. "Well done! I can't think when I've seen a lady shoot so well."

Will Elliot laughed. "One can't play Robin Hood without proficiency with a bow and arrow. From the time we were Bennet's age, Grace insisted Maid Marian should have a bow and Guinevere a sword."

"If they had, the legends would have turned out quite differently," she said crisply.

Arkwright laughed. "You prefer the romance of earlier days, do you, Lady Grace? Something you and Everdene have in common. You'd think my practical friend would be proficient with pistols, but he seldom bothers to practice. However, present him with a sword and you'll see him in full flower."

"A sword?" Avery—the one who had first thrown a mudpie—exclaimed, his button-bright eyes looking at Lucien with new interest.

"Indeed," Arkwright continued. "I've seen Everdene divest an opponent of his buttons, and clip a lock of hair from our sword master as if it were nothing."

Lucien felt a trifle uncomfortable. "Really, Arkwright, we are occupied with archery. No one is interested in such tales at the moment."

"We are!" the boys cried in unison, Bennet leaping up and down on the toes of his shiny black boots.

Cassandra shot Lucien a condemning glare. "My brother was always running about playing knights when he was a boy. Once, he insisted on hoisting Jane high up in a tree, pretending it was a tower. He was supposed to rescue her, but he forgot to retrieve her until after dark."

Lucien had been pulled out of the game by Father, who'd taken him to meet with a visiting MP, but what followed was an appalling example of heedlessness on his own part. Lucien frowned, remembering Jane's pinched white face when he'd raced out to the orchard and found her, too frightened to climb down.

"No swords here," Bennet complained. "*She* locked them away."

There could be no question as to whom 'she' was. The boys cut a glare at their stepmother.

Will gave him a stern glance. "Only because you held the vicar at sword point when he stopped by unexpectedly."

"He was looking suspicious," Avery told Arkwright.

"Squinty eyes," Ethan confirmed. He attempted to mimic the expression, but his mischievous face ended up looking like he'd taken a bite out of a lemon.

Arkwright cast a pleading look toward Lady Elliot. "Perhaps we could bring the swords out this once," he wheedled in that tone that made every woman over thirty want to give him sweets. "An exception, so that Lord Everdene can give the lads a quick demonstration."

Lucien straightened his cravat. "I've no desire to disrupt our archery practice."

Lady Elliot immediately set down her bow. "I daresay we'd all love to see it."

The boys shouted with delight, the rest of the party a clamor of encouragement.

Damn Arkwright for even suggesting such a thing. There was nothing for it but to acquiesce and maintain some measure of dignity, or continue to refuse and seem rude. His lips thinned as he nodded assent.

Will Elliot hastened to the house, returning with two rather battered fencing foils, buttons on their points. "I'll give it a go!" Will grinned, eager as a puppy as he handed one blade to Lucien.

Lucien leaned the sword against a chair, then stripped off his frock coat, and unfastened his cuffs, rolling up his sleeves to bare his forearms. Hefting the blade, he turned it over and back to free any tightness in his wrist. Everyone was staring in anticipation. Even the servants had edged nearer. Only Cassandra stood apart, watching under hooded lids.

Selecting a level area, he saluted young Elliot, then began. He restrained himself long enough to save the lad's pride, then divested him of his sword. The foil went flying, landing with a thud on the turf.

One of the boys whistled his approval.

Will laughed. "One minute more and I'd have had him."

Arkwright slapped Will on the shoulder. "My lad, the minutes you *did* have were a gift. He was holding back out of sheer politeness."

Lucien scowled at his friend. While his father had sought every opportunity to show his superiority at any social gathering, Lucien had come to loathe vulgar displays when people made much of their own talents.

Even so, Will's eyes shone with admiration. "I'd heard of Captain Harcourt's exploits but had no idea you were so skilled."

Simon laughed. "Who do you think I honed my swordplay with?"

"Shall we return to our archery?" Lucien suggested, setting the foil aside, but suddenly Cassandra stepped forward.

"Perhaps you would be willing to indulge *me* with a little swordplay first?" she said.

The others laughed and Lucien could tell that they thought Cassandra's challenge a show of sisterly teasing, but her eyes were steely as the button on the tip of the swords.

"I think we've had enough," Lucien said. "Shall we withdraw to have some refreshment?"

"I insist, brother."

Was this dare to cross blades the most honest encounter he'd had with her? Was it possible that lashing out at him this way might ease some of the tension that sizzled in her like a coming storm?

"If you wish. I will use my left hand, to even the odds." He slid his hand around the hilt, lifted it.

"How remarkably *honorable* of you."

Lucien didn't show that her verbal thrust had struck the mark.

Her maid appeared at her side, silent as a wraith, the bit of silk covering her left eye, the other so keen it might have belonged to some oracle in myth. Cassandra stripped off her gloves, and handed them to the woman, then removed her cambric undersleeves, baring her arms. Her sleeves were not in fashion, the puffs allowing freer movement. She tucked her skirts up in the belt at her waist with practiced ease, then scooped up Will's abandoned foil.

Cassandra saluted Lucien as he switched hands. Let her bash away at him for a while, he thought.

The first clash of swords startled him with its force, and it must have shown on his face. She bared her teeth in a rictus of a smile. In a flurry of silver and movement, she went on the offensive. He was vaguely aware of gasps from the onlookers. But as he fended off blows, he realized he had seldom fought a more skilled opponent. This was no game to her. She was fighting in earnest, every muscle in her face tight with exertion.

Sweat broke out on Lucien's brow as they moved about the field. *Come on, then Cass*, he thought, grateful there were buttons on the sword tips. *Get the poison out*...He had greater upper body strength, but she was quicker, light on her feet. He didn't want to accidentally hurt her, but it was harder and harder to parry her thrusts without putting his whole weight behind it. Her footwork was flawless, with a skill he'd seldom seen.

She executed a brilliant combination, the crowd applauding.

Their swords gave a metallic twang, grating against each other's length hilt to tip, sticking for a moment before they could yank them free. He and Cassandra sprang apart, circling each other. Her eyes burned now with something he couldn't name. Pleasure? Triumph? No. There was almost a blindness, as if she were in a trance. Something that sent a chill crawling up the back of his neck.

He was frightened for her.

"Cassandra, I forfeit." He started to lower his blade, but she came at him like a fury, slipping under his guard. Pain burned his chest, glancing off his sternum.

What the hell? He leapt back, whipping his own blade up, knocking hers aside. His shirt tore, Cassandra's sword point carving a fiery line across his chest.

He heard Lady Elliot scream from the sidelines. "He's bleeding!"

He could feel it, warm, sticky flowing from the cut Cassandra had made. The button on the point of her foil had fallen off, but Cassandra didn't know it. She kept coming at him, her eyes vacant. Chilling. As if his sister wasn't there...

CHAPTER 10

The clash of metal on metal, the flash of light on the blades, filled Lucien's senses, his left-handed swordplay a poor match for Cassandra's skill. His stomach clenched with the horrifying possibility that he might wound his sister or die by her hand.

Suddenly a hard voice snapped something in Italian. Cassandra hesitated for a heartbeat, long enough for Simon to lunge in and grab her wrist.

"Cass, stop!" Simon barked in the tone that had halted battle-drunk soldiers. Her hand was shaking, the blade trembling. Its tip, red with blood, swam in front of Lucien's eyes. His vision blurred in a combination of shock and pain as Simon pried Cassandra's fingers off of the hilt and slipped the weapon from her hand.

The minute it was free she gave her head a shake, as if startled awake. Her eyes widened as she stared at the bloodstain spreading on Lucien's torn shirt.

"The guard came off your sword," Simon explained, curving one hand over Cass's shoulder. "I know you didn't mean to hurt him."

Didn't she? Lucien wished he were as sure as she dropped the sword and buried her face in her hands.

Chaos erupted, Lady Elliot fainting into her husband's arms, the terrified Elliot boys clinging to Will. Simon, Penelope and Paola clustered around Cassandra while Arkwright and Grace rushed toward Lucien.

Grace, pale, yet calm, examined the wound.

"How bad is it?" Arkwright asked her. "Do we need to summon a surgeon?"

"It's just a scratch," Lucien growled, his cheeks starting to burn. "The sword point glanced off."

"You're dashed lucky it's not worse!" Arkwright exclaimed.

But it was Grace who filled Lucien's vision. Her cheeks flushed, gaze intense as she pressed her wadded up handkerchief upon the slice to slow the bleeding. It had violets embroidered on it or some such. Absurd to notice that now. She motioned to a maid whose cap had slipped askew. "Susan, run ahead to heat some water and have it taken to the morning room then fetch a fresh shirt. Will, take everyone to the tents and have Ives set out luncheon. I'll take Lord Everdene to the house and get him cleaned up."

Lucien frowned. Strange, that Grace should be the one escorting him to the house instead of presiding over the tea tables set beneath cloth canopies. Yet he was glad. Her grip on his arm was gentle, yet firm as she guided him toward the manor.

"You'll get blood on your frock," Lucien warned.

"It won't be the first time. Or have you not met my brothers?" She kept her tone light, but he could see the worry creasing her brow as she looked at her stepmother who lay in a fluttering heap, being plied with smelling salts, demanding far more attention than the one who was actually bleeding. "What am I going to do with her?" she huffed in exasperation. "She faints at the sight of blood."

"She'd best get used to it if she's to play mother to those little hellions," Lucien observed between gritted teeth.

"Blood and toads. What more could a stepmother ask for?" She smiled to herself. "Bennet is quite enamored with the little creatures. Lady Elliot not so much."

Grace and Lucien had reached a set of doors in the terrace, and she led him inside. He had visited The Willows as a boy, but it was wholly different now. The tasteful mural he remembered had been obliterated by silk wallpaper boasting a flock of vulgar peacocks that glared out at those who entered. He blinked, wondering if his eyes were playing tricks on him. He'd swear one or two of the birds wore a black moustache. A number of furnishings were obviously new and garish. There were scrape marks on the floor where the older furniture still stood, as if the heavy pieces had been dragged to and fro.

By the time Grace and Lucien reached a rather pleasant room at the far end of the hall, he was feeling queasy from a combination of the wound and the memory of his sister's eyes. Hate-filled, yet also frightened. So vacant it chilled him. What had put that expression on her face?

Grace settled him on a wooden chair beside a table that the maid had prepared. Steam rose from a basin of water. Beside it, a stack of clean bandages sat next to the kit of medical supplies no mistress of a household could be without.

He thought of how long that battered, leather case had been in Grace's charge. Had Grace become skilled in such wifely duties when she should have been reveling in all the pleasures the London season could offer a lovely young debutante? The thought troubled him.

"Let us get this shirt off of you so we can see just what we have here," she said, quickly unknotting his cravat and moving to the placket of his shirt. He caught her hand.

"Perhaps a footman might aid me. You, a young, unmarried woman—"

"Lord Everdene, I shed my innocence about medical matters five years ago. You needn't fret about my sensibilities."

He said no more because she was already making quick work of his buttons, the fabric falling open, her soft knuckles brushing against his chest. He shouldn't have noticed when she grazed a flat nipple. He was bleeding, for Christ's sake. But the intimacy was undeniable. "I can unbutton the rest," he said to spare himself the sensations.

At last, he finished and tugged the shirt tails from the waistband of his breeches. He set aside the blood-soaked handkerchief that clung to his wound, then carefully pulled his arms from each sleeve.

Grace surveyed the wound with a discerning eye, dipped a cloth in the basin, and began to carefully clean the blood away. Glancing down, he saw the slash from the center of his breastbone, tapering off to just above his left pectoral. The edges of the wound were purpling.

"You were very lucky," Grace said. "I won't need to stitch it."

She said it as if stitching a man's chest was little different than the samplers women were forever embroidering.

"This will sting a bit," she warned, applying some sort of salve from a tin. It did. But not in the way she meant. Those delicate, deft fingers moving upon his bare skin distracted him from the discomfort. His breath quickened, and she caught her bottom lip between her teeth.

After setting the salve aside, she took up clean bandages and formed a pad the length of his wound.

"I'm glad it's no worse," she said. "I couldn't see everything that happened clearly, but I think it might have been disastrous."

"It wasn't."

Grace took hold of his hand and raised it, bidding him hold the pad and one end of a rolled of bandage in place. Once he did so, she began wrapping a long strip of cloth around his torso. Once. Twice. Three times. Her fingertips brushed beneath his arm, across his back, and he couldn't help imagining them doing so under very different circumstances. Circumstances he had no business envisioning.

"Cassandra seemed…not quite herself," Grace said, so close to him that her breath warmed his shoulder.

"She has been under a great deal of strain."

Grace was gliding those fingers against the sensitive skin under his arm again. He flinched away.

Her gaze leapt to his. "I'm sorry. Did that hurt you?"

"No."

It was a lie. She was killing him with her tenderness, the concern in her eyes, the satiny pink of her lips mere inches from his own, awakening feelings he hadn't ever experienced before.

No one had ever looked at Grace the way Lucien Harcourt did now. He was staring down at her with those ice-blue eyes as if he could see to the very core of her, all of the guilty secrets she kept locked inside. Anger and grief at her mother for dying, hurt and the sense that Papa had betrayed her with Helen, that urge she sometimes got to charge out the front door of The Willows and keep running…

God knew, she saw truths in Lucien's eyes that left her shaken as well, his defenses torn away in the aftermath of his sister's attack. Lucien Harcourt, stripped bare in more ways than just the magnificent breadth of his hair-roughened chest.

As she pinned the ends of the bandage and tucked the ends in snugly, she looked up at him and forced a smile. "That should hold. I had Susan fetch one of Will's shirts for you. I'm not sure you'll be able to button it all the way."

"It will do. Thank you."

"If you wish, you can rest in one of the guest rooms, or I can have Susan summon the coach to take you home."

"No. I will return to the picnic."

"To make certain Cassandra knows you are all right," she said softly.

He stared down into her face, his gaze a tangible force, as if he were a predator caught in a snare, while someone tended him. He cocked his head just a trifle to one side as if her understanding confused him.

She stilled, his intense gaze pulling her in.

"What is it about you?" he murmured. "Your kindness, humor? The way you deal with the world…capable, unflinching? It's like I can't help myself." He framed her face with his hands, his fingertips masterful, and Grace felt warmth spread from the skin he touched to her breasts, her belly. He focused on her—not her whole face—but one feature at a time, the freckles on her cheekbone, the vulnerable curve where her earlobe brushed her jawline, the swell of her bottom lip, as if he were choosing the sweetest berry to taste. She pressed her thighs together, feeling her secret places soften.

He smelled of the herbs in the salve, the soap she'd used to cleanse him, and something uniquely his own. And she wanted to discover all of the secrets of that sensual mouth.

"No," he whispered against her hair. "It's not that I can't help myself. I just don't want to stop."

She had no idea what he was talking about, until he lowered his mouth to the hollow behind her ear, tracing a warm path down to the cove where her collarbone arched. Fire trailed in his wake as he tasted her. The tip of his tongue found her pulsebeat. Then his lips were on hers, exploring with a skill that made her knees melt. She flattened her hand on his bare chest for balance, felt the edge of his bandage and pulled away from him, clutching her hand against her breasts.

"Your wound," she stammered. "I shouldn't have…"

"You didn't. I did." Those piercing blue eyes regarded her as if she was a puzzle he was attempting to solve. "It seems every time I see you, I take the most appalling liberties. I'd ask your pardon, but I'm not sorry."

She swallowed hard. "Neither am I."

He drew away from her, solemn. "And that is why we had best return to the tent." He offered her his arm, and she laid her hand gently upon it as the two of them headed down the hallway. Partway through the corridor, he paused, staring intently at the objectionable wallpaper. "That peacock *is* sporting a mustache," he exclaimed.

"I'm afraid it's the latest fashion for wallpaper hereabouts," Grace said.

"I thought I was hallucinating, perhaps going into shock." The ghost of a smile touched his lips, then he squared his shoulders and stepped out into the sunshine.

The rest of the company was beneath one of the awnings, the adults speaking a little too heartily to cover up their distress as they picked at the repast Grace had planned. Cassandra sat beside her maid in a breach of etiquette, the Italian woman peering out with her lone, fierce eye like a raven guarding treasure.

Grace saw Cassandra's gaze fix on Lucien, the strange vacancy of earlier gone, replaced by wells of pain and confusion. What was wrong between brother and sister? Between the Harcourt children and their father? She remembered her own father's warning about the family's havey-cavey doings. The countess vanishing for decades, then reappearing. The daughters swept away from England. Rumors swirled as to the reasons for their banishment, and where the countess had been.

If only Mama were here, Grace could ask what had happened,

sure she'd receive a forthright answer instead of her father's evasions. But Mama was gone.

Grace did her best to play hostess, despite the crackling of tension beneath the overly polite conversation and half-hearted games.

Two hours later, when the last of the Harcourt horses and carriage were brought around, Lucien lingered. He drew her aside as the others traded farewells.

"Thank you," he said, only the deep lines in his face betraying that he was still in pain.

"Thank you for what? Tending your wound? I was worried you'd been hurt badly."

"Once again, you managed an uncomfortable situation with grace, humor, and a skill I've seldom seen. This is the second time I owe you my thanks."

Her cheeks burned at his praise. She glanced down at the thickness of the bandage visible beneath the borrowed shirt and a lump formed in her throat. "You *will* keep the wound clean, won't you? Have your valet change the dressing often."

"He will not be such a tender nurse as the one I had today."

"Lucien…"

He touched her cheek. "You mustn't fret. I have taken care of myself for a very long time."

He looked so alone, even with his friend and his family. Solitary in a way that twisted her heart. But there were moments she glimpsed the man behind the mask, the man she'd come to know in those stolen times when his guard had been stripped away. Rare moments, when he'd seemed more real, more vulnerable, something in his eyes she couldn't forget. The farthest thing from cold.

What would it be like to be the woman who stepped past those walls, drew out the man she'd glimpsed so briefly when he'd caught her in the kitchen at Everdene Hall, when he'd kissed her in the morning room just hours ago. When his eyes had glowed, bluer than ever, with a spark of longing he couldn't hide. Not just physical desire, but something deeper.

Her pulse fluttered, as she met his ice-blue gaze. "Penelope has invited me for tea next week," Grace said. "Perhaps your cook could make more of those pink cakes."

He looked down, twisting the signet ring on his finger. "I won't be there," he said. "It's best if I return to London as soon as possible."

"Lucien, I don't understand…"

"Surely you can see the effect I have on my sisters. I make Jane so nervous she can barely speak when I'm in the room, and Cassandra…well…you saw what happened today." After a moment he looked at her. "Perhaps the one thing I don't regret about this interlude at Everdene Hall is my time with you, my Lady Grace."

His voice turned husky, tender, worlds away from those echoes of boyish mockery. He smiled, a smile that buried itself deep in her chest. He took her hand, bent his dark head to kiss her fingertips. Then he swung up on his golden horse and rode away.

CHAPTER 11

The clock was chiming ten by the time Bennet loosened his grip on Grace's hand enough that she dared to slip her fingers from his grasp. She froze in the glow of the candle he'd insisted be left burning and watched the slight flutter of his lashes against his cheek, fearing his eyes might pop open again. Thrice she had thought she'd managed to soothe her brothers to sleep. But when she tried to tiptoe away from their bedside, the creak of floorboards had awakened them. This time, thank God, they seemed well and truly asleep. *For now*, a voice whispered in her head.

She rubbed the back of her neck, weary to her bones from dismantling picnic accoutrements, calming the servants' rattled nerves over the fencing accident, and answering Nanny's plea for help with the frightened boys. When she finally stepped out into the corridor, she was surprised to find Will standing like a sentry, blocking the stairway that led to the nursery.

"You look like the very devil, Grace. I was beginning to wonder if you'd ever be able to pry Bennet's fingers off of yours."

"What are you doing here?" she asked, swiping at her burning eyes.

"I assume you received the paternal summons to dissect the happenings of the day." Will raised his dark brows.

The meeting. Her heart sank. She longed for her bed. A nice cup of tea. Pulling the coverlets over her head…

"Father sent me to see what was keeping you," Will explained. "I took one look through the door and decided that he and Helen could dashed well wait." An unaccustomed seriousness shadowed his youthful features. "Poor little fellows. I've not seen them so upset since Mother died. I wouldn't count on getting much sleep tonight, Gracie. I have a feeling you'll have company."

In the weeks following their mother's death, Grace's room had been haunted by three little night-shirted wanderers seeking answers she couldn't give them, Avery joining in under the guise of checking on his younger brothers. They'd burrowed into the four-poster bed like puppies, their small, warm bodies smelling of soap and strawberry jam, their silky hair tickling her cheek.

She'd cuddled the boys close in the vast stretch of empty hours that had remained after the long days of caring for Mama. Slowly, oh so slowly, she'd felt the coils of fear and confusion loosen, then melt from their rigid bodies as the jagged grief inside her softened, too.

If they *did* come wandering later tonight, she would welcome them with open arms. After the events of the day, she could use a hug as well.

As if he understood without words, Will looped an arm around her, and she leaned against his shoulder. "You are the best sister who ever lived, you know," he said in that deep voice that still surprised her. "We're all blasted lucky to have you."

His unexpected praise made the corners of her mouth turn up. She nudged him with an elbow. "You're not so reprehensible yourself."

He smiled back at the word she'd oft used to describe him when he'd teased her in the past. They made their way down to the study together.

Their father was pacing the confines of the room Helen had begun to redecorate in sea-sick green and gold. Smears of paint samples blotted the walls and swathes of sample fabrics were draped about.

"Here you are at last!" their father said sharply. "I sent Will up to fetch you an hour past."

"It took this long for Bennet to fall asleep," Will explained.

Helen fanned herself with her handkerchief. "No wonder, after the day we had!" Her gown was crumpled, tendrils of blonde hair curling about her cheeks.

"This is what comes of interactions with the Harcourts," Father growled, pouring himself a glass of port. "It will be a miracle if the whole county doesn't learn of this debacle with the swords before the week is out."

Grace felt a surge of defensiveness. "The guard came off of the blade. It could have happened to anyone."

"The Harcourts aren't 'anyone.' What if he'd been killed right on our front lawn? The Viscount Everdene—by his own sister! The scandal would have destroyed us in good society!"

Grace frowned. "Society's reaction is what concerns you? Not the fact that a man was injured and his poor sister was obviously distraught?"

"She belongs in a madhouse!"

Grace choked back a gasp, stunned at her father's harsh reply. "Cassandra was overwrought! Surely you think a little compassion is called for?"

"What is *called for* is a solid boundary walling off this family from any contact with the Harcourts. Viscount Everdene is just like his father! Showing off his skills, not caring who gets hurt."

"Lord Everdene was pressed to take up the sword by Lord Arkwright," Grace exclaimed. "When Will and the boys insisted he do so, he had little choice but to comply. Didn't you see how careful he was? He could have divested Will of that sword in a heartbeat."

"Let's not give the man too much credit," Will said in a huff.

"You are ascribing traits to Everdene that don't exist," her father replied. "You've seen him—what? Thrice in the past twenty years?"

That much was true. And yet, the way he'd reacted at the lake, the way he'd accepted her little brothers' apologies, the moments alone, in the kitchen at Everdene Hall, and in the morning room... she'd seen glimpses of a man she wished to know better.

Her father lifted his glass of port. "I understand the fascination women feel toward the viscount. Lucien Harcourt is rich, powerful, and fine looking enough to turn women's heads. But so are snakes."

"Papa!"

"You must accept that I know best," he bit out.

Hurt and anger flared inside her. She stared at her father as if he'd suddenly transformed into a stranger.

At her reaction, he seemed to check himself, speaking to her in measured tones that irritated her. "My dearest girl, you don't know Viscount Everdene. My judgement should be enough for you."

Her chin bumped up a notch. "Considering the changes around here of late, I prefer to trust my own," she said.

Her father's face flushed brick red, while Helen stifled a sob.

"I can't think why you would invite the Harcourts to The Willows to begin with," he blustered. "There was bound to be trouble! The only reason I allowed you to attend the dinner at Everdene Hall was because of Captain Harcourt's work on the village, and because the earl himself was never in residence there. I prefer you not pursue old friendships."

"Whatever ill happened between you and the earl all those years ago has no bearing on us now," Grace said. "I'm not a child in need of protection."

"No, you are in a far more precarious position as an unmarried gentlewomen, yet you would insist on dealing with his wound." He glared over the rims of his spectacles. "You were gone a very long time."

Grace thought of the kiss, the way the taut skin of Lucien's chest felt against her palm. Her cheeks burned. "*Someone* had to perform a hostess's duty here at The Willows. You could have attended our guest yourself, Papa, but you were too occupied with a wife who was carrying on more than the man who was actually bleeding!" The moment the words came out of her mouth, she regretted them.

Too late. Helen looked at her, aghast. "I'm sure the first Lady Elliot would have handled things flawlessly." She dabbed at her tears with the lace-edged handkerchief. "Barbara was everything I am not!"

A strange mixture of grief, defensiveness, and torn loyalties warred in Grace's father's eyes as he patted her shoulder. "It is no wonder you were overset. Any woman of proper feeling would be. But I will make certain you will not be put in such a position again." He turned to Grace, his expression darkening. "Helen informed me that you and she have been invited to for tea by Captain Harcourt's wife. You will send your regrets and do the same for any other invitations that come from Everdene Hall."

Grace's temper flared. "Why should I do so? They are my friends."

Her father slashed his hand through the air. "My decision is final. I'll not have you in the company of Viscount Everdene."

"Lucien will not even be at this tea!" Grace flung back.

"*Lucien!*" her father sputtered in outrage. "Since when have you two been on such informal terms?"

"Since we were eight and in dancing lessons. And you've naught to worry about regarding his lordship's presence at Everdene Hall. He intends to return to London." A sense of loss surprised Grace.

"Dearest Grace," Helen said. "I beg you see reason. Your father and I love you very much."

"Love me?" Good heavens. The woman barely knew her.

Helen reached for Papa's hand, giving him an adoring smile, before turning it to Grace. "It is because of that love that I wrote to my dear friend Deborah and explained that it is imperative that you depart for Scotland at once."

The world seemed to tilt at her stepmother's words. Grace heard Will blustering his objections as if from a distance. "Scotland?" Grace stared at her father, certain he'd object. When he did not, she turned her attention back to Helen. "That is hardly for you to decide!"

"You *will* show your stepmother *proper* respect," her father said. "Helen wrote at my direction."

"Not at mine!" Grace wheeled to face her father. "I'm not a child to be ordered about."

"You are a woman who should have been married long ago!" His words fell like stone.

Bitterness spilled poison inside her as she glared at him. "Now that Mama is dead, and you have no more use for me as a nursemaid, I'm to be married off? Do you feel even a qualm about sending me so far away from everyone I love? From the little boys?"

Her father reared back as if she'd slapped him. "I saw the way that Lord Everdene was looking at you, even if you did not!"

But she had. The confusion, the sensual attraction, the deep pull of understanding she could not deny. Despite multiple emotionally fraught encounters, she felt a kind of ease with Lucien she'd not encountered with any man she'd ever known.

Silence filled the room, her father's gaze challenging her to deny what they both knew was true. At last, he tugged at his cravat. "I am sending you away for your own good," he said. "I wish to see you married with a household of your own."

"In *Scotland*? With a man I've *never met*?"

"Deborah assures me that the local belles find her son most amiable!" Helen interjected.

"Then they are welcome to him!" Grace crossed her arms and gave a sharp nod.

"You will leave for Inverness within the week and remain there until the season begins. If a betrothal is not forthcoming from that quarter, I have also made it known to Neville's father that you are, as yet, unwed should Neville wish to renew his addresses."

Grace stared at him, feeling sick. "How could you?"

"Why should I not? You have fulfilled your duties to your mother. The impediments that separated you and Neville have dissolved."

"He's married."

"His American wife succumbed to yellow fever while he was surveying business interests in Louisiana."

"You contacted his family without a word to me? Mama would never have sanctioned this."

"Your mother is not here."

Her hands balled into fists. "I know that better than anyone! I was with her when she died, while you—"

She stopped herself just before she said the words she could never take back, but they hung in the air, unspoken. Her father's face went ice white. Helen snuffled in her handkerchief.

He patted his wife's hand, his gaze locked on Grace. "This discussion is over until you can conduct yourself as a dutiful daughter should."

"I will. As my *mother's* daughter." She turned on her heel and stormed from the room. Will caught up with her at the top of the stairs. He grabbed her elbow, spun her around and gathered her against him, clinging as they had after their mother died.

"Of all the abominable interference!" Will said. "Helen is shameless! And father—I'd never have believed he was capable of this. What are you going to do?"

Grace fought back angry tears. "I don't know. But I'm done having my choices decided by someone else. I'm not a—a chess piece to be shoved about at their whim."

She froze, her mother's voice whispering in her memory, sending strength and resolve through her veins. *A man may believe they control the chess board. But never forget...the queen is the most powerful piece of all.*

Her jaw hardened with resolve, her heart raced.

The next move—whatever it was—would be hers alone.

CHAPTER 12

*L*ucien knew where he would find his sister. She had disappeared the moment the carriage reached Everdene Hall and hadn't been seen since. But then, they'd all had the sense to scatter, Penelope and Simon to the nursery. Arkwright to the stables. Lucien to his room to bathe and change from his borrowed shirt and bloodstained clothes. Now, clad in his perfectly tailored trousers and coat, his black silk neckcloth pinned with a gold stick pin, and not a hair out of place, he climbed the stairs to the studio.

The cut on his chest burned.

The door was partially open, light from dozens of candles spilling out across the floor.

He'd always heard artists needed natural light to paint, but that hadn't stopped Cassandra. A paint-splashed smock covered her dress, as she filled a section of canvas with vivid red. She didn't notice him, so focused was she, painting as feverishly as she'd wielded the sword.

"Leave the tray on the table, Paola," she said without turning, her body so tense it seemed as if the tendons must snap.

"I'm not Paola," Lucien said softly.

Cassandra wheeled without first lifting her brush, leaving a streak of red upon the canvas like a wound. He saw her hand tremble, but she swiftly stilled it. She dumped her brush into turpentine, and grabbed a rag to dab at her hand.

"I startled you." He gestured to the red smear.

"Fortunately with oils I can paint over my mistakes. Life is not that simple."

"No," Lucien agreed, crossing to the easel. "After what happened at The Willows, there are things you and I need to discuss."

"Are there? I thought I made my feelings clear. Your sudden show of concern makes me sick. You threw Jane and I away, flinging us the occasional bank draft to sooth your guilty conscience. Now you can look us in the eye." Cassandra's mouth curled in bitterness.

"Twenty years…Did you ever think about us?"

"No." Truth was he'd tried not to think at all. The weeks following that hideous night, he'd had all he could do to keep Simon sane. Lucien had been horrified, as if he'd set a stable afire and could still hear the horses screaming…

That dark light shone in Cassandra's eyes. "I thought about *you*," she said. "What I'd say to you. What I'd do to make you suffer a small portion of what Jane and I suffered. You swept us out of Everdene Hall like yesterday's rubbish. Last time, I didn't know how to fight back. But I taught myself. Every moment I could steal away, until I mastered the skills…"

A raw, wary admiration rose in Lucien. As a girl, Cassandra had been all ribbons and dancing slippers and delight. The kind of girl adults smiled indulgently at, and eyes followed. Spirited, pretty, with quick intelligence. Loyal and protective toward their mother.

God, how different things might have been if he'd listened to her long ago.

"No man will ever find me helpless again."

She looked so fierce, and yet, society itself set forces against a woman that no sword could match.

"I wish to discuss arrangements to insure that," he said evenly.

Her upper lip curled in a sneer. "It is not your part to *arrange* anything for me anymore."

"Society's strictures say otherwise."

"I hate you for what you did to mother and me. But mostly, I hate you for what you did to Jane. Do you know she didn't speak for two years? I was afraid they'd lock her away in an asylum. I worked day and night to coax her to speak. *You* did that to her."

"I know." Lucien stood, impassive, schooling his face into a stoic expression that didn't show the knife to the heart. "What I did was wrong."

"If you're looking for absolution, you'll never get it from me. Why don't you go away and leave all of us alone? You're not one of us. You never were."

For a moment, he could picture how it was years before…Jane, Simon and Cass with their mother…that awkwardness he'd felt mixed in with the sense of pride in being set above them as the firstborn son and heir. He'd remained silent when the earl shared his scorn for the rest of the family.

It was as if Cassandra was remembering the same scene. "Go off and do whatever important business father's great heir has to do," she said, wiping her hands on a rag as if she would scrub him from the family as well. "Leave Jane and Simon, Mother and me in peace."

"That is my intention." Lucien straightened his cuff. "I have written my banker to instruct him that you may withdraw whatever funds you and Jane require—"

"Don't tell me you hope to send us away from Everdene again! I'll not be discarded like rubbish so you can be comfortable."

He cut her off in cool, firm accents. "Everdene Hall is your home, for as long as you wish to remain here. *I* will stay away unless pressing business compels me to return. If it does, I will give you fair warning so you and Jane may take a brief holiday or join Mother in Galen's Well if you prefer."

For a moment, she looked taken aback, a hint of softness in her face, then her expression hardened. "Good. You cannot leave soon enough for me. Now, I need to repair my painting." She wheeled back to her work, scooping up palette and brush.

He stared for a moment at the slash of red upon the canvas, then turned to leave. At the door, he paused and looked back at his sister. Her stiff shoulders, the aura of vigilance, as if she were waiting for a blow.

"Cass," he said, low, "for what it's worth…thank you. For looking after Jane."

He could see her catch her breath. "Your thanks are worth nothing since you are the one responsible for Jane's wounds. Just keep your promise and stay away from here."

"I give you my word."

As he made his way downstairs, an unexpected image flashed in his mind. Grace Elliot, her curls a-tumble, her eyes lifted to his. He could still feel the way she'd touched him, completely unintimidated by the stony armor he'd drawn about himself since the night he'd stood by as his sisters were banished.

Permanently leaving Everdene Hall was the only way to ensure his sisters could live in peace. It also ensured that he'd not chance to run into Grace again, picking berries…picnicking at the lakeside…or in the kitchen at midnight when the rest of the world was asleep.

He closed his eyes, remembering the feel of her fingertips, gentle, so capable, on his bare skin. Her tenderness. That innate kindness was more genuine than any he'd ever experienced.

Distancing himself from her was for the best. One more regret to pile on a lifetime of regrets.

He found Arkwright and Simon sitting in the billiard room, their cues leaning against the wall, a bottle of fine whiskey on the table between them.

Their gazes snapped up to Lucien, then to his chest. Worry creased Simon's brow. Both men knew better than to ask after his health.

"Luce, sit down, man," Arkwright ventured. "Have a drink. We were just about to pull out the playing cards. Care to join us?"

"No. I only wish to inform you that I've had a change in plans. I leave for London in the morning."

"What?" Simon started to rise from his chair. "You can't be serious."

Lucien pinned him with the implacable gaze that had kept rival MPs in their seats. "I wasn't asking for your opinion. I was informing you of my decision. Arkwright, you needn't chafe. You can stay for as long as we originally planned, of course. Enjoy the horses, the country."

"That is not my concern!" His friend actually seemed offended. "Surely it's not wise to be jolting around in a coach."

"Rhys is right, Luce. You're not invincible," Simon cautioned. "The wound will break open or become putrid."

As he looked at his brother, a vast chasm seemed to open up between them.

How could he explain the wound already had?

THE TRUNKS WERE STACKED AT THE ENTRANCE, WAITING TO BE loaded when the coach was brought round. He'd penned instructions for the latest repairs on the grist mill, hoping that he could delay the necessity of the far more expensive, permanent solution Simon favored. Everyone must economize until England—hell, all of Europe—shook off this run of poor harvests, potato blight, and crofters on the edge of rebellion who did not understand the challenges landlords faced.

"My lord," a footman announced from the door. "Someone is here to see you, the matter most urgent, I'm told."

Lucien shut his ledger and suppressed a sigh. "Someone about estate business?"

"Lady Grace Elliot."

Just her name was like a bracing breath of sea air. Whatever this was about, an unreasonably powerful wave of pleasure washed through him. He would be able to see her one more time.

"She awaits in the blue parlor," the footman said

Lucien stood, straightened his cravat, then went to meet her. She was wandering about the room as if she couldn't keep still. A riding habit of cerulean-blue velvet clung to her curves, gold braid across the front and rows of brass buttons giving it a military flair. A top hat with a streamer of net veil had been abandoned on a piecrust table, and she'd stripped off her gloves. But it was her face that arrested his attention. There was something almost frenetic in her eyes and flushed cheeks. Those lips that had haunted last night's dreams were drawn in such a desperate expression he crossed to her, taking her hands in his.

Her eyes went wide at the sight of him, and she stammered. "I'm sorry to—to arrive unannounced."

He smoothed his thumbs over her knuckles, wanting to ease the tension thrumming through her.

"Is something amiss? Please tell me you've not misplaced one of your brothers," he said, hoping to tease a smile from her.

"No. Not yet, anyway. I need to speak to you."

Lucien's brow creased. He had seen her in the most stressful circumstances imaginable. Half-naked in his arms by the lake. Alone in her nightgown with frosting clinging to her skin...In the party when the earl himself had swept in like a hawk and at the archery range when Cassandra had wounded him.

But never had he seen her so rattled. It sent a chill down his spine. Concern puckered his brow. "I am at your service. Come in. Sit down. Would you care for some refreshment?"

"N—no. But perhaps..." She glanced at where a decanter stood on his desk. "Perhaps just a—a taste of...of spirits."

He poured her some wine, then pressed the cut glass tumbler into her hand. She was trembling. He felt an unexpected twinge of concern—an unfamiliar tug in his chest. "Lady Grace, are you quite well? Whatever it is, you had best out with it."

She sipped the drink. He watched her pink tongue lick away a red droplet that clung to those rosy lips. She closed her eyes, her lashes curled on her rose-blushed cheeks. "This is so much harder than it seemed when I first thought of the idea," she said. Swallowing hard, she rummaged in the pocket of her gown and drew out a newspaper clipping, laying it on the table before her.

He frowned as he looked down at the image. It was one of the cartoons, the 'Elusive Viscount E' with alligators in bridal veils snapping at his heels.

"Not a particularly flattering likeness of me," Lucien observed.

"Is it true? That you are plagued with women seeking your hand?"

"I've had a narrow escape or two." He pictured Arkwright rolling his eyes. Were it not for pure luck and skill, Lucien might have been leg-shackled half a dozen times. Fortunately, he'd earned the enmity of those he'd outwitted, rather than gaining a wife.

Grace withdrew a handkerchief and seemed in danger of rending it to bits. "My lord, I have come with a—a business proposition I believe will be to both of our benefits."

"Indeed?"

"You need a wife and I…I need a husband."

Lucien stared at her, rendered speechless for, perhaps, the first time in his life. "I confess, of all the matters I thought I'd discuss today, this is the last," he said after a long moment. "You seemed a reasonable creature when we spoke before. What in God's name made you come up with this idea?"

"I know that this is an unusual proposition, but it could suit us both, don't you think? We get on well. You would no longer have marriage-minded mamas plotting to snare you for their daughters. I would be an asset to you in town, if that is what you desire. Otherwise, I would be quite happily situated here near my family."

But *I* won't be here. Lucien considered the promise he'd just made his sister.

Grace was willing to marry him to remain close to her family, when all he wanted to do was escape his own.

"I learned at my mother's knee the skills that are necessary to be an exemplary political hostess."

"Lady Barbara Elliot was a remarkable lady. Her talents in that realm are still talked about in London."

She glanced away briefly, her eyes glossed with tears. "Thank you for saying so," she said with aching sincerity. "Mama had a gift for getting opposing sides to talk to each other. More importantly, on occasion *listen*. She insisted that all men are more amiable when they've been fed a good meal in the company of a woman who knows how to guide conversation and mediate disagreements." A shy dimple winked on Grace's cheek. "Mama likened it to juggling knives."

"Pardon me?"

"If you know how to manage it, you can impress the company and aim blows at the correct target. If not, the bloodstains quite ruin the whole endeavor."

Lucien laughed. His own mother had no talent for such machinations. Lenora Harcourt, Countess of Ravenscroft, had ever been a gentle spirit, shy in large gatherings.

There had been a time Lucien had understood the earl's frustration with his wife.

He'd watched his father's friends and fellow lords forge

alliances, plan legislation, bring opponents to their knees with the help of the aristocratic wives who brought elegance, grace and a light, feminine touch to men's affairs, sometimes with a clarity that astonished.

There were worse prospects than having Barbara Elliot's daughter at one's side.

"So you would be my political hostess," he said carefully. "What benefit might there be to you, my dear?"

"As a viscount's wife, I would be able to retain my independence, and pursue causes I am passionate about. I would have entry to any drawing room in the land, and be able exert my influence and help to shape conversations."

"And what are these issues you are so eager to champion?"

"The fate of children, women. Injustices like slavery and factory conditions. The Poor Law. The kinds of things my family has fought for since Wilberforce gave his first speech on enslavement."

"Very forward-thinking of you. But not the whole truth, I'll be bound." He gently disentangled the handkerchief from her fingers and set it aside. "What is the real reason?"

She drew in a shuddering breath. "It's just…Scotland is so very far away. My father and Helen are sending me there before the week is out, pressing me to marry someone I've never even met."

Arranged marriages were common enough. But the thought of Grace being forced into such a situation by her ungrateful father made Lucien clench his fist. He forced his hand to relax then curved his palm against her cheek. "Why such sudden haste to whisk you away from The Willows?"

"You."

Lucien raised one brow in surprise.

She began to twist her hands together, and he feared they would fair no better than the handkerchief. He caught the tender fingers between his own.

"Papa is convinced that—that there is something between you and me."

"Ah," he said, stroking her hands. "Score one for Lord Elliot's intuition."

"Last night, after your accident, Bennet, Ethan and Avery couldn't sleep," she rushed on. "Their whole world is upside down, yet Father would send me away and leave them no one to comfort them. If I desert them…" Tears coursed down her cheeks. "Lucien, I can't bear to be sent so far away. Bennet is so little and Avery is so angry. I'm afraid he might do something desperate. And Ethan…I don't know what he's feeling half the time, but I need to find out."

Lucien swallowed hard, astonished at how deeply her plea affected him. He remembered all too well the kiss that had left him so damned restless, and the way she'd touched his bare chest, tended the wound with capable hands, undaunted by family drama, the bloody gash, the fact that he was a man she barely knew.

Was he actually tempted to accept her proposal?

"My dear, I would make the very devil of a husband," he said gently. "Even if we were mad enough to consider this…arrangement…there is an impediment. If Lord Elliot is willing to send you to Scotland to escape my attentions, he would hardly consent to our union."

She raised her chin, and looked straight into Lucien's eyes.

"If Papa knew you'd compromised me, he'd have no choice."

CHAPTER 13

*I*f *Papa knew you had compromised me, he would have no choice...*

Lucien stared, her words reverberating in his head.

She wanted him to march up to Lord Elliot and tell him…what? That he'd licked pink icing off of her skin in the middle of the night? That he'd held her against him beside the lake when she'd been as good as naked, wearing nothing but a soaked chemise?

"I know I am asking a great deal of you to go before my father and—and admit to a breach of honor."

Lucien's lip curled. "On the contrary. My honor has seldom been of concern to me. Besides, there is something in the thought of confounding your father's plans to send you to Scotland that brings me grim satisfaction. However, I dislike using your reputation as a weapon."

"I want you to do this. It is the only way to get him to agree to our terms."

She looked so fervent, hopeful. How desperate must she be, turning to him, Lucien Harcourt, Viscount Everdene, and trusting him to make things right? He had to put some safe distance between them so he could *think*. He crossed to the table and poured himself a drink, then sampled it, trying to adopt a businesslike mien.

"And what exactly are those terms you speak of?" he said, "I never enter into contracts unless the particulars are spelled out."

She fretted her lower lip. "I need to remain close to my little brothers. As for the rest, I'm sure we can come to an understanding."

"You have outlined your expectations. It is important I clarify mine."

"Of course." She had a leaf caught in her hair, a small one that must have fallen there on her ride.

He wanted to pluck it out, set it aside, but he forced himself to remain where he was.

"If you are imagining the two of us sharing comfortable family outings or frequent holidays at The Willows, you must surrender that expectation at once. I am not a man who desires such ties."

Did he see a flicker of doubt in those large, dark-fringed eyes? Good. She should be wary of him and understand the kind of marriage she was considering.

"Should we wed," he continued, "you are welcome to visit The Willows as often as you like. I will not stand in your way, but I will not be accompanying you."

After a moment she nodded. "I understand. Of course, there will be special instances." She gave him a tremulous smile. "You will wish to celebrate Christmas with our children."

Lucien suppressed a shudder. Last Christmas, Simon and Penelope had attempted to bring holiday cheer to Everdene Hall for the first time in twenty years. They'd invited the villagers from New Everdene, the grateful tenants who now inhabited cottages Penelope had designed, and his brother had risked everything to build. There had been holly garlands and bright red ribbons, kissing balls of mistletoe and a flaming bowl full of raisins for children to snatch and play snapdragon. It had been chaos, children running about, people far happier than anyone had a right to be.

Lucien had sought refuge in the stables where Simon's golden horses had been under the care of their stable master, Jamie McLeod. McLeod had been a prisoner of war for two years, captive of the Afghan tribes that had massacred British troops at Kabul. He had no more stomach for celebration than Lucien did.

He turned his attention back to the present, eyeing Grace and that damned leaf, still in her hair. "I am forced to attend certain balls and routs with the ton because of my station," he said. "I would rather be dragged behind one of Simon's horses than endure a fete overrun with children. I prefer spending Christmas at my club."

The warmth in Grace's gaze faded, and she looked down at her hands. He waited to hear her withdraw her proposal, say she'd made a grievous mistake and race out the door.

Was that what he wanted her to do? It was, and he decided to drive the point home. "I admire your concern for your brothers, but is it a great sacrifice you make for them," he said. "You have an unusual capacity for affection, Grace. Wouldn't you rather marry a man who can return it?"

"I want you."

A shaft of desire shot through him. In her innocence, could she have any idea what those three words did to him? God knew what the marriage would be like, but he'd never desired a woman more. If they wed, he would have the right to take this woman to his bed. Explore her body as he wished to. He felt himself harden.

She would give him the heir and spare that duty demanded of him. He would enjoy getting those sons upon her lovely body and leave the raising of them to her. No doubt she would come to realize she'd made a devil's bargain…but until then, he could teach her the power of her own desires. She'd been so damned responsive when he'd kissed her. He'd felt the sensuality in her, passion denied far too long.

It would be so easy for him to take what she offered, and yet, she didn't know Lucien at all. Didn't he owe her the truth?

He put more space between them, his pleasurable thoughts growing dim. "You believe that you want me. But you don't know me at all. You must have some understanding about the man you would wed."

A shy smile played at the corners of her lips. "I would like to know you better."

"I doubt you would be pleased with what you discover. My mother, sisters, yes, and Simon, too, suffered great wrongs at my hands before we left Everdene as children and after. I regret it. But that changes nothing. You saw my sister's anger when she lashed out at me at the picnic."

"Yes."

"There are secrets that are not mine to share, but I will tell you this. Cassandra is right to hold me responsible for much ill that has befallen her. I deserve every scrap of her ire. Jane can barely look at me without her hands shaking. My mother forgives me…but—" He stopped, hiding the anguish in his eyes. "You heard Cassandra mention my obsession with King Arthur as a boy? I am Mordred, who brought the kingdom down. I may never know the full extent of the damage I did."

Her brow puckered, and he wished he knew what she was thinking. "When your sisters left Everdene, I remember you were a boy yourself, were you not?" she mused. "Fourteen years old?"

"My age is irrelevant."

"As is your past to me," she said. "I have given my situation much thought, and I am certain this marriage is what I want."

Silence stretched between them. Their gazes locked, held.

Seconds ticked away as he pondered the thought, tried to dismiss it, and failed.

"Then you shall have it," he whispered, his voice was husky to his own ears. He closed the space between them, angled her face up, and slowly took her mouth with his. She tasted of honey and strawberries and a deep well of goodness he had never known. When he drew away at last, he felt shaken to his core.

"I will come to see your father this afternoon," he promised.

For the first time, a dart of fear showed in her eyes. "Perhaps we could elope?"

"No." He cut her off too abruptly.

She peered up at him, startled.

Lucien drew a steadying breath and traced the vulnerable curve of her cheek. A wave of almost painful tenderness washed through him. "You will make a beautiful bride, my Lady Grace," he said and she flushed a lovely pink at his praise. "I want the world to see you become my viscountess."

If only that were his real motive. Somewhere deep within, he wanted to strike out at those who had hurt her. An elopement would make things too easy on Elliot. He'd forced his daughter into this untenable position. He could damn well watch her wed a man he hated and see what his selfishness had wrought.

Lucien stood on the front stairs, watching until Grace and her horse disappeared over the hillside, her veil streaming behind her. It was hard to believe what had happened in the past hour. His valet, Graves, had waited at a discreet distance until Lucien turned back to the house. "The coach is ready to be loaded, my lord," Graves said. "When will we be leaving for London?"

Not nearly soon enough to satisfy Cassandra, Lucien thought with a twinge of conscience. So much for his promise. He'd explain that this was a temporary delay, but he could already picture his sister's reaction.

"You may send the coach to the stables and take my trunks to the steward's house instead."

The servant blinked in bewilderment. "The steward's house, my lord?"

"Yes. But first, have my horse brought round. Be quick about it."

Graves was unaccustomed to such errands, but knew enough to obey.

Lucien returned to the house and went to where some of the family treasures were kept. By the time he descended the front steps to the carriage circle with a small, velvet box in the pocket of his riding coat, a stable boy was leading Atlas up to the mounting block.

The horse whickered as two familiar riders came into view. Arkwright seemed to be reveling in his time astride one of the Turkoman horses. But it was Simon who captured Lucien's gaze. The scapegrace brother who'd spent his youth one reckless act away from breaking his neck, rode as if he and his mount were forged of myths and legends. That gift with horses had saved his life in Afghanistan.

The two men obviously spied Lucien at the same time, and veered toward him, reining in at the foot of the stone steps.

"Glad we got back in time to say goodbye," Simon said as his golden stallion danced sideways on elegant hooves. "I thought you'd be on your way to London."

"I'm not leaving."

"What?"

"I've had a change in plans." Lucien swung onto Atlas, gritting his teeth at the stab of pain in his chest.

"Not more trouble with father, I hope."

"Oh, there will be. Not that I care." Lucien adjusted the cuff of his riding glove and picked up the reins. "You may be the first to congratulate me. I'm to be married."

"Married?" the pair of men echoed as if it were a jest.

"Yes. Married. Lady Grace Elliot has consented to be my viscountess."

Arkwright's jaw dropped, Simon gaping as if his prized stallion had transformed into a donkey.

Lucien spurred his horse toward The Willows and laughed, knowing he'd not forget their expressions for a very long time.

CHAPTER 14

Grace paced the morning room, every nerve in her body sizzling with tension since Lucien had disappeared into her father's study. It felt as if the two men had been sequestered forever, instead of the half-hour marked by the clock on the mantel.

"Whatever can they be speaking about?" Helen fretted. "Your father sounds quite angry, but I cannot make out what they are arguing over."

Grace knew, full well. Her father's fury was evident, despite the muffled words, yet Lucien's tone of voice never rose to betray any emotion.

"I cannot understand why your Papa dislikes his lordship so much," Helen said quietly. "He seems quite gentlemanly and is very rich."

She had been nattering on since the men had disappeared behind the study door, and Grace was beginning to consider the merits of using her handkerchief to gag the woman so she might have some hope of hearing what was going on behind closed doors. At that moment, the door opened, and the men came into the chamber. Her father's hair stood on end as if he'd torn at it with his hands, a devastated look on his face.

It reminded Grace of the day the doctor had told them Mama was going to die.

"Is it true what Lord Everdene claims?" Papa demanded, his eyes begging her to end this nightmare. "Did he compromise you?"

Grace felt as if she were swallowing a stone. "Yes."

Anger, shame and desperation flared in her father's face.

"We did not mean for it to—to happen," Grace said, "but we found ourselves quite carried away."

Lucien gave her a bracing smile. "You may be sure I would not pursue this, were it not for my high regard for Lady Grace. From the moment we renewed our acquaintance—"

Her father wheeled on Lucien. "All parliament knows that the Viscount Everdene never does anything without a self-serving purpose! Did your father put you up to this? Some sort of sick revenge? I should call you out!"

"Papa!"

"Vernon!" Helen cried.

"Far better to escort your daughter to the church to be wed." Lucien looked so tall, strong and in command that he made her father seem small.

"You will make Grace miserable," Papa asserted.

Lucien's jaw clenched. "I think Lady Grace would be far more so were she exiled to Scotland as you've planned." At the cutting remark, sweat beaded her father's face. Lucien crossed to her, took her hand. "No one is more surprised than I to discover Lady Grace is essential to me."

She looked at Lucien, stunned. Was he attempting to soothe her father's concerns? No. He met her eyes, just the hint of a wry smile curving those sensual lips.

"Speak to your daughter," Lucien said. "Ask what *she* wishes."

Papa sputtered in outrage. "Grace, tell me you do not wish to wed this man."

Grace drew a deep breath. "I do wish it," she said. "I know this is a surprise to you, and an unwelcome one. But the truth is, I am old enough to decide for myself. I do not to need your permission, Papa, but I hope I might have your blessing."

Helen rushed into the exchange, flushed with enthusiasm. "Of course you will give it, won't you, Vernon? Have we not been urging Grace to make a match? And now she has done so, with one of the most sought-after bachelors in the kingdom!" Helen turned to Grace. "When do you wish to marry?"

"We shall be wed as soon as the banns are cried," Lucien said.

"There is no need to rush," her father insisted. "Lady Elliot and I planned to give Grace the pleasure of a London season after her own was cut short. To pamper her with gowns from the best modistes, the finest parties and entertainments. That will give you time to consider whether this match is wise."

Lucien slipped his arm around Grace's waist. "As my viscountess, Lady Grace will have her choice of invitations, her choice of modistes and milliners. I can see no purpose in delaying our nuptials now that we've decided to wed."

Helen clasped her hands, blissful. "Oh, Vernon. Never mind new gowns for the season! We can plan her trousseau instead! We will leave for London as soon as may be! Just think, our Grace—a viscountess, and someday, Countess of Ravenscroft!"

***

Few things had given Lucien more pleasure than seeing the look on Vernon Elliot's face when he'd realized he would not have the power to control Grace's future. God knew, Lucien had seen that dictatorial attitude visited often enough on his mother, his sisters, and other women he'd encountered. What a hellish space to inhabit, the reality that the reins of your life would forever be in the hands of someone else, merely because you were a woman.

It felt damned good to put a stop to it in this one instance. He could hear whoops and footsteps pounding in the hall just outside the door, the young Elliots running riot, no doubt. That was all this contretemps needed. Three pirates who hated him. Please God, let them veer off and torment someone else, Lucien thought.

Of course, Lady Elliot trilled out an invitation. "Children, come hear the wonderful news!"

It was all Lucien could do not to clap his hand over the woman's mouth.

The boys thundered into the room, jostling each other in a jumble of arms and legs, their clothes askew and some unidentifiable substance smearing the littlest one's nose.

"Your *sister* is to be *married!*" Lady Elliot exclaimed. "She is to be Lady Everdene! A *viscountess!*"

If Grace's father had looked dismayed, the three boys looked stricken. Avery's freckles stood out like pox on his ashen face. Ethan huddled close to his older brother while fat tears welled on Bennet's lashes.

If this was an example of Lady Elliot's mothering skills, no wonder the boys were in full rebellion. Doubtless, Grace had wanted to tell her brothers she was to be wed herself, breaking the news in her own reassuring way. There could be no chance of that now. Lucien doubted a cannon salvo could have had greater impact.

Avery glared at Grace, betrayal flashing in his eyes. "You promised you wouldn't leave us."

Lucien could see Grace try to gather herself, groping for some way to repair the damage Helen had done. "That is the wonderful thing about this marriage," she said, giving him a gentle smile. "I won't be moving far away. Lord Everdene lives close enough that you and I can visit as often as we like."

"Will you read stories to us and tuck us in?" Bennet asked. His bottom lip trembled.

Ethan elbowed him. "Course not."

"We're too big for that anyway," Avery said gruffly. "We only let Grace do it because…because she's used to it." If he'd been a head taller, Lucien thought, he'd have been calling for pistols at dawn.

Grace knelt, trying to gather them into her arms. None of the boys were having it. They strained back as if she'd slapped them.

"You'll be going off to school yourselves soon," she said, burying her empty hands in her skirts. "But when you come home for holiday, I'll be close enough to visit for dinner, to hear all of your news. We'll still have outings by the lake, and—"

"You promised you wouldn't leave," Ethan asserted stubbornly.

She swallowed hard. "It was wrong of me to promise that."

"So you lied!" Avery snapped.

Lucien could see Grace's throat constrict. "Sometimes, life… changes in ways we—we can't predict," she began.

Helen cut her off. "Why, look at your dear papa and me! Who would have thought we would marry and be so happy?"

Oh, yes, that will help, Lucien thought. Remind them of the last catastrophic change in their lives. Could the woman not see she was making things worse?

"A promise is a promise!" Avery cried, then spun to face his sister. "You can't leave us with *her*!"

A shudder went through Grace, and Lucien sensed she was fighting back tears.

"Avery!" Lord Elliot boomed. "You will not speak of your stepmother that way! I demand you apologize this instant!"

But Avery was beyond fearing his father's wrath, the focus of his heartbreak on the sister who had always sheltered him. "I'll never forgive you if you marry him!" he vowed, then he spun to run out of the room. At the last moment, Avery veered toward Lucien and balled a fist, slamming it into his stomach with all the strength in his small arm. Lucien doubled over in surprise as pain radiated from the fencing wound Cassandra had dealt him.

"Avery!" Grace cried. "Oh, Lucien!"

He straightened, one hand on his chest. "Let him go," he said, trying to suck in a steadying breath as the other boys pelted after their brother. "Emotions are rather high at the moment. I think we could all use some time to cool down. Perhaps…a bit of fresh air in the garden would not come amiss." He eyed Lord Elliot. "My man of business will wait upon you with the marriage contracts," he said. "If there are any other matters to discuss, I will be in the steward's house near Everdene Hall."

Helen's brow puckered. "Surely as lord of the manor, you reside in the manor itself. If it becomes too crowded, others in your family can decamp to another location."

Lucien leveled her a chill look. "I am not in the habit of debating my choice in living arrangements with anyone, Lady Elliot."

Helen's hand fluttered to her ample breast. "Of course…I only… I just…"

"Lady Grace?" Lucien said extending his arm. Grace slipped her hand through it, and he led the way through the hall. Partway down, he eyed a black mark on one of the silk peacocks.

"No wonder your brothers deface the wallpaper," he muttered under his breath. "She's lucky they don't draw a mustache on her while she sleeps."

Though he wanted to lighten her mood, she gave a soft sniff. He was the very devil when it came to dealing with crying women. But somehow, the notion of Grace in tears chafed.

He led her to a small arbor in the garden where they would be concealed from the house. There, he handed her his handkerchief.

She accepted it gratefully, dabbing at her eyes. "I am so sorry you had to endure that family scene," she said. "Helen's prattling… my father's outburst…I don't know what got into him."

"Probably an understandable sense of caution."

"And my brothers…they were distraught, but I'm appalled that Avery struck you." Her voice cracked. "You must let me look at your wound again to make sure he didn't break it open." She reached for the front of Lucien's waistcoat, but he gently grasped her fingers in his.

"My dear, much as I look forward to your lovely hands on my bare chest, I prefer to wait until our wedding night. I fear your touch would undo me."

She flushed. "You are trying to distract me."

He canted his head, eager to prevent feminine waterworks. "Is it working?"

"Oh, Lucien…" Her voice cracked. "The boys…my heart aches for them. It was wrong of me to promise them that I would never leave. I know that now, but at the time, I would have said anything to soothe them."

"Even had you not agreed to marry me, it was inevitable that you would leave—or *they* would grow up and leave. They'll get over it in time."

"Did you?"

"Did I what?" he asked, taken aback.

"When your sisters left for Italy. Did you get over it?"

Jesus. Lucien looked down into those hurting, haunted eyes. "My dear, there is no comparison between my sisters and your brothers."

She fidgeted with the signet ring winking on his finger. "Do you think before the wedding we might be able to show them where we are to live? Remind them of how close we'll be living?"

Lucien recoiled inwardly, but said, "Of course—preferably when I am not at home."

She gave a watery chuckle. "Thank you. Perhaps seeing the horses again will ease things. I don't suppose you have a supply of toads available?"

"Horses will have to do."

She stood on tiptoe and kissed his cheek. "Thank you! You won't regret it!"

He already regretted the confounded family complications his decision had produced. But those lips…so tempting and pink, the sparkle of tears on her spiky lashes, and the hint of a smile were too much for him to resist. He framed her face in his hands and lowered his mouth to hers. He kissed her slowly, thoroughly, felt his blood heat as he traced the seam of her lips with his tongue. She opened to him, and then he was tasting her, sampling deep secrets yet to be revealed. She pressed her body against him, and he knew she could feel him harden against her. He trailed kisses down her throat, had a fleeting thought…they should have eloped. If they had, he could have her in his bed by nightfall.

At last he drew away. Her gaze found his, her eyes hazy with desire.

Possessiveness shot through him. Soon she would be his wife… "Perhaps this marriage is not what you imagined, but I think we will deal well together," he mused. "From the moment I pulled you out of the water, I wanted you in my bed."

He reached into his pocket, drew out a small velvet box, and opened it. A ring gleamed against the blue velvet. It was a large diamond, square cut, fit for a future countess. Lucien lifted her hand and slid the cool circlet onto her finger, vaguely displeased with the way the diamond looked on her hand. Some instinctive reaction to a step he'd sworn never to take?

"In three weeks' time you will be my wife," he said, as much to himself as to her.

Grace gave him an uncertain smile, and he suddenly wondered if she might change her mind. Her father might talk her out of it, or his sisters might…No. This is what she wanted. She was the one who had proposed to *him*.

"I hope you will be satisfied to stay in the steward's house for a brief time after we wed," Lucien said. "My presence in Everdene

Hall makes it uncomfortable for my sisters at present. I wish for Jane to be able to settle in."

She peered up at him with a softness in her eyes, as if he were doing something selfless. "Yes, of course," she said. "How very kind of you. I'm sure the steward's house will be quite lovely."

Don't look at me that way, he thought. *I'm not the man you think I am...*"Of course, we will depart for Raven's Court, my townhouse on Curzon Street soon after the ceremony," he said.

"It will be a relief to have all this wedding fuss over with. Truth is, I am rather dreading the trip to the city with my stepmother," Grace confided. "I'm fearful I might end up in a gown scattered with peacocks."

"Mustachioed or not?"

She smiled, slightly. "Helen is most enthusiastic, but all I can think about is the fact that the last time I went shopping for garments in London, it was with Mama. Just before my first season."

Lucien's instinct was to change the subject away from something painful. Instead, he said, "Tell me."

"She was so excited. One of the happiest memories I have is Mama and I alone for once, without any of my brothers. I had her all to myself as we reveled in selecting gowns and slippers and bonnets. The shopkeepers treated her like the queen, and she was so warm to them all. I think...perhaps...she already had some inkling she was ill, though she never let on to me."

Grace twisted the diamond on her hand, as if it chafed. "There was this bit of Honiton lace, the most exquisite I'd ever seen and so expensive. She said it would be perfect to trim my wedding gown when I met a man worthy of my love."

Lucien felt a twinge. Had Grace dreamed of wearing it for her former betrothed? What was the blackguard's name again? "Did you mean to wear for Freyne?"

"No. He hadn't paid his addresses yet." She looked away, and he wondered if the deepening shadow over her countenance had to do with that disappointment in love. But then, she continued, the true source of her heartache evident. "I imagined my mother and I would have all the time in the world. Trousseaus to select.

Baptismal gowns for babes when they came and clothing as they grew. She would have been the most wonderful grandmother."

I wonder what she would have thought of me. Lucien could well imagine. Barbara Elliot had been notorious for her forthright speeches. He could picture her reaction to the way he had secured her daughter's hand, and it would not have been pleasant.

"We never know what will come, do we?" Lucien mused. *I never imagined you.*

"No. There were so many things I took for granted."

The sudden loss, the grief, the wistfulness in her eyes tugged at that place where his heart should have been.

He imagined what this trip with her stepmother would be like for her.

A better man wouldn't let her face it alone.

CHAPTER 15

Never, in all her years, had Grace imagined she would be counting the hours until she could escape The Willows. But then, between her father's grim censure and the boys' reproaches, she felt as if someone had painted a T for Traitor on her breast.

In the two days since her betrothal, gloom had overtaken her as well, and she knew, with sudden certainty, that 'home' would never be the same.

She peered down at the newspaper she'd been trying to distract herself with in the study, but even the news of revolution spreading through the continent and unrest fomenting in England couldn't distract her from her own troubles.

There was a problem with perceiving the situation with her family clearly, instead of through a haze of self-deception. She couldn't unsee the consequences of her father's second marriage and feign ignorance.

Difficult as her father's anger and her brothers' heartache was to witness, Helen's enthusiasm was hardest to bear, as if new gowns and the title of viscountess could sweeten the bitterest draught. Her stepmother's eagerness to stamp her own wishes on this wedding made the pain of Mama's absence more acute.

"If only you were here," Grace whispered to herself. "You'd know just what to do."

But her mother was gone and 'home' would never be hers again.

"Lady Grace?" a mournful voice called through the closed door. Pevensey, the old butler as grief-stricken as everyone else.

A spark of temper fired in Grace. "Yes," she said more sharply than intended. They were preparing for her wedding, not her funeral, for pity's sake.

"The Viscount Everdene has *unexpectedly* come to call."

"Send him in," she said, stung by that slight disapproval in Pevensey's tone.

Lucien strode in and suddenly the entire room seemed brighter. She almost flung the paper onto the table at the sight of him, wanting to spring from the chair into his arms. "Lucien." His name felt so right, and for the first time that morning, she felt able to breathe.

He crossed to her, scooped up her hand and kissed it. "Are you quite well, my dear? You look rather pale." He examined her face then looked her in the eye. "I take it, your family's mood regarding our betrothal has not changed?"

"Let us just say that it's lovely to see anyone who isn't scowling at me."

"I think you should reserve judgement until I apprise you of the reason for my call," he said dryly. "I bring news you may not welcome."

Her stomach sank. Was it possible someone had thrown up an impediment to their wedding? Had he reconsidered? And if he did...She couldn't bear the thought. "What news?" she asked, wary.

"In light of our betrothal, my mother has voiced a desire to know you better. Hence, she would very much like to accompany you and your stepmother to London to select your trousseau. I understand this might pose an inconvenience to you. Should you agree to include her—"

"No!" Grace cried.

He looked taken aback by her vehemence. "I will tell her your plans are already set. Perhaps you could call on her for tea, instead? She had hoped to invite you and your stepmother stay with her in our townhouse on Curzon Street."

"You misunderstand me! Your mother's presence would be no

inconvenience at all! We—I would love to stay with her. In fact, it would be a relief."

"Indeed?"

"Helen suggested we stay in London with her friend, Mrs. Kemble. That would have been pure torture! She is an insufferable, bitter…" Grace flushed. "Forgive me, my lord. Truth is, I cannot wait to leave for London. I only hope that by the time I return home, this tempest has calmed down."

Home…she felt a twinge at the word. The Willows didn't feel like home, not anymore. From the peacock wallpaper to the constant flutter of Helen's drama, all of the undercurrents Grace had done her best to gloss over became more glaring with every day that passed.

Lucien fixed that piercing gaze on her. "Has it been very bad?"

"I am not used to being the subject of disapproval. It has given me a most uncomfortable glimpse as to what my brother Avery endures."

"Hmm." Lucien crossed to where she'd left newspapers she'd been reading. He gazed down at the etching of a factory with an angry crowd outside. "It happens that I have business in the city as well. Perhaps I will join your party, at least for some of the time. My mother insists I be on hand to take you to Gunter's to eat cherry ices when necessary. She informs me that trousseau shopping is quite exhausting work."

Grace managed to laugh. "You have no idea—especially with my stepmother involved. Please, tell the countess I remember her fondly from childhood. I know Mama liked her very much." A lump formed in Grace's throat. "Lady Ravenscroft's company will be the closest I can come to having Mama with me. Thank you for this, Lucien."

He looked up from the newspaper. "These plans are all my mother's. I have nothing to do with this arrangement—save providing ices when necessary."

THE COUNTESS GREETED GRACE WITH MOTHERLY WARMTH AS THEIR trunks were loaded into the Harcourt traveling coach. She linked her arm through Grace's as the two women walked toward the elegant equipage. "To think when your mother and I paired you and Lucien up for dancing—who could have imagined that that you would make a match all these years later?" A dimple appeared in her soft cheek. "I seem to remember you stomping on his toes from time to time...we will not say on purpose."

"It was on purpose," Grace confessed, with a teasing nod toward her betrothed who was issuing orders to the coachman. She lowered her voice, leaning in. "But he deserved it. He looked so put out when he had to dance with me."

The countess laughed, and Lucien looked over his shoulder, startled, as if the sound was far too rare.

A shadow crossed the countess's face as she watched her son. "I wish, above all things, for my children to be happy and loved. With Lucien, I feared—" She caught Grace's hand and squeezed it. "Yet, here you are," she whispered, her voice thick.

Grace's own throat ached with emotion. While it was not the same as having Mama with her, from the moment Grace saw the gentle countess who had once been her mother's dear friend, she'd felt a link with those precious times of her childhood.

Those halcyon days before the rift between their families, before Mama's illness and death had darkened Grace's world, reminding her of a time she had not felt encumbered with the cares of everyone at The Willows. When she'd felt free. Happy and loved...

How could she tell this woman with her hope-filled eyes, that this marriage was a business arrangement? How any hope of love and happiness was a complete unknown for this bride and groom, considering the terms they'd agreed to?

Feeling an awkward silence that needed to be filled, she was glad when Helen suddenly scurried toward them, beaming as she addressed the countess. "I cannot tell you how very grateful we are that you wish to accompany and host us on our trip. We shall have such a wonderful time. Isn't that right, Grace?"

"Wonderful," Grace said, pasting a matching smile on her face.

GRACE PEERED UP AT RAVEN'S COURT, THE ELEGANT TOWNHOUSE ON Curzon Street. The façade was the color of terracotta, trimmed in crisp white, the door dark green. A black iron gate and brick walls divided it from the other, similar structures that marched up the street.

To think…this would be her home when she was in London from now on. As such, the staff gathered to greet at her, their intense scrutiny making her feel a bit like one of Bennet's forest creatures being examined beneath a magnifier. Doubtless they were wondering what their new mistress would be like.

It made the marriage seem real in a way it had not before.

The countess and maids saw to Helen, while the housekeeper, Mrs. Brumby—a stern-faced matron who seemed reluctant to surrender her ring of keys to a new mistress—showed Grace about.

The rooms were pleasant, yet with nothing personal to show who Lucien Harcourt was. At last, Mrs. Brumby led her upstairs, in the opposite direction the other guests had gone. At the farthest end of the corridor, she opened a door and ushered Grace inside. The furnishings were simple, a large four-poster bed with pale blue curtains, a dressing table and escritoire tucked beneath a window. A single chair with Prussian-blue cushions beside the fireplace.

"This is to be your chamber, now and in the future." Mrs. Brumby's mouth pinched with a hint of disapproval as she eyed the door that led to the adjoining chamber. "The master ordered that you be placed here rather than with the other ladies."

The notion was a trifle unsettling. No wonder Mrs. Brumby regarded Grace with a touch of censure. Whatever could Lucien be thinking lodging Grace here? Did he plan to avail himself of that door even before they were wed? Her cheeks burned at the thought.

Mrs. Brumby must have sensed her discomfort. "If you object to these quarters, my lady, I can have the maids move you."

"Thank you, Mrs. Brumby." Lucien's deep voice came from the corridor as he strode inside and joined them. "My future viscountess is not one to indulge in such missish nonsense. You may go. Close the door behind you."

"As you wish, my lord." The woman dipped a stiff curtsey, the keys at her waist jangling as she left. Grace wondered how long it would be before Mrs. Brumby and the butler would be bemoaning such lack of decorum. Lucien, however, seemed not to notice his servant's disapproval or Grace's own discomfort.

"I know this arrangement is a trifle unusual, but it seemed only practical to situate you in this room, in case there are alterations you wish to make before we take up residence," he said.

Grace felt a shiver of emotion at the images his words conjured. This would be the chamber where she would begin her new life as Lucien's wife, share his name, and his bed…"Perhaps we could plan any changes to the room together," she ventured. "It would be lovely to have a pair of comfortable chairs by the fireplace where we could sit together of an evening."

"Two chairs will not be necessary. This suite of rooms will be yours alone. I will maintain my own next door."

The abrupt words startled her. She hesitated a moment before she said, "I see."

"Are you displeased with the room?"

"No. I was just thinking…For thirty years, my parents shared a bedchamber until my mother got sick. She had difficulty sleeping and so my father moved into a different room."

"Only practical."

"Was it? Because sometimes at night, I heard her weeping over the distance he'd put between them." Why had she told Lucien that? Suddenly she felt the need to add, "Of course, their marriage was far different than ours will be. But…I always thought my father couldn't bear to see her suffer, and his moving into a separate bedchamber was…somehow wrong."

Cowardly, she added silently, old resentment flaring. She'd moved a cot into her mother's room soon after, because she couldn't bear to leave her alone late at night when doubts and fears of death crept in among the shadows.

Lucien's ice-blue eyes fixed on hers. "Perhaps it is best that we will have no such expectations," he said.

Shoving those memories aside, she glanced around at the room. The heavy drapes blocked all light. What would her own marriage hold? She wondered. To be so *very* separate from the day they wed…

The dark of the room seemed suddenly overwhelming, and she

crossed over to the window, threw the drapes open, letting the light in. She'd had far too much darkness in her life, and this was one small thing she could do on her own.

AFTER TWO DAYS IN THE CITY, GRACE'S FEET ACHED WITH SO MUCH traipsing from linen drapers to milliners, fan shops and shoemakers, then back again. Helen had been in ecstasy as they'd pored over fashion plates, attempting to convince Grace to choose the outrageous colors and patterns Helen favored. Not that there was any chance of Grace doing so, and she was thankful to find an ally in her soon-to-be mother-in-law who managed to gently redirect Helen's attention to the far more understated shades that Grace preferred. Lady Ravenscroft was so changed from the countess she'd known as a child, and yet, in her deep kindness, still the same —and still beautiful, despite the years.

What had changed was the hint of sadness in the countess's eyes whenever she looked at Lucien. It seemed brittle and tentative. An underlying current of painful and exquisite carefulness in their dealings with each other.

All might have seemed well to anyone less intuitive. Helen certainly had no clue anything was amiss. If Grace had to guess, however, it had much to do with Lucien's need to fill every minute of his day with business, meeting them during the afternoons without fail out of duty. He would escort them to luncheon or Gunter's and then take his leave. Grace, herself, might not have noticed the delicate way they interacted, if not for the occasional, unguarded glances she caught between the two. No doubt about it. Lucien's mother moved through her son's world as if picking her way gingerly across uncertain ground…

Helen, on the other hand, pushed her way through heedlessly, as if clearing a path for 'our soon-to-be viscountess.'

Today, they wove their way through the vendors hawking posies and embroidered kerchiefs, Helen chatting away with the countess about the wonders of the shop recommended by Mrs. Kemble. "Have you ever shopped there?" she asked, then nattered on without waiting for a reply, as was her habit. "Apparently, this is *the* shop that is the most fashionable, and dear Mrs. Kemble insists that if we are to have *the* wedding of the season, we *must* acquire Grace's wedding gown from there."

Grace, determined to get it over with as soon as possible, glanced up at a bird sitting atop the raised sword of a bronze cavalier. The sense of familiarity on seeing it, reminded her of her last trip to London years ago with her mother. A warmth spread in her heart at the forgotten memory, her mother pointing high up to the statue's stalwart gaze locked on something across the square. "That's how I found my favorite modiste," she'd said. "I thought to myself, what's he looking at? Whatever it is, that's where I want to go. And there she was. Madame Lavoie, her shop newly opened, and I one of her first customers."

Grace stopped mid-step, following the statue's gaze across the square toward the very establishment her mother had frequented so long ago. The paint on the exterior was not as she remembered it, but the sign dangling above was unforgettable. A unicorn with a gauzy veil draped around it. Beneath, in gold letters: M.m. Lavoie, Modiste.

"I wish to go there," she exclaimed, her heart pounding.

"We are going to the shop down the street!" Helen protested. "Mrs. Kemble was most particular—"

But Grace was already hastening across the square toward the blue-painted door. Behind her, she heard the countess' voice. "It is Grace's wedding. If she desires—"

Grace didn't hear the rest. She opened the door, and stepped in. The scent of dried roses hit her, and with it vivid memories of her trip here with her mother. A rainbow of fabrics and trims were arranged around the charmingly outfitted room, completed gowns displayed on dress forms. Gleaming mirrors with distinctively carved frames still graced the pale pink walls, the same color as the dried rose petals filling the crystal cut bowl near the leaded window. She could see her younger self, selecting fabric, then retreating to the fitting room, her reflection in the mirror as she stood on the small, raised platform, seamstresses fluttering about...

Mama peering over her shoulder, her face glowing with love and pride.

A movement at the back of the room brought her swiftly back

to the present. The modiste, in the midst of giving orders to a young girl about beads to be stitched on a bodice, looked up and froze.

The woman's features were so familiar to Grace it wrenched at her heart. "Madame Lavoie...?" Grace said, her voice cracking. She barely noticed as the countess and Helen swept in. "I'm sure you don't remember me, but—"

"*Mon Dieu*, can it be?" Marie Lavoie pressed a hand to her heart and rushed forward. "Lady Grace Elliot! I would recognize you anywhere. So like your dear *maman* you are."

Tears stung Grace's eyes. "I am sad to say that my mother is not with me, she..."

"I knew..." Madame gave a deep sigh. "When I heard dear Lady Elliot had left town so suddenly, I knew what she dreaded had come to pass. She was so hoping to have more time with you."

Grace's eyes widened. "How did you know? She'd told no one."

"Madame had a spell during a fitting. She must confide in someone, no?" Madame clucked her tongue, her face filled with empathy. "She would not worry her husband or her so-lovely daughter who was on the brink of taking the ton by storm."

A whirl of emotions swept through Grace. Had she known her mother was sick earlier, she would have forced her to go back to The Willows and rest. Perhaps she and the boys could have had a few more precious months with her. How lonely she must have been, keeping her secret from the family those early days.

Grace's throat ached, her tears pushing against her lashes as she thought of her mother's silence.

The modiste gave a wistful smile. "Your *maman*, she loved you so very much. She was eager to see you through your first season. It wounded her that she might not be here when you became a bride."

"Oh, my..." Helen said under her breath.

Recalling she wasn't alone, Grace schooled her features and turned toward the two older women standing behind her. Helen, who no doubt heard the entire conversation, looked distinctly pale. The countess, her gentle face filled with empathy stood stalwartly next to her as if to lend her support.

The gesture wasn't lost on Grace, and she felt the first twinge of guilt that perhaps Helen deserved a modicum of respect from her, at least in public. "Pardon me for not introducing my companions sooner," Grace said. "Madame Lavoie, may I present the Countess of Ravenscroft and my stepmother, Lady Elliot."

"Stepmother?" Marie's nose wrinkled just the tiniest bit. "Ah, well…Your ladyship, your ladyship, welcome." The Frenchwoman curtsied.

Helen puffed up, her earlier discomfort immediately banished as she announced the reason for their visit. "We are about the business of selecting Lady Grace's trousseau. She is to be married to the Viscount Everdene."

"*Mais oui!*" Madame smiled as she set aside her pin cushion. "Of course I heard the news. The match is all anyone talks about. Lady Grace, you are quite the sensation since the Elusive Viscount E chose you for his bride. I have seen his lordship about. He is most handsome, and fierce. And now, the young ladies come into the shop, weeping, because he is to be wed! That you have tamed such a man…oh la la!" Madame said with a sweep of her elegant hand.

Grace's cheeks flamed, aware the countess was hearing her son described so.

The modiste smiled kindly at Lady Ravenscroft. "To think the day has come when his lordship will confine himself to hearth and home must warm a mother's heart. And he has chosen a diamond, I can see." She glanced at the over-large gem weighing down Grace's finger, then looked up at her, her dark eyes sparkling. "When I saw the announcement of your betrothal, I told myself, Marie, the day you have awaited has come! I meant to dispatch a note to The Willows, but it seems you already knew that I have something for you here. Is that not why you're here?"

"Something for me?" Grace echoed, as she and her companions stared at the shopkeeper in confusion.

"Ah, so you do not know! Your dearest *maman* left a gift in my keeping before she left London the last time. A so-precious secret for the daughter she loved."

Grace's breath caught. "From my mother?"

"A gift?" Helen said. "What could it be?"

The seamstress gave a benign smile toward Helen, before turning her full attention to Grace. "Why, the gown for your wedding day. Tucked away for so very long, I will need to find it, and have it delivered…to where?"

The countess replied, "Raven's Court on Curzon Street."

"Of course."

Helen's expression was a mixture of mortification and worry. "A gown? Dear me. It will be hopelessly out of fashion. As a viscountess, our Grace must be at the pinnacle of style."

Tears sprang to Grace's eyes, and she quickly brushed them away. "My mother's gift is far more precious to me than anything we could purchase."

Helen gasped as though stung. "I only mean you must take care, now that you are to be a viscountess. You have your brothers to think of. And your father."

Madame Lavoie stepped between them, her calm smile immediately quelling the growing tension. "I do so agree, my dear Lady Elliot. But I assure you, with a few simple alterations, Lady Grace shall be the epitome of fashion. Which means you will need to look to your own gown for the upcoming wedding. You must have a care or some might think you wish to outshine the bride. You know how gossipers love to prattle."

"Endlessly," Helen said with a nod, her golden curls bouncing.

Lady Ravenscroft walked over to a bolt of peach watered silk. "This would be perfect with your complexion, don't you think, Helen?"

The seamstress picked up the bolt, unwound a swath of the shimmering cloth, then held it to Helen's bodice, draping it over her shoulders. "Perfection."

Grace, recognizing the diversion for what it was, looked at her stepmother's reflection in the mirror. The soft peach, so different from the garish persimmon that Helen favored, accentuated the soft pink of her lips and cheeks. "It's quite beautiful on you."

"Is it?" Helen stared at the mirror almost in wonder. "I suppose it wouldn't hurt to look around."

Madame smiled knowingly. "Look around all you care to. But this…This is your color. Shall we start a fitting?"

Helen glanced at the watch pinned to her bodice. "It *is* near time for luncheon. We will never reach the shop we were to visit before we meet Lord Everdene anyway."

As the seamstress led Helen to the fitting room, the countess regarded Grace with a worried aura. "You look very pale my dear, and no wonder. Would you care to sit down?"

"I think I just need a bit of fresh air."

"Would you like me to come with you?" the countess asked.

Grace shook her head. "I need a moment alone." She turned and fled out the door, scarce seeing the shoppers bustling about, baskets looped over arms, footmen carrying packages for their mistresses.

As she wandered through the smattering of vendors hawking their wares, she glimpsed a bench near the towering bronze cavalier. But before she could reach the seat, a high-pitched shriek split the air. A young girl stood at the base of the statue, her arms skyward.

Just above her, clinging for dear life to the raised sword arm of the bronze cavalier, was a small boy, his feet dangling midair.

Grace's heart raced as she hastened across the square through a maze of carriages and shoppers to reach the children, fearing the boy might break his neck at any moment. He was likely half Bennet's age, she thought as she reached them. The red-haired girl, perhaps all of seven years, strained on tiptoe beside the statue's tall marble base. The nosegays she was trying to sell from the box that hung by a leather strap around her narrow shoulders were spilling to the ground.

Her head craned so far back it looked as if her fragile neck might snap as she tried to reach the boy who had scrambled onto the cavalier's shoulder and now clung to the statue's raised arm. How he had managed to climb to such a precarious perch, Grace had no idea. But there was no way the little girl could haul him down without likely cracking one, or both of their skulls on the cobbles below. And no one in the throng of fashionably dressed people pouring up and down the street was paying them the least bit of mind.

The little girl, apparently, was more upset over her fallen nosegays than the lad's predicament. "Now look at what you've done!" she said, crouching. She scooped up a handful of tiny bouquets, her bright green eyes going wide at the realization of Grace's presence. "Me brother didn't mean nothing by climbing up there. He's a pig-nosed, stubborn blighter who's going to get us both in trouble," the girl said in a lilting Irish accent.

Grace, after assuring that the 'stubborn blighter' had a firm grip on his perch, gave his beleaguered sister a commiserating smile.

"Brothers! I have four of them at home. What are your names?"

"I be Sibby Rose Nolan an' he be Scrap. *The wickedest brother in the world!*" she shouted, no doubt for his benefit alone.

Grace stifled a smile. "Is your mama or papa about, Sibby Rose? I think your brother might need some help getting down."

Sibby Rose glanced up at her brother, than back at Grace. "Ma and me brother Robert are at the factory workin', and me da…well, he's been gone lookin' for work for ever so long." She paused, her attention focused so intently on Grace's head, she wondered for a moment if she'd sprouted horns.

"We got to sell these flowers if we're to have any supper, an' all Scrap wants is to play pirates."

"He's doing a brilliant job. But maybe we should get him off the crow's nest and to the cannons."

"Not the cannons," Sibby Rose whispered. "He once fired off a loose cobblestone, nearly hit someone with it."

"Indeed. What sort of pirate fare might bring him down?"

"Treasure, of course." Her gaze landed once more on Grace's hair. "Me Da's going to bring me a ribbon just like the one in your hair when he comes home. I hope it's exactly that color. I think that's the prettiest I ever saw."

Grace reached up, touching the scarlet ribbon her maid had wound in her hair that morning. "I doubt this is a worthy enough treasure to bring him down. Something better, I'd think."

Sibby Rose tugged her attention away from the pretty bit of silk and glared at her brother. "I'm not sure treasure'd do this time. He's never climbed that high before."

"Lady Grace?" A familiar masculine voice came from somewhere in the crowd.

She glanced over her shoulder, relieved to see Lucien striding toward them.

His coat of black superfine fit his broad shoulders to perfection, not a crease in his trousers or the almost blindingly white shirt he wore. His hat was perched on perfectly combed jet-black hair. "Is there some difficulty here?" he asked, looking up at the boy, then at her.

Even little Sibby Rose seemed impressed. "Gor…" she muttered under her breath.

Grace smiled. "I fear we have encountered a problem with pirates," she told him.

Lucien looked around the area thronged with shoppers, a crease between his brows. "Pirates?"

"If you could just disentangle this young gentleman from the crow's nest, Sibby Rose and I would be most grateful."

Lucien, in his pristine coat and crisply knotted cravat regarded the two children with something akin to horror. "What, pray tell, does that have to do with pirates?"

She couldn't help but laugh.

"This is Lord Everdene, Sibby Rose," Grace said by way of introduction. "He has had some experience with pirates of late. My naughty brothers, was it not?"

"And I came away with ruined boots and mud in my face, as well as a runaway horse," he grumbled. "Where are you parents, girl?"

Sibby Rose scooped up another nosegay, this one crushed, and gave a long-suffering sigh. "Like I already tol' the lady, me da is gone, an' brother and mammy are at the factory. Widow Dunne usually minds Scrap, but she's off helpin' with a birthin'."

Grace, noting the boy's paling face, leaned toward Lucien, saying softly, "I truly think Scrap is frightened, but pride won't let him admit it. Surely, you can get him down?"

<hr>

LUCIEN LOOKED AT GRACE AS IF HER HAIR WERE ON FIRE. SHE DIDN'T actually expect him to…what? Scale the statue in the middle of a crowd? He could easily summon a footman or anyone else with a lordly wave of his hand. And he might have, but Grace was looking to him, provoking some ridiculous urge he would have quashed at any other time.

He glanced up at the boy and cleared his throat. He reached up, his arms not quite able to touch the child. "Come down here at once. It is very wrong of you to worry your sister so."

The boy clung tighter, drawing his little legs closer to his body, further out of reach. He shook his head.

Lucien, glimpsing a mixture of stubbornness and fear in the child's eyes, tried to remember his name. He glanced at the girl. "Scrap did you say?"

She nodded.

"I can't call the boy Scrap," he grumbled. "What is his Christian name?"

"Darragh," Sibby Rose said. "After our da."

"Darragh, let go this instant," Lucien ordered in the voice that sent the most powerful men in parliament scurrying to obey. The boy seemed to focus on him at the sound of the name, so intently it was dashed uncomfortable. "I will catch you."

"You can trust him," Grace said.

Lucien's chest felt too tight at her words. The boy stared down at him, then, without any warning, released his hold.

The suddenness stunned Lucien for a moment, the filthy bundle hurtling toward him. He had intended to catch the boy by the arms, hold the squirming child as far away from his own clothing as possible, then set him down. But the instant his hands closed on the child's spindly little body, the lad twined around him like the monkey one of his mistresses had kept as a pet.

"Dado!" The boy curled his fingers in Lucien's cravat and buried that filthy little face in Lucien's neck. There was no way Lucien was saving his coat.

"Yes. Darragh," he said with a frown, trying to disentangle himself from the boy. "Now, you have caused quite enough trouble for your sister for one day."

The boy merely clung all the more fiercely, jabbering to Sibby Rose in Gaelic.

"What is he saying?" Lucien asked.

"He thinks you're our da. Ye look a bit like the picture we have o' him. And when you said Darragh..."

"Well, I'm not his father! Tell him..."

"Willn't matter. Stubborn, he is, when he gets somethin' in his head."

Lucien looked at Grace, but she was not about to help him, he realized with some umbrage. The woman was grinning at him, so radiantly he'd have felt bathed in sunlight were it not for the ripe stench coming from the boy's bottom. The child was nearly strangling Lucien with his own cravat—which was all he needed. Giving the broadsheets a new way to mock him, he thought, imagining the cartoon.

A hostler with bits of harness over his shoulder stopped a few feet away. "What's that nob doin' wi' the boy?" the hostler said. "Draggin' him to the poorhouse! What he'd do wi' all o' us if the fine folk have their way."

"I'm not...dragging...him anywhere," Lucien growled as he worked to uncurl the little fingers. "I'm trying to...get him...off me." The boy's grip finally gave way and Lucien set the lad on his feet.

"Best check your pocket," a smirking dandy in a high crowned beaver called out. "The boy probably nicked your watch!"

The watch was the least of Lucien's worries. It would be a miracle if he hadn't acquired a case of the lice or fleas doubtless crawling among the boy's rags. Lucien's scalp itched at the mere thought.

"Infernal Irish!" the dandy's friend called. "Like rats, infesting England's streets."

"Because we're damn well starving across the pond!" a burly man who looked as if he could twist iron bars shouted back. He glared at Lucien, his teeth bared in raw hatred. "I know who ye are, Lord Everdene, and ye and yer like will get what's coming to ye. We ain't going to stand by anymore while lords like ye bleed us dry!"

Lucien leveled the man a hard glare. "You were standing by when the boy was about to break his neck climbing the statue." He drew coins from his waistcoat pocket, heartily wanting to send the urchins on their way. "I'll take the rest of your flowers," he told the girl—Rose something, wasn't she? "Here. Buy yourself a meat pie and take Darragh home for the day."

"Gor'!" The girl's eyes went round as plates. "Thankee, me lor'." She stuffed the coins in her pocket, then scooped up her somewhat wilted nosegays and thrust them into Lucien's arms, smearing pollen and petals and drops of less-than-clean water down his front, finishing off the coat once and for all.

She turned to Grace. "Thank ye, fer helpin' with Scrap, me lady." Sibby's gaze clung wistfully to the scarlet ribbon Grace's maid had wound in her hair that morning. "I think that's the prettiest ribbon I ever saw." After a moment, she tugged her attention from the pretty bit of silk and grabbed her brother's hand.

As she wheeled away, Grace called out. "Sibby Rose, wait!" She reached up and drew the ribbon from her hair, then carefully tied it around the child's ragged braid.

If anything, the girl appeared more thrilled with the ribbon than she had been by the coin.

"Thank ye, miss, me lor'," she said, with a curtsey, then poked her brother. "Make a leg to milor'."

"Dado," Scrap cried and flung himself at Lucien's leg, clinging to it. Startled, Lucien dropped the bouquets. He gave his leg a little shake, shooting a helpless glance at Grace. "What does he want? Get him off me."

But it was the sister who grabbed her brother's hand, tugging him along with her empty box still slung over her shoulder. "C'mon, Scrap! Meat pie!"

Before they disappeared around a corner, a man in a flat cap started after them. Someone from the rookeries that trained young thieves and pickpockets or some procurer eager to lure Sibby Rose into a brothel?

Before he could pass, Lucien extended one boot, tripping the man who fell into a pile of horse dung.

Grace started to exclaim, but Lucien stepped between her and the man, blocking way the children had headed. The bounder shoved himself to his feet, glaring up at Lucien with gin-glazed eyes.

"Watch 'ere yer goin'!" he barked.

"I could say the same for you."

Swearing, the man loped off in the opposite direction. At least the children had a head start now, Lucien thought. During that brief exchange, the vast city had swallowed them up.

"One would almost think you did that on purpose," Grace said. She was looking at him with an expression far too wise.

"And risk a nasty scuff on my boot? I don't think so. I'll have to make a trip to Hoby's to replace it." Lucien discreetly sniffed his sleeve to distract her.

"What is it?" Grace inquired.

Lucien grimaced. "The distinct smell of a chamber pot. My valet will be aghast. I'll never hear the end of it."

She stepped in front of him, so close he could see the tiny wisps of curls that had escaped when she tugged off her ribbon. She straightened his cravat in a wifely gesture, her fingers brushing his throat. The intimacy stirred his desire. When had anyone touched him so easily?

After a moment, she examined the knot she had wrought, then frowned. Rising on tiptoe, she pressed her nose into the nook beneath his jaw, her warm breath tickling his neck.

His muscles tightened in response, desire spearing through him. For a moment, he forgot the crowd around them and felt the impulse to pull her into his arms, kiss those pink lips that were curled in approval.

"You still smell of bay rum and shaving soap," she said, breathing him in.

Perhaps the risk of a flea bite or two was a small price to pay to see her eyes shine up at him. "Where are Mother and Lady Elliot? You were supposed to be ordering gowns, not wandering out here alone minding some stranger's children."

"There was some rather startling news. I needed a moment to— to sort through my feelings. I couldn't help but stop when I saw the children in trouble. Not when Sibby Rose and Scrap remind me of Avery and Bennet." She gave one last adjustment to his cravat, adding, "Thank you for sending them home with meat pies. They were so small and thin."

Lucien hoped the little ones might get to eat after all, since he'd intercepted the man in the cap who had tried to follow them. Had Grace realized what the man was doing? He wasn't sure. He couldn't fathom how she had seen the distressed children in this crowd in the first place.

But then, Grace saw—truly saw—the people around her, their faces, their feelings. He'd spent years looking through them. No, that was not true. Looking *away* because he knew how families shattered.

He fingered the betrothal ring she wore, shoving back the emotions that scratched at the gates he'd slammed down.

"Grace," he warned softly, "you cannot save them all."

"I know." Her poignant smile slayed him. "But someone should."

CHAPTER 17

$\mathscr{P}$eople were staring. Grace had noticed such curiosity before, in truth, ever since the viscount's party had arrived in London. But she had never felt the scrutiny more intensely than she did as they arrived at Gunter's Confectionary. Patrons peeped from beneath the brims of their high-crown beavers or around the rim of their bonnets, whispering as if she and Lucien were exotic animals caught in the throes of a mating ritual. And the reason for their fascination sat beside her, totally oblivious to the attention.

Even in his rumpled coat, Lucien, the Elusive Viscount of scandal sheet fame, drew every eye, men envying the aura of power he exuded, women hoping to spark passion in his penetrating gaze.

A blonde, over-generous-with-the-rouge-pot, attempted to catch Lucien's eye by licking the creamy dessert from her spoon as if promising him far more carnal delights. Grace felt an uncharacteristic sting of jealousy, adding to her already strained nerves.

She couldn't help but be grateful when one of her stepmother's friends beckoned. "Can you forgive me for stealing dear Helen away?" the woman asked Grace, clasping Helen's hand. "I have missed her so!"

Helen's eyes lit up and Grace could have kissed the woman when she insisted the countess join them, too.

Even Lucien seemed uncharacteristically quiet as the ices were served at their separate table, as if he was still mulling over the tumult in St. James's Square.

Hoping to escape for a walk alone to sort through her conflicted feelings, Grace ate her ice as fast as she was able—a fine idea until too much cold made her feel as though someone was driving an ice pick through her eye. She massaged her temple, stifling a groan as a portly man with a florid face planted himself in front of Lucien.

"By Jove, look at you, Everdene! Emerald waistcoat and all!" The stranger twirled his silver-headed cane with such exuberance he nearly knocked crystal dishes from a server's hand.

Lucien eyed the cane in a way that left no doubt as to his disdain for such excessive displays. "I can't imagine why the color of my waistcoat should be a topic of concern to anyone but my valet."

"It's proof that Chuffy was right! It *was* you we saw earlier, pulling that street urchin off of the statue! And then tangling with some nasty character moments later."

She could see Lucien's hand tighten on the base of his crystal ice dish, but the stranger rushed on, undaunted.

"Chuffy said it looked like you, but I wagered a crown that Viscount Everdene was the *last* person in all England who would soil his gloves in such an endeavor! Yet now that I see your waistcoat and your lovely companion's blue gown, there can be little doubt!"

Lucien regarded him with a frosty gaze. "How fortunate that you've settled such a vital question. Now you can turn your prodigious mind to some other matter."

"Aren't you a droll one! You know many would find the event most diverting. Give the caricaturists something amusing to draw, wot?" The man gave a hearty laugh. "Lord Ignatius Pinchbeck at your service, my lady. And you are?"

"Lady Grace Elliot," Lucien said.

Grace felt Lord Pinchbeck's gaze sharpen.

"Ah the very miss who snatched The Elusive Viscount from beneath the other ladies' noses. You must have cast quite a spell on my old comrade to get Everdene to dirty his gloves on street urchins."

"His lordship was most helpful," she said, disliking the blustering fool. "I was grateful. So were Sibby Rose and wee Darragh."

Pinchbeck's eyes near popped out of his head. "You know the urchins' names? How singular! Do not be turning Everdene into a blasted Whig, now." Good humor vanished into a scowl. "Bad enough he built that village and made tenants in three counties more discontented than before. If it weren't for the Harcourt voting record over the years one might think—"

"I vote as I see fit."

"It is just hard to know what side you come down on nowadays. Making both sides angry is hardly the way to—" Pinchbeck flinched under Lucien's hard gaze. His mask of amiability returned. "Well, those are subjects for another day. Today let me offer congratulations to your betrothed." He turned to Grace. "I lost a large sum at Whites, betting that his lordship would not be leg shackled before he turned fifty. I hope to make up for the loss through the expertise of my new business partner. In these troubled times, one must cast a wider net to draw in profits."

"Indeed?" Lucien said. "Then I suggest you get to it and allow us to enjoy our ices."

Unperturbed, Pinchbeck slid into the seat across from him. "I am quite fortunate to have such an astute partner in business. No man of discernment could resist the excellent connections this gentleman has made. More wealth than one could imagine, ripe for the plucking." He turned and called out, "Come here, my good man. There is someone you must meet!"

Grace glanced that direction as his companion turned and wove toward them through the crowd.

She froze.

"Lord Everdene," Pinchback said, beaming. "May I introduce you to the most forward-thinking industrialist you will ever meet. The Honorable Neville Freyne."

A hundred shards of memory burst through Grace in that moment. She stared at the man who might have been her future, recalling with chagrin that fizzy feeling of excitement, of first love, and the heartbreak of the letter that had dashed all her hopes.

Now, here he stood, familiar, yet a stranger with sun-bronze skin, and eyes so altered. They had been forthright when she loved him, but now there was an opaque quality, something harder. But then, she was much changed as well.

"Lord Everdene," Neville said with a bow.

"And may I present Lady Grace Elliot," Pinchbeck began.

Neville's gaze lit on Grace. Held for a moment. "We need no introductions," he said softly. "My dear Lady Grace!" He took her hand and lifted it to his lips, holding the kiss there for a little too long.

She stared at the crown of his head, remembering what it felt like to touch those golden locks, fine and feathery soft. They were, perhaps, thinner than she remembered. Or did it only seem so because she had run her fingers through Lucien's thick dark mane?

When he let loose her hand, he straightened his frockcoat that was cut in the latest fashion. "So, what do you think of your old friend, now that he's seen the world?" he asked. "I hope you are suitably impressed with the change."

His waistcoat dazzled, embroidered with gold and silver thread. Cufflinks and shirt studs glinted with gemstones, and a diamond stick pin shone in his cravat. Rings flashed on each hand. It was as if he wished his clothes to trumpet his importance the moment he walked into a room.

Egad, had he been but ten years older, he could have been Helen's male twin.

She wondered how she'd ever thought herself in love with him. In truth, he'd been more a boy when she knew him. Young and freshly minted without a hint of the shallow, garish man he'd become. "You look…well," she said.

He smiled. "I was hoping I might run into you here in London. Your father wrote to me that you would be in the city. I could hardly believe my good fortune when he confided that you are not yet wed."

Humiliation flooded through Grace as she imagined her father's letter, as if he were reminding a potential buyer at Tattersall's that a mare was up at auction once more.

Lucien curved one hand over her shoulder. "Perhaps you had not heard that Lady Grace has done me the honor of agreeing to become my wife."

"I suppose I had heard something of the connection." Neville laughed without humor, his gaze locked on Grace. "Now that I am returned home, perhaps I can persuade her to change her mind."

"As I understood it," Lucien replied, his voice cutting like steel, "you were the one who faltered."

Neville eyed Lucien, then swallowed. "Beg pardon, my lord. It was meant as a jest." He gave the slightest bow. "I have discovered that bold actions are required to succeed in life and in business. In fact, your father, the earl, was someone I always admired."

"My father?" Lucien replied, his hand still firmly on Grace's shoulder.

"I thought of him during my time in the West Indies and Americas, where I saw the opportunity for wealth beyond imagining. Plantations in Georgia and Mississippi with cotton fields that go on forever. Sugar plantations in Brazil and the Caribbean. I'm surprised he hasn't started investing there."

"Places where people are still enslaved?" Grace asked.

"Lord Pinchbeck," Neville continued, "has informed me there is a troubling movement to forbid trade with such countries. England must embrace the benefits free-trade offers or lose its rightful place in the world."

Grace bristled. "Even if that trade involves the suffering of thousands?"

Pinchbeck gave a dismissive wave. "They produce sugar more cheaply because of it," he said. "And without American cotton, every mill in England would turn its workers into the street."

The thought made Grace queasy. She thought of the children they'd just left, both so thin, their father desperate for work. Neville had always known how she abhorred enforced servitude and slavery. Had she really never noticed this side of him?

"I know it sounds hard, Grace," he said, his voice softening. "God knows, we all benefit from the tender hearts of our angels of hearth and home. But that very tenderness is why men must protect the gentler sex from the world of commerce. Permit me to point out that you have never seen these plantations with your own eyes as I have. It is not nearly as bad as abolitionists claim. The slaves fare better than our own working poor. Their people have warm cabins, food to sustain them, work to keep them busy—"

"Their children ripped from their arms at a master's whim!" she countered, indignant. "They are whipped and hunted. As for the condition of our own poor, we should do better by them as well! Children like the little ones we just encountered on the street—" She pictured little Scrap and Sibby Rose. Grace turned to Lucien, thinking he would surely agree with her, but the expression on Lucien's face never wavered as Neville spoke over her and Pinchbeck nodded in agreement.

"Englishmen *do* have a choice," Neville reasoned. "That's the whole point of Free Trade. Anyone who's conscience troubles them can choose *not* to buy the cheaper sugar from Brazil or cotton fabric for their homes. Sentimentality can have no part in business decisions if England is to survive. Am I right, Lord Everdene?"

"Is that how you feel, my lord?" Grace turned to Lucien, once again searching his face, hoping for him to refute Pinchbeck's claim.

He frowned, a deep line forming between his brows. "It is complicated, as so many things are."

"Far too complicated for the fairer sex to understand," Neville added with a gentleness that infuriated her.

"Never mind the masses!" Pinchbeck banged his cane on the table, rattling the dishware. "All this nonsense about common men getting the vote. Last thing we need is for landed gentlemen to lose their hold on the government! Imagine the chaos! We must extinguish this reform nonsense as soon as may be."

Grace felt a pang when Lucien made no counter to such an argument. How very different from her own parents, who had risen to the defense of reformers. Her mother always said that one should lead by example, and so Grace tilted her chin up. "Times are changing, Lord Pinchbeck," she said. "We live in an age of factories, trains and more industry than our forebears could have imagined possible. Surely it is only right that we change, too."

"Indeed we must, Grace!" Neville said. "Small crofts are a thing of the past, running estates into the ground. No one knows that better than Lord Everdene, after the expense he incurred on his model village."

She felt Lucien stiffen. "New Everdene is none of your concern," he warned.

"I am merely saying we all have ill-fortune when we gamble from time to time. It is not too late to make up for your losses. Invest some of the Harcourt fortune in our new factories."

Lucien's expression was unreadable. "It certainly bears further exploration."

Was New Everdene truly in trouble? Grace thought of how she'd admired the progressive village and Lucien's sardonic reaction when she'd praised it. The past decade had been the hardest in recent memory, with blights and crop failures, industrialization shifting the balance until there were times their world was unrecognizable. Was it possible New Everdene could be a failure?

She was aware of the weight on Lucien's shoulders.

"Perhaps, Lord Everdene, I can present our business plans to you," Pinchbeck offered.

"Perhaps." Lucien gave a slight nod in Grace's direction, before returning his attention back to Pinchbeck. "I have reason to believe we will be returning shortly to the country. As for the investment you suggest, there is much to consider. As Lady Grace mentioned, times change, and we must change with them. But I am not yet convinced as to what those changes should be, nor do I think one should rush into it."

Neville's brows rose in surprise. "On the contrary. The House of Lords must take decisive action!"

"With the malcontents stoking fires among the populous, it's out duty to stamp them out before it's too late!" Pinchbeck thumped his fist on the table.

Grace, surprised by Neville's vehemence, thought of Sibby Rose and little Darragh. Their father searching for work, their mother struggling. She glanced at Lucien, hoping the incident by the statue had given him faces to remember. Small, wan, pinched with hunger, running from those who would force them into servitude. But when he failed to counteract Neville's argument, her heart sank. This was the man she was to marry? She searched his face for something she did not find there. Any expectation of knight's errant shattered at his impassiveness.

Realizing that she would have to wield that imaginary sword herself, she stood and squared her shoulders, drawing on her mother's zeal as she faced the three men. "Perhaps before you stamp those fires out, you should discover why they are burning?" Without waiting to hear their response, she excused herself and walked away.

CHAPTER 18

The carriage ride home from Gunter's strained the last of Lucien's patience, and he wondered how long it would take for his mother to forgive him if he jumped out right there and then to walk home. Knowing he'd never hear the end of it, he pretended to sleep, instead. How could he not? The confines of the equipage seethed with tension. Grace, arms crossed, a militant set to her jaw, Lady Elliot nattering on about some gift to Grace that was doomed to be hopelessly out of fashion and would spoil the stepmother's plans for an elegant wedding. And his mother sitting gracefully through it all, her gaze on him as if she expected he should do something to put a stop to the turmoil.

God's teeth, he hated feminine drama. Between his mistresses and the women eager to trap him into marriage, he had been subjected to his share and remained unmoved. Why then, was he feeling guilty now? Not guilt. Irritation. Surely they'd all be over it by dinner?

But when Grace pleaded a headache and disappeared for the rest of the day, he sought someone to blame. First on his list was Neville Freyne. The shock on Grace's face on seeing her former beau made Lucien wonder in that moment if she'd harbored any lingering feelings for the man. It didn't take long to discover otherwise. The pompous fool was completely unaware of Grace's growing ire the longer he spoke.

To think Grace's father had ever considered Freyne a suitable match was confounding. But then to write to Freyne and invite him to court Grace even after the man had jilted her? Lord Elliot certainly lacked some common sense, as evidenced by his marriage to his current wife so soon after losing his first. How Grace managed to endure her stepmother was beyond him, recalling the way she prattled continuously about Mrs. Kemble this, Mrs. Kemble that when it came to planning the wedding gown, the wedding breakfast, the flowers and God knew what else. Lady Elliot had no idea how the very name of this so-called friend of hers grated on Grace's nerves.

Lucien paced his bedchamber then looked at the door that separated his room from Grace's. There was one thing he could do for his betrothed. Stop them from tormenting Grace once and for all.

Put her between his shoulder and his shield...

Where the devil had that come from? He hadn't thought of that phrase since he'd been a boy, still naïve enough to read the tales of King Arthur and the knights he'd once aspired to emulate.

It was ridiculous for him to think of such a thing.

Yet, now that the house was quiet, he stood, stripped to shirt sleeves, two glasses of brandy in his hand. Strange, but he was almost unaware of pouring them. And yet, here he was, standing in front of his future wife's door, propriety be damned. No leash so fragile as Society's dictates could keep him away.

He raised his fist and knocked, heard a clatter of some object falling on the other side of the door.

"Y—yes?" Grace called out, her voice uncertain.

"May I come in?"

A pause. A bit of a scuffle, then again, that voice. "Yes."

He pushed open the door, feeling a strange tightness in his chest.

Grace stood beside her dressing table, clutching a silver-backed hairbrush against her breasts, her expression wide-eyed with a mixture of shock and wariness that he would enter her bedchamber before they were wed. "Is something wrong?"

He stepped into the room, his mouth going dry. Her hair streamed down the back of her nightgown, her bed neatly turned back, but untouched. He imagined what that bed would look like if he made love to her, coverlets in total disarray. He cleared his throat, forced the image from his mind, then held out a glass to her. "I saw the light under your doorway. It seemed as if you might be in need of a bit of fortification after today."

She set down the brush and took the brandy. "I'd offer you a seat by the fire, my lord, but as you know, you didn't think a second chair necessary."

He raised an eyebrow at the subtle barb. "It was not very sporting of you to abandon me at dinner with your stepmother," he said.

"I had a headache." While her expression gave nothing away, he thought he saw the slightest tremble in her fingers as she lifted the glass to take a sip. When she licked away a droplet that clung to her ripe lips, the arousal he'd felt a moment ago tightened its grip.

He dropped his gaze from her mouth. "Perhaps absenting yourself from the dining room was for the best, with your stepmother all aflutter over…whatever it was she was going on about." Was he just imagining it, or could he just make out the faint shadow of Grace's nipples beneath the cloth? "After spending an entire meal with her, I understand your proposal to me on an entirely new level."

She paced toward the hearth, and the firelight filtering through the long skirts of her nightgown cast slender legs in shadow. Her feet were bare, pink and tender. Lucien wanted to scoop them up and warm them in his hands.

She stared at the flames for several long moments. "Sometimes I feel like a clockwork Helen keeps winding until my spring is about to break. I know she means well, but when she disparaged the gift my mother left me, it was more than I could bear at the moment."

"A gift from your mother…?"

"Apparently, Mama commissioned it at the modiste's shop during my first season." Her voice cracked with emotion and it was a moment before she continued, her gaze still on the flames. "She left instructions for…"

"For what?"

Grace turned to face him, the firelight reflecting off tears that threatened to fall. "My wedding gown. She asked that it be delivered just prior to my marriage. She must have known she would not live to see me wed."

Once again, Lucien was struck by an absurd wish to shield Grace. It was damned disconcerting. "Clearly, you have had an overabundance of shocks today. Your mother's gift. Rescuing urchins. Colliding head on into a man you thought to marry."

He'd thought it better to have the subject out in the open, yet the moment he said the words, he wished he could take them back. Her cheeks went scarlet, and he imagined the pleasure he'd take in throttling Freyne and Lord Elliot.

She set the brandy on a small table. "I'm so sorry for my father's interference."

"No need for you to apologize for *his* actions. My own father's interference is nigh on legendary."

"But to think my father wrote Neville that I was in London and still on the marriage mart? Who does that?"

He recalled how his father had tried to marry a far-too-young Cassandra to Thornsby, something far worse in his mind. "You'd be surprised."

"Perhaps, but I know it was awkward for you as well."

"Not nearly as awkward as the conversation I had with my valet," Lucien observed, attempting to lighten her mood. "I'll have you know that he found no less than three fleas on my coat. I fear he may never recover."

The corner of her mouth tipped up. God, that smile was like the sunshine after rain. It reached past darkness inside him.

"Merely three fleas?" she said. "You should have passed them on to Neville. He could do with an itchy bite or two."

He suppressed a smile at the spice in her tone. "Did you love him? Freyne?" The words slipped out, startling Lucien as much as they did her.

"I thought I did," she said softly, turning back to the flames dancing in the hearth. "After the conversation today, I feel as if I didn't even know him." She was so close, he could almost touch her. But before he could do so, she paced back to the dressing table, laughing without mirth. "I seem to have a penchant for becoming engaged to men I don't really know. It is a trifle alarming, realizing how little I know about you."

"Judging from some marriages I've observed, that might be best." He'd intended it as a jest, but somehow, he didn't find it amusing. "What do you wish to know? Ask and I will tell you, if it's in my power." Dangerous territory, and yet he found he would risk it to ease her mind.

She fidgeted with the ribbon at the neckline of her nightgown. "I don't know…What—what is your favorite color?"

"I've never taken the time to choose one."

She regarded him with a curious look in her eye. "What about your favorite book?"

"Treatise on Law."

"I meant a novel." That smile peeked out again. "Something that touches your emotions."

"I don't read novels."

Her eyes went wide with something akin to horror. "Never?"

"Being occupied with parliamentary business and running estates, I have never had time for frivolous pursuits."

"How sad." She sank down into the chair, a pensive shadow falling over her lovely face.

"Do you have a favorite?" he asked, needing to distance himself from the pity in her eyes.

"Oh, so many! Jane Eyre, The Tenant of Wildfell Hall…" Enthusiasm sparked, as if he'd struck flint to tinder. "Sir Walter Scott and Jane Austen are delightful. And I just began a remarkable novel by Mr. Charles Dickens." She gestured to where a book lay, open amidst the neatly turned bedsheets. "From the time I was small, my family would gather at night and read a chapter of some book aloud. We'd sit by the fire, sharing the stories, and when the chapter was done, my brothers and I trying to guess what would happen next. Sometimes," she said, her eyes lighting with the memory, "I even crept into the room and read ahead on my own. When Papa discovered it, he put the book on a high shelf I couldn't reach."

Lucien pictured her as the child he'd known all those years ago, hair ribbons askew and jaw set with determination as she clambered onto a chair to reach the forbidden book, eager as if she were trying to steal sweetmeats. "So your rebellious streak did not begin with thievery in Everdene Hall's kitchen?"

She actually laughed. "Indeed, no."

"Well, as my viscountess you may order however many books you like and race through them."

She favored him with a brighter smile than he'd seen since the debacle at the modiste's shop.

Unable to resist, he crossed to where she sat, and curved his strong hands over her shoulders. The warmth of her seeped into his palms, the scent of jasmine drifting up from her hair. He meant only to give her a goodnight kiss, something simple to close out their day, but he was surprised by how stiff her shoulders were. "You really have had the devil of a day," he said, every fiber of his body aware of hers.

"The past week has been more strain than I realized," she confessed. "My father trying auction me off like a mare at Tattersall's. My brothers feeling as if I betrayed them. Helen up to her neck in elaborate plans I loathe…And the absence of my mother is like a hole in my heart. I'm buying all of these new clothes, but all I can think about is that nothing about my old life fits."

"You are so tense your muscles are like iron. After a match at the swordsmanship academy, we knead out the tightness like so." He pressed his thumbs into her rigid shoulders. "Allow me?"

She nodded and he began to work the knots out. Her skin was creamy velvet, so smooth beneath the pads of his fingers. Her hair streamed over his knuckles like silk ribbons. Slowly, her shoulders relaxed an inch or two. Her head drooped forward to allow him better access and he stared down at the dainty curve of neck, the vulnerable bumps of spine.

"Better?" he asked.

She gave a soft moan. "I'm so very tired of it all…The truth is, I wish this wedding were over."

"Then I will make it so."

Her head snapped up. He could see the faint pink marks of his fingers on her skin and wished to hell he still had her beneath his hands. "Would you?"

"If you truly wish to forgo the formal ceremony, I can have a special license in hand by tomorrow. Of course, if you wish to be married from the chapel at The Willows…"

"I keep picturing my family glowering in the pews and my father interfering and Helen making all of these elaborate plans I do not wish." She scrabbled for her glass, took a deep drink of her brandy and coughed. Finally, she nodded. "Marrying now would put an end to it, would it not?"

"If you are certain, I will see to the arrangements in the morning," he said.

Perhaps some men would feel insulted that she wanted to get the wedding over with, but that would only hasten bedding his bride.

Then it would be too late to change course.

Too late for Neville Freyne or any other man to interfere.

A surge of possessiveness such as he'd never known jolted through him. He closed what little space was between them so the back of her head brushed his chest. He could see both of their reflections in the mirror, his dark, saturnine face, hers a fine porcelain touched with peach. A pulse fluttered wildly at the base of her throat. Unable to resist, he reached over her shoulder to touch that fragile hollow, trailing his finger down. He slipped his hand beneath the lacy neckline of her nightgown, exploring the warm secrets that were hidden beneath the cloth. The wing of her collar bone, the topmost curves of her breasts. He felt her heart race as he edged his hand lower but she didn't pull away.

"Pink," he said softly as he traced a circle on the velvety skin.

Her gaze locked with his in the mirror, breathless and confused. "What?"

"Now that I think on it, pink is my favorite color. Ever since our encounter with the cake."

He could feel her shiver in awareness. "Now you are teasing me," she managed to say. "If we were still at dancing lessons, I would step on your toe."

He leaned closer to press his cheek against hers—faint stubble brushing smooth silk. "I am quite serious. I keep picturing pink icing against your skin. Indeed, I am hungering for it, and I never particularly liked sweets before."

Silence filled the room, then he spoke, his voice low. "I haven't been able to get you out of my mind since we met in the kitchens that night. I could not forget the taste of you when I kissed you…" His thumb brushed over her nipple, and he felt it pearl as if eager for his mouth. "I wondered what it would be like to sample every inch of you."

Her throat convulsed. "I—I wondered, too."

The confession surprised him. The fact that she wanted to explore what lay between them was the headiest aphrodisiac.

He drew her to her feet and turned her to face him, the desire flooding his body burning into something hotter than he'd ever felt.

"Imagination is no match for the reality, sweet," he promised. He'd seduced his share of women, but this was different. Deeper. Dangerous as diving into black waters with fathomless depths. He felt off balance, so unlike himself.

But she was *his*.

Some primitive drive made him need to wipe any memory of Freyne away. Taking hold of the satin ribbon tie of her nightgown, he pulled it slowly through the loops, laying the delicate fabric open to her waist.

He slid one side off of her shoulder, and it caught in the crook of her elbow, draping there, baring one perfect breast. He cupped that lush swell, and it was even sweeter than he'd imagined, the nipple puckering, berry pink, as he teased it with his fingers.

Grace moaned and arched into his hand, her body warm, her skin fragrant from her bath, smelling of jasmine…

He slipped the nightgown off of her other shoulder. She met his gaze, and slowly let her arms fall to her sides so that the sleeves slipped down, past her elbows, her wrists, then slid free. A cloud of cloth drifted to pool around her bare feet.

God, she was beautiful. Her skin glowed, pale gold with candlelight, her areoles ripe for tasting. He wanted to curve his hands around her waist, slide his palms down the flare of hips to where the dark curls beckoned at the apex of her thighs. His cock strained against his trousers. "I want you," he said, his voice passion-rough. She blushed, and he half expected her to pull away with maidenly shyness.

But her fingers went to the fastenings of his shirt and for a moment, Lucien couldn't breathe. She'd unbuttoned the placket before tending his wound, but this was far different. She concentrated so hard, catching her plump lower lip between her teeth as she spread the shirt open, exploring his chest by touch, lightly stirring the dusting of dark hair, the flat disc of his nipple. She traced his scar, all but healed. Her tenderness undid him.

He kissed her, coaxing her lips apart, his tongue sweeping inside. She twined her arms around him, her fingers threading through his hair at his nape, her mouth opening to him, as eager as he was. Impulsively, Lucien swept her off of her feet, feeling her naked side against his own bared chest, skin to skin. The need to bury himself inside her beat a wild rhythm in his veins.

Why wait? Why shouldn't he carry her to the bed? Make damn sure he drove thoughts of any other man out of her head, out of her heart…He could lose himself in her. Draw from her the responses he wanted…no *needed*…He needed to taste every inch of her, suckle her breasts, explore her sex, lose himself in her—body and soul…

He stilled, with something akin to alarm. No. He couldn't *need* anyone, lose his iron grip on control. Any weakness was a weapon to be used against him. And this woman…she could have the power to make him lower his shield, if he let her in…

Lucien broke the kiss, drew back so that he could stare down into Grace's desire-hazed eyes. He forced emotional distance between them, willing her soft, beckoning warmth away from him, closing the dangerous gate deep inside him that had begun to slip open. When had it happened? During the time she'd cared for his wound? When she'd had the courage to propose marriage to him? When she'd looked to him for help with those ragged children? Or afterwards, when she'd gazed up at him with gratitude that warmed him to the cold center where his heart should have been?

He lay her gently on the bed, but remained standing beside it. His whole body clamored to join her.

"I have disturbed you long enough," he said with a coolness he didn't feel.

Hurt flared in her gaze, mingled with confusion as he drew coverlets over all of those tempting feminine curves.

"Did I…do something wrong?" she asked, a slight tremor in her voice.

"No."

You did something far too right…

He loathed the edge in his voice. "This marriage is to be a business arrangement. As such, we must honor the parameters agreed upon. We will negotiate a schedule for conjugal visits that is agreeable to us both. After the wedding."

She gathered the coverlets above her breasts. It didn't help. The memory of her nakedness was imprinted on Lucien's mind.

"Oh…Yes," she faltered. "I see."

He doubted it. Fear thrummed in his chest. It was as if the world he'd inhabited had been shadowed, gray and still, and had suddenly become so bright it hurt his eyes. He knew full well what a true bond with such a woman would cost, a price he wouldn't pay.

"I will inform you when the special license is in hand," he said with a detachment he didn't feel.

He bowed, his gaze fixing for a moment on the nightgown pooled upon the floor. It was all he could do to turn and walk away. His own bedchamber was dark, spartan, empty of silver hairbrushes, the soft, feminine scent of flowers, the warmth that Grace seemed to bring into every room. But the wanting, deep in his core, remained. "I should have the license tomorrow by noon. Will that be enough time for you to…ready yourself?"

She clutched the bedsheets even tighter, nodding.

He shut the door behind him, leaned against it, his heart racing. Surely he wasn't falling in love. Whatever this strange sensation in his chest was, he could feel it luring him toward the cliffs like a siren song. He would have to be careful. Very careful to get control of it.

Before it was too late.

CHAPTER 19

The click of the door closing between them reverberated in Grace's head as loudly as if someone had struck a hammer to a gong. What had just happened? One moment Lucien's mouth was on hers, the heat of his touch even now still lingering, and the next he was pulling away as if repulsed by her very presence.

Only when she was certain he was not about to return and see her in all her humiliation did she let go of the bedsheets, then retrieve her nightgown from the floor. Her fingers shook as she tied the ribbon, then smoothed the fabric, trying not to think about the feel of his fingers on her skin. She looked at her unfinished brandy on the dressing table, tempted to finish it in an effort to erase the pain and utter embarrassment from her mind. Instead, she stared into the darkness until, at last, she slept.

She awoke the next morning when a maid knocked upon her door, announcing a visitor. She'd scarce tightened the sash on her dressing gown when Madame Lavoie herself walked in, a small army of seamstresses following in her wake, bearing packages tied with crisp ribbons, one package far larger than the rest.

"His lordship's emissary woke me in the middle of the night with news of today's wedding," Madame Lavoie said. "He gave most specific instructions to muster every seamstress in my employ." She waved to the other women, and they began opening boxes. Grace gasped at the contents, silk stockings, ribbon garters, and lace underpinnings so exquisite they seemed woven of fairy magic.

She stood rooted to the spot, watching them unveil the beautiful articles of clothing

She heard a soft knock on the door, and braced herself, dreading that it might be Helen trying one last time to dissuade her from eloping.

But it was Lady Ravenscroft who entered, her arms filled with pink roses. The scent filled the room as she laid them on the bed. "The moment Lucien informed me that today would be your wedding, I sent word for these to be delivered."

"*Mon Dieu*," Madame Lavoie said as she lifted the gown from the box, a folded card drifting to the rug. "As beautiful as I remembered." she said.

Lady Ravenscroft picked up the note, placing it next to the roses. Madame shook out the gown, then looked at Grace. "We have much to do and very little time. Shall we begin?"

The style was timeless. The wide neckline was trimmed with the Honiton lace her mother had chosen, it's pattern fine as fairy-wings, the sleeves full and graceful.

"All that needs to be done is a tuck here and there," Madame said. "Perhaps a bit more lace gathered at the bodice."

Grace stood upon a stool as the seamstresses fluttered about her, pinning and stitching until it was perfect. She heard the clock strike the hour Lucien had designated when they filed out the door.

Grace took a steadying breath and looked to Lucien's mother.

Lady Ravenscroft scooped up the flowers from the bed. "I thought you might like to carry these. They grew from cuttings your mother shared with me years ago." She paused mid-step, her gaze sweeping from the crown of Grace's head to the embroidered slippers that peeked out beneath the hem. "Oh, my dear, you look lovely. Turn around so that I can take it all in."

Grace cradled the roses in the crook of her arm, then spun slowly, the gown flowing around her in exquisite waves. Every ripple of the shot silk caught the light, changeable as a twilight sky, the color shifting from rich blue to a dark pink whenever the fabric moved. The hem and bodice seemed to twinkle, embroidered with shimmering gold stars.

"So very lovely," Lady Ravenscroft said, then handed her the note. "From your mother, I believe…She'd have been so proud."

Grace tucked the note on her dressing table, wanting to read it in privacy, trying not to imagine her mother's disappointment regarding her unconventional marriage, even if she might understand Grace's reasons…"I hope so."

Lady Ravenscroft straightened a bit of lace at Grace's throat. "I have rarely seen my son pause long enough to look at anything or anyone until he became entranced with you."

Grace swallowed hard and forced a smile, unable to bear lying to this woman with her kind, haunted gaze. "You are mistaken. This marriage…it is…a very practical…"

"You needn't try to explain. Lucien has made certain I understand this is merely a marriage of convenience between you. So emphatically that I believe he is trying to convince himself." The countess smiled, a rare, sweet curve of her lips. "He is not half so cold as he seems. He never loved as easily as my other children, and my husband did his best to stamp out any hint of tenderness in his heir."

Lady Ravenscroft paused, as though unsure whether or not to continue, but continue she did. "After the trouble that divided our family, Lucien resolved he would not love at all. And, yet, I catch glimpses of longing in him so poignant it breaks my heart." This time, she looked Grace in the eye, perhaps to make sure she was truly listening. "Do not be mistaken. He *will* resist true attachment in your marriage. But I believe that you may awaken him to life once again, challenge the dark places in my boy's past. It is a chance I had all but despaired of. A hope…that my son will not remain trapped in this self-imposed prison." Her voice cracked, and she paused for a moment, seeming to gather herself as she glanced at the clock. "Well, that is enough of my rambling. The carriage is waiting. Lucien went ahead to make sure everything is in order."

For a moment, Grace felt a flare of hope. She remembered the moment in her bedchamber, how passionate Lucien had been, until that last moment.

Was it possible the countess was right? That he was beginning to care for her? Moreover, what was this feeling she had for him?

SHE WAS ABOUT TO BECOME LUCIEN HARCOURT'S WIFE, THE DAY passing like a whirlwind, almost a dream…one she half-expected to wake from at any moment.

In truth, it did not even feel like a real marriage at all, with no friends or family attending, only Lady Ravenscroft at her side. St. George's Church on Hanover Square seemed so empty, the barrel-vaulted ceiling echoing Lady Ravenscroft's words of praise and affection, Lucien and the bishop waiting, as reflections of the stained-glass window scattered on the floor like broken pieces of the family she had yet to confront.

Lucien took her hand and Grace forced her own to remain steady, while her heart raced…

The bishop looked past them to Lady Ravenscroft, the lone witness sitting in the pew. "Does anyone know of an impediment why these two should not be joined in matrimony?"

The bishop's query released a litany that ran riot in Grace's mind. *Does it count if our fathers both hate this union? Or that Lucien does not love me…? That I do not know him…?*

She could not shake off a feeling of dread when she pictured her father's face once he learned of the elopement, the hurt and betrayal to come.

A moment of echoing silence pressed down upon her, then Lucien made his vows in a brisk voice, placing his ring on her finger.

"Be kind to each other," Lady Ravenscroft said, embracing Grace, and then her son, before bustling ahead to Raven's Court to prepare a wedding luncheon.

The bishop led them to the church register, and Grace watched Lucien sign his name, his signature bold, confident. She took the pen in her own hand, inscribing her name on the page that would link her to Lucien Harcourt until death…

As they left the church, she looked over at the man who was now her husband. He was under complete control, every inch the Elusive Viscount, all hints of the man who, last night, had all but made love to her hidden away.

"We will still return home as planned, won't we?" she asked, eager to get the confrontation with her father over with.

"We will remain in town. It is enough to send a note with your stepmother."

She grasped his sleeve, distressed. "That won't do. I must tell my father and my brothers myself before anyone else can."

He looked over at her, his brow furrowed. "I understood that you wished to avoid more family drama—"

The words were cut off by a thick brogue bellowing from the crowd. "There 'e be! Lord Everdene, greedy bastard! Death to land-lords!" She saw a blur as something hurtled toward them.

Lucien whirled her away, shielding her with his body as a missile hurtled past, catching in a flounce of her dress. Pain shot through her foot as something struck her slipper, then rattled to the cobbles.

A shout went up from the onlookers, Lucien's footmen giving chase, but the perpetrator vanished in the crowd.

Lucien turned Grace in his arms, the controlled veneer gone. "Are you hurt?" he demanded. the hard planes of his handsome face fierce with protectiveness.

"Jesus, Grace!" Another familiar voice cut in as a man pushed through the startled onlookers. She looked up to see Neville racing toward them.

Lucien stiffened at the sight of her former betrothed. "What are you doing here?"

"When Pinchbeck stopped by to present you our business plan this morning one of your servants let slip where you'd be. I wished to be on hand if Grace…changed her mind."

"As you can see," Lucien said, his voice taking on an edge she'd not heard before, "she did not."

Neville reached down and retrieved a half a brick with some-thing wrapped around it. "And, yet, you are already putting her in danger."

Before Grace had a chance to protest that she was fine, the footman arrived, breathless. "I saw the man who flung it. Garbed in black, a felt hat dragged so low over his brow I couldn't make out much of his face. Disappeared in the alleys before I could collar him."

"Slunk back to the slums he came from, no doubt," Neville said. "We'll never find him in that mess of vice. I vow, it would be better if they tore such hell holes down."

Lucien snatched the brick from Neville's hand, and Grace saw it was covered in paper, tied with twine. He withdrew the paper, handing the brick to the footman to dispose, then unfolded the note, frowning.

"Did I not tell you this rabble is dangerous?" Neville said, glaring at him. "Attempts to kill the queen. Factories vandalized and manor houses burned. Chartists marching down St. James's Street, shattering windows. Now your own wife endangered on your very wedding day. What will it take to get you to join us in crushing this anarchy once and for all, Everdene? They must be shown who is their master!"

Grace placed her hand on Lucien's arm. "May I see the note?" she asked.

He handed the bit of paper to her, and she felt his gaze on her as she read the note.

Deth to Ristocrats.

We hav not to loos but ar chains.

She ran her thumb over the grinning skull drawn where a signature should be.

Neville looked on, aghast. "Are you truly involving your wife in this dangerous matter, Everdene?"

Lucien wanted to give him a set down, but the man was right. To involve Grace—and on her wedding day, no less—was a step too far. He could only be grateful his mother had gone on ahead. He waved toward the waiting coach. "We should probably get back."

But she shook her head. "I don't believe you will find whomever threw this stone in the stews." She leaned close to Lucien, and he could feel her intensity, her sleeve brushing his as she returned the note to him. "Clumsy writing can be mimicked," she said. "But someone poor would use a bit of newsprint, or some other scrap easily scrounged. This paper is as fine as any in my writing desk at The Willows. I think you are likely to find the culprit in far more comfortable circumstances."

"Don't be absurd!" Freyne scoffed. "There are any number of ways someone could get their hands on such paper! If they were in service, stealing it from their master's desk. Perhaps a maid or boot boy, pinching it from a room at an inn when some nobleman has stayed there. A person who worked in a stationers."

Lucien ran the missive between his fingers, testing the quality of the page. "Perhaps we'd be wise to listen to Lady Everdene's reasoning."

Lady Everdene...

He met her gaze as he used her title for the first time. "What else did you notice?"

"The writing. If you look closely, you will see here and there a very clear letter," she said, pointing to an example. "A bold, confident stroke."

Narrowing his eyes, he examined the script more closely. "You are most discerning."

He could feel her warm to his praise, her voice lighter as she teased, "That is why you married me."

"In part." He caressed her hand, wanting to gather her into his arms, explore her body to be sure she was unbruised...to claim her as his...

But that would have to wait.

"Let us be quit of this place so I can show you the other reasons." He handed Grace into the carriage, then felt Freyne catch hold of his arm. He turned to face the man. Again, that loathing welled up. "You are crumpling my sleeve," he said in accents that could cut ice.

"Damn you, Everdene. If that brick had struck her in the head, she could have been killed. Whoever is stalking you—"

"Will be dealt with by me. As for you—my wife is none of your concern. You gave up any right to be involved when you jilted her."

Freyne glared at him. "If it came to a choice between business and a woman, you would have done the same."

The words landed like a punch in the gut, but damned if Lucien would let Freyne see it.

"Keep her safe, Everdene."

Every fiber in Lucien's body knotted with tension, and with it, something he had not felt for as long as he could remember. Fear. "I will. Now, if you will excuse us, I have a honeymoon to enjoy." He climbed into the coach and shut the door before a servant could do so.

Grace was sitting on the squabs. She'd all but taken his breath away when she'd walked toward the altar. Yet now, tears glittered on her cheek as she fingered a tear in her skirt, where the brick had hit.

He would see it mended, made perfect again, he thought, taking her hand in his. "I am sorry this happened. You are sure you are well?"

"Quite sure. We agreed to have an unconventional wedding. I just hadn't anticipated something like this." She forced a laugh, then regarded him with that gaze that probed too deep. "Has this happened before? Strangers hurling things at you?"

"There has been unrest, as you know." Yet somehow, this attack felt more personal. To Grace, he said, "I intend to see you well guarded whenever we go out. In the meantime, I've considered your wish to return to the country to break the news of our marriage to your family.

We shall depart as soon as may be and stay for a brief time. Can you be content with that?"

"Yes."

He wanted to get her out of town, determine what this direct attack on him might mean. And whether it would throw her into danger. He was not a man to believe in omens, and yet…

Some brides were pelted with flowers and good wishes.

His had been struck by a brick.

CHAPTER 20

*O*nly a rakehell would deflower his wife in the back of a coach.

Lucien had been hard pressed to remind himself of that inalienable fact on the hellish trip back to the country. He had summoned two coaches, one for his mother and Lady Elliot, one for the bridal couple. Damned if he could endure being cooped up with Grace's stepmother, who was still in a tumult at the thought of facing her husband in the wake of the elopement. He had pressed the coachmen to drive through the night, because he damned well didn't intend to spend his wedding night in even the finest room of some coaching inn with his mother and Lady Elliot next door and the raucous cries of drunken patrons echoing through paper-thin walls. But knowing he had the right to all the delights of Grace's body had made him feel a carnal need unlike any he'd experienced before. No question it would be best to wait until he had her at the steward's house where they would be staying briefly on the Everdene estate. But there was nothing he wanted more than to strip her gown away.

He admired her, damn it. Her cleverness, her calm in the face of upheaval. Her ability to delve beneath the surface, intrigued him. No, fascinated him, truth be told.

But it was more than that. He was still shaken by the unexpected feelings that had stunned him when he saw her walking toward him down the aisle of St. George's. The gown, with its scattering of stars fit her elegant figure to perfection. Even her skin had seemed to reflect the light spilling from the window. Tendrils of russet-brown hair had curled against her swan-like neck. He'd wanted to dip his head down to kiss it, the jasmine in her hair filling his senses.

When she'd placed her hand in his, so soft, yet so capable, it was all he could do to speak his vows with the briskness he thought necessary for a wedding untrammeled by sentimentality. Then, Freyne outside the church. The brick hurtling toward Grace...

The reality had struck Lucien. It was inevitable that he would disappoint her. It was possible that just being his wife would endanger her.

He thought of his sisters' faces. His mother's...

He had ruined lives before. Now, as he and Grace mounted the steps to The Willows to face Grace's father with their news, he had to wonder. Had he condemned Grace to the same fate when he slid on her wedding ring?

Helen swept up ahead of them, past servants, and even her concerned husband, pleading a headache.

He'd expected nothing less than a coward's retreat from the woman, he thought as she disappeared up the curved staircase. But this time, Grace would not be facing the repercussions of her stepmother's histrionics alone.

GRACE LAID THE LUMPY PARCEL SHE'D BROUGHT FROM LONDON ON the demilune table she'd moved to conceal Avery's mischief what seemed a lifetime ago. She touched the mustachioed peacock on the wallpaper and wished the confrontation with her father could be so easily solved. But the only way through this tangle was to spill out her news as soon as possible.

With Lucien at her side, she drew her father into the library.

"Your stepmother seems very weary," her father said. "After your wedding, I must take her to Bath to recover her spirits."

Grace stiffened her spine. "You and Helen may leave as soon as

Susan finishes packing my things to take to Everdene. You see, I am a married woman now."

Her father went ashen. "You cannot be serious."

Lucien cut in, his voice crisp, masterful. "The bishop himself performed the ceremony at St. George's in Hanover Square," he said, then glanced down at her and fell silent, honoring her wish to deal with her father in her own way.

"Why would you do such a reckless thing?" her father groaned.

"After I encountered Neville at Gunter's and learned that you'd written to him, revealing that I was going to London, I had no more stomach to endure such manipulation."

Her father flushed at her accusation, yet still looked defiant. "But the celebration! The breakfast…the dancing…"

"We both know you would not be celebrating." She met her father's gaze, unflinching. "You have made no secret about your feelings in regard to my marriage, and Helen has shown no consideration for my wishes regarding the celebration afterward. Why suffer through a charade before friends and neighbors with pasted on smiles and false good wishes?"

"Of course I wish you happiness!" Her father pressed a fist to his heart. "As for writing to Neville…What kind of father would I be if I did not do all in my power to stop a beloved child from making the worst mistake of her life?"

She could feel Lucien tense beside her, knew it cost him to remain silent.

"I am no child," she said, crossing to where a small framed portrait of her mother and the three youngest boys sat upon a miniature easel. "I have not been a child since Mama got sick and you ceded all responsibility for her care and the boys' wellbeing to me." She ran her fingertips over the frame. They all looked so happy in the image, Bennet on Mama's lap, Ethan curled up with a toy horse at her feet and Avery caught in the circle of Mama's arm, a cricket bat in hand.

Her father blustered, "I loved your mother too much. I could not bear to see her in pain."

"And I could? I was eighteen." She forced herself to keep her voice steady, saw shame flood his eyes. "What matters now is this: I would have you trust that I know what is best for me," she said.

"This marriage is my decision. I choose to be close at hand when the boys need me, rather than exiled in Scotland."

Her father pressed his fingers to his brow. "I pushed you to take this reckless course."

She could not deny it. And yet the truth was more complex. "You set up conditions that forced me to face the fact that my life must change. It was inevitable, once you married Helen. But I have the right and the will to choose this path."

"Grace?!"

The three adults all startled as Bennet's cry rang out through the corridor, the boys obviously returned from their outing. The trio of brothers pelted into the room, breathless, their hair wind-tousled, cheeks flushed. "I knew I heard your voice!" Bennet whooped and Grace gathered him close, smelling the sweet scent of his hair, meadow grass, sunshine and sweat. His clothes were rumpled from play, a smear of dirt on his cheek. She instinctively brushed bit of grass from his hair and wondered how long it would be until she would be able to hug him again.

He pulled away enough to peer up at her. "Did you bring us a surprise from town?" His eyes gleamed in anticipation, and her heart squeezed.

"Lord Everdene and I left the present in the hall." The boys rushed out, squabbling. Ethan and Avery were still tussling over the lumpy bundle when they carried it in.

"Good thing you insisted on buying the sturdiest item," Lucien muttered.

Grace smiled as they unwrapped their new treasure unveiling a toy boat just the right size for their lead soldiers. "I thought it was time Lord Admiral Nelson had a ship that was seaworthy," she said.

They crowed in delight as they furled and unfurled sails, admired the tiny cannons and fiddled with the hatches that led to captain's quarters below. She had to swallow the lump in her throat before she continued. "I have another surprise as well."

They turned to her, expectant. "Boiled sweets?" "Candy sticks?"

She stepped over to Lucien, linking her arm with his, needing to feel that strong presence bracing her. "You see, Viscount Everdene and I got married while we were in London."

The boys stumbled back as if she'd struck them, but she went on, determinedly cheerful.

"It will take us some little while to get settled at Everdene, but as soon as we are, I shall visit for the day and we will have a grand time." She fought to keep enthusiasm in her voice, but the slightest tremor slipped through.

Nanny burst into the room, breathless, her plump cheeks red with exertion, her bonnet askew atop curls growing ever more gray. "There you be, you little rascals! Begging your pardon, my lord. We crossed paths with Matty from the stables, and the lads *would* race ahead the moment they heard Lady Grace had returned." She dipped into a curtsey, looking from Grace to Lucien. "Welcome home, my lady. My lord. You three lads, up to the nursery to wash up and then you can show me this lovely ship your sister brought you."

But the enthusiasm had drained from their little bodies. Even the precious toy listed at a melancholy angle as they followed Nanny's orders. Their compliance was far worse than any fit of temper could be.

Grace felt her stomach lurch, the walls seeming to squeeze too close, as if she couldn't breathe. All she could think of was getting away. From her father, from the boys, from the home that was no longer a haven.

"I have an errand to tend to as well," she said, determined not to cry. "While Susan finishes packing my things, I wish to go visit Mama."

"May I accompany you?" Lucien's brow furrowed in concern.

"Not this time. I wish for a moment alone."

He nodded. "Very well. Your father and I have matters to discuss, your marriage portion to settle."

Normally, she would have bristled and wished to be a part of such a discussion, but not today. She hastened outside, still trying to draw air past the knot of grief in her chest.

Pausing at the carriage that stood in the crushed shell drive, she took out the book she'd left on the seat, the unopened note from her mother and a sprig of roses from her wedding bouquet pressed between the pages. Then she walked alone to the church where her wedding was supposed to have taken place. She stopped beneath a willow tree in the fenced-in cemetery where a simple memorial marked her mother's grave.

She'd waged her first battle without her mother by her side when the vicar had tried to thwart Mama's last wish.

You must inter Lady Elliot inside the family crypt with the dignity due her name…

But Grace had refused to be bullied. Her mother couldn't bear the thought of being in the crypt. She'd wanted flowers near her, willow fronds waving. Life still bustling around her. The scar on the earth had healed now, and wildflowers Grace had planted there thrived. She laid her pressed wedding flowers on the grave, and touched the epitaph carved in the stone.

Lady Barbara Elliot, beloved wife, wise counselor, loving mother.

A small bench had been built beneath the curtain of willow leaves, and she'd sat there often in the months after her mother had passed, praying for guidance. Now, she unfolded the rather faded missive that smelled of lilacs.

She bent her head to read.

My dearest Grace,
I hope that I will be able to watch you walk down the aisle of The Willows chapel to wed the man you love. But, it seems that is not a wish that will be granted me. I pray this gown will remind you on your special day how deeply loved you are, as well as carry my prayers for all the happiness you can hold. Love bravely, my precious daughter, and demand the same courage from the man you choose. Know that I am always with you. Just look up at our star.
Your own Mama

The familiar script blurred before Grace's eyes, and a tear dropped onto the page. She swiped it away with her thumb, smearing the ink.

How many times had Grace told her brothers just that? Looked at the stars…imagining that their mother was there.

By the time Grace returned to the manor house, the footmen had loaded a trunk into the back of the carriage and the time for parting was at hand.

Helen had remained in her room, and Papa had gone to comfort her, but Will and the three boys had come into the courtyard to see them off.

"Come now, sailors," Will urged the forlorn little crew. "Let's give Captain Grace a proper send off as she sets out across the seas. In line. Attention! Salute!" The three boys obeyed, looking heart-breakingly young.

She leaned down to kiss Ethan who was struggling manfully not to cry, then Avery who stood rigid as if facing a firing squad. Bennet, the tender-hearted, flung his arms around her legs and clung tight.

"G-Grace…I have something for you." He thrust something hard and lumpy into her hand. She looked down and saw the chipped toy figure he called Lord Admiral Nelson.

"Oh, oh Bennet!" she gasped, touched by the offer, yet dismayed. "I can't possibly take this!"

"You must!" he insisted. "Promise you will keep him in your pocket all the time. Lord Admiral will keep you safe from bad men."

Bennet looked at Lucien, as if fearing Grace's new husband could rival Bonaparte himself.

Ethan wrinkled his nose, though there was a hint of fear in his grimace. "*He* thinks you won't come back, but if you have Lord Nelson, you'll have to visit us."

"Of course I'll visit you! That's why I—" she cut herself off, began again, "—why I am happy I will be living so near."

Avery made a scoffing noise. "Don't lie! You'll be in London and having babies of your own and you'll forget all about us like Papa did!" Avery balled his fists. "I *hate* you for leaving us."

"Whoa, there!" Will protested, but Grace clung to her calm, hiding how hurt she was.

"I *love you*, Avery," she said. "Always. No matter what. And I *will* visit. You'll see."

Will scooped the boy up, flinging him over his shoulder despite Avery's size and age. "I think I'll dump this one in the horse trough to cool his temper!" The boys always delighted in brotherly horseplay, but this time Avery wrenched free. His face crumpled with anguish. "I hate you, Grace!" he cried again, then turned and bolted.

Grace took a step after him, but Lucien touched her arm. She looked up into ice-blue eyes.

"Best to let him go," he said softly. "You'll only prolong the pain."

It was true. But that didn't make this severing hurt any less. Lucien slipped his arm about her waist, firm yet gentle. Warm.

She bit her lip to keep from crying.

"Go on, Gracie," Will said, the childhood nickname one more stab to her heart. "I'll see to Avery."

She climbed into the coach with Lucien and the horses set out at a brisk trot. Grace turned in her seat, aching at the sight of Ethan and Bennet leaning against Will. She pressed the tin soldier against her heart and watched her brothers until they headed back to the home they'd always known.

The home that would never be hers in the same way again.

CHAPTER 21

Grace climbed down from the coach outside the old steward's house, still heartsick over the painful encounter at The Willows that afternoon. In the two days since their wedding, she and Lucien had not shared a bed, and even the countess's best wishes were edged with concern. Grace had hoped to drive back some measure of her sorrow by being welcomed by the Harcourts. She would have given anything to be embraced by Jane or Penelope, to have someone assure her she'd done the right thing. But she sensed that the precipitous London wedding had rattled Lucien's family nearly as much as it had done her own.

His mother had continued on to her cottage in Galen's Well, saying newlyweds needed time alone. The rest of the family had, apparently, left Everdene Hall immediately after the messenger Lucien had sent ahead informing them of the elopement.

A note in Simon's scrawled hand was the only greeting they received, stating that he and Penelope were delivering Cassandra and Jane for a visit with friends met on the voyage from Italy. He then planned to go on to evaluate a stud he was considering adding to the Everdene stables. Simon and Penelope would not return to Everdene for a fortnight. They would celebrate the marriage then.

Yet, something in Lucien's expression when he shared the news made Grace suspect some darker tension simmered beneath the note's surface.

She tried to smile and greet the staff installed at the smaller brick residence as Lucien made cursory introductions, but it seemed he knew what that cost her.

"Tomorrow is soon enough to begin taking charge of the household," he said. "Today, you will want time alone to unpack and settle yourself."

Under the circumstances, she could hardly expect a tender interlude like most bridal couples shared. Yet, after the night he'd come to her bedchamber in the townhouse, some part of her imagined that she might hope for more than this dismissal. Her new husband was an enigma. At one moment, controlled, commanding a room and everyone in it. The next…there had been something almost charming about his discomfiture with Sibby Rose and Scrap. A hint of vulnerability that had called to her.

"I have a pressing appointment with my solicitor, so I will be gone for dinner," he said, consulting his pocket watch. "I will come to you at ten of the clock if you find that agreeable."

He was just leaving her? She felt a frisson of alarm but reined it in firmly. What had she imagined? That he would spend this first day they'd been truly alone with her, as bridegrooms were wont to do? Apparently Lucien meant to begin as he would go on.

"Ten." She almost imagined him noting it down as if it was one more obligation in his appointment book.

Lucien bowed and strode away.

The maid assigned to attend her was named Ruby, an affable country girl, eager to please as she took things out of Grace's trunk.

"His lordship gave strict orders you are to have every comfort. A bath, supper served in your chamber, books lining your shelves."

Every comfort, it seemed, except familiar company in these strange new surroundings, she thought. She lifted her chin and set herself to spreading her belongings about this room, longing to make it more like home.

They'd worked for nearly two hours when Grace saw Ruby remove a flat rectangle bundled up in a shawl. Before the maid could unwrap it, Grace took it from her hands.

The startled girl flushed. "My lady?"

"I will finish the rest on my own," she told Ruby, then tempered her voice. "Thank you so much for your help."

The maid gave her an uncertain smile, bobbed a curtsey and left.

As soon as the door was shut, Grace sat down at the dressing table. She unfolded the silk until it lay open on her lap like the petals of a flower, at its center, a framed sketch she had made of her brothers and mother four summers ago. It was only a fair likeness drawn by a girl with some small talent. But it captured the joy in her loved ones, the warmth. A frozen moment when all had been right with her world.

She propped it on her dressing table then set the toy soldier beside it.

It was so very, very quiet here. Almost as if the house were a tomb and those inside it were unable to wake up.

The Willows had always been bustling with noise and people. Even the times she'd squirreled herself away in the study, it had been with the understanding that, at any moment, her brothers could burst in and carry with them delicious chaos, quarrels for her to mend, injustices to put right, toads and rocks and any number of treasures to be admired.

It all felt so strange, as if the events of the past week had happened to someone else and she was watching some other Grace from a distance, vaguely perplexed.

At least she had the books she'd brought for company, letters she could write. She sat down at the desk, drew out a sheet of stationary. Dipping her quill in ink, she tried to form the words to sooth her brothers. But what could she say to ease the anger, the hurt, and their feeling that she'd deserted them? The one thing of which she was certain: they would all be changed when next she saw them. Avery and Ethan. Bennet. She would be changed as well. Blinking back tears, she set down her quill.

She'd never felt so alone.

THE NIGHT'S PREPARATIONS HAD BEEN FIT FOR A BRIDE. A BATH WITH scented rose petals, hair brushed until it shone, a gauzy nightgown donned. Even the coverlets had been turned down, before a blushing Ruby curtseyed and left Grace alone with the ticking clock. Was this to be her life? Grace wondered. Lucien even scheduling the hour he would come to her bed?

She read and reread passages of a novel, unable to recall what they said from one page to the next. When she finally heard the low rumble of masculine voices beyond the door to Lucien's bedchamber, she grew more on edge than ever. She recognized her husband's voice, though she could not make out what he was saying. His valet answered, no doubt readying Lucien for bed... knowing what the night would hold? Her cheeks burned.

She attempted to focus on her book, but she surrendered, staring into the fire until she heard the valet leave. Lucien's room went quiet for what seemed an eternity, her nerves on edge.

She was almost ready to go to his room herself when she heard footsteps nearing the adjoining door, the handle turning, the panel opening. Her heart raced as Lucien entered her room. He was garbed in a silk brocade banyan of midnight blue fastened with gold silk frogs. His hair was slightly damp from his own ablutions, and he was freshly shaved. He looked every inch a prince, carrying an inlaid chest in his hands. Pandora's box? She wondered.

"Good evening, Lady Everdene." The syllables rolled over his tongue as if he were savoring the finest whiskey.

Her mouth suddenly went dry, her heart racing. "My lord," she answered, a shiver of anticipation and unease mingling as she imagined what was to come.

LUCIEN GRIPPED THE BOX IN HIS HANDS, TRYING TO THINK WHAT TO say. That Grace was so beautiful she took his breath away. That he'd been counting every moment until he could strip away the last barriers between them, take the lovely body that had haunted his thoughts since the moment he'd left her, naked in her bed. That she deserved every luxury he could give her, the softest linens, the warmest fire, to be made love to with a tenderness he could never hope to possess, drawing out pleasure to an exquisite edge. He wanted to tell her that and more. Yet all that would come out was, "I trust you have had sufficient time alone to unpack and settle into your role as mistress of the household."

"I did. Quite too much time, actually." Her hand fluttered to her throat. "I mean, I finished unpacking long ago."

Lucien glanced around the room. "Everything is to your satisfaction?"

"It is." She rose from the chair by the fireplace, setting the book down. "Though I confess, I have had trouble convincing myself that this marriage is real."

"I bring proof that it is," he said, opening the chest. Light sparkled on countless gems. "I had my solicitor deliver the Everdene jewels."

She crossed to the dressing table, looking down at the glittering adornments, but there was no joy in her eyes at the sight. "They are very beautiful."

"Are they not to your liking?"

"I'm just not sure why…they're here?"

"Because you are my viscountess."

"I'd rather be your wife…"

Her words, uttered so soft, undid him, melting part of that shard in his heart, affecting him like the strongest of aphrodisiacs. "After tonight, I will leave no doubt in your mind that you are." He drew her toward him. His lips found hers, her mouth stiff with nervousness. But she softened as he coaxed her lips apart.

She fit so perfectly in his arms, her breasts pressing into his chest, causing his skin to hum with that energy in the air before lightning strikes.

"We are both in uncharted seas," he murmured, "but I find myself eager to explore, chart every island and shore, every soft, secret harbor that promises pleasure. Tonight, there are no boundaries we cannot cross, as long as you are willing." His ran his finger down the column of her throat, looking into her eyes. "Do you know what happens between a man and a woman, Grace?"

She laughed, startling him, and he drew back, frowning.

"You find the question amusing?"

"Forgive me, but I couldn't help myself. Surely, you knew my mother? She thought it inexcusable that young girls were sent out into the world without the slightest knowledge about their bodies, or notion what to expect with their husbands. In fact, she not only made certain that *I* understood, but many of my friends as well.

She made it her crusade to dispel myths about how one fell pregnant."

"I'd imagine that stirred up quite a tempest among your friends' own mamas at times."

"Yes. Especially when she insisted that even our own… instincts…were not to be feared or ignored." Her cheeks went pink. "Yet now…I expect it is a trifle more complicated than she claimed. I am not quite sure what it is I should do. I—"

"What do you want to happen? Tell me."

He waited with a patience that only made her more nervous. Could he really expect her to say the words aloud? Was that a gift? Or a burden? He saw her lick her lips, swallow hard. Knew she was struggling to answer. "You have seen all of me," she said at last. "I want to see all of you."

His cock hardened, every primitive male instinct in his body straining to break free. He wanted to crush her in his arms, strip her nightgown away with one fierce yank, bury himself inside her as he'd been longing to do. But he kept tight control. "As you wish," he said. "Tonight we choose how much to conceal or reveal."

He led her to the bed, then paused, taking her hand and placing it on the topmost gilt silk fastening at his chest. "Go on, sweet…I want you to."

Her breath hitched.

GRACE SLIPPED THE FIRST KNOT OF SILK CORDING THROUGH ITS LOOP, then the next, and the next, her fingers unsteady as she reached his narrow waist, lower. When the last fastening was undone, the garment gapped open, revealing a slice of hard masculine body. He was naked beneath the robe, and she trailed her gaze from the pulse in his throat, to the dark dusting of hair on his chest, following it as it arrowed down his flat stomach in a dark ribbon, leading to mysteries below. She spread the cloth open, then ran her hands up to his shoulders to slip the garment off. His body seemed made for sin.

He stood there, shameless as Adam in the Garden of Eden, fire-light limning his body. He was beautiful, all powerful muscles, long bones and sinew. He seemed so patient, and yet, his arousal left no doubt he was eager for this joining, his shaft erect in its nest of dark hair.

"Touch me," he urged, half command, half plea.

She did so. His jaw knotted as she ran her fingers over his chest, learning him by touch. All that power, strength, so still. He was coiled like a tiger one breath away from pouncing. She reveled in the contrast, steel sheathed in silk, his skin so hot, smelling of bay rum and soap. She reveled in the thrill she felt, her own power to elicit such a reaction from Lucien. She wanted to snap that control, make him feel the need she felt. Remembering the spear of desire she'd experienced when he'd touched her nipples, she skimmed her fingertips over the flat disks, heard his breath hiss between his teeth.

He reached for her, divesting her of her nightgown. A chill ghosted over her bare skin, but only for an instant. His fingertips traced the curve of her breast, lightly at first, circling her nipple, but not touching the hard point until she was aching. He drew her so tightly against him she could feel every plane, so hard, so blatantly male. His mouth found hers, hot, skilled, his hands drawing her into currents that swept her away into a world of sensuality, of yearning, every nerve seeming to cry out for what he alone could give her.

She twined her arms about his neck. Her breasts flattened against his chest, the hair teasing her with its delicious texture, his shaft a hard ridge between them. He kissed her, his tongue slipping between her lips, stroking there, as if a prelude to what their bodies would soon join in. Sliding his big hands down, he cupped her bottom and pulled her onto her tiptoes, tighter, until his shaft was cradled against the place that ached to be filled. It seemed impossible that something so large would ever fit inside her, and yet, she wanted it to, so much.

He slid his mouth to her ear, his voice hoarse, tickling the tender flesh. "I want you very badly, Grace. All of those miles from London, I was picturing things that may shock you."

A delicious shiver rippled through her as she whispered, "Show me."

He smiled, a smile so sensuous her knees melted. He slid his hand down her arm, the tips of his fingers slightly rough on the sensitive skin as he reached the inside of her wrist where her blood was rushing. "Come to bed."

He scooped her up as he'd done before, but this time he followed her down, the mattress sinking under his weight.

His mouth was on her throat, his teeth skimming the fragile skin in tiny nipping kisses, his tongue teasing her as he trailed kisses down to take her nipple between his lips. She gasped as he suckled her, and she threaded her fingers through the black silk of his hair, holding him to her breast. One long leg curved over her thighs and he half covered her with his body.

She shifted, restless, eager as he smoothed his hand past her waist, along her hip, down her thigh. He circled his fingertips against the intimate place behind her knee, then gently eased her legs apart, and charted a path upward, to the soft down, and the place that felt slick and swollen.

When he found the pearl at the top of her sex, stirring it with the tender-rough pads of his fingers, she gave a little cry, the sensation almost too intense to be pleasure, and yet, it was.

"Oh...oh, my...that feels..."

"It can be even better, if you'll let me..."

"Yes..." *Anything...everything...*

"Open for me, Grace. I need to taste you."

She thought she'd known what to expect. But this? Lucien settling his big body between her legs. The slow, hot journey of his mouth downward, the dark silk of his hair brushing her belly, his broad shoulders spreading her wider, all of that heat and strength pressing against her inner thighs.

He threaded his fingers through the soft tuft, his fingers opening the petals of her sex. Dear God, what was he doing? He stared at her most secret places, his breath teasing the sensitized flesh. He smiled, a tiger's smile, his gaze blazing with a heat so intense it thrilled her, frightened her. She stiffened, clutching handfuls of the sheets to anchor herself in a world tilting off its axis. Something altered in Lucien's face, and he kissed the downy mound, then drew away. She made a soft sound, needing him to fill an aching emptiness, and he slipped his finger inside her. Grace arched her back, deepening the sensual invasion. His thumb circled the sensitive nub his breath had warmed moments ago.

Tension built, and she strained toward it, lost in waves of pleasure as he slid a second finger into her sheath, thrusting and withdrawing, stretching and opening her. He found a place inside her, deep, that she hadn't even known existed, and she cried out, and he renewed his efforts, his thumb circling, teasing, taunting the nub at the top of her sex, driving her higher on the crest of something she could not name.

She lifted her hips, desperate to get closer, the sensation building until she gasped his name, the pleasure breaking over her in huge waves. He pulled away, and she moaned in protest, but he was atop her, his shaft hard against the slickness. He reached between them, guiding his blunt tip to her entrance, then braced himself on his elbows above her. He pushed into her, just an inch, then paused, sweat beading his brow.

"There will be pain."

"I know." She slid her hands down his back, urging him deeper.

He shifted his hips forward, shallow thrusts, then deeper, filling her inch by inch. She felt the tearing, the sting.

One last thrust and he was buried deep. "Are you…well?"

She nodded, not able to put into words the feelings rioting inside her. Pain, yes, but far more pleasure.

"You feel…so tight…so perfect…Wrap your legs around me." She did so, twining her legs around his narrow hips, lifting herself against him. Her arms drew him even closer, and he kissed her, as he began to move. He was trying to be gentle.

She could feel what it cost him to keep his desire tightly leashed, sweat glossing his skin. "Lucien…I want…I need…more…"

He drew back, just far enough for her to see the taut planes and angles of his face. "More?"

"More of this…more of you…just…more…"

He cursed low, kissing her fiercely, then set himself into a rhythm, driving deep, all but withdrawing, then driving deep again. She clutched him, grasped the hard curves of his buttocks, arching closer and closer, urging him with her hands, her body, her soft cries.

When she could bear no more, she pressed her teeth to his neck and Lucien gave a groan of surrender, his own body like iron against hers as he grasped for his own pleasure.

He reached between them, circling the sensitive bud with his thumb, and she felt a new crest rising, one far more overwhelming than the first. "Come for me, Grace. I can't wait any longer…"

The climax burst over her, and she sobbed in completion, felt him drive deep, pulse inside her. He arched his head back. A raw, animal sound tore from his throat, his body shuddering in release. When the last tremor of pleasure fell still, he collapsed atop her, his breath rasping, his body slick with sweat. He buried his face in her neck, and she could feel the hammering of his heart against her breasts. After a moment, he rolled off of her, both of them laying on their backs, their breath still rasping. She felt the loss of him, his weight, his warmth, the emptiness and ache where he had been inside her. She wanted him to gather her against him, wanted him to hold her, but the space between them seemed to fill with a distance she could not name.

"There," he said, pulling the coverlet over her. "It is done."

"Done?" She stiffened, hurt.

He was ruining it. The excitement, the passion, the breathtaking pleasure she'd found in his body and her own.

"Next time there will be no pain."

She wanted to believe that was what he meant, but there was a tightness in his voice that made her wonder if there was more he was not saying.

"I have never been with a virgin. I hope it was not too uncomfortable."

What was she supposed to say? That she'd felt as if he'd split her in two? That it stung and burned and then all she had been able to do was hold on while he seemed to launch her into worlds unknown? Swirling heat and exquisite sensation where her body strove to keep up with the pleasure he gave her? That she had felt wild with it, giving herself so completely? But now, with his coolness, this distance he'd put between them, she felt as if she were suddenly lost, more alone than she had been when he walked through the bedchamber door.

She caught her lip between her teeth.

He swung his legs over the edge of the bed, stood and scooped up his banyan, covering his nakedness then crossing to the wash-stand and dampening a cloth. When he returned to the side of the bed, his face was once again impassive, so distant it chilled her.

What was he thinking? Had she been a disappointment? She hated how much she needed reassurance, needed him to hold her. The room was so unfamiliar, the wound of leaving her home, her brothers too fresh.

"You will be wanting this," he said, retrieving her nightgown, the folds appearing even more fragile in his strong masculine hand. Once she had slipped the filmy garment on, he passed her the damp cloth. His gaze dipped to the place still tender after his possession. "You are sure that you are…quite well?" He looked as if he wanted to say more.

"Quite. A trifle cold."

He crossed to the hearth. Taking up the poker, he stirred the embers into a brighter blaze. He stood with his back to her, his head bent, staring down into the orange flames. After a moment he turned, "That should warm the room. Now I will leave you to your rest."

"Will you not stay?" she asked softly.

"No." Lucien clamped his jaw tight, then turned and strode out the door.

CHAPTER 22

$\mathcal{L}$ucien poured a glass of brandy from a cut glass decanter then drank it, waiting for the spirits to quell the clamoring in his head, but neither the liquor, nor glaring at Grace's bedchamber door could blur the images that kept swirling in his mind.

Grace, her body silken, eager, so responsive he'd nearly pushed their first love play beyond what a new bride would expect. He'd wanted to do it all, all of the sensual things he'd been imagining since he'd tasted pink frosting on her skin, seen her naked as a pagan nymph in the townhouse. He had avoided virgins his whole life. Not because he was troubled by noble scruples, but because first lovers sank hooks into a person's memory, even with a man as jaded as he. And physical pleasure was all he had ever cared to offer.

Tonight, when he'd nestled between her creamy thighs, his mouth mere inches away from her sex, he had stopped. Not because he didn't want to shock her. But because he had known with Grace the act would be different. He would be crossing a threshold of intimacy impossible to retreat from.

He had been unnerved by whatever the hell *he* was feeling. Primal triumph at being Grace's first lover, yes, but far more perilous. Hunger for something he could not even name.

The sensation of sinking into the heat of her body had undone him, this craving for her…for *more*…closed about him like a fist.

Those moments after he had rolled out of her bed, stared into the fire in her room…he had fought the need to return to her, gather her into his arms, press that delectable body against him. He still felt an inexorable pull.

Won't you stay…

Grace's plea echoed in his head, and he could see those wide eyes that were so filled with compassion and *life*. The sadness he'd seen as he turned away from her now haunted him.

He had given her the Everdene jewels, and she'd not touched a single bauble. She was seeking something far more dangerous, prying at the place he kept locked tight in his chest.

Just by leaving her bedroom, he had hurt her. What would happen when he left her to live separate lives as he intended…

When she'd escaped her arranged marriage and come to him, she had been so naïve. She had no idea what she'd bargained for wedding a man with no heart to give her.

There was only one thing to do. Get Grace with child as quickly as he could. A babe would comfort her, amuse her, love her as he could not.

And once that child was in her arms, he could do as he planned —put miles between them, go back to his solitary life.

Until then, he had to keep a tight leash on his passions because God knew where it would lead if he were ever reckless enough to let go.

Lucien swore.

It didn't matter that he had spent countless sleepless nights in his study, buried in work. Tonight he damned well could not sit still. He yanked on clothes, thrust his feet into boots. Securing a lantern, he stalked out into the night air, down the path to the Everdene stable. The building lay quiet, the grooms and stablemaster asleep in their quarters above the stable, the smell of horses and hay and leather driving back the scent of Grace's skin.

Atlas, Lucien's favorite mount, thrust his head over the stall door and shook his cream colored mane, his gold coat shimmering in the flickering light. The gelding whickered and Lucien hung the lantern on a hook, then went to the horse, stroked his velvety nose.

Once Atlas was out of the stall, Lucien tied him to the post and went to fetch the tack, hoping a ride would cool the fever in his blood.

As he stepped out of the tack room, a voice cut through the quiet.

"Hands in the air. Turn around. Very slowly."

Lucien raised his hands, turned, and found himself staring down the barrel of a pistol. Jamie McLeod, garbed in naught but hastily donned breeches, sleep tousled and hard eyed, pointed a weapon at Lucien.

Recognition flared in the Scotsman's battle-hardened eyes. He lowered the pistol, bare feet shifting in discomfort. "Your lordship! What are you...? I didn't expect—I thought I heard someone meddling with the horses."

It wouldn't be the first time thieves had attempted to steal one of the valuable animals.

"Is something amiss?" McLeod asked, running a hand through his dark red hair.

"No. I am going for a ride."

McLeod frowned and looked out the stable window. "It's the middle of the night."

"I ride when I please." The certainty eased some of the tension inside him. He was a viscount. In command of this stable, this estate. His own goddamned body.

Their gazes locked, held for long moments, McLeod's bitter. The stablemaster made no secret he had contempt for the landlords he'd left in Scotland. Men who had turned him off his family's land. Lords, like Lucien, who did as they pleased. But at last, the Scotsman laid the pistol atop a barrel and took over the task of saddling and bridling the gelding.

When Atlas was ready, Lucien swung up into the saddle, but McLeod held fast to the reins. "There have been incidents between angry workers and some other landlords to the east," he warned.

Lucien thought of the brick that had been thrown at him in London. The threat tied to it.

McLeod held out the pistol. "Take this."

Arabic symbols inlaid in the pistol glinted silver in the lantern light, mysterious words from the years McLeod had spent as a prisoner of war in Afghanistan.

Lucien took the firearm and thrust it into the waistband of his trousers. McLeod opened the stable door and Lucien spurred off into the night. He had faced a far more lethal threat than horse thieves or rebellious crofters in Grace's bedchamber tonight.

GRACE'S HUSBAND WAS AVOIDING HER. FOR SEVEN DAYS LUCIEN HAD come to her bed at precisely ten of the clock, made love to her with a fierceness that left her breathless, then vanished behind his bedchamber door, transforming back into the reserved stranger she had once known him to be.

Oh, there were those rare times during the day when she caught him watching her with those hooded ice-blue eyes as if he were a wolf, in the dark of winter, glaring at the beckoning warmth of a fire, but unable to draw near.

Her own world felt cold as well. She had tried talking to the servants, though the maids seemed nervous and the housekeeper jealously guarded her territory. After those failed forays, she had decided to turn her attention to the crofters at New Everdene. But searching the pantry for jars of jam and other treats to share with them met with the cook's denouncement that Captain Harcourt's wife had already distributed this month's largess. Remembering Helen's mistakes with the staff at The Willows, and not wishing to tread on Penelope's toes, Grace relented and puttered about the garden, wrote letters, read books, and generally tried not to let her unhappiness show.

The one place Grace had not been regarded with suspicion was the stables. She'd walk over there every day, lean against the fence, the sight of mares and foals in the pasture reminding her that she would not always be so alone. This marriage might soon grant her a babe to love and care for. She imagined a child with Lucien's eyes, his dark hair, that child in his father's arms. Lucien smiling down at his son or daughter with a tenderness and wonder all the more precious because he allowed that side of himself to show only to her.

She had seen glimpses of what could be if this enigmatic man let her into his closely guarded heart. And that hope had filled her with longing—no, more than that. *Love.* She felt a shiver work through her, somewhere between thrill and fear. She was falling in love with Lucien. And yet, once she conceived their child, would he disappear altogether?

As the stable yard came into view, she was grateful for the sight of Eli, the young groom who was brushing a two-year-old mare named Guinevere.

"Your charge is doing very well," Grace said softly. She picked up a brush from the bucket at Eli's feet and gently began smoothing the little mare's mane.

"My lady," Eli said, pulling his cap. "Mr. McLeod is letting me help with her training."

"She obviously trusts you," Grace said.

Was the weight of that responsibility the reason for the shadows under Eli's eyes? In the seven days since her arrival, he had grown noticeably paler.

"Have you been ill, Eli?" she asked, gently stroking the mare's nose.

"My lady?"

"I can't help but notice you are not as hale as when first I came here."

The boy ducked his head. "Oh, I never get sick. It's just sleepin' in the tack room that's worn me out."

Grace's brow furrowed. "Is one of the horses ailing?"

"No." The boy pulled a face. "Leastwise, not yet."

She tipped her head in puzzlement. "I don't understand."

"We're all of us scared Atlas is goin' t' take a tumble, what with his lordship ridin' out late every night."

Grace stiffened. "What?"

"Somebody's got to be down here, t' get his lordship's horse saddled an' cool Atlas down after he returns."

"In the middle of the night? How long has this been going on?"

"Ever since ye came to the brick house. Mr. McLeod says I can sleep while 'is lordship is gone, but I'm worrit Atlas will step in a hole an' his lordship'll be hurt. We're all holdin' our breath each night 'til they come back in one piece."

That was what Lucien had been doing after he left her bed? Riding his poor horse in the darkness? Keeping this poor boy up half the night? Was Lucien so determined to get away from her that he would risk breaking his own neck?

She bid Eli and the mare goodbye, leaving before the lad saw how outraged she was. She fumed the rest of the day, stalking about Everdene Hall's grounds, deadheading roses in the garden with a vengeance, invading the kitchen and helping knead bread to the horror of the cook, getting angrier by the minute until she heard her husband enter the house.

She swept into the entryway to meet him. He didn't look like a man who was riding all night like some unquiet spirit. He was perfectly turned out, cravat starched, not a crease in his coat, while she felt as if one of the stable's cats had been batting her about ever since her encounter with Eli.

"I have been waiting to speak to you," she said.

"Can it not wait until tonight? I have an accounting matter to consider. This horse Simon wishes to purchase—"

"Does the horse come with lanterns on its bridle so it can see in the dark?" she demanded in heated accents. "Because if that is so, I say any coin spent would be well worth it considering that night is your favorite time to roam the countryside."

He froze, looked at her sharply. She had never expected to see the Viscount Everdene discomfited. But red crept up from that perfectly tied cravat. "Who told you that?"

"That doesn't matter. It is obviously true."

"I have nothing to hide. When I choose to ride is of no concern to anyone else."

"As your wife, I disagree," she said. "I would rather not be made a widow. After what happened in London and the threats you received, you must be aware of the danger you are in. Is it truly so difficult for you, having me here in the house, that you have to go for midnight rides?"

"Riding helps me think."

"I want to be a help to you, as my mother was to my father. Would not talking to me help you think without the risk of broken bones—for you or the horse?"

He clenched his jaw. His eyes glittered with something dangerous. Good, Grace thought. Anything was better than the cool politeness that made her want to scream.

"No," Lucien said levelly. "Talking to you would not help me think."

"How would you know?" Her hands knotted in fists. "You have not even given me a chance!"

His ice-blue eyes locked with hers, the connection sizzling between them until it was nigh unbearable. She refused to look away.

He paced toward her, more like a tiger than ever, his gaze never wavering. "Talking to you would *not* help clear my mind, wife," he said, as he grasped her by the arms, "because when I see you, the only thing I can think of is *this*."

His mouth crashed down on hers.

CHAPTER 23

*L*ucien could feel the wildness leap up in her. All the words he could not say were like a whirlwind in his mind. That he'd needed the knife-edge of danger riding in darkness to ease the driving need he felt right now.

Her anger at him only heightened it, the fire beneath her compassion, that fierceness that dared him…

He pressed his tongue between her lips, and kissed her the way he had been longing to, with nothing held back. Her fingers delved into his hair, her body against his as if she had been formed just for him.

"It is not ten yet," she said.

She was baiting him.

It only served to make his cock harder than it had ever been before. "I don't give a damn what time it is." There it was. The truth.

From the first moment he'd kissed her in Everdene Hall, he had fought this battle to maintain the dam he'd built to hold back the feelings she unleased in him. He'd surrounded himself with rigid rules in an effort to retain control. He could feel the walls cracking, yet in this moment he didn't give a damn. He'd shore them up later…after he'd buried himself, not just in her body, but in all that was Grace, her compassion, her humor, her courage. This woman who was life and light and—God alone knew why—wanted *him*.

He took her hand, drew her up the stairs to her bedchamber

before caution could intrude. Once inside, he locked her door, fumbling with the laces up the back of her dress, eager to strip away any barrier between them.

"God, you are delectable," he murmured as he pulled down one side of her bodice and chemise, revealing a creamy shoulder. He pressed hot kisses to the skin he'd bared as he backed her toward the bed. The ropes squeaked as he lay her on the mattress and followed her down, shifting his body atop hers. His hand slipped under her skirt. "I want to devour every inch of you."

Suddenly she went absolutely still, her gasp anything but one of pleasure.

"Lucien…Lucien, wait."

He didn't think he could. His hunger for her surged as his hand reached the thin skin of her inner thigh above her stocking, but he forced himself to stop, confused. A moment ago, she had seemed as eager for their love play as he was.

"What…what was that sound?" she whispered, tugging her bodice back into place.

He froze, listening. Then he heard it, too. A shuffling beneath the…*bed?*

Threats he'd received the past months echoed in his head. The idea Grace might be in danger hardened in a knot in his belly.

Lucien rolled off the mattress onto the floor, crouching on his hands and knees, to peer beneath the bed. There was a smudge of something pale in the shadowy space, a sound like the squawk of a beast in a snare. He thrust his arm beneath the bed, grabbing something warm, writhing. Alive! Whatever he had laid hold of fought like a demon as he dragged it toward him. Suddenly pain spiked through the fleshy part of his hand as the creature sank its teeth into Lucien. He swore, tightened his hold, dragging his assailant out into the open—a kicking, cursing…*boy!*

He collared the lad, hauling him upright into the light. The child was a grimy, smelly mess, his face smeared with something that might have been food at one time.

"Avery!" Grace cried, shocked. "What on earth? How—how in the world did you get here?"

Lucien's eyes narrowed. One look at his attacker was like being plunged in that chilly lake again, the shock, the dismay. The boy wrenched free, scrambling onto the bed and into his sister's arms.

Lucien rubbed the place on his hand where a half-circle of tiny cuts stung. "He bit me!"

"You frightened him," Grace said, holding the boy tight.

"Finding someone under my bed when I am about to make—er, be with my wife startled me as well, but I didn't sink my teeth into the boy." Lucien found his handkerchief and wrapped it around his bleeding hand.

It stung, but not so much as the strange loss of balance he felt inside. Did he glimpse the slightest hint of her dimple winking in that pink cheek?

"Avery, whatever are you doing here?" Grace asked. "How long have you been…?"

"Dunno. After breakfast. Hid under the bed after the maid made it up. Fell asleep."

"Well, it's almost dark. We'll have to send a note to The Willows telling them that you're here. We can't take you home until morning."

"I'm not going home! Not ever. I'm going to join the navy."

Lucien winced, remembering Simon in the heat of anger.

I'll join the cavalry. You cannot stop me. It was a choice that had all but destroyed him.

Lucien expected Grace to quell her brother's nonsense at once. Instead, she said quietly, "Lucien, may I borrow one of your shirts for him to sleep in?"

Lucien pressed his handkerchief to the wound and glared for a moment. "Are you actually suggesting I hand one of my bespoke, perfectly tailored shirts to this little fiend?"

The lad would probably dump the nearest ink pot onto it out of spite.

"We can hardly dress him in one of my pelisses."

With a grim set to his jaw, Lucien went into his room and retrieved one of his least-favored shirts.

The boy took it with a grudging expression.

"Avery, are you hungry?" Grace asked. "When is the last time you ate?"

"Something other than my hand," Lucien muttered.

The boy ducked his head, but not before Lucien saw a look of triumph. "I sneaked into the kitchen and took some hot cross buns and apples under the bed."

Wonderful. No doubt the crumbs would be the perfect lure for mice.

"How did you even guess where my room was?" Grace asked.

"I peeked in all the bedrooms and saw that." The boy gestured to Lord Admiral Nelson on her dressing table.

Damned resourceful little scoundrel, making his way all the way from The Willows and sneaking in with none of the servants noticing. Lucien would have to have a word with his staff.

He could have rung for the servants, but left the room to cool his temper, finding a maid and ordering food for the boy and a pitcher of warm water so he could wash up. When the servant delivered what was necessary, she didn't quite close the door. Lucien knew he should get as far from the scene unfolding as possible, but something held him in the corridor, as Grace helped settle her brother into the bed Lucien had been eager to share with her.

From the first moment the lad had hurled a mud pie at him, there had been a boldness in this pint-sized hellion who had tormented him. There was no doubt he was the leader of the brothers. And when Lucien and Grace had announced their marriage, Avery had actually struck him, something no grown man of Lucien's acquaintance would have dared, leaving no doubt he planned to be a formidable adversary.

But now, he seemed so young and small, something about him making Lucien damned uncomfortable. Something familiar…He remembered chasing after Simon after their mother disappeared. Finding him huddled in the treehouse they'd built, shivering, hungry, trying to hide his tears. Knowing that when they returned home, he would receive a beating from their father.

Lucien shifted in the hallway until he was able to see brother and sister more clearly. Grace leaned over Avery, stroking his tumbled hair, his face red and hot and shining with tears.

"There, there…," Grace said. "Tell me, why are you crying?"

"I hate Stepmama for marrying Papa and I *hate* Lord Everdene for taking you away. I want things to go back to the way they used to be."

Lucien saw Grace take a deep breath. "I know," she said. "So do I sometimes. But things can't always stay the same. Even if Mama were still alive and I hadn't married, things would change. Look at how you've grown, just since this spring."

Avery wiped his nose with the sleeve of Lucien's borrowed shirt. Lucien remembered the defiance when he'd dragged the boy from beneath the bed. He'd fought like a wild thing—hell, bit like one as well—but there had been no tears.

Now, the boy and Grace both looked so vulnerable it made Lucien's gut knot. He wanted to turn away, go to the study, lose himself in the piles of work waiting for him there. He wanted to go to his own bedchamber, shut the door, and pour himself brandy, do whatever he'd always done on the nights that sleep eluded him. But he stood there, feeling as if he was looking back in time to the boy he had been.

The boy who shrank away from any comforting touch. Steeled his shoulders, hardening any tears into an icy lump that grew harder and harder over the years until any tears were sharp as broken glass and the shell around him so tough he could no longer feel the touch of his mother's hand.

Lucien wanted to turn and walk away, pull free of the thread that seemed strung between his chest and Grace.

The woman whose body he'd come to know, but whose heart… whose spirit had been beyond his long-hardened mindset to comprehend, even if he ever became reckless enough to want to discover its mysteries.

Her partially unlaced gown drooped off one shoulder, baring a creamy expanse he'd tasted just before they'd been interrupted. Tendrils of rich brown hair, threaded with red-gold strands, curled against her throat.

She crooned a poignant melody, one Lucien had never heard, a tale about stars. The lad quieted even more. But he didn't sleep.

"Grace, am I going to hell?"

The lad's soft query drifted to the door, burying itself in Lucien's chest.

"Of course not! Why ever would you think such a thing? Where in the world did you get such a notion?" Grace asked.

"I heard Mrs. Kemble tell Stepmama that I am the wicked one and I'll drag Bennet and Ethan down with me. She's right, I'm the one that gets the others into trouble. I boosted Bennet up through the window to ruin the luncheon. I'm the one started moving things back where Mama had them. I'm the one who told Stepmama there was a ghost. Sometimes the *angry* just boils up inside me and has to come out. So I have to join the navy, you see?"

"Bennet and Ethan wouldn't know what to do without you. And Will and Ethan and Papa would be so sad. So would I. You would be far away on a ship somewhere. Whole years would go by and we'd not see you. We'd not even spend Christmas together. Who would play snapdragon and help cut down the Christmas tree?"

That seemed to make the boy stop to consider. He sniffed, then looked up at his sister. "Don't you miss us, Grace?"

"Of course, I do. I miss tucking you into bed, and reading you stories."

"And playing at the lake."

"Yes, that, too."

"Don't you get lonely?"

Lucien heard Grace hesitate. "Yes. I do get lonely. I am so used to chasing after all of you, busy all of the time. But we'll become accustomed to the changes in time. You know, Will and I were alone in the nursery until you came along. Then Ethan and Bennet. You cried a great deal. Colic, the nurse said. But it didn't last. Soon, you were smiling and knocking over towers of blocks and now, I can't imagine life without you."

"I can imagine life without Lord Everdene just fine."

Grace swept the fall of her hair over one shoulder, baring the nape of her neck, the pale curve so vulnerable. "I know he can be… rather alarming, but you shouldn't have bitten him."

"His face was all…all so mad it looked like he'd eat me alive!"

"Oh, Avery. You know he would never—"

"I don't! He scares everybody. Ethan and Bennet. And the footmen and maids, too. I heard them talking. Even Papa. He didn't want you to marry him either."

"You mustn't let your imagination run away with you. Lord Everdene is my husband."

"It was like he—he changed into a monster when he found me under the bed, just like the ones in the stories Nanny told us."

Hearing Avery talk, Lucien couldn't stop childhood memories from crowding in. His father's face suffused with fury, his eyes hot coals, teeth bared, his huge body seeming to blot out the sun as he raged, and Simon…So small and slight in his grasp. Something bitter rose in Lucien's throat.

"A monster?" Grace said. "To be fair, I was the one who was scared, when I heard something under the bed."

"Aren't you afraid of him?" Avery asked.

She seemed to ponder it a moment. Lucien held his breath. "No. I just picture him the way he was that day at the lake, with mud dripping all over him, and a lily pad on his shoulder. And then he's not so scary at all, don't you think?"

"He was angry then, too. Looked like he'd explode."

"He was also cold and wet, and we'd ruined his boots. But he dove in after me because he thought I was in danger."

"He doesn't even know how to have fun. Anyone would have known we were playing."

She sighed. "Sometimes…I see him watching everyone else while they are talking or laughing or having fun…and he looks a bit…puzzled as if he doesn't quite know how to join in."

Even from a distance, Lucien could see the lad huff. "Maybe because nobody *wants* him to."

"I do."

Two simple words that cut Lucien off at the knees.

He turned gently and shut the door before he went to his own bedchamber. He sat down at the desk.

The room was quiet. Spartan. Just the way he preferred it.

But not what Grace was used to.

Aren't you lonely? Avery had asked Grace.

Lucien would never forget her face in that moment, the haunting sadness, her soft answer.

Yes.

Yes, she was.

NEARLY AN HOUR HAD PASSED WHEN HE HEARD A SOFT RAP AT HIS bedchamber door. "Come in."

Grace entered. She was carrying a small medical kit. "Avery is finally asleep. I need to look at your hand."

"Don't mind it," he said. He'd washed the blood off and bound it in a clean handkerchief.

"I won't rest until I attend to it. Bites easily become putrid."

She set the kit on a table then gestured for him to hold out his hand. After a moment, he surrendered. *Not* because he wanted her to touch him, he assured himself as her deft fingers untied the makeshift bandage. She cradled his hand in both of hers and examined the wounds. The flesh around the bite was purpling and swelling.

"It looks painful. I'm so sorry."

"You aren't the one who bit me."

She flashed him a pleading glance. "I'm sure Avery is very sorry."

Lucien arched one brow in disbelief. She flushed prettily.

"At least, he knows it was very wrong of him...," she amended. "Perhaps he will feel more at ease with you once he grows used to visiting us here at Everdene."

That will never happen, he thought, *because I won't be here.* But for the first time, the resolution gave him a twinge. How often had he behaved thus? Avoided people who threatened his solitude, escaped...That had been his plan with Grace as well, and yet, he was haunted by the sadness his withdrawal had caused her. Pain that would grow greater still, if he let it.

He watched her as she crossed to the washstand and dampened a length of toweling, the soft curve of her lips, the glow of tenderness in her eyes. Would he be able to block her out as he had so many others? Even on the midnight roads, she had been with him, in the stars overhead, in his thoughts...No, pulling away from her wouldn't change this uncomfortable sensation inside him. And yet, could he ever change this instinctive reaction? Do something different this time? *Maybe...*a voice whispered inside him.

Maybe not.

She returned to him, and his breath caught in his chest. "This was all an unfortunate mistake," she said as she dabbed away the dried blood. "We have all made them."

"Some worse than others," he observed wryly.

"Surely you will give Avery a chance to make things right," she said. She spread the puncture wounds open just a little and poured whiskey into the cuts.

He welcomed the sting. "I was not speaking of Avery's transgressions. I was merely considering past errors of my own."

She regarded him with that sharp discernment he found unnerving. "You know, in medieval times they used to whip people through the marketplace so the whole village could see them do penance for their sins. You are a fine looking man, so you would draw quite a crowd."

He frowned. "I don't consider it a jesting matter."

"Of course you don't since you are using it as an excuse."

He felt as if he'd grasped white-hot iron. "What?"

"If your mistakes are unforgiveable, you can use them like weapons to keep people away. You do not have to take risks."

"You were just complaining that I was riding at night."

"I am not speaking of physical risks. Those are easy enough. Risks of the heart are another matter."

"Easy to say when one's conscience is as clean as yours. You know nothing about what I have done."

"Then tell me."

God, she was so beautiful, so earnest, so tempting. As if she were some mystical being who might wash his sins away. But there was no such healing magic. Not for a man like him. And she'd best understand that now.

"I am what destroyed my family," he said. "I spent years after my mother and sisters disappeared believing my father's lies. My father insisted that Mother was not in her right mind. He enlisted me to be his spy. Alert him if anything strange happened. I performed my duty well. I discovered my mother, Jane and Cassandra, attempting to run away in the middle of the night. They begged me not to tell, but I was my father's creature." His lip curled in disgust. "I raised the alarm, and they were captured."

He watched Grace, searched for the change in her face, to see her disgust, her horror at what he'd done.

She paused, as if trying to take it in, and he waited for her to recoil from him, turn away. But she only peered up at him with those eyes that seemed to penetrate to his deepest core, her face sorrowful, filled with understanding. "You trusted your father. Most children do," she said so gently his hands knotted into fists.

"Father said Mother deserted us." His voice grew rough. "Years later, when I began to ask questions, he said she had died somewhere on the continent."

"That is on his conscience. Not yours."

"Three years ago, Penelope discovered that our mother was alive. That she had spent years in an asylum. A kind doctor got her released. But father warned that, if she contacted us, he would cut Cassandra, Jane and Simon off without a farthing."

Only now did Grace's eyes widen. "No wonder you were all so shocked when he turned up at the welcome dinner."

"It was only after I was reunited with my mother that I learned the true reason they had been fleeing that night. My father intended to force Cassandra to wed his political ally, a renowned lecher thrice her age. Cassandra was not yet fifteen."

Grace pressed her hand to her mouth, as if she was about to be ill. Well, she should be, considering the ugly truth. "How horrid."

"My mother risked everything to stop the wedding. In the end, she managed to do so, despite being interred in that asylum."

"So that is why you and Cassandra clash," Grace said. "But you were a boy when all of this occurred. Yes, you were involved, but your father was responsible. You were his victim, too."

"I was no child when Penelope determined to find out what really had happened to our mother. I tried to stop her. I threatened her." The words were like knives scoring his skin. "I am not proud of it."

"Why would you do such a thing?"

"I didn't want Simon to find out the truth. I do not...form attachments easily. But my brother..." He stopped, swallowing hard. "For years we'd only had each other. Then, he finally learned that I had been lying to him the whole time."

"Oh, Lucien...it all must have been horrible for someone as

young as you were then." Empathy filled her gaze, along with something he couldn't quite name. "I still believe you can make things right with Simon and Jane. Even with Cassandra. Ask pardon, make amends."

"I have done. As best as I am able."

He could see Cassandra's face, hear the loathing in her voice. *You want to make amends? Stay away from Everdene Hall...*

He could tell Grace about his promise now. Would she be so compassionate when she realized that he would live at one of his estates in Lancashire, hundreds of miles away. And she would likely have to join him?

No.

He had seen the betrayal in Cassandra's eyes, condemnation he richly deserved. He needed more time before he had to witness that emotion in Grace.

But it was inevitable, wasn't it? Once she learned how he'd 'made amends' to his sisters by vowing to stay away from Everdene Hall. Grace had only married him to live here, close to her brothers.

He watched her, silent as she tenderly spread salve on the wounds, then wrapped them in a clean bandage. Impulsively, she kissed the knuckles of his injured hand. Her bodice slid off one shoulder. "Oh, bother!" she said and Lucien gently slid the cloth back into place.

"The laces in the back of my dress became hopelessly tangled when I tried to pull my bodice up and refasten it after we heard the noise. There is no way I can sleep this way. Would you be willing to help unfasten them—if it wouldn't pain your hand too much."

"It wouldn't pain me." Not exactly true. It would be exquisite torture, awakening all of those tumultuous feelings that had boiled to the surface before Avery had appeared.

Yet Lucien would take any excuse to touch Grace's velvety skin. His need for her was fiercer than ever.

With an endearing smile, she turned away from him, scooped the silky tresses out of his way, baring her neck and a tempting slice of her back. Perhaps it was best that they had been interrupted earlier. He'd teetered on the precipice of something that alarmed him then. The conversation he'd overheard with Avery made the danger greater still…

With great care, Lucien began to untangle laces and hooks and eyes, picking loose the knots. He let his fingertips linger on the pearl-like bumps of her spine beneath the muslin of her chemise, the delicate wing of her shoulder blade. When the task was done, he imagined unfastening her corset as well and lifting the chemise over her head. But no.

She turned to face him and glanced at his bed. He could see his desire echoed in her eyes, her curling lashes at half-mast. He clasped her wrist with his thumb and forefinger, rubbing a slow circle on the sensitive place where her pulse beat.

Her tongue darted out to moisten her lips, and he wondered if she had any idea what the nervous gesture did to him. He wanted to gently nip that full lower lip, kiss his way to her earlobe.

Forget…

"I—I had better go," she murmured. "I need to be there when Avery wakes up.

I wouldn't want him to be frightened."

"No." Lucien's voice roughened with unspent need. He forced himself to uncurl his fingers from her wrist.

He opened the door to the adjoining bedroom, and she disappeared through it. He watched her cross the room to sit in the chair she'd drawn over beside her bed. She picked up the boy's small hand.

*Aren't you lonely here…*Avery's question to Grace seemed to taunt Lucien. More poignant still, her answer.

Yes. I am…

What could Lucien do about it?

Certainly nothing here, even with his family returning soon. Simon had written that Cassandra was in a state when they left. It had not taken much imagination to guess why. Had Cassandra planned to tell Grace the role he'd played in the destruction of their family?

He had told Grace that much himself.

But he'd left out one key piece of information. The devil's bargain he had made with Cassandra. That they would quit the Everdene estate, move far away…

He knew that Grace would learn what he'd done. Maybe she would hate him for it.

But not yet. He remembered the tender brush of her lips on his knuckles, as if she could kiss away his pain. An uncomfortable feeling clenched around his chest.

No. He'd not tell her yet.

CHAPTER 24

Grace had spent a sleepless night longing to vent her righteous indignation on Avery's behalf and upbraid her stepmother for the pain she'd inflicted by allowing that awful Mrs. Kemble to say such horrible things about Avery. But as the Harcourt carriage pulled to a stop in the drive at The Willows, it was harder to maintain all of that fury.

Will and Father bolted down the stairs to reach the runaway, while Helen stumbled after, obviously distraught, her face suffused with guilt, eyes cherry-red from weeping.

Will reached the boy first, giving Avery a shake filled with affection and relief. "I will kill you if you ever scare me like that again!"

Father scooped Avery out of Will's arms and clutched his son against his breast, choking out words Avery alone could hear.

The other two boys must have been watching from the nursery, for they spilled out of the door and fell on Avery as if he had returned from the wars. Tears brimmed in Grace's eyes as she watched Avery's welcome. Flushed and rumpled and thoroughly hugged, her wayward little brother could have no doubt how deeply his family loved him.

Grace noticed that her father's eyes were glistening, over-bright as well when he turned to Grace and Lucien. "Ethan told us Avery intended to sign on as a cabin boy," Father said. "Will and I would have been on our way to Portsmouth and Liverpool if Mr. McLeod hadn't arrived with your message before dawn. I am in your debt, Everdene." Grace could see his heartfelt gratitude as he held out his hand to Lucien. After a moment, Lucien took it.

A lump formed in Grace's throat.

While Will took the boys to raid the kitchen for fresh scones, the others gathered in the drawing room. Grace and Lucien sat on the settee across from her father and stepmother. Grace struggled to find a modicum of patience despite the anger that still pulsed inside her. Venting it would not help Avery and Helen to get along in the future. And that was the most important goal.

She drew a deep breath, sharing with Helen and her father the events of the night before and Avery's reasons for running. It was both painful and heartening to see how deeply the tale affected them.

"I had no idea Avery overheard Mrs. Kemble saying such things," Helen choked out then shook her head, her lips curling in self-disgust. "No, that's not exactly true. Ethan tried to tell me, but I didn't want to believe him. It made me feel guilty."

"He needed you to defend him," Grace said.

"I know that now. Instead, I listened to Mrs. Kemble, who claimed that children spin stories and a parent must crush such dishonesty before it takes root. When Ethan told us that Avery ran off to join the navy..." Her voice broke, and she pressed her handkerchief to her mouth. "The thought that I drove a child to such desperate actions sickens me. We might never have found him." Hands shaking, Helen turned to Grace. "Will I never get this right? Please, tell me how to make this right."

Sincerity and regret shone in Helen's eyes. Grace did not know if that resolve would last, but she prayed it might. "If you really wish to mend things, go to Avery. Ask pardon. Promise to listen to him in the future and begin again."

Grace felt Lucien watching her with those intense tiger-eyes, as if trying to decipher some unknown language he wanted to understand. She could sense it, as she did so many of his unspoken feelings. Was he like that wary creature she'd imagined, taking another step toward the warming fire?

Hope flickered inside her as he made conversation with her family and accepted Helen's invitation to stay for tea, and yet—was that hope merely her own invention because she so longed for that connection?

When it was time to leave, she noticed that Lucien had drawn Avery aside. She wanted to hasten over to them, to manage whatever their exchange was to be. But she curled her fingers in her skirts and remained where she was. She did not know what her husband said, but after a few minutes of conversation in low voices, Avery looked up at Lucien and nodded solemnly. She watched, stunned, as they shook hands.

The pair approached her, and Lucien's mouth curved in a hint of that smile that went straight to her heart. She looked at Lucien. "What are you two plotting?"

"I was just telling Avery that I am taking you to London in the next few days."

"London?"

"I have some business to attend to, and you could benefit from some diversion. There are purchases to be made so you might make the townhouse your own, entertainments to be enjoyed."

"But surely you'll want to wait until your family returns?" She regretted the words instantly as a guarded expression clouded his face.

"There is no telling when they will actually return to Everdene Hall. When Simon is looking at horses, he is apt to become so engrossed he loses all sense of time."

"But…" She cast a helpless glance at Avery.

"I'll be all right, Grace," Avery said. "You will write to us. And you could even take Lord Admiral Nelson around London, so it will be almost like you are taking us along." The boy looked as if he had grown taller somehow in the time since his conversation with Lucien.

She could barely speak through the lump in her throat. "I will carry the Lord Admiral with me wherever I go, I promise. And I will write about his adventures."

Avery brightened. By the time she bade her family goodbye and climbed into the carriage with Lucien, she was feeling a strange mixture of gratitude, nerves, and anticipation.

She could not stem a flutter of hope that she might recapture what she and Lucien had shared in those charged moments before they had been interrupted in her bedchamber and afterward, when he'd confided to her about the shattering of his family. She had known from the look on his face what he'd expected—for her to be repulsed by what he'd done, to reject him as he had rejected himself. He had looked so confused when she had not, seemed younger, somehow.

As the carriage jounced down the drive, she asked, "You and Avery seemed to have a serious conversation. May I ask what it was about?"

"We reached a gentleman's agreement and a gentleman never betrays what was said in confidence."

She took his hand in hers, her heart swelling, feeling certain that the armor he'd worn for years had cracked, just a little.

Maybe, just maybe, that crack might let her shine a spark of light into Lucien Harcourt's darkness. And maybe she could begin to seek light of her own as well.

OF COURSE ARKWRIGHT WOULD SHOW UP ON RAVEN'S COURT'S doorstep the moment he heard that the newlyweds were in their London residence, Lucien thought with more than a little relief. As his friend lavished them with congratulations, he had to admit he had rarely been more grateful to see his friend's face.

Everything had changed since the night Lucien had found the rascally stowaway under Grace's bed. He felt as if he was walking on uncertain ground and might, at any moment, plunge through. To...what? He couldn't fathom. He only knew he disliked the sensation immensely.

Going to his club would be just what he needed to recapture some of his old, familiar life—that was, if Arkwright would be sensible again and stop grinning at him like he had stolen sweets.

"You'll forgive us, my dear, if Arkwright and I go to the club."

"Surround myself with a pack of dull men in their cups when we can spend the afternoon showing the lovely new Lady Everdene off to the ton? Unthinkable!" Arkwright's boundless enthusiasm reminded him of the retrievers that were always scampering up whenever the friendly bastard passed by. "I've come to spirit you newlyweds away to Hyde Park."

Lucien would have loved to clap a hand over Arkwright's mouth, but there was nothing for it. Not when Grace's whole face lit up. It was go to Hyde Park or behave like a cad.

It would be a miracle if he didn't end up strangling his friend.

They left the carriage in care of the coachman to stroll along the Serpentine, Grace's skirts swaying like a bluebell, her face beneath her bonnet drawing Lucien's gaze again and again.

She watched the families on the shoreline of the man-made lake, a smile dimpling her cheek as little girls tossed crumbs to the swans, and boys sailed toy boats beneath the indulgent gaze of proud fathers or mothers. Arkwright walked to the vendor and purchased a stale bun, presenting it to Grace with a flourish so she could join the fun. Lucien knew damned well what Arkwright was doing as he watched Grace join the throng of children.

"You're an arse," Lucien muttered.

"Yes. Well, how else am I to find out what's been going on? You have been glaring until I expect the lake to start boiling at any moment."

Lucien watched Grace laugh in delight as a toddler took three steps, then clapped his hands so enthusiastically he plopped down on his rump.

"Out with it, my friend," Arkwright prodded. "How is married life?"

Stray curls were teasing the velvety skin of Grace's neck. Just watching them made him want to press his lips there. It was unnerving, the sudden, irresistible urges he felt whenever he was near her. Even when he was not, his famed concentration was shaken. "It is not what I expected."

"How so?"

"Someone shouted my name as we exited the church after the wedding. They flung a brick and struck Grace."

"Bloody hell…"

"It tore her skirt and landed on her foot. Could have been far worse. There was a note attached to the brick. A warning."

Concern furrowed Arkwright's brow. "Any idea who was behind it?"

"None. I insisted we leave at once for Everdene."

"Not the most romantic wedding night."

"That had to be postponed under the circumstances."

Arkwright stared. "You didn't bed her? The way you were looking at her that day at The Willows, I'd have thought you'd barely wait until the ring was on her finger."

"Of course I've bedded her, you dolt! After we arrived at Everdene and broke the news of our elopement to her family."

"I'm just astonished at your…restraint. There is more to it than this. I can see it in your eyes. What the devil happened? You know I won't let up until you tell me."

Lucien sucked in a deep breath. "I presented her with a box containing the Harcourt jewels. I thought it would please her after having to deal with her father. She cared not a whit about them."

"You did what?"

"She is entitled to jewels as my viscountess. Any woman I've ever known would have been delighted. She barely looked at them."

"Exactly when did you present this box of trinkets?" Arkwright asked.

"When I came to her bedchamber for the first time."

"Right before you bedded her?"

"Can you think of a better time?"

"Any time but that," Arkwright burst out. "One lavishes pretty baubles on one's mistress as payment for services rendered. A wife is a different matter. If you would like my expert advice…"

"What I'd like is for you to sod off."

Arkwright stared, and Lucien didn't like the keen edge to his gaze. "Can't do it. I'm your best friend. No one knows what a bastard you can be better than I do. I'm bound to notice when you start acting human. It's damned disconcerting."

Lucien hesitated a moment, then said gruffly, "She's lonely."

"You've only just now figured that out?" Arkwright's animated grin softened, and he looked at Grace, who was sharing half of her bun to a child who had none. "What did you expect, going from a house full of family to being your wife?"

"I have told her to go to the shops and buy anything she wishes." He frowned. "Giselle and my other mistresses were always pleased when I offered them such things."

"Trinkets are not the kind of thing Grace would be pleased with." Arkwright picked up a pebble and flung it into the Serpentine. "Your brilliancy is so blinding, I'm surprised you can see your nose on your face."

"What do you even buy for a woman who turns down jewelry?" Lucien asked.

"I know the perfect gift." Arkwright clapped him on the back, his enthusiasm jarring as a trumpet blast.

"Out with it, man. Lest you find yourself walking back to Curzon Street."

"A dog."

"You mean a coursing dog or a hound?"

Arkwright looked so damned pleased with himself Lucien wanted to shake him. "Not a hound, you dolt. A wee little thing to tie ribbons on and lavish with kisses."

Lucien's jaw dropped. "Are you mad?"

"Grace misses her brothers. Puppies and boys are much the same."

"Indeed. They shed all over everything."

"I think my publisher just whelped a litter. Spaniels."

One more set of pleading eyes begging for something Lucien couldn't give? "Absolutely not."

"Either get her a puppy or you'll have to spend time with her yourself."

"How is that even a choice?"

"Yes, such a hardship. She clearly likes you, though I cannot guess why." His face sobered as he gave Lucien a long, searching look. "Everyone needs affection."

His friend had an insufferable ability to poke things Lucien preferred to ignore.

Lucien turned his gaze back to the lake, watching as Grace threw the last crumbs into the water, then brushed her hands. He ran a finger under the edge of his cravat, which seemed suddenly tied it too tight. A picture from his past flashed in his memory. They were at a Christmas party at The Willows, Grace's parents so tender beneath the kissing ball. Lucien's mother looking on, wistful, her eyes shimmering with unshed tears. Though he was but ten years old at the time, he had known something was very wrong that night, that his mother had changed. Feared it was the melancholia his father had warned against. He knew better now. She had wilted from neglect before Lucien's eyes.

What if Grace wilted, too?

FOUR DAYS LATER LUCIEN SAT WITH HIS WIFE IN THE DRAWING ROOM, a place that might have been inviting to anyone who wasn't watching his wife for signs of unhappiness. In the time since the memory of his mother's decline had stolen into Lucien's head, his concern seemed to lodge in a knot of pulsing pain behind his left eye. One he badly needed to ease before he and Arkwright went to their club an hour from now.

Grace sat in her chair, her work basket beside her as she stitched on some bit of embroidery. He had managed snippets of conversation, then pretended to read a newspaper, though the words swam before his eyes. At last, he set the daily aside and pressed his fingertips to his left eye.

"Your head is aching." Grace's voice broke into his thoughts.

Startled, he looked up to find her regarding him with concern, her dark hair pretty beneath a lace cap. She seemed to be waiting for an answer.

"A bit, yes."

"Perhaps your eyes are strained. I could read the newspaper aloud to you." She picked up the daily that lay folded on the table. "It seems there is a new branch of Chartists, willing to do whatever is necessary to have the vote and improve working conditions."

Even if that meant resorting to violence…Lucien thought.

Of course Pinchbeck had given the journalist his opinion regarding that development. The man could never resist seeing his name in print. And yet, Lucien had more difficulty dismissing Pinchbeck's concerns since some elusive bastard had nearly hit Grace with a brick.

He winced. "The goings on in London only make my headache worse."

Grace interrupted his troubled thoughts again. "What if I read you a novel to distract you?"

God, no, he almost groaned, but managed to stifle it as she continued.

"There is a book I was starting to read again by a man named Charles Dickens. Have you heard of him?"

"Complaints mostly from Pinchbeck and his like. He claims the author is trying to shake down the very pillars of decent society with his tales. Arkwright likes Dickens well enough." He did not add that Arkwright was far too amiable in general. Lucien was trying to be more attentive, wasn't he? At least, if Grace was reading aloud he wouldn't have to make conversation while wrestling with this abominable headache. "I suppose I could listen for a bit," he said.

She smiled at him, like dawn after darkness. "Come. Lie on the settee while I fetch the book." He eased himself down, his boots dangling off the edge of the upholstery so as not to smudge it.

She placed a cushion beneath his head. "Shall I take off your boots?"

"No."

Her eyes widened at his sharp tone, and he felt an uncharacteristic impulse to explain himself. "I have a meeting at the club with Arkwright soon." Lucien frowned, bemused. He had never had anyone fuss over him in quite this way. Oh, mistresses and women hoping to snare him in the marriage mart had paid him attentions, but there was always an undercurrent beneath such actions, an exchange to be made. With Grace, it felt different, but it set him off balance. He could not seem to get comfortable. She took up the book, the gilt in its binding glowing in ribbons down the leather spine.

"Would you care to lay your head on my lap?" she asked.

Instinctively, he was ready to refuse, then he reconsidered.

"I suppose I would be able to hear better," he grumbled.

He raised up on his elbows while she slid onto the settee, then he laid his head on the soft nest of skirts, felt the warmth of her skin through the petticoats, her faint scent of jasmine and cinnamon surrounding him.

"The Old Curiosity Shop," she began.

He hadn't suffered listening to someone read since he'd had

schoolmasters who thrashed him if his mind wandered, but her voice was melodious, oddly soothing.

He closed his eyes and let his muscles relax.

He didn't have to really listen, he told himself. Grace would never know.

And yet as the hour passed, pictures began to form on the canvas of his mind, like mist, faint at first, then clearer…drawing him in. An old man tending his shop full of antiques…a money-lender tempting him to gamble…and a little girl named Nell whose face unsettled him…shifting into that of much younger child, a flower seller with Grace's scarlet ribbon in her hair.

CHAPTER 25

$\mathcal{I}$t had been one thing to attend a small house party at Everdene Hall with people Grace had known as a child— quite another thing entirely to be swept back into the social whirl of London again after three long years. On this crisp September night, tension thickened the air even more than usual. Since Lord Pinchbeck was among the guests at Lady Downe's soiree, Grace dreaded the possibility that Neville might be attending as well. Another meeting with her former betrothed was inevitable, but she loathed the prospect that anything might upset the balance she and Lucien had achieved.

She forced a smile when the French ambassador absconded with her husband to discuss the furor of unrest in Paris, but chose not to await the next salvo of impertinent questions alone. Slipping into an alcove, she lingered there until Arkwright appeared with a grin.

The man had an uncanny knack for noticing when Lucien was called away and stepping in to fill the void. "Are you all right," he asked with an arched brow. "Or is there someone I need to trounce?"

"I am fine."

"But glad I am here?" Arkwright said with an infectious grin.

"Very." She'd been unable to suppress the butterflies in her stomach from the moment of their arrival. "I fear I'll scream if I'm forced to fend off one more question from yet another prying, smiling hostess."

"Who no doubt scarce conceals bared teeth?"

"Indeed." She leaned toward him, conspiratorially. *"You have been absent from society for so long...You must tell us how you brought Lord Everdene up to scratch."*

Even the dailies featured caricatures lampooning the marriage, while anyone who had been attempting to enchant his lordship themselves, or secure him for their marriageable daughters, was eager to find fault with his chosen bride.

She looked at Arkwright. "I promised Lucien when we agreed to wed that I would be an asset to him politically. But I feel like the dark horse that triumphed at Newmarket. Everyone suspects I must have cheated to win."

"Let them gawk and gossip," Arkwright said with a dismissive wave of his hand. "You are an asset to Everdene in every way." He grinned, his gaze fixing on Lucien who was now surrounded by a cluster of colleagues near the punchbowl. "I daresay, the real joke is on him. I confess, it is amusing to see him so confused. Only once before in all the years I've known Everdene have I seen him this bewildered. He has always been so sure of himself while the rest of us mere mortals were bumbling about. But with you, there are times the old fellow looks as if he's teetering on the edge of a precipice."

She felt the sting. "I hardly take that as a compliment."

"Oh, it most definitely is. With you, he has finally met his match." He gave a soft laugh, his gaze still on Lucien. "In fact, I think he could fall in love with you, if he'll allow himself."

Grace's heart skipped a beat. "Do you truly think so? Sometimes I think he might have tender feelings toward me, but then, it is as if he slams a door shut inside him, and barricades it more securely than ever."

"Excellent. You are making progress, then."

"That hardly seems like progress."

"It is. I have some experience, truth be told." Arkwright turned a solemn gaze her direction. "Everdene behaved quite the same way with me as we became friends."

She pressed a gloved hand to the bodice of her glacé silk gown, almost daring to hope. Was it possible Lucien cared for her as well? "How did you finally break through?" she asked.

"It was a rather messy business, I am afraid." A spark of humor lit Arkwright's eyes as he thumbed his lapels. "I am a very likeable fellow, if I say so myself, but Lucien would barely talk to me. At Eton our beds were next to each other, in the far corner of the dormitory. Late at night when the other boys were asleep, I saw him with this blue tin box. He'd take something out of it and run it through his fingers. I couldn't see what he held, but I thought it must be something wicked or at least interesting. One night, while he was sleeping, I dug the box from under his bed. He woke while I was holding it. I'll never forget his expression. He grabbed for the box and planted me a facer."

Arkwright rubbed his eye with a rueful grin. "The tin fell and made a deafening noise and boys around us woke. It was quite the melee, but when the prefect came, I edged the box under Lucien's bed with my foot. Neither of us would tell what we had argued over, even when they thrashed us."

Honor among boys…How many times had Grace see it in her brothers?

"Later, after everyone else was back asleep, I saw him by moonlight, holding the box. It is the only time I have ever seen Lucien cry."

Grace's heart ached as she pictured the boy Lucien had been. "What was in it?"

Arkwright shrugged. "Dashed if I know. It was too dark to see. And afterwards, well—I never found out what it was. I made reparations as best I was able. I had discovered a nook behind a loose board between our beds where I would hide the bits and bobs boys collect. I removed my things and gave the space to him, promising I would never pry again. To solemnize the vow, I nicked my palm with my penknife and swore a blood oath that I if I ever told I soul I would drop down dead." His mouth crooked in a rueful smile. "So, if I choke on a fish bone this evening, you will know what happened."

She gave a watery laugh, so deeply moved by Arkwright's words that she squeezed his arm. "I am so glad that Lucien has you for a friend."

"He is the truest I've ever known. Don't give up on him, Grace. He cares about you more than he knows."

She *had* noticed a change in the weeks since she'd begun reading to him. He rarely missed their time together. He would sit across from her in his big chair as she read, his long legs stretched out before him, a glass of brandy in his hand. As he listened, she'd detected sparks of interest, a crease between his brows, the hint of a smile or frown.

Grace smiled up at Arkwright, tingling with hope that this 'business arrangement' of a marriage might turn into something more.

Arkwright offered her his arm. "Perhaps we should go rescue Everdene from that cadre of our 'honored opposition.'"

But Grace and her escort had scarce stepped from their alcove when Lord Pinchbeck blocked their way, the golden-haired girl at his side staring up at Grace with cornflower blue eyes.

"Mr. Arkwright, Lady Everdene!" Pinchbeck enthused far too heartily. "Pardon our exuberance! My daughter very much wishes to be presented to the belle of the evening." He gestured to the girl in the rose-hued gown beside him. "Lady Everdene, my daughter, Lady Alice Pinchbeck."

Pinchbeck's daughter was very young and very pretty, her cheeks flushed pink as she fidgeted with the fringe trimming her sleeve. "I am—I am so glad to meet you," she said in a breathless voice then turned to her father. "Papa, do go find Mama or she'll never forgive either one of us. I know she wished for an introduction to Lady Everdene as well."

"How should I know where your mother got off to," Pinchbeck complained.

"You might find her in Lady Downe's conservatory," his daughter suggested. "She wished to see some rare plant her ladyship's son sent from Brazil."

Grace heard the creak of corsets as Pinchbeck made his bow, then headed off. The moment he was out of earshot, Alice coughed, and batted her gold-tipped lashes at Arkwright. "May I trouble you for a glass of ratafia? I fear I have a—a catch in my throat."

Arkwright regarded her with suspicion, but there was nothing for it. He bowed like a gentleman and set out in search of punch.

The moment Grace and Lady Alice were alone, the girl turned to her, breathless. "I pray you forgive me for sending Mr. Arkwright away, but I so desired a moment alone with you. I could not say what I wish otherwise."

Grace regarded her warily as the girl looked in the direction her father had disappeared.

"You will hear that I was among those distressed over your elopement. But it isn't true," she said fiercely. "Mother and Father wished the match to gain a political ally. Mother even plotted to catch Lord Everdene and me in a compromising position at the ambassador's ball, but luckily the viscount foiled her plan."

It was shocking to hear such confessions from someone Grace had barely met. She struggled to think of something to say.

"I always knew my parents would choose a husband for me and it was my duty to obey, but I confess, I am quite afraid of Lord Everdene." Lady Alice fretted her lower lip. "There are times his lordship looks as if he could turn one to stone with a glance."

"He can be intimidating."

"I mean no offense," Lady Alice said, turning wide blue eyes back to Grace.

When she saw Alice's soft chin quiver for a moment she felt anger on the girl's behalf as well. Lady Alice's parents would have wed her to a man she feared. In society's view, a daughter was nothing more than a chip to gamble with. "No offense taken."

Grace glanced across the room at her handsome husband. No wonder he alarmed the girl. He had the aura of a jungle cat, all coiled power, ready to pounce at the slightest threat. "His lordship does have a formidable scowl. Before I came to know him better, I wondered if he practiced it in the mirror."

The embarrassment on Alice's face fled and she giggled, ducking her head to hide her merriment.

Grace laid one finger along her jaw as if considering. "I wonder what would happen if I tickled him with a feather. Do you think I might coax a laugh out of him?" She meant it to put Lady Alice further at ease, but suddenly an image seared itself in her mind. Hiding a plume beneath her pillow, then daring Lucien to lie still while she trailed the downy tip down the tender side of his ribs, across his flat belly and lower. Her own cheeks burned.

Lady Alice clasped her hands in delight. "Oh, Lady Everdene! I do like you immensely. I so hope we can be friends." Then the girl froze, rather like a pup whose leash had been yanked. "Mother!" Alice warned under her breath.

A woman in silvery satin sailed toward them on Pinchbeck's arm, the plumes in her coiffure waving like battle flags. "Why, Alice, you naughty gel! Meeting Lady Everdene while I was otherwise engaged." Lady Pinchbeck rapped her daughter sharply with a folded fan. "You knew how anxious I was to welcome her ladyship back into society after such a precipitous departure years ago."

The woman made it sound as if Grace was in her dotage. "It has only been three years."

"But the circumstances! The scandal of a broken engagement can hardly help but cause one humiliation when all of society—"

"Mother!" Lady Alice exclaimed in horror.

"I am merely stating a well-known fact. And it seems both parties involved have moved on, have they not?" Lady Pinchbeck said with an indulgent glance at her daughter that puzzled Grace. Pen-stroke thin eyebrows arched toward a roll of graying curls as the redoubtable matron regarded Grace. "Quite a triumph to attend tonight's revels as Viscountess Everdene. It is a title many aspired to."

"But," Pinchbeck cut in, patting his wife's beringed hand, "this shy country blossom has eclipsed them all."

"Shy? Country?" Arkwright's merry laugh was never more welcome as he approached with the punch Lady Alice had requested. "If you can find a lady anywhere in England to match Lady Everdene for wit and charm, I will leap off of London Bridge."

"We must all rejoice that Lord Everdene has wed," Pinchbeck said. "Nothing like an angel at his hearth to make a man realize how vital it is to keep fires of rebellion from spreading. Why, these vermin intend to turn God's natural order upside down. I am sure Lady Everdene will remind her husband where his loyalties must lie. His lordship has a distressing propensity for changing his mind."

The anger Grace had felt on Alice's behalf burned even hotter as she came to Lucien's defense. "I admire Lord Everdene for his ability to alter his stance on issues. Especially in light of new information he discovers about those fighting for change. That takes courage as well as intelligence."

"Well said!" Arkwright exclaimed.

Pinchbeck began to bluster, but Grace went on as if she hadn't noticed. "Loyalty to a false statement does not change the truth," she said. "When Galileo discovered that the earth orbited the sun, the inquisition threatened him with torture and execution unless he recanted. Still, the earth continued to orbit the sun."

Pinchbeck blustered. "A man without loyalty is nothing."

Grace looked across the room at Lucien, and wondered who, save Arkwright, had been loyal to him.

"In the past, Everdene's vote could always be counted to do whatever was necessary to maintain order in the kingdom. Why, the rabble feared him as much as his father. It will be so again. We must put an end to this upheaval the Chartists and Irish scum are stirring up or there will be revolution here as there is in France."

"As I understand it," Grace observed, "the Chartists wish to have some say in parliament, a vote regarding labor conditions, and the Irish food for their children. It hardly seems unreasonable to consider—"

"They should be grateful to be employed." Pinchbeck made a scoffing sound. "As for the Irish, what would you have us do? Fling open the doors of the granaries? I say, let them work harder if they want their bread. Labor dictating working conditions? Of all the nonsensical ideas."

"I would very much like to see the conditions myself," Grace said, maneuvering the conversation as her mother might have done. "Perhaps you would give me a tour of your factory, Lord Pinchbeck?"

She disliked the nasty flicker in his eyes.

"I am sure my partner, Mr. Freyne, would be happy to meet with you and tell you anything you wish to know."

Alice caught her breath and Grace felt Arkwright stiffen. She laid a hand on his arm.

No doubt, Pinchbeck meant to silence her by mentioning Neville's name, but Grace was not so easily cowed. "I prefer to see conditions for myself," she said. "You attempted to enlist my husband as an investor in your business ventures, and I imagine that process must be a trifle like courtship. You are unlikely to point out flaws."

"My dear Lady Everdene," he replied. "You do make one wonder at the comparison to courtship considering the fact that you are so lately wed. What flaws you may have hidden—"

"Flaws?" Lucien, his eyes glinting steel, appeared out of nowhere. "My wife has no flaws save extending politeness to some who do not deserve it."

Poor Alice took a step back. Her father guffawed. "Ah, Everdene, here is the happy groom at last! A bit of teasing is allowed in addressing a new bride, is it not? I was merely suggesting that a married man has a different perspective from a bachelor's. When one has a wife, and the prospect of being blessed with children, civil unrest is doubly upsetting. Take your father for example. He knew how to protect his own. Send in the hussars and be done with it, like we did in Manchester in 'nineteen."

"*Such* courage!" Grace said, wondering if Pinchbeck was even clever enough to note her sarcasm. Peterloo, the papers had called it, the carnage named after the battle of Waterloo. Sixty thousand English men, women and children had gathered to hear speeches about bettering their working conditions and gaining the vote…"As I understand it, all was completely peaceful until hussars charged into the panicked crowd with their sabers swinging," Grace observed. "You must be so proud."

"We are charged with keeping the peace," Pinchbeck retorted. "Protecting the Crown and the interests of propertied men. The common herd will not be satisfied until they're suckling at the Queen's own teat."

Lady Alice gasped, and her mother nearly choked herself, clutching the opals at her throat.

"I think," Arkwright said, his jovial aura holding an edge, "that Prince Albert might object at such liberties."

Pinchbeck rounded on him. "You know what I mean! This is what comes of nonsense like that village Everdene's brother built. Coddling the rabble just makes them more discontented with their lot in life. Surely you don't expect all landlords to empty their coffers like Harcourt did?"

Lady Downe approached the group with the instinctive skill of a hostess sensing trouble, but even her presence didn't dissuade him from continuing to spout his point of view. "I'd wager, should you ask Everdene how his investment is doing now, he'd tell a different story."

"Come, come Lord Pinchbeck," Lady Downe said. "You must not plague our newlyweds with disagreeable subjects on their honeymoon. This is a time of celebration."

"Indeed it is," Lucien said, curving an arm about Grace's waist, his expression unreadable as he addressed their hostess. "Your ladyship, perhaps you can persuade someone to play the piano forte. I feel the irrepressible need to dance with my bride."

Lady Downe beamed. "Of course! You must lead the first waltz!" She bustled off in search of a musical guest.

Grace still simmered with outrage as Lucien guided her to the center of the floor. He swept her into his arms as the first notes rang out, cutting the tension that swirled in the air. He danced divinely, with athletic grace, his hand splayed on her back.

At the next turn, he pulled her just a little too close. "I think you made quite an impression tonight, Lady Everdene. Your mother's tutelage was on fine display."

"Sadly, she neglected to advise me in one particular area."

"And what was that?"

"What to do when I want to fling ratafia in some pompous wretch's face."

Lucien's brows rose. A grin spread across his handsome face, then he laughed. The rich, rare sound rang out across the room, guests craning their necks to stare, voices trailing off mid-conversation.

Grace couldn't help herself. She laughed with him until tears stung her eyes.

"You are quite beautiful, you know," he said, an unexpected tenderness softening his severe features. "And most convincing in your arguments. Perhaps it is easier to swallow a bitter truth if it is spoken by a beautiful woman."

"I meant what I said about going to see the conditions in Pinchbeck's factory. After all, he asked you to invest."

"I have already dismissed the idea of doing so."

"In spite of that…would it not be best to actually *see* what people are unhappy about for ourselves? My mother always said we should observe circumstances with our own eyes if we wish to understand them. I could go—"

"No," he snapped so harshly she stiffened. He tightened his arm about her waist, guiding her flawlessly in the dance. "Forgive me for being strident," he said, "but considering the current climate on the streets, it would be unwise for you to visit such a place."

"Surely I can spend an hour there."

"With the threats I have received? And what happened at our wedding? No." Her resistance must have shone on her face, for his voice gentled. "I am much occupied with state business at present, but I will try to make time in the future."

Would he? Or would more pressing matters distract?

One thing she knew for certain was this.

She would not wait to go to the factory forever.

CHAPTER 26

*R*ain was dampening the October evening as Lucien strode into the townhouse, feeling a trifle sheepish. He'd had an engagement scheduled at Whites but canceled it. How Grace would laugh if she knew he had turned down meeting men at his club so he could spend the evening with his wife. Not only because he enjoyed her company—which he did to an increasingly alarming degree—but because of that damnable novel she was reading to him. It was a bit like the opium dens he had heard of, luring a man in, weaving a dreamworld so real one did not want to leave it. Last night they had broken off just at the most exciting part, and he needed to find out what happened next to Little Nell, and whether that scheming bastard Quilp would be crushed at last. But as Lucien handed his cloak and hat to a footman, a strange hush blanketed the house, reminding him of the days when he had lived alone.

He frowned. He would never be the kind of man who lived in his wife's pocket, but in the months since their wedding, he had become accustomed to her smile, the swish of her skirts, the soft, feminine touches about surroundings that had once been bachelor quarters.

Perhaps she had gone out. Women had been seeking her friendship of late. Lady Alice Pinchbeck had even sent an invitation to the theater in two weeks' time. Lucien grimaced at the prospect. He would have to be sure not to accidentally look at the girl, lest she leap out of the box like a frightened hare.

Confound it, where was his wife? He searched the library and drawing room before encountering a maid, the startled girl all but dropping a tray of prism-decked candelabrum candlesticks she'd polished, the crystal teardrops jangling.

"Your pardon, sir. Wasn't expecting anyone to be in here. Graves said you were to be dining at your club."

"A change in plans. Has Lady Everdene gone out?"

"Oh, no, my lord. Her ladyship has kept to her room since this afternoon. Had her meal brought up on a tray and everything."

What the devil? Lucien felt a surge of protectiveness that startled him. If one of those society women was plaguing her, they'd deal with him.

"I fear she is not feeling well," the maid continued.

But Lucien was already halfway up the steps. When he was ill, he wanted nothing more than to be left in peace. But this was his wife who'd seemed perfectly fine that very morning. When he opened the door, saw her curled up on her side with a pillow held against her belly, he rushed to her side, alarmed. "I shall summon a physician at once."

"No. You mustn't!" Her cheeks turned pink.

He put his hand on her forehead, grateful when he found it cool to the touch. Still, her face was somewhat pale. "You don't look well."

"At the risk of sounding indelicate, I am…having my monthly courses."

"…Oh."

He couldn't quell a jab of disappointment—not about fact that she hadn't fallen pregnant exactly. He wasn't even sure if he'd been hoping she was with child or relieved she was not. He couldn't quite fathom why he felt this sinking sensation, nor did he want to. It wasn't just that he would not be enjoying her body tonight. Nor that they would not sit cozily by the fire while she read from Dickens, which was even more disappointing. No. It was something far more disconcerting. "You won't want to read this evening," he said, seizing on the least dangerous option.

"I'm afraid I'm not quite up to it right now."

"No. Of course not…" At a loss, both from seeing her in this state, and the jumble of his own thoughts, he felt an irresistible urge to help. "I could…read to you," he said. "If you wish…?"

It was several seconds before she answered, and the smile she gave him did something strange to his heart. "I would like that very much, a welcome distraction, perhaps."

Lucien went to fetch the book and shed his jacket, cravat, waistcoat and boots.

He rolled up his cuffs, then lay down atop the coverlet beside her, his back propped up on pillows. "Would you like to rest your head on my shoulder?" he asked, and she scooted her body closer, nestling against him. He could feel the sweet weight of her cheek through the fabric of his shirt, her breath warm. That languor came over him, a melting sensation as the tightness in his muscles relaxed, the guard he kept up softening just a little.

Opening the book, he cleared his throat and began to read, not one chapter, but two…three…At last, he stopped to pour himself a glass of wine.

"Is your voice growing tired?" Grace murmured as he took a drink.

"Not at all. Unless you wish to sleep?"

She shook her head. "I love the sound of your voice." Her eyes sparked with amusement. "I can see why you win so many arguments in parliament."

"Perhaps I can argue that we should finish this book tonight?"

"Because…?"

He smiled. "We are nearly to the end. I have to find out what happens."

She laughed. "It is a good thing you didn't read this when it was released as a serial. We had to wait a full week to find out. Then Avery got measles, and Papa made us wait even longer, until he was well to finish it."

A scene flashed in his mind. Something Lucien hadn't thought of since he was a boy. A sick room, the light bothering his eyes, his skin itching…and Cassandra…

Grace's brow puckered. "Is something amiss? You look rather done in all of a sudden."

"No...I'm fine. I was just remembering something. Cassandra and I had the measles at the same time when we were small." His mother had never left their sides.

She pushed herself up on an elbow, her nightgown dipping just a little to expose the topmost swell of one breast. "How old were you?"

Why had he even opened that door to her question? He could still brush it off, but somehow felt compelled to answer. "Six." As long ago as it had been, he still remembered clearly..."They put us in the same bed away from Simon and Jane. I was burning with fever, but Cass insisted on covering me with that infernal blanket she dragged about." And yet, he hadn't complained. Even at six, he'd known sharing that blanket was a gift his sister had given him. "My mother had embroidered the corner of it...Pansies, Cass's favorite..."

He wasn't even aware he'd spoken this last bit out loud, until Grace said, "That sounds like a lovely memory."

Only because he'd had decades to dull all that happened. Even to this day, it burned like the sore throat that had tormented him. When he and his sister had finally recovered and were allowed out of the sick room, his father had taken Cassandra's blanket to burn. Might have destroyed all of it except...he shoved the memory away.

"Shall we continue the book?" he asked briskly, returning to the bed. He lit a fresh candle to give himself more light.

The rustle of pages and the bedchamber with its warm fire and rich accoutrements faded as he lost himself in the story once more. Relief filled him as Nell and her grandfather found safe haven. Lucien's chest felt tight, and something prickly seemed lodged in his throat as the little girl was tucked in a warm bed at last. He swallowed hard, his voice sounding strange as he read Nell's words. *"When I die, put near me something that has loved the light—'* What the devil?!" He slammed the book shut. Startled, Grace jerked her head from his shoulder. "Nell *dies*?" He glared at Grace in indignation. "What was this Dickens fellow thinking?" It took a moment for his head to clear enough to see Grace's face. A tear welled on her lashes, trickled free. His outrage faded away, leaving him appalled at his behavior.

He smoothed his thumb across her cheek, gathering up her tears. "Forgive me for being churlish, sweetheart."

"It's not you." Her voice broke. "It's Nell…"

Lucien gathered her into his arms, experiencing a surge of relief that he wasn't responsible for her tears. Cursing Dickens for drawing them from her. He kissed the crown of her head, rubbing her back, wanting above all things to soothe her pain away. Her hand curled in his shirt, her hair spilling across the pillow, smelling of flowers and compassion…

"Nell isn't real, sweetheart," he murmured. "You are weeping over the death of a child who never existed."

"And, yet, you were upset as well."

"That's different. You knew how the book would end. I did not."

She lay her hand upon his chest, her touch penetrating far deeper than the surface of his skin, sinking through to muscle, bone…to the place where he should have had a heart. "The real reason I'm upset is that there are a thousand Little Nells all over London. They just have names like Sibby Rose."

He felt a throb of something that made his throat go dry. How was it that he had thought he could simply get her with child, then walk back to his own life unchanged?

"I will leave you to rest," he said, needing to put distance between them so he could think straight. Think at all. He gently untangled her fingers, slowly slipped from her bed and doused the candle flame. Shadows surrounded him, but he was used to darkness. He made his way to his bedchamber door, his shirt still damp with her tears; his imagination filled with images he could have gone his whole life without noticing…and feelings too new to understand.

Grace leaned close to Lucien as the Harcourt coach waited its turn to draw up to the Theater Royal, the line of equipages and lanterns stringing out before and after them like a glittering necklace.

She peered out the window at the spectacle. Tonight, Drury Lane was filled with contrasts. Jewels sparkled, fashionable gowns and bonnets a rainbow of color. Vendors were scattered about, hawking their wares, meat pies and slices of orange, trinkets and ribbons and fans. Here and there, scrawny, sharp-featured waifs wound through the crowd, ready to pick pockets, and hard-eyed men milled about ready to do worse, were they not held at a distance by towering footmen in livery.

It was a strange patchwork that changed whenever she looked, not unlike the man sitting beside her. In the weeks since they had finished the Dickens novel, her husband had seemed uncomfortable. Sometimes silent as a sphinx, watching her with a sharpness that made her feel bare to the skin, others so distant, his eyes guarded as if he expected her to slip a penknife between his ribs. He had been so tender that night, but now…even their lovemaking had changed, with a fierceness, but a wariness as well.

She put that troubling picture from her mind, looking over at her husband. "Wasn't it kind of Lady Alice to send tickets to the theater?" she asked. "I am so excited."

"So excited you nearly forgot?" Lucien observed and she winced inwardly. "I return home expecting to find my wife garbed in her theater finery, only to discover her elbow deep in a plethora of crates instead."

Was he angry with her? Or teasing? She wasn't sure. She had learned of a school set up for factory children to learn ciphering and reading on their Sundays off, and she had determined to do all she could to help. A calling made sweeter when she had found Sibby Rose Nolan outside the building where school was held, waiting to walk her older brother, Robert, home. The child's earnestness as Grace had shown her how to write the first two letters of her name was fresh in her mind, the little girl repeating with adorable seriousness. *'S' is a snake…'i' is a candle with a dot of flame.*

"I do apologize," she said. "But the slates and pencils I'd ordered arrived just as I was going upstairs to change. If you knew how delighted the children will be, you might have got distracted, too."

"I doubt it," he said.

She sucked in the corner of her lip. But before she could think what to say, gloved fingertips brushed her cheek, Lucien's deep voice starting a tremor along her skin.

"If playing Lady Bountiful makes your eyes shine like they did over those crates, I would consider purchasing every slate in London."

Her heart skipped, grateful as he smiled warmly. "Securing supplies for the school is my favorite thing about living in London. *Almost*." She dared a wicked smile and squeezed his thigh. "As to my garb, I do hope it is up to your very fastidious standards."

"I will like the dress better when I have stripped it off of you later tonight." Lucien regarded her with eyes so intense they made her nipples burn. His lids fell to half-mast as he leaned in close, lowering his voice. "Perhaps we can leave at intermission."

The coach rumbled to a halt, the door suddenly opening, the footman letting down the coach steps. It seemed every eye in the surrounding crowd was turned their way. As Lucien descended and handed her down, she couldn't suppress a laugh.

"What do you find amusing, Lady Everdene?" Lucien asked.

"I was just recalling how it was during my first season. How my friends and I clustered together, imagining what it would be like to enter a room on the arm of a handsome escort everyone else had been swooning over."

"I never imagined you were the giggling, swooning type," Lucien said.

"You're partly correct. I told myself I was my mother's daughter —far above such fol-de-rol. It turns out, I am not nearly as dignified as I wished to be. I am quite enjoying all of the envious glances thrown my way."

The severe lines of Lucien's face softened in a way she had seen so rarely. He covered her hand with his. "My dear, I am the one to be envied. You look lovely tonight."

She was turning her face up to his when a piping little voice rang out, the Irish brogue like a song. "Posy…posy for milady, sir?"

Grace wheeled toward the sound, glimpsing a small girl in the crowd, a faded red cloak swathing her body. A box hung from a strap around her narrow shoulders.

"Sibby Rose!" Grace released Lucien's arm to wave at the little girl who took up the end of her plait, displaying a somewhat droopy, yet still-bright red ribbon. But before Grace could make her way to the child, Neville's voice jarred her.

"Ah! If it isn't the happy couple!" he said. Her former betrothed approached with an exquisite woman on his arm. "Lord Pinchbeck mentioned you were to come to the theater with Lady Alice."

"Unfortunately," Lucien said stiffly, starting to steer Grace past the couple, "Lady Alice has a megrim and sent her regrets."

"Yes. Most unfortunate. I was hoping to see her myself. However, the lovely Miss Marchand has volunteered to ease my disappointment."

Neville's companion caught Lucien's arm with a familiarity that set Grace's teeth on edge. Sultry violet eyes regarded Lucien with ill-concealed amusement, the woman's tongue moistening pouting lips. "*Ma chère* viscount, surely you do not mean to ignore an old friend?"

Grace saw the muscle in Lucien's jaw tighten, then he gave her a curt nod. "Miss Marchand."

Neville pushed on. "The lovely bride and I are friends as well. Allow me to introduce Miss Giselle Marchand, Lady Grace Elliot, er, Harcourt."

She heard Lucien's breath hiss between his teeth, felt his muscles knot beneath her hand. "Lady Everdene." His words were steely as a blade.

But the French beauty only looked up at him with a knowing laugh. "All these years you always swore you would never marry, and yet scandal snared you at last. Something about a house party, a tryst after midnight, and the parson's mousetrap snapped shut?"

Miss Marchand's tone made it a question, but there was a knowing light in those sly eyes. Was this pure conjecture, or had what transpired between Grace and Lucien somehow leaked out? Heat rose in her cheeks. "My lord, perhaps we should find our seats —" she began, trying to draw him away.

Lucien would not be moved. "Let me dispel your delusions at once, Miss Marchand. I wed Lady Grace because she is without peer. She puts every other woman of my acquaintance in the shade with her beauty, intelligence and kindness. If fools think I would wed for any other reason, they do not know me at all."

With a curt bow, he swept Grace toward the rotunda. She peered up at him, daring to hope. Was it possible what he had said was true?

WHAT THE DEVIL WAS GOING ON HERE? LUCIEN SEETHED, NOT EVEN seeing the actors on the stage. Neville Freyne showing up with Lucien's former mistress? Here at the theater on the very night Lady Alice Pinchbeck invited Grace? And that snide comment of Giselle's—that Lucien had been forced into marriage because he'd compromised Grace…Was that just a swipe of cat's claws? Or something more?

Lord Elliot was still in contact with Freyne. Had Grace's father felt the need to explain why he agreed to the marriage and had Freyne told Giselle? Or had some servant witnessed their indiscretions at Everdene Hall or at the townhouse and started rumors?

These thoughts made Lucien's blood boil.

Yet, his answer to Giselle's jibe had unnerved him even more. Because the words had spilled out with the ring of truth…because of the way Grace had looked at him as he spoke them, the emotion he'd seen flare in her eyes…The hope…Love…

Fierce protectiveness mingled with a fear so raw he had to clench his hand to keep it still. At intermission Lady Downe came to visit Grace, and Lucien excused himself. He hunted down Freyne and drew the bloody bastard away from the crowd.

"What game are you playing, Freyne? Flaunting Giselle in front of my wife. Spewing rumors about the circumstances of my marriage? I swear, if you say another word to anyone—"

"You think I am the only one who knows what you and Grace were up to? You avoided marriage so long. It's easy enough to reach that conclusion with pure conjecture, let alone when one is privy to—"

"To what?"

"Anything I say would only be the truth."

"If I ever hear you are maligning my wife again, I will see you in hell."

"And here, I thought your brother was the Harcourt with a penchant for dueling," Freyne said, his gaze narrowing. "Pistols at dawn from the Viscount Everdene, the man with ice in his veins? That *would* give credence to the rumors about your marriage for sure."

Lucien loathed him for speaking that simple truth.

"As for pistols," Freyne continued, "you had better keep one close. You have developed a talent for making enemies." Freyne looked toward the box where Grace sat. "And it seems the iron-clad viscount has developed a weakness at last."

CHAPTER 27

*A*rkwright had once claimed Lucien's mind was like a steam train, barreling through whatever problem confronted him with no notion of the countryside flashing by. That had never been more true than tonight.

The burst of applause seemed to come out of nowhere, the red velvet curtains and soaring ceiling of the Theater Royal swimming back into focus as actors took their final bows. Lucien looked at Grace, his jaw tightening. Vulnerability still clung to her lovely features after Freyne's jibes earlier. Damned if Lucien would let such a situation stand. He had waged campaigns to change public opinion before and seldom lost, but this battle to douse rumors Freyne and gossips like Giselle might try to ignite could be the most important he'd ever waged.

Anyone who distressed his wife would discover just how ruthless the Viscount Everdene could be. Grace deserved so much more from him than he would ever be able to give her, but this much was true: Lucien had wed Grace by choice. And it was time all of London society knew he held her in the highest esteem.

He usually made haste to exit the theater and avoid mere social prattle. But tonight, he tucked Grace's arm in his with a possessiveness impossible to mistake, determined to seek out the crème of London society and set a few things straight.

The conversations bled together as they made their way down

the sweeping stairs to the rotunda, Lucien stopping about every step to show off his wife:

"May I introduce you to Lady Everdene, the woman I am fortunate enough to call my wife…" alternating in one form or another with "…Had I known what pleasure marriage to this lady would bring, I would have reconsidered my position long ago…"

It was obvious Grace knew what he was doing. Her dark-fringed eyes found his time and again, and she smiled up at him with amusement and something a trifle poignant.

Chill night air rippled the blue ribbons of her bonnet as he finally escorted her outside.

Gaslights shone in pools of gold in the haze of coal smoke that perpetually blanketed the city, lanterns hanging from hooks on the endless line of coaches and hackney cabs that waited to carry theatergoers away. Some of the vendors still waited for late-night commerce while opera dancers and courtesans hoped to catch a rich man's eye.

"Oh, Lucien," Grace exclaimed, straining on tiptoe to see over the crowd. "Over there! Sibby Rose is still here selling flowers!"

As he followed her gaze to where the child stood, looking very small amidst the throng, his wife's voice echoed in his memory: *There are Little Nells all over London…*

He managed a smile. "Consideration for my valet's nerves demands that I ask: Is the little miss accompanied by her brother?"

Grace's laughter drove back some of the anger Freyne had stirred within him. "Scrap is nowhere to be seen," she promised.

"Then I will happily buy every last petal and send the child home."

She squeezed his arm, pressing it into the soft pillow of her breast. A shaft of heat went through him and he was suddenly impatient to get Grace back to Raven's Court and make love to her in a way that would drive Freyne and Giselle's vile insinuations from her mind. But that pleasure would be have to be delayed since Lord and Lady Downe were sweeping toward them with determined smiles, one more social connection that could only help dispel ugly rumors.

Lucien glimpsed the Harcourt coach part way down the road, the coachman on the high seat with the footman watching for them to appear. Perhaps he wouldn't wait for the privacy of the bedchamber after all. He pictured Grace in the dim coach, her skin, creamy, glowing as his hand skimming up her stockinged leg…

"Everdene! Ho, Everdene!" A shrill voice hailed him from the crowd. Lucien ground his teeth, the enticing image of ravishing his wife fading. Sir Edward Allen barreled toward them, his loose-jointed arms waving like a marionette. "Your pardon, Lady Everdene," the man gasped as he reached them. "I must speak to his lordship alone."

"Then make an appointment to do so." Lucien leveled him a quelling glare. "My wife has a particular errand in mind and surely you cannot think I would leave her unaccompanied in a crowd."

Lady Downe bustled up to them with a bright smile. "Perhaps my husband and I could serve as her escorts. We were hoping to find you in this crush and inquire about Lady Everdene's work with the Sunday Schools."

Lucien had known that Lady Downe had a philanthropical bent. It seemed Grace might draw another patroness to her cause.

Grace smiled at the aristocratic couple, even though Lucien sensed she was worried that Sibby Rose might slip away. "That would be lovely, your ladyship," she said warmly. "I was just going to buy some flowers."

Lucien pressed coins into her hand before the Downes swept her away to make the purchase. "I will join you directly," he told her. He waited until she was some distance away. "What is this important matter?" he demanded of Sir Edward. "I am recently wed and eager to be with my wife." He glanced in Grace's direction, noting that she, too, had been detained some ways from her destination as Lord and Lady Downe paused to introduce her to a dowager in scarlet plumes.

"My friend Carlisle did not arrive here until intermission," Sir Edward said.

"I cannot see why Carlisle's tardiness should concern me."

"He had to take a longer route because some Irish ruffian outside the Crook and Bull was riling up the common herd. You saw what happened on St. James's Street when the gentlemen's clubs were attacked?"

He hadn't been present, but he had seen the aftermath. Learned just how quickly a mob could get out of hand.

Sir Edward mopped his brow with a handkerchief. "Carlisle said they were shouting something about Drury Lane."

The back of Lucien's neck prickled and he glanced beyond the line of grand coaches and footman to see the shadowy streets beyond. Was there some threat simmering beneath the usual hubbub of the theater crowd?

He searched for Grace in the sea of bonnets, top hats, and plumed turbans. He spotted her just as the first warning split the night.

"'Ware! A mob's coming…"

Shouts penetrated the cacophony of sound, like thunder building before a storm. How the devil had he not noticed?

Ragged men suddenly took shape in the shadows, pushing into the street flanking the theater, their faces distorted as growing numbers loomed in the gas light. Crude weapons were clasped in their hands.

"Death to blood-sucking 'ristocrats!" a guttural voice called. "Gi' us bread!"

Cries of alarm rippled through the crowd, people shoving and jostling, trying to get to their coaches or flee down Catherine Street. Lucien's gut clenched as he pushed his way through the mass of panicked theatergoers and tried to reach the place where he'd last seen Grace moments before. But all he saw was Lord Downe hastening his wife away, Grace nowhere to be found. A moment of panic swept through Lucien as he looked around, then saw her making her way toward the child as the mob boiled toward them like an angry sea.

Objects pelted through the air, a rotting vegetable splatting against a nearby woman's velvet cloak. Stones and bottles and God knew what followed.

He heard names being called, people crying out in pain and panic, desperate to escape the hail of objects. He needed to get Grace.

"There 'e is!" someone shouted, "Lord—" A crack of gunfire split the air. Lucien heard a scream from where Grace had been a moment ago, but she had vanished in the panicked crowd.

Something glanced off his back as he shouldered his way to where he had last seen her. He trod on what looked to be her bonnet, crushed on the ground, then saw the bright splash of blue ribbons before the crowd converged in once again.

"Grace!" he shouted.

"Here! Lucien!"

Relief shot through him at the sound of her voice. She was curled above what looked to be a small bundle of rags, protecting it from the panicked throng. Sibby Rose Nolan lay on the ground like a broken doll, blood streaming from a cut on her brow. The box with the last of her flowers had splintered, and the strap that had held it around her shoulders twisted.

"Something struck her!" Grace cried. "She can't...can't..."

He reached them at last. With an oath, Lucien disentangled the broken box from the girl, then scooped her up. She weighed little more than a kitten. "I'll get us out of here," he told Grace. "Hold tight to my arm." He had marked the place where his coachman sat on his perch, searching for him in the churning crowd. He pushed his way toward the coach, Grace stumbling beside him as the coachman gestured to a footman who came wading toward the embattled group. With the servants' help, Lucien managed to get his wife into the coach, then handed Sibby Rose to her.

Grace cradled the child against her, heedless of her gown as Lucien pulled a box from beneath the coach seat and withdrew a gleaming pistol.

The coach rocked dangerously as it lurched into motion. Bottles smashed against the vehicle's walls. The crack of the whip and whinnies of distressed horses seemed to go on forever as Lucien guarded the window, pistol poised.

Bit by bit, the roar of the crowd faded into the distance, the bone-jarring jolts lessened, the blows to the coach stopped. Only the jingle of harness, the clop of the horses hooves and the thundering of his heart continued to strain Lucien's nerves.

He knocked on the roof of the coach, and the equipage shuddered to a halt.

"I think we've lost them, my lord," the coachman called. "Where are we to go?"

The girl roused in Grace's arms, her tears streaming down her dirty cheeks. "I want me mammy."

"Of course you do, sweeting," Grace soothed. "We will take you to her as soon as may be." Lucien glanced down at the child. Grace had wrapped her shawl around the girl's trembling body. One stick-thin leg stuck out, the cotton stocking carefully darned. It was a miracle she wasn't hurt worse.

"Child, where do you live?" Lucien asked.

She looked at him in the light of the coach lantern, her eyes too large in her pinched face. "L—Little White Lion Street."

One of seven streets that made up a hell of crime and poverty and vice.

He turned to Grace. "I'd not send the devil himself into the Seven Dials tonight. We'll take her to Raven's Court, and then, once the streets are quiet, we'll return her home."

"Did you hear that, Sibby Rose?" Grace said, stroking the little girl's hair. "You'll sleep tonight in a princess bed with velvet curtains and eat all the cake you want. Then, as soon as the angry people are gone, Lord Everdene and I will take you to your mama ourselves."

Not quite what Lucien had envisioned, and yet, he suddenly thought of the daughter he and Grace might have one day. How vulnerable any child would be.

Grace peered up at him, her face so drawn it made his chest ache. "Her mother will be frantic," she whispered.

Would she be? Lucien wondered. Or would the child's mother be one of those gin-soaked, hate-filled women Pinchbeck so often spoke of? The type of woman urging the mob on?

CHAPTER 28

"**I** have dismissed the servants," Lucien explained, once the child was bathed, wounds tended, then put to bed in yet another one of his shirts. "I intend to examine you myself, make certain you are not hurt. Sometimes, in heightened excitement, one does not feel pain until the crisis is over."

He led her to the chair beside the fire and she sank down, wincing, her gown smudged, lawn undergarments peeking through rents in the fabric. "Nothing but a few scrapes and bruises, I'm sure," she said, "but I am glad to have you here. I have never been so frightened."

He knelt, slipped off her shoes one by one, then rolled down her stockings seeing a crescent-shaped bruise, likely from someone's bootheel, some scrapes where someone in the crowd had bumped her as they tried to get away. Her skin was warm as he gently felt the bones in her foot, her ankle, her calf. Satisfied that nothing was broken, he urged her to a standing position, unfastening her gown with deft fingers. As he peeled away the layers of cloth, he found more bruises on the creamy white skin, a long, raw scrape marred her left side—from the jagged edge of Sibby Rose's shattered box, perhaps?

When she was naked, He traced the outline of the abrasion with his fingertip, his voice low, rough. "God, when I think about what could have happened when you disappeared in the crowd...."

"I knew you would find us."

Her faith in him made his gut clench, and he knew he would fight his way through lions to reach her.

"Sibby Rose is so little...," Grace said, a catch in her voice. "I tried to shield her..."

"You did." He kissed her bare shoulder. "The child's wounds will heal in no time."

But would Grace's? Lucien wondered. She'd nearly been trampled, experienced violence unlike anything she'd ever seen.

He drew the pins from her hair one by one, her silky locks tumbling over his hands. Gently, he felt her scalp for any lumps or abrasions.

"I fear the cuts will sting when you get in the water, but they must be cleaned."

He took her hand and led her to the copper tub before the fire. The water was still steaming. He held her hand to help her balance as she stepped in, and she gave a soft moan of pleasure as she sank down in the hot water. Lucien rolled his sleeves up past his elbows, he scooped soft, jasmine scented soap into his hands and smoothed it over her skin. He had never performed such a task. Her drawn-up knees were like little islands in the sudsy water, and he noticed bruises darkening the creamy flesh. She must have fallen hard to hurt herself through all of those petticoats.

"Mmm." She closed her eyes and leaned her head back on the rim of the tub as he skimmed a cloth over every inch of her, his little finger straying off to brush the silky, damp skin. He had only ever seen his mistresses after they'd been polished and pinned and rouged to perfection. Never this way. Like Eve in Eden, naked and tousled and so very vulnerable. The slopes of her lovely breasts were just visible, her nipples a mere hint beneath a crest of foam. He couldn't resist lingering over them, his cock hardening beneath the fastenings of his trousers. He wished he could wash away the memories of the altercation at the Theater Royal from her mind as well. Freyne's insinuations, the ugly shouts of the mob, stones and rubbish hurtling through air thick with danger.

And the sudden stomach-churning fear that he wouldn't reach her in time.

"Shall I wash your hair?"

She looked up at him, smiling. "No. I am too tired to dry it by the fire. Perhaps another time."

Lucien felt a jolt of desire at the prospect that there would be another time. He imagined slipping into the tub behind her, cradling her naked body between his legs. Soaping each other languidly until the fire they kindled became too hot. But tonight was for Grace alone.

"As you wish," he said softly, then retrieved the towel warming by the hearth. He helped her from the tub, her skin was rosy with heat, a few stray froths of suds clinging to her breasts and the curve of her hip.

He dried her with a tenderness he hadn't known he possessed. Every scrape and bruise sickened him. He wanted to press his lips to them, cover her with his body, protect her.

But she seemed so fragile as he slipped a nightgown thin as mist over her head. The fabric cascaded down her lissome body, and a wave of scent drifted up to him—jasmine, fresh, clean cotton, and that scent that was Grace's alone. He brushed out her long hair then guided her toward the bed.

"Will you hold me?" she asked softly.

Lucien swallowed hard. It stunned him to realize there was nothing he wanted—no, *needed*—more.

He turned back the bedcovers, and she slid beneath them, her hair soft on the pillow. He tucked the warm coverlet over her and stood beside the bed. He pulled off his boots, then stripped off his damp shirt and trousers still smudged with dirt from the night's misadventures, leaving only his drawers in place.

He gathered her into his arms. She nestled against him, resting her cheek on his bare shoulder, her breath warm on his chest. The sigh she let out was pure trust, and she melted into him.

"I was afraid something would happen to you," she said softly.

"Me? I was not the one battling the crowd to shield an errant flower girl. You were quite brave."

"Lucien...I—I heard one of the mob yelling something..."

He tried not to reveal the foreboding that trickled down his spine. "And what was that?"

"Someone shouted 'Find Everdene,'" she said.

This was the second time someone had struck out at him specifically. Someone with a particular grudge, no doubt, but who? The house of Harcourt had crimes enough laid to its score during his father's time. And Lucien had made enemies of his own.

What if the rioter seeking him had realized Grace was his wife? The very thought sent a sliver of fear into his chest. Not wanting to worry Grace, he kissed the crown of her head. "Doubtless someone saw me enter the theater. It is naught to worry about."

"But it is! When I heard the rioters searching for you, feared they might injure you…I knew…"

He tightened his embrace, wanting to protect her from the world. "Knew what, sweet?"

She lifted her head, looked straight into his eyes with an expression that pierced him to the core. "This is not an arrangement anymore. Not for me. I love you, Lucien."

Something inside his chest leapt at those words, as if he had been starving to death and she had offered him life. As if he were stripped bare, overwhelmed by a rush of sensations too exquisite to bear. Elation. Anguish. Disbelief. Fear.

He knew how to take care of *things*. Business, estates, finances. People…he'd failed when they needed him most. Yet the tumult inside him wouldn't let him go. He remembered his promise to Cassandra, that he had vowed to live far, far away from at Everdene Hall. *You have an estate in Lancashire*…she'd said. That was not that far from Scotland after all.

"You must not…" *Love me.* He could not even say the words, the weight of the beliefs he'd carried his whole life pressing down on him. "I warned you not to…" Were those his words? Or were they a belief his father had instilled him? A lash of punishment Lucien had wielded on himself?

"We can't help who we love," she said, an angel's voice, inviting him to step out of his own hell.

He cupped her face in his hand, her cheek warm against his palm. His throat burned as if he'd swallowed thorns. He should tell her now. Tell her about the vow he'd made to take her far away from here, away from his sisters. Confess. But all he could say was, "You are…precious to me."

She smiled, softly, a little sadly. "I love you, Lucien," she breathed again, the words searing into him. "Don't leave me tonight."

He lay awake, holding her until her breathing rose and fell, soft in sleep. Stayed until the fire became a glow of embers. Could a man learn how to love the way he learned to ride a horse or play faro? he asked himself as dawn squeezed through the break in the draperies.

God help him, he would try.

* * *

Taking his wife into the Seven Dials was a decidedly bad idea, despite an armed coachman, a brace of brawny footmen and the pistol Lucien had tucked in his coat pocket. He had sent a rider ahead to make certain the violence from the night before had ended, but resentment still thickened the air like the miasma of smells that assaulted the senses: unwashed bodies, open sewers, rotted food and despair.

Avid faces stared at the coach as it squeezed down the narrow streets, shops and street vendors selling secondhand wares to the ragged denizens of the rookery. The Old Curiosity Shop could have been any one of them, and Grace's words echoed in his head. *There are Little Nells all over London. They just have names like Sibby Rose…*

He glanced across the coach to where his wife sat in a soft blue day dress, Sibby Rose dozing on her lap. The child's little frock had been washed and pressed, a clean white bandage wrapping her head. Even so, angry bruises were visible beyond the strip of linen, the fragile skin beneath her eye purpling.

When the coach reached the location Sibby Rose had given them, the street barely wide enough to allow entry, Lucien rapped on the roof of the coach to signal the driver to stop. "Wait here," he warned Grace, checking the pistol in his coat pocket.

A footman opened the door and Lucien stepped out onto the filthy street.

A woman with a face like a shriveled apple squinted up at him. "Well, if it isn't another swell slinkin' round. Lookin' fer a bawdy house or a gaming hell to lose a fortune? Or did ye just come t' gawp an' laugh at us like animals in a cage?"

While Lucien was doing nothing of the sort, he couldn't help the swift feeling of shame. God knew, misery always drew crowds —hangings at Tyburn, houses made famous by grisly crimes or famous criminals who once lived there, asylums where the quality entertained themselves by gawking at the wretched inmates. His father dragged him on such an excursion once to frighten him, no doubt, warning that melancholia was overtaking his mother…

He shoved the gut-wrenching memory away. "Can you direct me to the Nolan family. I've brought their daughter here. The little flower seller."

"Yer got Sibby Rose? Moira's been tearing up the neighborhood since she didn't come home last night. The last thing she needs, with her husband up and gone." The woman's eyes sparked with disdain. "Won't believe what the rest of us know. Darragh Nolan is not comin' back. Come along, an' I'll take ye there."

Lucien, thinking she could full well be leading him into some sort of trap to be robbed, was a bit surprised when the old woman made a clucking sound with her tongue, her expression one of compassion. He glanced over to see Grace already framed in the carriage door, the little girl in her arms.

Though he wanted to take the child from Grace as he helped her disembark, Sibby Rose looked so comfortable there, so secure… God, what would it be like to feel so damned…safe? Was that what Grace would look like with his child one day? The babe that might even now be growing in her womb? He felt a sting of panic at the possibility.

The old woman rapped sharply on a nearby door. "Moira, some swells got Sibby Rose here."

A woman flung open the door, saw her daughter and Grace, then rushed at them. Lucien could taste her fear and the flood of relief as she tearfully cried out, then stopped, as if too afraid to approach. "Sibby! Oh, Sibby!"

She had been beautiful once, he guessed, her face heart-shaped, her wide green eyes and glowing coppery hair like her daughter's. But hunger and worry had etched deep lines in her skin and sharpened her cheek bones. Those traits, a stark contrast to the sprinkling of freckles dusting her nose, which made her look more like Sibby Rose's sister than a mother barely holding her family together.

A boy older than Sibby, but just as spindly, wedged his way through the door and glared at Lucien. "What have you done to my sister? Run her over in the street?"

"Robert!" the mother cried.

Young Robert put hands on hips. "Why else would they have her?"

"There was a riot last night," Lucien explained. "She was hurt, so we carried her out of the mob." He wanted to get his wife away from here, but Grace carried the girl inside. He followed her in, taken aback by what he saw. He had seen poverty before as he traveled the city streets and on farms struggling through bad times. But he'd never stepped inside such poor quarters. This was unlike anything he'd ever witnessed. Rush lights gave a faint, oily glow to the single, cramped room. It was dark, what passed for a window boarded up and covered with scraps of old newsprint. Even so, Lucien could see that what little was there was as clean as possible. Carefully mended clothes far too large for anyone there dried on a rack drawn up by a rope to the ceiling. A kettle hung on the hearth. Three chairs, a lone bedstead, and a scarred table were crowded into the room.

"Mammy?" Sibby Rose's little voice broke in.

Mrs. Nolan bent over her. "*Mo chroi*, oh, treasure, are you well?"

"My head aches."

At that moment, there was a blur of motion from a nest of rags beside the hearth. Worried eyes lit up as they locked on Lucien. "Dado!" Scrap squealed. He ran over, trying to scale Lucien's leg like a kitten escaping a hound. There was nothing for it but to disentangle the boy before he tore the fabric.

"Scrap!" the oldest Nolan boy shouted. "Get off him, ye daft bugger!"

Something about Robert Nolan's disgust brought out the contrariness in Lucien and he lifted little Darragh into his arms.

"Robert, stop yer yellin'," Sibby said. "These're the nobs I tol' ye about—the gent 'at pulled Scrap down from the statue and the lady who gave me my ribbon."

"Well, we got ye home, so they can go now." Robert jutted his chin up at Lucien. "It's hard enough around here without folks thinkin' some milor' is tupping me ma."

"Robert Nolan!" his mother said, her voice sharp. She turned toward Lucien, her cheeks red. "Your worship, he doesn't mean it."

"Ye know full well I do." He balled his hands into fists. "Swells come around here only after one thing! Ye can't have Sibby Rose, or me ma!"

Lucien had always loathed the idea of how vulnerable women were in such situations, ripe for procurers should they become desperate. But now that he had met Sibby Rose and Moira Nolan, those women and children had a face, a voice…The thought suddenly hit home. He could feel Sibby Rose in his arms as he carried her to the coach, picture Sibby Rose at Raven's Court, Grace brushing and freshly plaiting the tangle of coppery hair and tying the end with the cherished red ribbon. The child was such winsome little thing with her pointed chin, rosebud mouth and eyes that did something strange to Lucien's chest.

Moira's eyes darted fearfully to Lucien. "My lad, he means no harm, your worship. Listens too much to troublemakers at the factory."

"Robert, is that your name?" Grace inquired in a voice that might soothe an injured fox. "This is the Viscount Everdene and I am his wife, Lady Grace. Perhaps you've glimpsed me when you let out from Sunday School. I have seen Sibby Rose waiting for you there."

"Got better things t' do than gawk at ladies who shriek when I brush by their dress. And what's that have t' do with Sibby not coming home?"

Grace, unperturbed, continued on, "Your sister was alone, in the midst of a violent mob. We took her to our home until the streets quieted down for her own safety, and then brought her here, that is all." She turned to a drawing in a crude homemade frame at the mantel, a rosary draped over it. A man's face. It was the work of an obviously untrained artist, but the natural gift was evident and compelling. A man of about thirty years, with a shock of dark hair and a scar on his chin.

"Is this your father?"

"Aye," Robert said.

"Sibby mentioned he is away at present."

Mrs. Nolan lovingly touched the worn rosary adorning the sketch. "He'll be back any time now, my Darragh."

"Where is he?" Grace asked.

She stared at the drawing a moment more, before looking at Grace. "Saw a strapper whipping a child at the factory. Couldn't bear it and interfered. Mr. Freyne fired him."

Grace's eye widened as she turned to Lucien. "Neville? Is he not involved with Pinchbeck's factory?"

"He is."

Young Robert curled his lip in disgust. "Even that weren't enough for 'im. Put out the word so naught in London would hire me da."

Lucien looked at the picture of Darragh Nolan, wondering if he'd simply left his family to search for work so they could survive. Or had he deserted them like the old woman said?

Grace moved beside him, examining the drawing as well. "I have to admit…he looks a bit like you."

"Aye, if ye strangled him in one o' those stupid neckcloths an' made 'im look like a peacock," Robert sneered.

The similarities were a trifle disconcerting, but then, it might have been any one of a hundred other dark-haired men in London. However, to a little boy, longing for a father he didn't remember, it was enough.

"Darragh's friend Tom O'Malley drew it," Moira said. "He's a fair hand with capturing likenesses, when he can get the paper."

Robert thrust out his thin chest. "O'Malley doesn't need to be muckin' about here either. I've got things well in hand."

Lucien felt a pang, seeing the boy trying to be the man of the house.

"Do you, now?" Moira Nolan scolded, not unkindly. She brushed a limp curl away from her forehead. "We're lucky to have Tom's help, Robert." Then, to Lucien, added, "The three of us grew up together in Connemara. He and my husband worked together on the railroad up north for a while before coming here. When my husband lost his job at the factory, Tom wrote a letter for Darragh to give to a foreman in a mine up near Glasgow. Said there was no steadier hand at blasting than my Darragh."

Another possible explanation for the father's absence, Lucien thought as he adjusted Scrap in his arms. The mines lost so many men on the job that they were always looking for someone else to send into the warren of caves beneath the ground. One misstep, cave in, or explosion, and no one would ever know.

There was a flurry of noise in the street, then Lucien's footman, Wells, shouting as a man shoved his way through the door.

Wells was a step behind him. "Sorry, my lord. He just pushed his way past."

"Moira! There's a carriage out front…" The man's face could have been a map of Ireland. He looked like he'd been dragged through hell. "God, tell me Sibby's not…"

"It's all right, Wells," Lucien told his servant. "Wait outside." Whoever the Irishman was, he obviously knew the family. He saw Sibby Rose on the bed and rushed over to where the child sat. "Jaysus, Mary and Joseph," he cried, taking in the swath of bandages around her head, "how bad is she hurt?"

"They say she'll be fine," Mrs. Nolan said, with a nod toward Lucien and Grace.

The man wheeled on Sibby Rose, his relief changed to anger. "What the devil were you thinking, girl? I've turned over half o' London lookin' for you! Ye promised t' leave for home when the crowd went in after intermission!"

"I waited 'til the play was over to see my lady. She's my friend."

"No *lady* is your friend!" O'Malley all but spat the word. "Jaysus, girl, when I heard some nob scooped you up in a coach, I thought you'd be locked in some bawd's house an' we'd never find ye! What the devil happened?"

"The angry men came an' knocked me over and hit me in the head. My box broke an' the strap got all tangled and I couldn't get loose. Then my lady was there and put her arms around me, and people were bumping her and stepping on her an' tryin' t' run right over me, but she wouldn't let them." Her voice broke, then she turned a wary gaze toward Lucien. "He grabbed me up an' next I knowed I was in a coach."

Scrap had found the chain to Lucien's pocket watch, and pulled the timepiece free, his chubby hands opening it and closing it.

The Irishman spun to glare at Lucien, no hint of deference in his eyes. "Who the devil are ye?"

"Lord Everdene. My wife became acquainted with the children through one of young Darragh's misadventures. She was going to speak to Sibby Rose just before the mob overran Drury Lane. We thought it best to take the child to our townhouse until it was safe to bring her here."

If anything, O'Malley looked as if he trusted them less.

"They've a house big as a castle," Sibby piped up, "An' a bed with curtains, an' my lady teaches me letters…S is a snake and I is a candle—"

"See, Bippy Wo? Pwitty." Scrap dangled the watch toward his sister. "See?"

O'Malley's gaze flashed to the boy, and his gaze locked on the gleaming gold. "For Christ's sake, Scrap!" he swore, stalking over and pulling the child out of Lucien's grasp.

"Dado!" Scrap flailed, reaching for Lucien, but O'Malley held fast to the child.

"Let go o' the bauble." O'Malley pried the watch out of the little hand. "Next y' know this swell will be tellin' the Charlies you pinched it!"

"The devil I would," Lucien replied, the child's wails raking his nerves.

The man thrust the watch at Lucien. "You're not needed here. You're not wanted here. Take this and go back to where you came from."

Gritting his teeth, Lucien took the timepiece, returning it to his waistcoat pocket.

Grace extended her hand in a placating gesture. "Mr. O'Malley, I fear you misunderstand—"

"Oh, I understand quite well. The famous Lord Everdene. In the broadsheets, aren't ye? One more rich bastard tramplin' workin' folk under yer boot. But we'll get what we want sooner or later. Give us voice in parliament or we'll take it from your hands. It matters not a damn to me."

O'Malley smoothed one half of his worn coat to the side and

laid his hand on something that gleamed above the waist of his baggy trousers. Lucien's gaze locked on the worn, battered butt of a pistol.

A threat or a warning? He thought of the news article, the branch of Chartists willing to resort to violence. Was O'Malley one of them?

Lucien felt the weight of his own pistol. Was O'Malley merely trying to survive in this hell hole? Or was he something more?

CHAPTER 29

Grace attempted to paste a polite smile on her face as Lady Alice Pinchbeck and her mother perched on the edge of the settee at Raven's Court, sipping tea with almost avid expressions.

"You poor child!" Lady Pinchbeck commiserated, toying with the diamond-studded pendant she wore on a gold chain. "We came as soon as we heard about that dreadful business at the theater. I can only thank heavens dear Alice was stricken with a megrim and unable to attend."

Alice's teacup rattled as she replaced it in her saucer with a trembling hand. "The reports Mr. Freyne regaled us with were terrifying!"

In the confusion, Grace had all but forgotten Neville had been there, along with the French cyprian he'd flaunted before Lucien. Putting that from her mind, she gave a bland smile.

Lady Pinchbeck preened. "I vow dear Neville was very relieved you were not present, Alice. He has been most attentive to our dear girl of late. I believe happy news will be forthcoming."

Grace thought of the cyprian that had been on Neville's arm and heartily hoped Lady Pinchbeck was wrong.

Unfortunately, Alice flushed and pressed a hand to her cheek. "Mama! You mustn't speak of it yet!"

"I'm only saying that your suitor was most relieved you were safe."

"As am I," Alice said. "If I had been caught in such a riot, I fear I would have taken to my bed for a month!"

Lady Pinchbeck selected another tea cake filled with apricot jam. "And I would have seen to it you did. You do have such delicate nerves." She looked up at Grace. "Alice was so very concerned something had happened to you, Lady Everdene. She insisted she must see for herself how you fared."

"As you can see, I am well."

"I must disagree." The older woman sampled a bite of her cake, wrinkled her nose and set the sweet upon her saucer. "I am quite sure once your dear father-in-law, the earl, learns what you endured during that horrendous riot he will see to it that the most stringent measures be taken against the perpetrators. Why, Lord Everdene himself must be wild with rage, considering the danger you were in. Any gentleman of proper feeling would be."

Grace resented the flicker of triumph in Lady Pinchbeck's eyes.

Pointless rage was the last thing Lucien would indulge in. As to 'proper feeling'…Grace thought of Lucien hastening her to the coach, little Sibby Rose crushed against his chest. His gentleness once the child was asleep when he finally took Grace into their bedchamber tending to her own injuries. That night it seemed so much had changed.

Ever since, Lucien had not left her before first light. She warmed at the memory of nestling against his long, lean body once their lovemaking was through. Mornings she would wake to find his face on the pillow beside her, his hair tousled, his mouth tender, those ice-blue eyes peering at her with something akin to wonder. She felt that nearly painful connection as well, pleasure almost too perfect to be real. If only she were with him right now instead of enduring this interminable visit.

Lady Pinchbeck's voice intruded. "Since you've no mother to attend you, poor lamb, I feel duty-bound to offer advice. Until his lordship takes necessary steps to make certain you—and every decent woman—is safe from riots on London's streets, you must stay well clear of the unwashed masses you've tried to be patroness of. Yes," she said before Grace could get a word in edgewise. "Lady

Downe has told me you have been catering to the waifs at *that school*. You must mind your nerves as my Alice does. A woman of childbearing years can easily slip into hysteria. A womb that is jiggled about can subject one to all sorts of travail."

Grace might have laughed out loud if it weren't for a sudden awareness stealing through her. She pressed a hand to her stomach. How long had it been since she'd…? She brushed the thought away before she could fully form it. And as for hysteria—she knew exactly what the term was used for. It was the perfect excuse to dismiss a woman's point of view when she disagreed with a man. She thought of the countess's gentle, haunted gaze.

"It is imperative that you surround yourself with proper society from now on and take care not to exert yourself," Lady Pinchbeck insisted.

Taking to her bed in a fit of vapors was the last thing Grace's mother would have advised her to do. Not when she could take action and do some good. She pictured her mother's face in her mind, fiery resolve igniting inside her. "I believe I shall host an event at Raven's Court three weeks from today. A charity event to benefit the schools for factory children."

Alice gasped. Lady Pinchbeck's cheeks puffed up, scarlet as she sputtered in indignation. "Well, I never! I have never wasted my good counsel on such an ungrateful girl."

"Ah, that is how we came to cross purposes," Grace said with a perfectly schooled smile.

"I am no girl. But I *am* the Viscountess Everdene. Alice, do note on your social calendar the date. Three Wednesdays hence. Seven of the clock. Raven's Court. I promise it will be a night you'll never forget."

Grace's chin bumped up a notch. Lady Pinchbeck could stuff her patronizing concern into that capacious cleavage of hers along with the gaudy pendant she wore.

TWO WEEKS LATER, THE VISIT FROM ALICE AND HER MOTHER STILL chafed Grace. Lady Pinchbeck had left in high dudgeon, the pompous woman like a thorn festering beneath her skin. For the life of Grace, she couldn't figure out why. Yes, she had felt a trifle unwell since the incident at Drury Lane, her emotions honed to a sharp edge, but she had done her best to forget the horrors of that night, and had immersed herself in the maelstrom of activity needed to host an event for the ton: Invitations written and sent, planning the delicacies cook would prepare and the entertainment to be offered, composing the appeals she would make for donations.

Donations she feared would be far less than she'd hoped, thanks to Lady Pinchbeck's interference.

But at the moment, it wasn't her frustration with the meddlesome woman or the notes of regret on her escritoire that made Grace's stomach clench. It was the missive that lay atop them, words written in Avery's cramped hand.

It has been three weeks since you told us what Lord Admiral Nelson is doing. Did you take him to the Tower of London to see the headsman's ax as you promised?

Not only had she failed to take the Lord Admiral to the Tower, she had no idea what had become of her brothers' cherished toy. For the past hour she had pawed through pockets and drawers, spoken to maids, and even crawled on the carpet to search beneath the bed and armoire. But the dented tin soldier that was the link to her brothers was nowhere to be found.

In truth, she'd not even thought of the toy since before the riot at Drury Lane. Thought of little, save the planned charity event and her happiness with Lucien. A happiness she handled like a spindle of glass lest the slightest pressure break it. Pressure that might, even now, threaten...She peered into her mirror, touching her stomach with a flutter of excitement, confusion and dread, uncertain what changes this new possibility might bring. She shook away that fear, pinched her cheeks to give them color, then descended the stairs to search for her husband in his study.

She was surprised to find Lucien was not alone.

Arkwright stood in rakish disarray beside the hearth, doubtless to drive the late November chill from his long limbs. He shot her that irrepressible grin. "I stopped by to tempt Everdene into a game of chess since he's eschewed the club of late. Not that I blame him, considering the lovely company he has at home." He turned toward

Lucien. "It seems marriage agrees with the Elusive Viscount Everdene. Dare I say it, Luce? You look almost happy."

"And you look annoyingly smug." Lucien rolled his eyes at his friend, then held out a hand to Grace. She slipped her own into his, grateful to feel the warm strength.

Arkwright beamed. "You are only annoyed because I am right."

"I fear things are a trifle chaotic at present," Grace said. "I am preparing to host my first real event as a political hostess this coming Wednesday. A charity event with all proceeds to benefit the school for factory children."

"Indeed? That seems like a worthy cause. And who is to attend this event?"

"Anyone with the slightest bent toward philanthropy, though I have received some regrets as well." She made a face. "Alice Pinchbeck's mother scheduled an event at the same time. A musicale starring a famed opera dancer. I am rather sure she did it on purpose."

"Am I to receive an invitation to your fete?"

"Yes, of course! I did not know that you had returned to town. Lucien said you were visiting your grandmother in Lancashire. I hope you found her well."

"Terrifyingly so. I'm exhausted after trying to keep up with her." Affection radiated from Arkwright. "Attending mere London party will be a relief."

"I know I am a trifle early for the holiday, but I plan to make it a Christmas theme in hopes that will inspire people to be more generous."

Arkwright gave a hearty laugh. "You may put me down for a sizeable donation. As for Lady Pinchbeck—" He pursed his lips in a perfect mimic of the sour matron, but before he could finish, Lucien cut him off.

"The lady will prove no match for you," he said, and she leaned closer against his solid shoulder. "The ton is about to be dazzled by my new Viscountess."

"I have no doubt!" Arkwright addressed Grace. "Speaking of the upcoming holiday, will you be seeing your brothers for Christmas? Tell young Master Avery that he had best be keeping up his swordplay. I intend to challenge him to a duel when next I see him."

Grace looked down, reminded, not only of the lost toy, but of the holidays looming. Lucien's resolution before they married echoed in her head: *I would rather be dragged behind one of Simon's horses than endure a fete overrun with children. I prefer spending Christmas at my club.* But perhaps with the changes in their relationship, there might be reason to hope?

"We have not yet discussed where we will spend Christmas," she said, "but I fear I've sought out Lucien now to inquire about another matter regarding the boys."

"The boys?' Lucien echoed, feathering his thumb across her knuckles in a soothing path. "Is something amiss?"

"I'm afraid so. I have only just realized I misplaced Lord Admiral Nelson."

Arkwright gave his head a bemused shake. "Uh, I believe you'll find a statue of him in Trafalgar Square. Or perhaps you might visit his tomb at St. Paul's Cathedral—"

"Not the real Lord Admiral Nelson, you gudgeon," Lucien corrected with a solemnity that only made Arkwright appear more confused. "The toy soldier her brothers gave her. Grace has carried it all around London and written to them of his adventures."

Arkwright eyes widened. "Grace, you really *are* the best sister in Christendom."

"My brothers won't think so when they discover I have lost their favorite toy. I just received a letter from Avery demanding to know whether or not the Lord Admiral has visited the Tower. I fear when my brothers learn the truth they may be shouting *off with my head.*"

"Have you spoken to the laundresses?" Lucien asked, his brow furrowing. "Perhaps you left the toy in your pocket."

"I have searched everywhere and asked all of the maids. He's been on my dressing table a fair amount, so they know what to look for."

"When do you last remember seeing him?"

She fretted her lower lip. "I'm ashamed to say I'm not sure when I last had him in my possession. I remember showing the Lord Admiral to the children at the school and talking about the Battle of Trafalgar. I took him to the museum with a crowd of Alice Pinchbeck's friends. They laughed when I showed him the Elgin Marbles.

I wrote the boys that he'd observed plants from the South Sea islands in Lady Downe's conservatory. Her ladyship was talking quite wistfully about her son, and so I shared the tale of how I had come to carry the boys' tin soldier about."

"Perhaps you dropped it." Lucien was quiet a moment. Grace imagined his thoughts turning in his head, like the gears in his gold pocket watch. "Did you have the toy that night at the theater?"

"I don't know." She turned her hands palm up. "I fear I have grown lax about the poor admiral. I merely transfer things to my pocket or reticule by instinct…my watch, the toy wrapped in a handkerchief. It has become such a habit I rarely think about it now."

She had spent the first month of her marriage looking backward toward The Willows. Worrying. Wondering how her brothers fared. But a gentle severing of the old life had gradually taken place. Her gaze now turned toward Lucien and the future.

Arkwright piped up. "Maybe you could buy another toy soldier to replace it without them knowing the difference. I should buy a set for you to keep here anyway," he teased. "Considering how much time Everdene is staying at home, Uncle Rhys should start filling up the nursery with playthings. Must have it fully stocked when you provide me with a wee Harcourt to spoil."

Grace saw the corners of Lucien's mouth harden, and she quelled the instinctive urge to touch her stomach.

"Believe it or not," Lucien told Arkwright, "I cannot even spare time for a chess match, let alone indulge your ridiculous urge to spoil children that do not even exist. I was about to go on an errand."

"Excellent! I'll come along with you." Arkwright rubbed his hands together in anticipation and gave Lucien a crooked grin. "Where are we off to? Tattersalls? Bond Street? I could use some new boots."

"Pinchbeck's Factory."

Grace's breath caught. "Truly?" She pressed her hand to her chest, only half believing.

"Pinchbeck's factory?" Arkwright echoed, disgruntled. "What the devil do you want to go there for?"

That smile that had grown less rare tipped up the corner of

Lucien's mouth. "Someone very wise told me I need to find out why people are rioting, see the conditions they work under for myself."

"Oh, Lucien! Thank you!" She flung her arms around him despite Arkwright looking on.

He hesitated a moment, then returned her embrace, stroking his hand up and down her back. "I hope I might discover something about the fate of Darragh Nolan as well," he told her.

"Will you take me with you?" she asked.

"I will learn more if you are not present. They'll have no excuse to avoid certain subjects or areas to protect a woman's sensibilities."

Disappointment tugged at her, but she had to admit he was right. Much as she wanted to go, it would be better to get all of the information possible. "You will tell me everything when you return?"

He hesitated, and she got the feeling he did not want to make promises he might not be able to keep.

"You must not hope for too much," he warned instead. "I am not certain what I will achieve by doing this."

"I understand, but it means the world to me that you are trying."

He gently trailed the pad of his thumb between her brows, and she knew he was smoothing out the crease that formed there when she was worried. "You look rather tired, my dear. I fear preparing for this charity event has been robbing you of sleep."

"You needn't worry about the ton," Arkwright said. "I am certain you will convince them to donate to your cause. After all, you have got my curmudgeonly friend going to tour a factory."

She stretched on tiptoe, leaning in to whisper against Lucien's ear. "The party is not what has been keeping me awake at night."

She loved seeing the heat flare in his gaze as he angled his head to kiss her. His mouth lingered, his hand warm on her cheek. "You mustn't let anything trouble you. Not Lady Pinchbeck, your guest list or Lord Admiral Nelson. We will solve that mystery of the Lord Admiral together, or we will concoct an epic adventure to explain his disappearance—without Arkwright filling up rooms with toys we do not need."

He shot a quelling look at his friend, but Grace felt a flutter of unease at his words.

Perhaps it was time to get the answer to another mystery as well, she thought, her own unease heavy in her chest. After Arkwright and Lucien left, she went to her escritoire and wrote a note and sealed it. Heart hammering, she handed the missive to a footman.

It was time to find out the truth.

CHAPTER 30

race's smile…Lucien could not stop thinking about it as the hack rattled along the crowded street where factories and all manner of businesses crowded together. Wagons laden with bales and crates and barrels jockeyed for position, the drivers lashing out with whips and curses. Roofs speckled with chimneys belched coal smoke.

He had spent a lifetime believing that commerce was the lifeblood of the empire. But as they rattled up to the building with Pinchbeck and Freyne painted on the sign, he wondered whose blood was being spilled to make it so. Simon and his friend Jamie McLeod's in the war in Afghanistan that had scarred them both? Families like the Nolans?

And Grace believed he could change things, her eyes shining at him as if he were a far better man than he could ever hope to be.

"Not exactly Bond Street," Arkwright observed as they climbed out and walked toward a pair of wide doors that led into Pinchbeck's. "If someone had told me the Viscount Everdene would be touring a factory to view working conditions, I would never have believed it. Grace may be the best thing that ever happened to you, old friend."

He didn't doubt it. The observation made him damned uncomfortable. It remained to be seen whether he would benefit her as well.

A cacophony of noise greeted them, the clanking and whirring of machines, the shouts of workers. Sharp chemical smells assailed their nostrils, and he felt as if he needed to sneeze as bits of fiber floated through the air. They made their way to the glass-encased main office where they met a barrel-chested man whose eyes were all but lost beneath the formidable shelf of his brow. He had a well-fed look about him, muscles bulging nearly as much as his arrogance as he twirled a long staff in his hand.

"Good morning, your honors," he greeted them. "Name's Mr. Crimmins. I'm foreman here. How can I be of service to you fine gentlemen today?"

"I am the Viscount Everdene and this is Mr. Arkwright. We are here in search of Lord Pinchbeck or Mr. Freyne."

"Afraid you'll have to return another time if you wish to speak to them. They're both visiting Manchester, looking to buy another factory there."

"A factory for…?"

"Cloth, same as here. But there's far more industry up north an' the masters aim to raise production. Mr. Freyne has a source for the finest bales of raw cotton from Georgia and Louisiana for a price you'd not believe."

Oh, Lucien would believe it. It was no surprise you could produce cotton cheaply when you didn't pay wages to the enslaved people who harvested it. He remembered Freyne's assertion at Gunter's ice shop. People could choose to buy more expensive fabric with cotton grown by freedmen if they wished. But could they really? He looked out at the factory workers barely scraping by. What happened when you had to choose between your moral compass and survival?

"How unfortunate that the factory owners are unavailable," Lucien said. "You seem to know a great deal about the workings here. Is there any chance you could show us about?"

Crimmins puffed up at Lucien's praise but looked doubtful.

"Lord Pinchbeck offered me a chance to invest in the business," Lucien continued, "but my schedule is rather crushing, and I have another venture to consider. On to the next possibility, eh, Arkwright?" Lucien gestured to his friend, making it seem as if they were about to leave.

"We're turning a fine profit," Crimmins said hastily. "Come in, come in. I will give ye a look about. Hate t' have ye miss out on such a fine investment."

More likely he would hate to have his bosses find out he'd lost them the opportunity to bring in ready cash to offset the purchase of a new factory. "You are so kind…"

Crimmins led them out to the main floor.

It was like walking into the belly of some great beast. Darkness crowded every corner, candles providing the only light.

"These machines are a wonder, m'lord," the foreman said as he led Lucien and Arkwright onto a narrow walkway along one wall, high above main floor. From that vantage point Lucien was able to see the whole factory and the people working below. The metallic sound of the machinery and roar of engines grew deafening, the smell of chemicals thickening the air. Lucien pictured what could happen if one of the candles tipped over. Fire engulfing the building with terrifying speed? An explosion?

"These machines can do the work of countless people in half the time. We're livin' in an age o' marvels."

He could see the frenetic actions of the workers more clearly now. Women bent over their tasks, moving so quickly that their hands seemed to blur. Children darted in and out under the machines or climbed on shaky stools to do God knew what. Men wheeled carts hither and yon, shouting and banging on machines trying to fix them.

"Can you tell me about your workers?" Lucien asked over the roar.

"What about 'em?" Crimmins scratched his pungent armpit.

"You have a lot of women and children working here. Many of them mothers, no doubt. What happens when a child falls sick or gets injured?"

The man looked genuinely puzzled by the question. "Never affects production, I promise you. If they're not back at their post the next morning, got a dozen new ones clamoring t' do the work."

A shout rang out over the clamor of noise, and Lucien saw a man lash out with a strap, striking a child who was darting beneath one of the machines.

Lucien's breath caught as the girl's head barely missed the whirring metal parts.

Even Arkwright noticed, saying, "That girl was almost caught in the moving gears. Why didn't the man running it turn them off?"

"An idle machine makes no money," the foreman said, following their gaze. "We hire children small so they can squeeze in and out while the machine keeps producing."

"And if those children don't get out of the machinery's way in time?" Arkwright asked.

"See one or two accidents an' the others'll move quicker, won't they? I can tell you think me hard, but better they do an honest day's work than run the streets." He shrugged. "Sure, some few might get caught in the gears, but they could just as easily get run over by a beer wagon or snatched up by some thieving Jenny to pick pockets or house break. Wind up at the end of a noose or deported t' a penal colony. What else they going to do if not work here?"

"Perhaps," Arkwright suggested, "if they could learn to read and figure sums they might better their lot?"

His friend's simple comment made Lucien see Grace's work with the school in a whole new light.

The comment clearly went over Crimmins's head. "Then who would work the machines? These folk are like the horses that pull the plow. It's what God made 'em for."

Had there been a time Lucien had accepted that was so? The thought turned his stomach now. No doubt, his father had certainly believed it, never more so than when he'd ordered Simon to level the village of Everdene so the view from the Harcourt manor house would be 'a pleasing prospect.'

He turned his attention back to the foreman. "How long have you worked here, Mr. Crimmins?"

"Six years, I'm proud to say. Foreman for three."

"I have an interest in a man who was once employed here. Darragh Nolan. I believe he was fired from his position two years ago. Do you remember him?"

The foreman's brow furrowed. "Aye. Fired him myself a' Lord Pinchbeck's order. Got into fisticuffs with one of our strappers.

We've no tolerance for troublemakers. Have to make them an example to the rest, like Lord Pinchbeck an' Mr. Freyne say."

"Have you heard any news of him since?"

"Don't know where he went. Only know that he did."

Lucien drew a coin from his waistcoat pocket and turned it over between his long fingers, the silver winking in the candlelight. "You're certain?"

The foreman swallowed as if his throat had gone dry, his eyes fixed on the coin. "Someone did claim to see him sometime last spring."

"Give me names."

"Don't have 'em. Just somethin' I heard in passin'. Didn't believe it. Boatloads of Irish pouring in causin' trouble. Who can tell one from the other?"

"I will pay handsomely for information that leads me to Darragh Nolan." Lucien handed the man the coin, then one of his cards.

"His wife and son work here. I could—"

"I've already questioned them, so no need for you to."

The man canted his head, shrewd eyes narrowing. "What's a man like ye want with Nolan, yer lordship?"

"That is for me to know. But understand this, I do not suffer fools. Deceive me and you will learn why people fear the Harcourts."

The man swallowed hard, his gaze darting away. Lucien and Arkwright strode toward the door of the building, workers staring as they passed.

Lucien never expected to find himself rapping at the door of Mrs. Watson's Boarding House for Men, but here he was, ready to beg a favor of a man who hated him. He pictured Tom O'Malley's face in the rushlight of the Nolan tenement, his eyes grim as the pistol he'd carried.

Steeling himself for a rocky reception, Lucien waited until the establishment's proprietress opened the door. Stout and stringently clean she had the look of a formidable mother, the kind that could keep a dozen sons sitting on a church pew without fidgeting at all.

Lucien could hear a voice from the other room, someone reading aloud perhaps? As Mrs. Watson paused before what looked to be a modest parlor, he glimpsed men of various ages lounging on worn settees, sitting backwards on spindly chairs or stretched out on the floor before the fire. Every eye was fixed on Tom O'Malley, an open book in his hands as he brought characters' voices to life. It was a tone Lucien recognized well from his time in parliament—compelling, hard to resist, one that could raise spirits or dash them, spur men into action. Mrs. Watson clapped and the reading stopped abruptly, heads swiveling toward the open door.

"Got a visitor for Mr. O'Malley," the proprietress said. "That Lord Everdene wots in the dailies." Everyone in the room craned their necks to stare, and Lucien felt a chill at what he saw on their faces.

The glare O'Malley shot past Mrs. Watson to where Lucien stood could have burned a hole in solid steel. "What the devil are you doing here?"

"I need to speak with you on a matter of importance. Alone."

The other men's gaze shifted to O'Malley, darkening with suspicion. Even Mrs. Watson regarded him as if he might carry some contagion.

"We'll finish the chapter later," O'Malley growled, carefully closing the book and setting it aside. He stood and stalked toward Lucien as if counting out paces in a duel. O'Malley took him to a room crammed with a narrow cot, a small table with books, Chartist pamphlets, a pen and foolscap. A small frame with a sketch of some kind stood off to one side. Lucien looked more closely. It was a sketch of a much younger Moira Nolan before Sibby Rose, Robert and Scrap, and the shabby room in the Seven Dials. She was on a swing, laughing.

O'Malley walked over to the table and turned the frame face-down, then crossed his arms over his broad chest and glared at Lucien. "How did you find me?" he demanded.

"It was not difficult. You have caught the attention of authorities, though they have no reason to arrest you—yet. I wondered if I could buy you a meal at a pub."

"Tryin' to ruin my reputation? Not on your life." He scoffed. "What'd you want? Our boy Oliver Twist just got mixed up with some pickpocket an' it's not goin' t' go well for him."

Lucien arched his brows in surprise. "You are reading Dickens? I would think books were too dear."

"Your sort'd like t' keep learnin' out o' our hands, wouldn't ye? Since that Dickens fellow started writing we pool our money together an' whoever is able t' read reads 'em aloud."

Lucien felt an unexpected spark of admiration.

"Got it just right, the way things are for us," O'Malley continued. "Not that it's any o' yer business. So, what the devil are you here for? Speak your piece an' get it over with."

Lucien had to hand it to the man. There weren't many who would dare address a peer this way. But then, just his sort had set up a guillotine in France seventy years ago, and there were plenty more across the continent who would be happy to do so again. The thought made him more cautious and he wondered if this had been an ill-thought-out venture.

"I have come about Darragh Nolan. What is the situation with his family?"

"Like ye give a damn." O'Malley snarled a bitter laugh. "Leave the Nolans alone. Moira has enough trouble with without folks seein' you muckin' around."

"I intend to find her husband and I need your help. Then again…maybe you want him to stay missing." He gestured to the overturned frame. "I saw the way you looked at his wife."

"Why you—" O'Malley's fists knotted. "What do you know about a woman like Moira, except that you can take her with just a crook o' yer lordly finger whether she will or no? She's fine as Irish lace, she is. Aye, I tried to win her before your sort threw me in Kilmainham Jail for speakin' the simple truth! If she was unmarried I'd try again. But I'm not willing to kill my friend for the chance."

"Even indirectly?" Lucien's gaze sharpened. "You sent Darragh Nolan to the mines, didn't you? You cannot control a blast. Light the fuse but keep your hands clean and let the gunpowder do the rest. Just like you goad men into riots like the ones at Pall Mall or outside the theater. The authorities told me what you do. Make speeches, then stand back and let others take the saber cuts or bullets when troops ride in. Then you are nowhere to be seen."

Two bright spots of color burned on O'Malley's cheeks. His chin jutted at a pugnacious angle. "Maybe some leaders do that, but not me. If it comes to physical force like some claim it will, I'll be at the head of those who fight, not in the rear like your fancy lords and generals." His lips curled in contempt. "All we want is a say in our own fate. Who will see to our needs while we're not represented in parliament? If we stay silent your sort will keep grinding us down until there is nothing left but dust. Some folks figured you might have a care for our plight, considering the village you built. People are talking about it, even here." O'Malley shot him a hard look. "But me? I know that you Aristos only think of yourselves."

Lucien thought of New Everdene, the creation Simon and Penelope had fought for. He'd thought it reckless at first, a huge expense when estates all over England and Ireland were struggling. God knew, it was still a challenge to pay for what had been done. And yet, there was something about New Everdene. Walking through the well-planned lanes, seeing the sturdy cottages with hearths instead of mere holes in the roof for smoke to be let out. Tidy gardens and green space for children to play…Had seeing the difference between his father's plan to destroy the village and his brother's dream of building something better been the beginning of this change in Lucien himself?

"New Everdene was my brother's doing," Lucien said. "He insists we can change things one family at a time. I want to understand the Nolans' story. I am asking you to tell me."

"Same as most of the Irish in London. We came here so we wouldn't starve when the potato crop failed. Here's no better. You English loathe us for bein' Irish, men like Pinchbeck give the jobs to women who work for pennies on what a man would earn an' children like Robert for even less. Pinchbeck'd have Scrap working if he could reach the looms. An' the way the foremen treat those babes…it's a wonder any see their first whiskers grow."

"Mrs. Nolan said a child was being struck and her husband intervened."

"That's the truth of it." O'Malley nodded. "But Darragh's rage was already simmerin', just waitin' t' blow. He was that far gone in drink, seein' the hell he'd brought his family to. Couldn't bear to see them suffer."

Lucien pictured Grace and the child they hoped to conceive.

"Something broke in Darragh, it did. He left London two Christmases ago an' I feared even then he'd never look back."

"The family needs help." Lucien kept his voice neutral, and yet, O'Malley winced, stung.

"You think I haven't tried everything I can to help Moira and the babes? She won't move out of that rat's nest because she's waitin' for Darragh t' come home. Keepin' the faith that he will. She says 'Here's where my husband left me, an' here's where we'll be when he walks through that door.'" O'Malley's voice broke. He stalked to the scarred boardinghouse table, and leaned his hands flat against it, his back to Lucien. "Jaysus, Mary an' Joseph."

Lucien paused a moment, letting O'Malley collect himself, then said quietly, "I spoke to a Mr. Crimmins at Pinchbeck's factory today. He says some men claimed to see Nolan in London last spring."

The Irishman whipped around to face him, something flashing in his eyes. Disbelief or deception?

"Do you think it is possible that Darragh is in London?" Lucien asked.

"I think that bastard Crimmins would say he'd seen Moses and the angels for coin."

But there was something unreadable in O'Malley's face.

"If Darragh *was* in London he would try to catch a glimpse o' Moira and the babes. Even if he couldn't bear to speak to 'em. Or he'd come to me. He knows where I lodge."

A sudden memory stirred and Lucien thought of the man he'd seen following the children the day he'd plucked Scrap down from the statue. "You say he couldn't bear to see his children suffer. Is it possible he might keep watch over them? That Sibby Rose or her brothers might have seen him?"

"Scrap wouldn't know him from Adam. He was barely toddling about when Darragh left. Sibby Rose not much older. I doubt even Sibby would recognize him after all this time."

Lucien rubbed his jaw with one hand. "I have devised a plan." He would write to his brother's business partner. McLeod had connections in Glasgow. "I will hire an agent of inquiry here in London."

"You are serious about this."

"Entirely."

The Irishman's gaze sharpened. "Why?" he demanded. "What is it to you?"

Lucien inhaled a deep breath. "Because my wife has a soft heart. She wants to help the family. Their situation can only be considered desperate with the little ones suffering."

"Like half the wee ones in St. Giles, an' every Catholic in Ireland." The Irishman's gaze clashed with Lucien's like sword blades. "I don't like you. I don't trust you. But if you can find Darragh…I'll work with you."

Lucien felt a wave of triumph. "Agreed."

"But on this alone. If you're thinkin' of pryin' into any o' my other business for your fine authority friends, you'll regret it. I'll know. You have my word on it."

Lucien hesitated, glancing down at the Chartist pamphlets. What if he stumbled across some plot that endangered lives? "Spying upon your more questionable activities is not my intent," he said with all honesty.

O'Malley seemed satisfied.

"If I hear any news, I will come to the boarding house," Lucien said.

"Be takin' your life in your hands t' come here again. Most people in the Dials would stab you as soon as look at you. I'll come t' you if I hear anything. An' if you learn something, just send word an' I'll get t' you fast as I can."

"You have my card. You can reach me at Raven's Court or at my office near Westminster."

"I just can't get my head around it." O'Malley regarded him with shrewd eyes, one work-battered hand rubbing his stubbled jaw. "Why would you do this? Why now? I know your family's record in parliament. Your father voted against every law that would benefit people like us. And so, my lord, did you."

It was true. There were past votes that filled him with shame. But now…images flashed through Lucien's mind. Grace's delight over the slates and slate pencils, Scrap Nolan who had trusted him enough to drop from the statue into his arms. The feel of Sibby Rose against his chest as they raced through the mob at the theater, then the child in the big bed at Raven's Court, the bandage around her head. He pictured Sibby Rose and her ribbon, remembered the feel of Scrap clinging to him with such trust.

Lucien had thought he had seen poverty in the years before. But he had not walked the peoples' streets. Spoken to them and seen their courage and their fear. Their love for their children. He had not seen their world through his own 'Little Nell's' eyes…

Who would have guessed that merely reading a novel could alter your world? He thought of O'Malley, his tale of how the poor pooled their coin to buy the book, to read it together….

Why now? O'Malley's question echoed in his head.

Lucien laughed just a little at himself. "You're not the only one who read Dickens," he said.

He started to walk toward the boarding house door.

"Your lordship." O'Malley's voice stopped him.

He paused and turned, regarding the Irishman's wary expression.

"About your wife…"

Every muscle in Lucien's body tightened. "What about her?"

O'Malley's eyes shifted away. "Speaks to everyone interested like. That ribbon she gave Sibby Rose…Moira says the child wears it every day and's been sleepin' with it under her pillow at night." He moved the pamphlets into a pile on his desk, the task taking longer than it should. "After you two left the day you brought Sibby home, she told us how the lady brings the Sunday School apples, an' soft rolls an' shows 'em toy soldiers an' such t' make 'em smile."

Lucien could picture Grace doing just that. After all, she had made him smile. Made him laugh when he'd thought he'd forgotten how. He wondered if she had found the toy soldier she'd lost.

"She's a rare one, she is," O'Malley said.

"Thank you."

"I ain't saying it to compliment her. It's more a warning. You'd do well t' keep her away from where the school is, Lord Everdene. That area's a hotbed o' discontent right now." He drummed work worn fingers on the pamphlets. "Sometimes it only takes one spark to set the world on fire."

The back of Lucien's neck prickled. "Is that a threat, O'Malley? Do you know something you're not telling me?"

"Like I said…Just givin' fair warnin'. Been caught in the middle of a donnybrook already, hasn't she? I'm not one for striking out at women, but there are plenty who don't give a damn. Be a shame if a kind lady like yours got caught in the flames."

CHAPTER 31

She was with child.

Grace pressed her hands to her stomach, joy, trepidation, and fierce protectiveness warring inside her as the carriage rolled through the streets toward Raven's Court. It almost didn't seem real, as if during the few hours since Lucien had set out for Pinchbeck's factory that morning she had tumbled into some strange new world, off balance and stunned though she should not be.

The signs had been there. The missed courses, tender breasts, the faint sense of nausea that never quite settled. Had she resisted seeing the changes in her body because she worried about what effect a babe might have on this new closeness she and Lucien shared? Now that she knew, truly knew, there was no avoiding whatever was to come. She wished, more than anything, for a chance to confide in her mother, glean some of her hard-earned wisdom. She had never felt her absence so keenly.

The coach lurched over a break in the cobblestones and Grace braced herself against the tufted leather seat. What would Lucien think when she told him of the impending child?

When they'd wed, he had made it clear he planned to keep distance from Grace and his child once an heir was born. At the time she had feared that resolve was due to his own preferences. Now she knew him better, those wounded places left by his own father, the earl corrosive, controlling, oft times cruel. She sensed Lucien's fear that he might hurt a child the way he had been hurt. What if Lucien held to that original belief?

The coach shuddered to a halt, and she waited for a footman to hand her down, wanting desperately to rush upstairs, retire to the room where she and Lucien had shared so much passion. Be alone to think of how to tell him he was going to be a father.

As she entered the townhouse, Smythe, the butler hastened up to her, wringing his hands.

"Thank goodness you're home. You have guests. They arrived an hour ago."

What in heaven's name had distressed him so much? Whoever had arrived threw the household into a tempest worthy of her brothers. Even if it was the queen herself, Grace would not be able to play the serene hostess.

"I fear I am indisposed. Please give them my regrets."

"Er, I am afraid that will be difficult. It is Captain and Mrs. Harcourt and the viscount's sisters, Lady Cassandra and Lady Jane. I placed them in the parlor."

So that was the root of his dismay. Had news of the discord in the Harcourt family reached the servants here? Heaven knew, household staffs seemed to have a line of communication faster than the palace itself.

She might have been glad to welcome family under different circumstances. But now? What had brought them to her doorstep with no warning? Had something gone wrong back home?

Discarding her bonnet and cloak, she pasted on a smile and swept into the parlor.

The four Harcourts were gathered around a tea table, partaking of the feast of teacakes and finger sandwiches provided.

They swiveled to face the door as she entered, Pen a trifle sheepish, Jane's lashes dipping shyly, and Cassandra with a sphynx-like gaze.

Grace swept toward them. "Look at you all here! What a surprise!"

Simon rose, favoring Grace with a wide grin. "Did you not receive the message we sent ahead?"

"N—no. I am afraid not. But of course I am glad to see you!" she fibbed. She could hardly tell Lucien her news with guests here. In fact, she had to wonder what he would say when he came home to find his family. "I trust all is right in the country?"

"Right as rain," Simon said. "A colleague of Pen's has just finished a building and she has come to London to see it. Since you did not wait for us to return to Everdene Hall after you wed, Cassandra insisted we must offer our congratulations to you and Lucien as well."

Something in the way he phrased it made Grace uneasy. Cassandra had made no secret of her resentment toward Lucien. That glaze-eyed anger when she'd wounded him with the sword.

Cassandra gave a catlike smile. "It was very inconsiderate of you to deprive us of a wedding."

There was nothing for it, but to tell the truth. "My stepmother was making me quite miserable with the preparations for a large society wedding. Lucien wanted to spare me further vexation."

Jane gave a delicate shudder. "No wonder you eloped. I would not want to be in front of so many people, either."

"Lucien being considerate," Cassandra said. "How…astonishing."

"That is love, for you," Simon replied, a look in his eye that made Grace think he was trying to smooth things over with bluff humor.

"Your arrival couldn't be better timed," Grace said. "I am to give my first entertainment here at Raven's Court three days from now. How nice it will be to have family attend. I will have the staff make up your rooms."

Cassandra laughed without humor. "Have you not got to know my brother yet? We would be about as welcome as the plague."

"We are staying at the Langham Hotel," Penelope said hastily. "It is your honeymoon, after all."

Grace tried not to let her relief show. "You must do as you like, of course. But rooms at Raven's Court are yours whenever you wish to use them." She took her place on the settee to preside over the teapot, deftly switching the subject. "Have you had any news from The Willows since I have been gone?"

"Indeed we have," Simon volunteered. "Will has brought your brothers to visit our stables several times, and we've had quite a bang-up time together. They've promised to help me cut down the tree for Everdene's annual Christmas fete."

She beamed, gratitude welling up inside her thinking how healing it would be for the boys to find themselves enfolded into a larger, loving family. "That is so kind of you, Simon."

Penelope's eyes sparkled. "He and our Kit are two of a kind. Dear Kit was toddling after a dormouse in the barn the other day. I live in fear of the day he's nimble enough to catch one."

Grace smiled at the antics of Simon and Pen's adorable little son. Kit would be cousin to the child she now carried. Would they become fast friends? She imagined the pair at Bennet's age, racing around the lovely parklands as Simon and Lucien once had, climbing in the hayloft, learning to ride on twin ponies.

"As for Christmas," Penelope continued, "I am quite determined this year's celebration will be the most delightful we have ever held." She selected a little cake and took a bite. "All of the crofters will come, and our neighbors. And you and Lucien, if you are able."

Grace thought how precious that would be, her first Christmas as Lucien's wife, familiar faces gathered around, children bobbing for apples and playing games like snapdragon. Would her own child be part of those traditions once he or she was born? "It sounds lovely."

Simon slid an arm around his wife. "Speaking of family traditions, is Lucien off at his offices in Westminster?"

"No. He and Arkwright have gone to examine conditions at Pinchbeck's factory."

Cassandra's lips pursed. "Looking for ways to squeeze more money out of the people who work there, are they?"

"Quite the opposite," Grace protested, stung. "He has gone to see the conditions workers are laboring under."

A strange expression came over Cassandra's face. "I'm sorry... you were talking about Lucien, were you not?"

Grace nodded, then regaled them with the story of how they met Sibby Rose and Scrap, and their visit on returning little Sibby home the day after the riot. "Of course, you should have seen the look on your brother's face when Scrap climbed into Lucien's arms like a wee monkey and pilfered his pocket watch." Her voice trailed off at the realization that Lucien's family was staring at her.

Suddenly Simon burst out laughing. "I would have paid good coin to see that," he said.

Penelope's eyes sparkled, and small smile played about Jane's mouth, the first Grace had seen on her since her return. Cassandra, however, looked at Grace as if she suddenly sprouted horns. "Pray tell what any of that has to do with his visit to Pinchbeck's factory?"

"The children's father, Mr. Nolan, was fired from his job two years ago for interfering when the foreman beat a child. He left London in search of work and has been missing ever since. Lucien has gone to find out what he can."

"Lucien, you say?" Cassandra gave something of a scoff.

If nothing else, the story seemed to ease the tension and Grace managed to keep the conversation flowing until, at last, she heard noise in the corridor, then the familiar rumble of Lucien's baritone. She flushed and excused herself, hurrying out to meet him and shutting the parlor door behind her.

Her heart squeezed at the sight of her handsome husband. He looked uncharacteristically disheveled as he shed his cloak and high-crowned hat. His cravat had wilted, his usually pristine frock coat marred by a light dusting of lint, the faint smell of something unpleasant clinging to his clothes. But his eyes were the most changed.

Weariness and relief filled his gaze as he saw her, as if Grace were everything that was warm after trudging through knee-deep snow.

Love, mingling with an unexpected shyness, rippled through her. She would have given anything to be alone with him so that she might share her news. A child—*their child*—would arrive come spring. Part of her and part of Lucien. If a boy, the child would be the heir he had needed for the title, but now, she dared hope for so much more.

"Welcome home." She slid her arms around him and pressed her cheek against his chest, feeling his heartbeat, thinking about the babe inside her, her heart welling with hope and trepidation. "As eager as I am to hear about your time at the factory, that will have to wait. We've had a surprise visit. Family come from Everdene."

"Family?" A muscle in his jaw tightened.

"Penelope and Simon were coming to London and Cassandra

insisted she and Jane come along to congratulate us on our marriage."

There was something in his face she couldn't quite decipher. "Let me put myself in order. I'll be back directly," he said.

Lucien was true to his word, returning in an exquisitely tailored superfine jacket, his cravat crisp, his hair combed. He smelled of spices and soap, and yet there was a stiffness about him, as if he were, once again, the man at that first dinner party at Everdene Hall when he'd faced the earl. Rigid with the people he should have felt most comfortable with.

Simon hastened toward him, a wide grin on his handsome face as he shook Lucien's hand. "We've spent a pleasant hour with your lovely bride. Congratulations. We wish you both happiness."

"We do." Penelope approached with a polite smile. "I fear this visit was more of a surprise than we intended. The note Cassandra sent to apprise you of our visit seems to have gone astray."

Lucien's gaze locked on his sister. "Unfortunate indeed."

Cassandra smiled, a glint in her eyes. "I cannot imagine where it got to. But we are here now, and that is all that matters."

"Grace told us you were touring Pinchbeck's factory," Simon said with a lift of his eyebrows. "You had some interest in an Irishman who once worked there?"

"Yes. Darragh Nolan. My visit was most enlightening." Lucien turned to Grace, and for a moment, she felt as if they were alone. "You must not get your hopes up too much, my dear, but it is possible he has been seen in London."

Grace caught hold of his hands. A bright flare of excitement burst within her. "Truly?"

"The foreman at Pinchbeck's said some of his men claimed to have seen Nolan at a London pub. It may be mere nonsense from men in their cups, but that's why I am so late. I went to the boarding house where Tom O'Malley stays and enlisted his help, then spoke to an agent of inquiry."

Grace turned to his siblings to explain that O'Malley was a friend of Mr. Nolan's back in Ireland. Her gaze suddenly snagged on Jane, who was no longer peering at the world through lowered lashes or darting glances fleeting as a bird's wing.

Surprisingly, Jane was actually *looking* at Lucien, perhaps for the first time since her return. "It is…quite kind of you to help them," Jane said softly.

Lucien's expression softened as he regarded his sister. "You, above anyone, know I am not kind by nature, Jane. I would have walked past them as if they were invisible if it were not for Grace."

Cassandra's lips pursed. "Tripped over them and been angry they scuffed your boots more like," she muttered. "I can't imagine what Father and his allies would have to say to you."

"Quite a bit, actually." Lucien went to the mantel where the portrait of an Elizabethan Harcourt ancestor hung, complete with ruff and the family coat of arms. "I have been inundated with missives and meetings attempting to sway me. Father's allies are as angry as the folk I saw in the Seven Dials. But the Tories have far less reason."

"Well said, Luce." Simon curved a hand over his brother's shoulder. "I would love to discuss matters later over port."

Grace saw her husband stiffen for a moment, his face guarded again, as if Simon's touch startled him. "The issues are far from simple," Lucien told him. "The threat of revolution spreading from the continent is real."

Cassandra joined her brothers at the hearth looking up at the motto painted on their ancestor's coat of arms. "*While I am vigilant, I am safe,*" she read. "There will always be those who would burn the world down to get their way."

Grace suddenly wondered if Cassandra was one of them.

Penelope rose, smoothing one of the silk tassels on her cream-and-green day dress. "I think we should give you the wedding gifts we brought from Everdene," she suggested, perhaps to break the tension.

Grace agreed, grateful for the distraction as they gathered where some bundles sat across the room. A beautiful embroidered cushion from Jane was the first they opened. The forest scene seemed almost real, with a doe and fawn drinking at a stream. An exquisite statue of a rearing horse was from Simon, Penelope and little Kit, Simon explaining, "This is Caspian, the stallion Jamie MacLeod and I sneaked out of Afghanistan. Without your gift of the Harcourt stables, Lucien, this bloodline would still be just a dream."

It was obvious Lucien was deeply touched by the gift. Grace began to hope the strain in the family might ease.

"My gift will be late." Cassandra laughed. "I wanted to paint something from a classic myth, but Jane objected. Apparently, Persephone being wed to Hades is *not* an appropriate image for a wedding gift."

Had she meant it as a jest? Grace didn't know. She could only be grateful not to receive such a painting. She looked from one sister to the other, remembering the gruesome painting Cassandra had shown the night of the dinner party. How closely Holofernes had resembled the earl, Judith's knife biting into his throat.

"Fortunately, for you," Cassandra continued, gesturing to a large, flat oval object draped in holland cloth, "Mother painted something far more fitting."

Grace leaned close to Lucien as he unwrapped the gift. Her breath caught as he unveiled a painting of a boy and girl facing off in front of their dancing master. The girl's eyes sparkled with mischief, the boy stiff and solemn, refusing to react.

Grace pointed to the little girl's blue satin slipper. "I do believe she is stepping on his toe," she teased, slanting a glance up at her husband. "On purpose."

"He deserved it." Lucien placed his hand on the small of her back, and for the first time since he had entered the room, a hint of his smile touched his lips.

She laughed. "We will have to hang this in the ballroom at Everdene Hall, where we took those dancing lessons!" She imagined their own child, one day, asking about that that painting, hearing the tale of their childhood rivalry. Would Lucien be there beside them?

"Everdene?" Cassandra said. "That won't do at all. You must hang it where you will be able to see it."

"I am sure we'll return home as soon as there is a break in parliamentary business," Grace said.

"Return *home*?" Cassandra leveled a pointed stare at Lucien. Grace felt tension coil between Lucien and his sister, a spring about to snap.

"Yes," Grace faltered. "Our family estates are so near…being able to—to spend time together is one of the reasons we are so happily matched."

"Lucien didn't tell you?" Cassandra asked.

Grace looked at Lucien. His beloved face was frighteningly still, emotions hidden beneath that mask of ice. "Tell me what?" she asked.

"My dear sister-in-law. Surely, you know about the rift between Jane, Lucien and me?"

"Yes. But, painful as it was, you were children then. You have all grown and changed. After so many years you can put it to rest."

"People do not change," Cassandra said, lifting her chin. "Not at the core of them."

Grace thought of the difference between the man she had first met at the lake and the man who had carried Sibby Rose into the room in Seven Dials, the man who'd let Scrap play with his pocket watch. The man who made love so tenderly and whose child now grew within her. "People *can* change," she insisted. She had to believe that. More than ever right now. "If they choose."

Cassandra crossed her arms over her chest. "Lucien and I cannot. We have dealt with the gulf between us in the only way possible. Hence his promise to me, before you wed."

A grim look hardened Cassandra's face, and Grace felt a creeping dread. She looked at Lucien, his eyes that could be so tender, so heated with passion suddenly stark, unfathomable.

"Lucien...?" The moment his name left Grace's lips, she saw the barriers form between them. "What promise is she talking about?"

"I vowed that I would never live at Everdene Hall again."

CHAPTER 32

Grace stared at Lucien, feeling as if the floor had crumbled beneath her feet. The future she had dared to imagine as she and her husband grew closer shattered: summers at Everdene and The Willows, a little boy with Lucien's ice-blue eyes and a daughter with his smile splashing in the lake with their cousin Kit, driving the wicker pony cart, playing hide and seek in the ballroom where she and Lucien had once had dancing lessons. He had crushed her dreams before ever placing his wedding ring onto her finger. She just hadn't known it.

Cassandra broke in brightly. "Lucien has a lovely estate in Lancashire. I am sure you will be happy there."

"Lancashire…," she echoed, her gaze holding Lucien's. "So far north it is almost to Scotland."

When were you going to tell me? she wanted to rail at him.

She felt like a fool. She had seen the expressions on the family's faces in that terrible moment she'd learned the truth. Jane stricken, Penelope shocked and desperately groping for something to say. Simon glared at Cassandra, who suddenly seemed smaller, as she had the moment after she'd snapped back into herself after wounding Lucien with the fencing foil. Her hand betrayed the slightest tremor.

Was she enjoying the discord she had wrought? Or was some part of her regretting it?

Grace saw Lucien regarding her with a somber gaze and wasn't sure who she was angriest at. Through his silence, he had opened her up to this humiliation, left her defenseless.

She needed to be alone, but she wouldn't give Cassandra the satisfaction of excusing herself.

Instead, she went to fetch a large work basket she always kept at the ready, determined to keep her hands busy as the Harcourts attempted to make awkward conversation.

"What are you working on?" Penelope asked with a kind of desperate cheerfulness.

"I am making Christmas gifts for the factory children who go to our school on Sunday."

"Perhaps we could help while the men discuss business," Penelope offered. "I know Simon had some questions about the estate he wanted to ask Lucien."

"Of course," Grace said as Lucien gave her one last, heavy look, then left the room with his brother.

As she laid the pieces of the project out on the table, Penelope murmured, "I am so...so...sorry. I had no idea what Cassandra planned."

Grace forced back tears. "I suppose I was looking forward to more time with my family so near Everdene. I thought..."

What? That she could change Lucien? That there was some sort of miracle unfolding between them and she understood Lucien better than the family that had known him all his life?

But they'd known him *before,* a stubborn voice insisted inside her. He had made that promise to Cassandra *before* Sibby Rose and the riot. *Before* he had begun spending entire nights in Grace's bed, *before* she'd awakened to that awed expression on his face...before she'd felt the spark of new life inside her. A wave of fierce protectiveness overwhelmed her.

What was real? What was not?

And what would happen when she told Lucien that she was carrying his child?

LUCIEN WOULD NEVER FORGET THE EXPRESSION ON GRACE'S FACE— shock, disbelief. He'd felt sick when Cassandra delivered her verbal riposte, dealing a wound he had known would come when he did not confess the truth himself. Why the devil hadn't he done so, those times when he'd come so close to admitting what he'd done? Trusting that they would work through it?

Grace looked so vulnerable when she'd turned to him after Cassandra's revelation, obviously hoping that he would make things better…And then her belief in him had changed to hurt and betrayal as the truth sank in.

He had wanted to gather her into his arms, try to explain…he would, God curse it, as soon as he was able to get her alone. He walked into the study with its scent of beeswax and leather, the scent of Arkwright's cheroots. What little time he had spent at the townhouse in the past, he'd spent here, before Grace had made Raven's Court something he'd never expected. A home.

"What was that all about?" Simon asked.

For a moment, Lucien wanted end the conversation before it started. Instead, he poured them each a brandy from the decanter on a nearby table and handed a glass to Simon.

"After the picnic at The Willows, Grace came to me. She had made a promise to her brothers after their mother died. Swore she'd never leave them."

He could see the flicker of understanding in Simon's face, both of them remembering those dark days when their mother and sisters had vanished and they'd only had each other.

"Lord Elliot was determined to marry Grace off to some friend of the stepmother who lives in Scotland. Clear the way for his new wife. Grace said we could help each other. If we married, she would be my political hostess and provide me with an heir. I would ensure that she could live at Everdene and keep her vow to her brothers."

Simon regarded him with that damnable patience he'd acquired in the past two years, just waiting for Lucien to go on.

"Just before Grace and I became betrothed, I tried to make amends to Cassandra. Told her I had been wrong in siding with Father all those years ago. I could not change the pain I had caused, but I would do whatever I could to make things right. Her price— that I never live at Everdene again."

Simon turned the snifter in his hand. "You didn't tell Grace what you had agreed to."

"No. From the first it was to be a marriage of convenience. I made it clear I would provide financially for her and a child, but I was not interested in being involved beyond that. I told myself the agreement with Cass changed nothing. I didn't expect…"

"Didn't expect what?" Simon asked quietly.

Lucien crossed to the window, braced his arm against its frame. He peered out into the street.

A ragged boy ran through the gate toward the servant's entrance, a parcel gripped in his hands. Once Lucien would not even have noticed, but now he wondered. Was it some delivery for the charity event or one of Grace's school children?

How could he begin to explain how she had changed him?

"I didn't expect to love her," he confessed in a low voice.

"But that is wonderful!" Simon exclaimed.

"Is it? Since she's been my wife, she's had bricks thrown at her, been caught in a riot. The people who made those attacks were trying to get at me. Even this entertainment she is giving on Wednesday has become a target for my rivals. Pinchbeck's wife is determined to make it a failure if she can."

"Then we will make certain it is a roaring success."

He turned to Simon. "You know as well as I do that I am not the husband she needs."

"That is for Grace to decide. I saw the way she looks at you."

He remembered just that morning as he'd left with Arkwright, the softness in her face, the strength, the love. Jesus, God, the love…

A lump formed in his throat.

"Tell her, Luce. Tell her you love her. Explain what happened with Cass. Grace has such a loving heart, she will understand."

She would. He knew it. So much compassion, kindness, so much love directed at him was a miracle…yet terrifying.

A soft scratch at the door made Lucien straighten, wiping any emotion from his face. "Enter."

The door slid soundlessly open, a footman hovering uncomfortably on the threshold, something in his hands. "My apologies, my lord. A young lad just delivered this. Insisted that I put it directly into your hands and that you open it at once. There was something about the lad's face. I thought it best to do as he asked."

Lucien frowned, remembering the boy he had seen running up the walk. He took the small bundle. "Thank you."

The servant bowed then left the room.

Lucien crossed to his desk and set the package down. It was wrapped in some kind of newsprint with a caricature of lords lashing a skeletal worker with their whip. A note was tucked under the string tied around it. He slipped it free, reading the words in blotted ink.

Spark to flame,
flame to powder,
lay waste what was,
new world order...

"What is it?" Simon asked.

"Another warning." Lucien handed Simon the note. "At least they didn't break a window this time."

"What is in the package?"

Lucien carefully peeled back the crumpled newsprint.

His pulse stuttered, ice flooding his veins as he recognized what lay inside.

Grace's battered toy soldier.

LUCIEN WANTED TO THROTTLE SOMEONE. HE HAD ALL BUT TERRIFIED the footman, demanding the description of the lad who had delivered the package. He and Simon had searched the nearby area with the servant in tow. But there were swarms of delivery boys thronging the streets of London, all but invisible in their worn coats with hats pulled low over their faces. In the end he had known it was futile. The lad had melted into the crowds.

There was nothing to do but break the news to Grace.

Windblown and frustrated, he and Simon returned to the parlor. Lucien's chest felt too tight as he surveyed the room where he and Grace had spent such warm, pleasant hours.

The women were industriously gathering groups of pages between covers of bright calico and stitching them in place. Lucien noticed for the first time that the pictures contained a tin soldier amidst various adventures. Stranded on a lily pad, sailing in a toy boat, facing down a fierce cat and defending some little mice in waistcoats or frilly bonnets.

Grace, offering children whose lives were bleak a glimpse of something whimsical. The thought that some cowardly bastard threatened to put that light out filled him with rage.

"We have had a change in plans," he said so gruffly the women all looked up, startled. "You will all stay at Raven's Court until the charity event is over."

Cassandra looked decidedly uncomfortable. "But I thought we agreed—"

"There has been an incident."

"What happened?" Grace rose and Lucien reached into the pocket of his coat, the toy soldier all but lost in his hand. Slowly he opened his fingers, showing it cradled against his palm.

"Lord Admiral Nelson!" Grace cried, so pleased Lucien winced. "Wherever did you find him?"

"It arrived today in a package with this."

He handed her the note, watched as the color drained from her face. The other women gathered around, reading over her shoulder with worried frowns. Even Cassandra seemed stricken.

Simon lay a comforting hand on his wife's back. "We'll go to the hotel now. Gather our things and return in the morning."

Lucien barely registered what was going on around him as the women said goodbye. When the last skirt had disappeared into the dark interior of the coach, Simon paused and turned to Lucien. "I am going to send word to McLeod. Have him come to London to help with the search for whoever is making these threats. There is no man I trust more."

Lucien swallowed hard. "I am in your debt."

"We're family. We will find these bastards and put an end to this together."

Lucien watched his brother climb up into the equipage and the horses swing out onto the road. Somewhere, in those streets, an enemy was waiting. An enemy who had targeted Grace because of him.

He turned and reentered the townhouse where Grace was already bustling around, giving orders to servants, her face taut.

He stared for a moment at the note laying there amid the innocent drawings, then ordered up his hat and cloak, fury he'd suppressed since boyhood pouring through him.

He would hurl all the power of the Harcourt name against whoever was threatening Grace. Use any method to find them.

And when he did he would kill them.

CHAPTER 33

By the time Lucien returned late that afternoon, Raven's Court seethed with words unspoken, anger unresolved, lies told. Unseen dangers made his spine tingle with a foreboding he had not felt since the weeks before his mother and sisters were swept away.

When he had left hours earlier, Grace had been rushing about like a dervish, airing guest bedrooms, amending meal plans and rearranging seating charts. She was the consummate political hostess she'd promised to be when she'd wed him, seeing to necessities despite her feelings of betrayal. A vise seemed to crush his chest at the memory of her hours earlier, her curls tumbling from their pins, her cheeks scarlet with fury and hurt. And he was grateful when Grace did not greet him now so that he could slip upstairs to his bedchamber alone.

Once there, he crossed to where a wooden chest stood on a shelf. Anyone who knew Lucien would assume it contained cufflinks, watch fobs and stickpins for his cravats, instead of those few keepsakes the most unsentimental peer in England carried with him wherever he traveled: Letters Simon sent while in the cavalry, a small ivory elephant from the Gold Coast, a hammered disc that had once decorated a Turkoman horse and a powder flask dropped by a tribesman in a skirmish.

But beneath those lay something that pained Lucien like

shrapnel buried beneath old scars. Tonight he needed that grim reminder to steel himself for what was to come.

He found what he sought at the very bottom of the chest: The dented blue tin box he had kept with him since the night his world had crashed down. How long had it been since he had looked inside it? He couldn't say. But he forced himself to pry the bent lid open, the metal squeaking as he revealed what lay inside. He took the bit of cloth out, ran it through his fingers, strengthening his resolve to see Grace safe.

Tonight's confrontation would be the hardest thing he had ever faced. Yet, if there was one skill he had mastered at his father's knee it was this: How to disguise what he truly felt.

He heard steps marching toward his room and stowed the scrap away, knowing who approached even before the bedchamber door opened. Grace glared at him, looking so beautiful he gripped the tin box until the edges bit into his palm.

"So you've returned," she said. "May I ask where you've been all this time?"

"I felt it imperative to speak to my agent of inquiry regarding new developments."

"A courtesy you did not see fit to extend to me." Her chin bumped up a notch.

Lucien set the tin box in its nest of old letters, then shut the chest's wooden lid. "You have every right to be angry."

"You owed me the truth before we wed." Two spots of color heated her cheeks, her eyes snapping fire. "When were you going to tell me that you had sworn we would never live at Everdene?"

He fought to keep his voice level. "I swore that *I* would not live there. Your residence at Everdene was never in question. As I remember from the day you proposed to me, that was always the agreement. We will merely situate you there sooner than planned. Surely you can see it is the only reasonable course after the package that arrived this morning."

"So these past months, as we grew closer…Was that also a lie?"

Lucien ignored her question, maintaining his impassive expression with his reply. "Whoever sent that note knows they cannot intimidate me so they are making you a target. They not only discovered how important that toy is to you, they were able to get close enough to take it from your pocket. They could have done far worse." Voicing that truth set fault lines rippling through his control. "They could have dragged you into a carriage, kidnapped you, driven a knife between your ribs."

She nearly trod on his toes she stepped so close. Her eyes blazed up at him. "I'm not afraid."

"*I am!*" he roared, all control forgotten. "Jesus, Grace. Whoever took that toy was inches away from you. Knew that nothing—*nothing*—would be a clearer message to me of how much danger you were in." Raking his hand through his hair, he said in steely tones, "The morning after the party on Wednesday, Simon will take you back to Everdene Hall and *you will go.*"

"What about the danger you are in?"

"That is just part of being in parliament. Make unpopular decisions and the opposition gets angry—"

"Well, I am plenty angry right now. I have been raking this over in my mind ever since you left today, and do you know what I think? I think you are using this threat as an excuse to put distance between us because you are beginning to care for me."

He couldn't look away as the words struck their mark, her eyes defiant, so fierce, yet revealing just a hint of fear. It thrust a spike into his heart.

He clenched his fists. "Can't you see I'm trying to protect you? It is pure luck that you weren't trampled in the riot or injured by a flying brick. I won't risk it, I tell you."

"Well, *I* won't keep being pushed away because of some mistake you made when you were just a boy. If you insist I leave you once the party is over, I will go. But know that I will be leaving you for good. I'll raise our babe alone."

"Babe?" Lucien felt as if he'd been poleaxed. Words snagged in his throat and for a heartbeat something flared inside him. Disbelief, then awe. He grasped the edge of the table. "You are with child?"

"You need not look so shocked," she said, crossing her arms protectively over her middle. "It cannot be surprising news, considering how often we lay together."

Lucien inhaled a deep breath. "No. I suppose not."

Now a brand new fear stabbed him, imagining the dangers she

faced in childbed, dreading that he would be a father like his own and scar his children. But a babe…his babe growing in Grace's womb…

"If I am no more to you than a bargain made, why didn't you tell me we'd not live at Everdene in the first place?" Grace demanded. "I will keep your damnable pact if you can look me in the eye and tell me these past weeks have been a lie."

"Grace—"

"*Tell me!* Are you the Lord Everdene so many people warned me about? The man who struck that cold contract? The ruthless man who lied to me. Or are you the husband who bathed me so tenderly after the riot? Who carried Sibby Rose to safety? Who let Scrap play with a pocket watch. Are you the man I see on the pillow beside me when I wake, looking at me as if…as if I am precious to him and he can scarcely believe…" Her voice broke, and tears brimmed in her eyes. "*Who are you, Lucien?*"

He scarce knew anymore. The man he'd once been would not have hesitated to deal a necessary blow to drive her away. But he needed her like he needed his next breath.

"You want to know why I didn't tell you I'd not live at Everdene? Because I am a man who has always taken what I wanted and I wanted you. When we encountered Freyne at Gunter's and I saw the way he looked at you, I knew telling you about my agreement with Cassandra might push you into that bastard's arms and I couldn't endure it. I didn't want to love you. Hell, I didn't think I was capable of any such feeling, but somewhere between the moment I pulled you from the lake and the night of the riot I knew." His voice broke. "I love you, Grace. The thought of you being hurt because of me…it's my worst fear come real."

Tears brimmed in her eyes. "Living without you is mine."

She took his hand, brought it to her stomach. "This babe…it's part of you," she said softly, "part of me, made from our love."

"When is the child to come?"

"Sometime in May."

He closed his eyes, cradling that spark of life in his palm. He had never known anything more worthy of defending than this woman, this child.

Sliding one hand around her nape, he drew her mouth to his, kissing her so gently he felt her smile.

"I'm not made out of glass, Lucien. You won't break me."

He was still afraid for her, and yet…this was Grace…"You are the strongest person I know. I didn't even know what love meant until I staggered out of that lake and saw you with your brothers. I only know that I want to be the man who sees your eyes shine. I want to be the man who kisses pink frosting from your fingertips and holds you when you weep over characters in books and children in factories. I want to fight alongside you to change things, things I've only seen because you wouldn't let me look away. Because if it is possible to change things for the factory children, it is possible for me to change as well."

She raised her fingers to his mouth, stopped him.

"You are not the only one who has changed since we've been together. I had lost myself after Mama died. I was so busy caring for everyone else. You…saw *me*. Dragged me back out into the world where I felt…felt everything. Anger. Grief. Passion. You helped me remember what it meant to see things through my own eyes, not everybody else's. You wouldn't let me keep surrendering myself to what other people wanted for me."

"You have the right to choose."

"I do." She cupped his jaw in her hand, and he felt those delicate fingers rasp against his beard. "I choose you. Whatever is to come."

She drew him toward his bed, the one they had never slept in. Slowly, he unfastened her gown, slid the bodice off of her shoulders, taking his time undressing her until she stood before him in all her naked loveliness. He skimmed his hands over the slight swell of her belly, the fullness of her breasts with their darkened nipples, and he wondered how had he not known she was with child.

"You are so beautiful," he praised as she helped him shed his own clothes, his skin heating with each brush of her fingers. "We will fight this together, my love. And when it is over…" He laughed suddenly, surprising himself, and she turned her sweet face up to his.

"I so love your laugh. When it is over—what?" she asked.

"For the first time in my life, I don't know what comes next. I have no idea how to be a good father. How to be the husband you deserve. But swear I will learn."

He scooped her into his arms, lay her upon the coverlets, then followed her down.

"We will fight whoever is behind these threats together," Grace said as he traced her cheek with his fingertips. "I love you, Lucien. We cannot have come so far in our love to have it snatched away."

Lucien buried his face in her neck, breathing in the sweet, jasmine scent as he covered her body with his own.

He worshiped her body like the miracle she was, infusing every-thing he felt into making love to her, his beautiful, brave wife who had dared love him.

But even as they lost themselves in release, he held her with a fierceness that nearly undid him.

He knew just how devastating it was when the one you loved was snatched away. And the man stalking Grace was still out there, somewhere.

A snake preparing to strike.

CHAPTER 34

*I*n three hours this interminable wait would be over, Lucien told himself as he paced the townhouse. Guests would arrive, the party commence, and at least some of the tension coiling in his belly would ease. Simon and McLeod seemed confident everything was under control, he reassured himself, and they had spent years in the military, on guard against ambush.

But, much as Lucien trusted their judgement, he had a wife and child to consider for the first time, love far too precious to lose.

He scowled as he searched the rooms for anything out of the ordinary—which was *everything* at the moment, he admitted with grim humor. Oh, he'd hosted gentleman's dinners at Raven's Court through the years, serving up simple fare, his best port and strategies for political schemes. But now, the townhouse was awash in swishing skirts, the fragrance of perfume and the hum of feminine anticipation.

Raven's Court had never felt alive in quite this way, not even when his mother had been hostess to events in the past. But then, she had dreaded them, while Grace possessed a unique gift for drawing people out, making them part of the good she hoped to do.

Cassandra had applied her artistic skills to the canvas backgrounds for the tableaux Grace had planned, painting star-spangled skies and vignettes from the Dickens novel A Christmas Carol.

Some, the exteriors, like Scrooge's famed counting house, others, interiors like Fezziwig's warehouse, and Bob Cratchit's home, each to be illuminated with candles and oil lamps that glowed.

Penelope had entertained little Kit while she organized serving pieces Lucien had forgot he'd even possessed and Jane had filled gauze bags with treats for the children who would be caroling among the guests. Gingernuts and boiled sweets, pencils and India rubber balls and colorful tin horns. When Kit escaped his mother's eye and began attempting to toot one, Lucien had muttered something about the fresh hell the women were unleashing. But he couldn't help imagining his own child delighting in such a toy, and Grace's laughter as he marched about.

Now, Simon's son was off with his nanny in the nursery that had stood empty for so many years. Simon and McLeod were doing one final check with their informants, and Lucien was trying to stay the devil out of the way as the women completed their toilettes.

He donned his own garb then retreated to his study, leaving Penelope, Jane and Grace hastening back and forth between rooms, exclaiming over jewelry and fans and making last-minute adjustments to gowns and hair.

Only Cassandra had not joined in the preparations with the same enthusiasm, seeming as edgy as Lucien as the hour for the party approached. They had not spoken alone since the revelation she'd intended to sabotage his marriage, but when he peered into the ballroom, he was surprised to find her there. She was garbed in a severe gown of black satin with red ribbon trim, yet she looked strangely younger, more uncertain. Once, he might have quietly slipped away, but he stepped closer. "You've done lovely work on these tableaux," he said, gesturing to the painted toy spaniel beneath a Christmas tree. "This looks like our old dog Flash. He even has one of Jane's dolls in his mouth. He led us on many a merry chase."

"It is so strange, is it not?" Cassandra mused, running her fingers over a candlestick decorated with the stars their mother had loved. "It's as if Raven's Court is waking up after some enchantment. I see the same silver, the same ballroom floor and paintings, and yet, it feels so different from the way it was when we were children."

"Yes."

"I had buried so much. Seeing mother's things brings it flooding back."

He saw her shudder and wondered what she was reliving. They each had their own nightmares.

"The last time I was here is when Father introduced me to Thornsby, insisting I waltz with him," Cassandra said.

Thornsby, the evil man their father had betrothed Cassandra to against her will. Mother had been attempting to spirit Cassandra to safety the night Lucien had sounded the alarm. He hadn't known of his father's machinations…and yet, it turned Lucien's stomach to remember that his actions had enabled their father to deliver Cass into the hands of the lecherous bastard who had preyed upon a girl not even out of the schoolroom. Thank God, their mother had managed to obtain Cassandra's release, even from the asylum the earl had imprisoned her in.

He tried to think of the words to say to his sister, but before he could speak, Cass's voice came, soft, uncertain.

"Have you ever wondered if our family is cursed?" She looked up at him, her gaze searching his face.

Lucien shook his head. "I don't believe in curses."

"I do. Do you remember Paola, my maid?"

Lucien pictured the grim Italian woman with the eyepatch who had looked at him as if he were the devil. "It would be hard to forget her, especially since she was the one who taught you to wield a sword. Strange, I hadn't marked the fact that she did not accompany you here."

Cassandra picked at her thumbnail, and shrugged. "She was called away. When we were in Italy, she introduced me to a Romany seer, an old woman who said…sins demand payment in blood. She knew a Sin Eater, said he could wash the curse away, but I refused. I wanted you and Father to pay for what you had done more than I wanted to be free of some evil spell…even if that could free Jane and Simon and Mama. Even if it could free me."

Lucien had felt the same kind of poison, eating away at him… before Grace.

"I always accused you of being like Father," Cass said. "But perhaps I am the one—"

She stopped at the sound of someone else entering the room, a footman looking irritated, red splotches on his face.

"Pardon the interruption, my lord, but there is a person at the front door who insists on seeing you."

Lucien glanced at the ormolu clock on a table. Possibly some news from one of the guards posted on the corners outside?

"He refuses to come inside," the footman huffed in high dudgeon. "I explained that lords do not address strangers on their doorstep."

The back of Lucien's neck prickled. "I'll see him. Cassandra, perhaps we can continue our conversation later."

"Heaven forbid." She waved her hand, shuttering that hint of vulnerability away. "Go on, before I say something even more foolish."

Troubled, Lucien made his way down to the front entry, the arches and nooks bedecked with holly and silver ribbon.

A hard-eyed man stood outside the townhouse door, his coat worn but clean, his soft cap pulled over mouse-brown hair badly in need of a trim. There was something vaguely familiar about him, though Lucien couldn't place him.

"I am Lord Everdene," Lucien said.

"I knows it." The man's lip curled in disdain. "I saw you the day you came pryin' around the boarding house looking for O'Malley. Stopped us right in the middle o' readin' that Dickens fellow an' O'Malley's not been around since."

"What do you want with me?"

"You? Nothin'. Wouldn't pour slops over yer head if yer hair was on fire, but I would fight my way through a horde o' heathens for O'Malley. He sent for me and told me to put this in yer hand without fail. Took long enough t' find yer." He thrust out a crumpled piece of paper, covered all over with print. A page torn from Oliver Twist. In the margins, someone had penciled the words:

Found Darragh. Come to Nolans now or people will die. O'Malley.

Lucien looked up sharply, remembering O'Malley's warnings about rebellion, then the note that had come with Grace's tin soldier.

Spark to flame.

He clenched his teeth. Soon, guests would be arriving, and yet, he dared not delay.

"How did you travel here?" he asked the man.

"How d'ye think. On foot."

"Can you ride a horse?"

"Well enough. Grew up on a farm before yer sort turned us out."

Lucien motioned to the footman. "Run to the mews with this man. Tell the grooms to saddle two horses and bring them here."

The pair set out and Lucien strode back into the townhouse, calling for his cloak and hat.

Cassandra stood in the center of the entryway, pale and drawn. "People will start arriving soon. Where are you going?"

"This is something that won't wait."

"Are you even going to tell Grace you're leaving?"

He glanced behind him at the sweep of staircase, wishing he could go to Grace, hold her once more in his arms. "There is no time," he said as he handed Cassandra the note.

She followed him as he hastened outside, passing servants preparing for the arrival of horses and carriages.

"This note…" Cassandra faltered, "it's from the people in the Seven Dials, isn't it?"

"Yes."

"Wait until Simon returns so that he can go with you."

"I need him here to keep all of you safe. I have to go alone. Cass, they won't trust anyone else."

She caught hold of his arm. The first time she had touched him willingly since she returned from Italy. "What if it is a trap?"

It could be.

He covered her hand with his own. "If I don't come back, there is something for you in my bedchamber…a blue tin box…"

"What?"

"Be sure to find it."

He heard the clop of hooves as a groom and the messenger trotted toward them, leading two horses. His heart wrenched as he pictured Grace and the babe he might never see. The child he had not even told anyone existed, the knowledge still a precious secret, too precious to share.

"Cass, no matter what happens, watch over Grace and the child. Promise me."

"The child?"

He looked at his sister, emotions stripped raw. "I am going to be a father…," he said. His voice broke. "Tell Grace I love her."

He swung up on the horse and raced toward Seven Dials.

THE CROWD GATHERED OUTSIDE THE NOLANS' TENEMENT SEETHED with agitation, the group parting with hostile glances as Lucien shouldered his way through them. The moment he stepped inside the single room, he smelled the coppery tang of blood and the sourness of fear. The table lay on its side, crockery shattered, a stool splintered as if there had been a fight. The children cowered in the darkest corner, the whites of their eyes visible in the glow of the rush light. Moira Nolan bent over the mattress on which O'Malley lay, his face ashen, blood oozing from a gash on his brow. His arm hung at a strange angle.

"I have a shilling for the first one to bring a surgeon and some whiskey," Lucien barked to the crowd then turned to the Irishman. "What happened here?"

"Darragh. He was talking wild—half out of his head. Clubbed me when I tried…tried to stop him."

"Stop him from what?"

"Damned fool intends to set off a bomb." O'Malley slurred his words. "Kill himself and a whole lot of people. Bastards convinced him…" He leaned over and retched onto the floor.

"Who convinced him?" Lucien demanded. "Radical Chartists? Irish rebels?"

"How many times do I have to tell you! Not us! Rich toffs been paying spies to incite mobs to violence. Darragh Nolan is not the first hired to do their killing. If they make it look like us, they can start another Peterloo and this time crush us completely."

Lucien had heard men in the House of Lords saying they wanted to end things…but to incite a massacre on purpose?

Lucien felt a sick sense of foreboding. "Where is this bombing to take place? Where did Darragh go?"

"Some party at a nob's house. Perfect place to fire up 'ristocrat's rage."

There were society gatherings all over the town tonight, including one at Lucien's own house. The target could be any one of those.

"Darragh is not—not a bad man," Moira Nolan wept. "The men who hired him promised they would take care of me an' the wee ones if he did it. They gave us coin enough that I'll never have to fear again."

"Did Darragh or those men say anything that would give you a clue where he means to strike? Think or people will die!"

"Some fine house is all I know."

Lucien felt a tug on his sleeve. He looked down and saw Sibby Rose, her eyes huge. She handed him a crumpled handkerchief. Blue initials were entwined in a spray of flowers. He'd seen a hand-kerchief just like it in Grace's hand when she'd pressed it to his chest after Cassandra had wounded him. "Da left this when he sent back the lady's tin soldier."

Lucien turned to ice. "Your father had the tin soldier?"

Sibby nodded.

"He's going to Raven's Court," Lucien said, balling up the embroidered square and thrusting it into his pocket.

Moira grabbed at his arm, her hands like claws. "Don't hurt him!" she sobbed.

Lucien thrust her away. "He's going after my wife! How long have you known?"

He would send the woman to the devil, but his gaze caught on Sibby Rose and Scrap. "Get O'Malley and the family the devil out of here," Lucien told O'Malley's friend. "Hide them well." He thrust pound notes into the man's hand.

Moira wailed. "But I—"

Lucien turned on her, fierce. "The men who hired Nolan won't leave anyone alive to implicate them."

O'Malley stumbled to his feet. "He's right, Moira. Darragh's a damned fool."

Lucien started for the door, but the Irishman called out. "Wait! Take this!" O'Malley staggered to where the framed sketch of Nolan's face stood on the mantel. He slammed the frame against the wall, breaking it, then pulling the paper free. He thrust it into Lucien's hands. For a moment their eyes caught, held.

Lucien jammed it into the pocket of his coat, then wheeled and shoved his way through the crowd, praying he was not too late.

CHAPTER 35

*L*ucien hadn't had time to say goodbye.

The harsh reality crowded in on Grace as she paced the ballroom, the crumpled note Cassandra had given her still clutched in her hand. It seemed a cruel jest that the note that had plunged Lucien into danger had been written on a page from a Dickens novel.

A make-believe London Street wound about the room, just waiting for the actors to bring A Christmas Carol to life: Scrooge and Marley's Counting House, the merriment of Fezziwigs and the Cratchit's humble, yet love-filled home set like jewels in the tableaux.

Yet when the lamplighter set Penelope's clever streetlights aglow, there would be no cutthroats lurking in the shadows, no mysterious enemies hunting for prey. In the dangerous slums where Lucien was going, God only knew what peril could be waiting.

*People will die…*Tom O'Malley had warned.

She felt a touch on her back and wheeled around, startled. Simon stood behind her, his face red from the cold. "You're back!" she exclaimed.

"Just in time to hear that Lucien's gone."

She handed him the note and he read it. His mouth set grim. "It was a damn fool thing for him to go off to the Seven Dials alone. I am sure it has been a shock to you."

"A shock. Yes."

"You should sit down for a bit before the guests arrive," Simon said. "The stress isn't good for the baby."

Grace eyes widened in surprise. "Lucien told you?"

Simon grimaced. "No. Lucien told Cass before he left. Made her promise we would take care of you and the babe in case—"

"He dies," Grace bit out, her stomach twisting.

"No one is more able to take care of himself than my brother," Simon attempted to soothe. "It's just—fatherhood is terrifying when you've had an upbringing like ours. You realize just how vulnerable your wife and child would be without you." He straightened one of the upturned barrels from which costumed vendors would serve refreshments once the guests arrived. "The moment the party is over, I swear I will find him."

Grace threw up her hands. "By then anything might have happened to him. You have to go after him *now*."

"You know I cannot do that," Simon reasoned. "Lucien entrusted me with your safety."

"Who is going to keep *him* safe? Fight for *him*?" Grace thumped her fist against Simon's chest. "No one ever has!"

Simon caught hold of her hands, his handsome face softening. "Until you."

"I am completely protected here, in my own home," she said fiercely. "I'm surrounded by family and you've posted guards around the premises. We *know* Lucien is riding into danger. *Alone.* Go to the Nolans', Simon. Help him." Tears filled her eyes. "He has a right to know his child. Lucien deserves this chance at happiness."

Simon's gaze locked with hers. Held. And she knew she had won.

"Happiness…," Simon breathed. "Yes, he does."

<hr>

THE TABLEAUX SEEMED SPUN OF MAGIC, BRINGING DICKENS' irresistible tale to life just as Grace had hoped it would. In the three hours since Simon had ridden after Lucien, Marley, decked in chains and cash boxes, confronted Scrooge. Bob Cratchit carried Tiny Tim on his shoulders. Ghosts of Christmas Past, Present and Yet To Come cast their ethereal spells, while carolers, vendors and shoppers laden with Christmas bundles wove amongst the guests, filling the chamber with music.

The lamplighter moved about the room, igniting the oil lamps Penelope had mounted on posts, the flames setting swaths of gilt-painted stars glittering.

Benches and chairs arranged at points around the room allowed guests to pause and listen to a selection from the story and drop coins into upturned top hats.

Yet despite the delight on the faces of her guests, it was hard for Grace to keep a smile on face. Her cheeks ached from the effort and she feared she might scream if one more person asked where Lucien was. But as Mrs. Camilla Aylcock swept toward her in a garish plaid silk gown, Grace was fairly certain her self-control was about to be put to the test.

"Wherever did you find these actors, Lady Everdene?" the baronet's wife gushed, waving her fan. "I vow, I'm tempted to stick them with pins to see if I can get them to break character. And the scenes you have created are quite exquisite."

"I hired the actors from a traveling troupe a friend recommended, and the painting was done by Lord Everdene's sister, Lady Cassandra," Grace said. "Captain Harcourt's wife helped with the structures and scenery."

"Did Mrs. Harcourt suggest positioning the barrels and kegs at different heights with the food spread upon them? It is quite effective!"

For a moment Grace's forced smile became real. "That was actually Lady Alice Pinchbeck's suggestion."

"Lady Pinchbeck's daughter?" Mrs. Aylcock scooped up a cup of ratafia from one of the keg tops she'd admired. "I own I am surprised she is even speaking to you. I must tell you, Lady Pinchbeck feels you are quite the bad influence and was most insistent that I not come here tonight. But I would not be deterred."

Nor would Alice, Grace thought warmly. Alice had turned up at the door of Raven's Court, windblown and defiant to apologize for her mother's ill behavior. When she had glimpsed plans for the party spread upon the table, Alice had added her own suggestions. *I know just where I can find you the perfect kegs.*

"You seem positively overrun with Harcourts, save one," Mrs. Aylcock said. "Where *is* the Elusive Lord Everdene?"

A chill ran through Grace and she stiffened her spine. "He was called away on some important business."

"What could be more important than the first event his bride has hosted?" the woman scoffed.

*People dying…*Grace bit off the words before she could say them out loud. "His lordship has many responsibilities."

"For your sake, I do hope this won't stir up gossip. My son confided that the wagers in Whites' betting book regarding who would trap Everdene into marriage have been amended. They are laying odds regarding how soon he will tire of his bride. Men can be so very wicked!"

Lady Downe frowned at Mrs. Aylcock from a seat on one of the benches, then rose and breezed over with a swish of her deep green skirts. "Truly dedicated Members of Parliament have no time for such trivial pursuits. One never knows when men like Lord Everdene and my husband will be called away to attend concerns of the crown. Committees to serve on, investigations to head. Why, the latest inquiry regarding public health…" She stopped and lay a hand on the Grace's sleeve with such tenderness her throat ached. "Suffice it to say, Lord Everdene is one of the hardest working men in the House of Lords. We will have a lovely evening despite his unfortunate absence tonight, and shall be able to do wonderful things for the school. Now, Mrs. Aylcock, perhaps you had best go to the retiring room. I fear you have spilled a bit of punch on your bodice, and silk stains abominably."

With a sour smile, Lady Downe steered Grace away, while Mrs. Aylcock examined her bodice for spots.

"That woman is a nightmare!" her ladyship huffed as she withdrew coins from her reticule and dropped them in a caroler's outstretched cap. "Pay her no heed. It is obvious to anyone who knows his lordship that marriage agrees with him. I have never seen Lord Everdene smile as much as he has these past months. Not since his mother disappeared. I do not think that the Harcourt children ever recovered from her absence all those years. I knew

Countess Ravenscroft before her disappearance from society. She was as kind and gentle a soul as you ever saw."

"She still is." The countess had remained in the country, doing good works, but Jane was like an echo of her mother, Lucien's gentle sister quietly speaking to a young widow dressed in half-mourning. A group of actors outside Fezziwig's Warehouse invited guests to join a country dance and her ladyship went to join them.

Grace glanced nervously at the clock then paused to take a paper poke filled with treats from one of the street vendors, something about the man drawing her gaze.

His chin was buried in the knitted scarf that swathed his neck, his greatcoat a cheerful bottle green. Fingerless mitts concealed hands that trembled.

His station had been made to look like he was roasting chestnuts. Flames of red and orange silk topped one of the barrels, while the others held refreshments.

One would think the fire was really burning, the way sweat trickled down his temples.

Had he become overly warm? He was standing very near to a brace of streetlamps.

He caught Grace's eye and looked down quickly.

"I fear it is growing far too warm in here to be wearing so many layers of winter clothes," she said. "I am very sorry if you are uncomfortable."

"'Tis not so bad, my lady," he said in a lilting Irish accent. Perhaps that was why he seemed nervous. Few people were willing to hire the Irish, especially with the unrest in the streets.

"If you are feeling ill from the heat, you are welcome to take a few moments outside to cool…" Something in his expression stirred her memory and she regarded him more intently taking in his tip-tilted eyes, the shape of his mouth…

A muscle spasmed at the corner of his eye, and he shuffled his wares, knocking one of the pokes askew. He looked as if he expected her to have him hauled out by the scruff of his neck.

"I am sorry for staring," she said gently, "but you remind me of a drawing I saw. It's of a man we've been searching for. Darragh Nolan."

He jerked his head back an inch, the scarf slipping, revealing a crescent shaped scar on his chin. She gasped in wonder, seeing the truth flare in the man's eyes. "It *is* you, Darragh Nolan!"

At that moment, she heard a familiar voice from the far side of the room. Her heart leapt with relief.

Lucien stood at the door, still wearing his greatcoat. His hair was mussed, sharp cheeks red from cold. Beloved. Safe. He clapped his hands, as ever, taking command of the space. "Forgive my tardiness," he announced. "I have arranged a surprise for my wife. We will withdraw to the back garden at once. All of you. Guests, performers and staff as well. This will be an exhibition you will never forget."

Grace's heart thrilled and a wave of excitement rippled through the crowd. People began walking out the door.

She was moving between Darragh and the display just as his hand shot out toward the pole of the faux streetlamp. She lunged instinctively, jarring the barrels themselves as she caught the falling post before the glass lamp could crash down and shatter atop them.

"Oh, dear! That could have been—" She froze as stared at the barrel top. The silk flames had slid aside, revealing a sprinkling of dark powder and a coil of fuse disappearing into a knot hole. Grace gasped, looking up in horror. Nolan's eyes widened, white-rimmed, almost mad. Terror clutched at her chest.

In a heartbeat his arm snaked around her, pinning her arms to her sides. He dragged her against him, his muscles ropy cords made even stronger by his desperation.

She struggled to get free, oversetting a small barrel. Black powder spilled at their feet. She jolted him backwards, then realized her mistake. He reached through one of the false windows, grasping a branch of candles with his other hand.

"Don't do this!" she pleaded. "Darragh, we've been searching for you. Want to help you. You and Sibby Rose and Moira."

His gaze held hers, tortured in the light of the flickering flame.

"No one can help me now."

CHAPTER 36

*I*t was taking far too long to reach Raven's Court, every beat of horse's hooves like a death knell. The fury and fear in Lucien's gut magnified from the moment he heard Simon's shout in the crowded London street, glimpsed his glistening Turkoman horse approaching. He'd entrusted his brother with one task, to guard Grace tonight. And Simon had left her—and everyone they loved most—in the townhouse with a man bent on murder.

He'd never forget the horror on Simon's face when he had roared out the truth. The pair pushing their mounts to the limit, eyes fixed in the direction of Raven's Court, dreading the sound of an explosion, the orange red stain of fire against the night dark sky.

At the gate, Lucien dismounted, the guards rushing toward their lathered horses.

"Nolan is here with a bomb," he warned. "After my announcement, move people outside as quickly and calmly as you are able. We don't dare alarm Nolan. It might spur him to ignite whatever hellish device he's smuggled in."

"*If* he managed to get past all of the safeguards we put in place," MacLeod averred. Lucien felt a slight bit of hope, but his gut told him differently. They had been guarding against rabble from the streets. If what O'Malley had said was true, whoever had planned this, had access to ton society. Could be anyone he'd seen across a ballroom or in the halls of parliament.

Simon raced inside, bound for the nursery to fetch Kit. Now, the other men fanned out to sweep the premises, searching for Nolan and evacuating the household staff and guests.

Lucien fought to keep the fear from his voice as he drew the crowd's attention. "…withdraw to the back garden at once…an exhibition you will never forget."

He heard a murmur of confusion, some faint protest that it was December…yet no one dared question him in his own home, thank God. Grateful for the power the Harcourt name could wield, he made his way through the crowd flowing out the door to the entertainment that didn't exist.

Lucien felt a jolt of relief to see MacLeod was with Cassandra, Jane and Penelope, something fierce and unreadable in the Scotsman's face as he grasped Cassandra's arm.

But where was Grace?

Lucien scanned the room, his gaze suddenly arrested by two figures beneath one of the street lamps. Lucien's blood froze. Grace was caught in the man's arm, a branch of candles wavering in his other hand. Something dark had spilled from an overturned barrel and spread in a pool beneath her skirts. Gunpowder.

He heard a soft oath from nearby guards looking in the same direction and saw them grope for their pistols.

If they fired, they could hit Grace or the candlestick would fall, setting gunpowder ablaze.

If Lucien moved closer, Nolan could well ignite the bomb. But he had to try to dissuade him. "Leave us," Lucien ordered, pulling out the crumpled sketch.

"But, my lord—"

"I said, *leave us.*"

Grace's gaze clung to his, her whole body trembling. Lucien held out the crumpled sketch, his hands, palms up, as he walked toward where Grace stood.

"Darragh Nolan. I've just come from Moira on Little White Lion Street. This is you, isn't it?" He held out the sketch, saw Nolan's eyes dart to the familiar drawing, a muscle jumped at the side of the Irishman's eye.

"N—No. I don't know who you are talking about."

"The children were frightened after the row between you and O'Malley. Sibby Rose and Robert and little Darragh. Scrap, the children call him. Scrap has grown a fair bit since you left to look for work. And Sibby Rose…she is going to be a beauty like your wife."

Nolan paled even further, the branch of candles in his hand shaking. Jesus, God don't let one of those candles fall.

"That red ribbon Sibby Rose loves? Did you see it in her hair?"

Had the man been sane enough to see anything?

"My wife gave that to your little girl. We came across Sibby and Scrap on Bond Street when we were shopping one day. He'd climbed too high and couldn't get down. Sibby told us that when you came home you had promised to bring her a ribbon."

Nolan's face contorted with pain.

"I hope one day I can bring my daughter a ribbon, too," Lucien said, suddenly knowing how desperately that was true. "You see, I just found out that I am going to be a father. Scares the hell out of me, to be honest. But I know I would do anything to protect my wife and babe. Even if it meant burning the world down…But then my child would have to live in the wreckage."

"They've been living in hell already! Now Moira and the babes will never have to worry again with the coin the swells gave us." The resolve in the man's face made sweat dampen Lucien's palms. He held Nolan's gaze, not daring to shift to Grace or the candles, as if by will alone he could stay that shaking hand.

"Do you really trust these men to keep their word?" Lucien asked. "Don't be a weapon in the hands of rich men who want to crush families like yours."

"I failed Moira and the babes. They made sure Moira has enough to make a fresh start. They swore—"

"Those men are liars. They'll do whatever they must to get what they want. I know, because my father is one of them. And once, so was I." The admission cracked something deep inside him.

"There is no way out," Nolan said. "Not for me."

Lucien looked at him, knowing he had to tell the truth.

"Maybe not for you. But there *is* a way forward for Sibby Rose. For Scrap and Robert and Moira."

"That is what you are willing to sacrifice yourself for, is it not?"

Grace said. She tried to turn to look at Nolan. The candles wavered.

Lucien fought to keep his voice steady. "I have seen what your family goes through. I know how wrong it is. My wife showed me…" His gaze flashed to Grace, his heart hammering in his chest. "Knowing Grace and Sibby Rose and Scrap…changed me. I understand that you don't want to hurt people, Nolan. You just want your family cared for."

"After today, I won't be there to look out for them anymore. No matter what I do, the magistrates will take me or I'll die."

"Surrender, and you will be sent away, true. But the person or people who put you up to this—they are the guilty ones. I swear on my wife's love that I will hunt them down and I won't let your children pay for mistakes you made."

"Why should I believe you?"

"I've made mistakes myself. I'd give anything to change them. I don't know what will happen to you. But I will hire the finest barrister I know to be beside you every step of way. I will move your family to my estate Everdene. If you are released, I'll have a job waiting for you."

"Sure, an' a pot o' gold as well."

"Not a pot of gold. An honest living."

"Why would you do this for me?"

"Because I've been where you are, used by someone else as a tool for his evil. I know you are trying protect the people you love the only way you know how. At the time, I believed that, too. But people I love paid a terrible price I couldn't fathom until it was too late."

Nolan was listening.

"Do you really think whoever is behind this will let your family live once you've done their bidding? They want you dead, Nolan, then they'll murder Moira and the children to wipe out any proof that powerful men were involved in this plot. Those men will silence Moira and the children forever to keep such treachery from coming to light."

He could see the truth bury itself in Nolan like a sword thrust.

"Help me help you," Lucien pleaded. "Tell me who these men

were who hired you. Who is threatening my family and intends to destroy yours. I will stop them."

Nolan's hand was shaking even worse now, threatening to topple the candelabra over into the black powder at Grace's feet. Lucien gauged the time it would take to launch himself at Nolan, knock him backward, but the barrels blocked his path. The chance that the candelabra would fall and the candles roll was too great.

"If nothing else, let my wife go," Lucien's voice broke. "My death alone would be enough to ignite whatever outrage those men are seeking. Grace has done nothing but try to help your children."

Grace's green eyes held his. "I won't leave you. No more than Moira would leave Darragh."

"Grace, for the love of God—"

"You and my husband are more alike than you know, Darragh," Grace said. "Forced by a ruthless man to make an impossible choice. Lucien was only a boy when it happened, but he believed his choice damned him for all time. I saw who he was inside, a good man. A man worthy of loving, of the kind of loyalty that kept Moira waiting for you for two years. In the end, here and now, it is up to you to decide. Who are you? A man someone else can use as a weapon? Or are you the man your family has been waiting for?"

Nolan's grip on Grace loosened, and he turned to the side, his whole body seeming to sag. Lucien watched the hand that had gripped the base of the candelabra sink a few inches, feared it would tip. Slowly, carefully, Grace turned to face Nolan. She reached out her hand, and Lucien saw all of the goodness, honesty, and compassion shining in her face as she waited. That expression that made even the wildest, most feral people dare to trust...

People like himself, Lucien thought.

Gently, Nolan placed the candlestick in her hands. The man's face convulsed, and he crumpled to the floor, a sob tearing from his chest.

Grace held so still, Lucien's woman of light. The gilt-painted stars glowed around her as Lucien went to her, curving his fingers around the candlestick's silver base over hers to steady it. The moment seemed to stretch into eternity. Gazing into her eyes he crushed each flame with his other hand.

CHAPTER 37

The guests were gone, the first entertainment at Everdene Hall having provided the ton with more fodder for gossip than anyone could imagine. The barrels of gunpowder had been safely removed and the premises searched for any more signs of danger, but every nerve in Lucien's body was still buzzing with the memory of the disaster they'd missed by one stray spark.

He wanted nothing more than to gather Grace in his arms. Assure himself that she was safe. Comfort himself by feeling her body pressed against his. Instead, he had directed Simon to gather the Harcourt women and try to calm their nerves. He remained with Darragh Nolan.

He looked across the study to where the Irishman sat on a chair, his face buried in his hands as he waited for the magistrates to arrive. Lucien had told Simon and the others that he hoped to learn who was behind the plot. But the truth wasn't that simple.

There was something about Darragh Nolan that hooked a claw in Lucien's chest. He knew that echoing silence of regret. Being alone with the horror as he faced the consequences of something he had done.

That sensation had crashed over him in a wave at the London docks on the day Cassandra and Jane returned from Italy.

Now, he could barely recognize himself, the man who had made an excuse and fled before they set foot on dry land.

But God, he remembered that barren wasteland he'd felt inside.

"I will engage a barrister on your behalf," he promised. "Tell me who is behind this so we can help you," he asked again, with little hope Nolan would answer.

The man did not raise his head. They sat silent. Lucien wasn't sure for how long. When they heard movement and voices outside the door, Nolan stiffened. *Waiting for the ax to fall*, Lucien thought.

When, at last, a soft rap sounded on the door, Nolan's eyes went wide. Lucien stood and crossed to the door, opened it. Guards still stood at attention outside the room, but it was Jamie MacLeod who whispered something in his ear. Lucien nodded.

"Show them in," he said, then turned. He saw Nolan's Adam's apple jump. "It seems someone followed you from Seven Dials," he said.

There was a rush of footsteps, a clamor of voices and Moira rushed in, flinging herself to her knees before her husband, clutching his hands. Robert marched after her with a scowl, looking far too old for his age. But it was the woman who followed them that held Lucien's very heart: Grace, leading a child by each hand. Sibby Rose, pale and shy. Scrap…his face tear-streaked and grimy. His cherry-red nose running.

The child's eyes went saucer wide.

"Dado!" he cried pulling free of Grace.

But instead of running to Nolan, Scrap launched himself at Lucien, wrapping thin arms around Lucien's legs, burying his damp face against Lucien's trousers.

Lucien could feel the boy sobbing, reminding him of Simon that awful night decades past.

Robert Nolan snorted in disgust. "Daft nodcock! How many times do we ha' to tell ye he's not your da!"

Something about the words drove deep into Lucien's chest. He paused for a moment, then scooped Scrap up into his arms, feeling the child's slight weight, the way his body trembled. Scrap hid his face against Lucien's shoulder.

"Ho, there, little man," Lucien murmured soothingly, Scrap's coppery curls brushing his jaw.

"Fwightened!" the boy sniffled.

A wave of protectiveness swept over Lucien as he rubbed the

child's back, every rib and vertebrae a bump beneath his hand. "There is nothing to fear. Not anymore."

He saw Darragh Nolan's face twist, anguished. Thought of his own failings, how close he'd come to denying Grace and the child to come. Angry as Lucien was at the danger Nolan had put them in, he understood the choice the man had made. Even the choice Moira had made, keeping silent in an effort to protect the husband she loved.

He looked at Grace. She had gathered Sibby Rose close, those hands that would one day comfort Lucien's child curved around the little girl's shoulder. Grace, who saw the world so clearly and yet, still was brave enough to love. She knew that he would make countless mistakes as a husband and father. But he would make amends. They would forgive him, and he would forgive himself. That was the price to be paid for this almost unbearable closeness, this wonder, this awe.

Lucien hunkered down with Scrap in his arms, gently setting the child on his small feet. "I will see that you are safe, Scrap. You, Sibby Rose, Robert and your mother. But I am not your father." He took Scrap's hand and led him to the man who sat, quaking with emotion. "This is your da. His first name is Darragh, just like yours."

The child popped his thumb in his mouth, regarding Nolan shyly. With his other hand, he gripped Lucien's fingers with all his might.

"Can you say hello?"

Scrap looked from Nolan to Lucien, then back to Nolan again. The boy pulled his thumb from pink lips and said, "'Lo."

"Y-you were just a babe when I left. Look at you..." Nolan reached out a hand to touch the boy, but Scrap shrank away.

"Give him time," Lucien said.

The Irishman looked up, desolate, and Lucien felt his pain. "Time is the one thing I haven't got," Nolan replied.

Another rap on the door, and MacLeod cracked it open. "My lord, the magistrates have come."

"Post a guard at the windows and door and tell the magistrates to wait in the ballroom. I will speak to them directly." Lucien turned to the Nolans. "We will give you this hour. Be wise."

"I swear it." Nolan nodded and looked up at him. "Thank you."

Lucien was almost to the door when he heard Nolan speak.

"Lord Everdene."

"Yes?"

"I will tell you who paid me."

The information electrified Lucien, a lightning strike of murderous rage, but he kept his voice level. "Do you have any proof?"

"He's the one who gave me the lady's tin soldier. It was at the Swan and Thistle. Roger, the barkeep, saw it, along with the barmaid, his daughter. She heard enough to ask me about it after. There was also a hack driver at the next table getting bubble an' squeak."

"Was there anything else you overheard? Anything that might help bring the bastard to justice?"

"Overheard 'm mention one other toff when they were arguing. I never saw 'm or heard a name."

"Is there anything more?"

"No."

"If you think of something…"

"I will send word."

Lucien feathered his fingers over Scrap's curls, then smiled at Sibby Rose and touched her cheek. With one last look at the family, he walked over to Grace and took her hand, leading her away.

The minute he was able, he drew her into a room, gathered her into his arms. "I almost lost you. You and the baby."

"You didn't. You never will."

"So…now we know."

Grace nodded. "I feared there must be some connection to the Pinchbecks, as soon as I realized the kegs held gunpowder. And the night of the riot at Drury Lane…Alice invited me, then made her own excuses."

A haunted aura shadowed Grace's face. "Do you think Alice knew?"

"I don't know, but I *will* find out. I intend to go to Pinchbeck's soiree and return the barrels he sent."

No footman in England would dare to refuse entry to Viscount Everdene and his brother, and tonight was no exception. Oh, they gawked at the Harcourts' sudden appearance and the strangeness of a keg balanced on Captain Harcourt's strong shoulder. One startled fellow attempted to announce them, but Lucien and Simon merely stalked into the Pinchbeck ballroom like an invading army.

The chamber was filled with guests of the highest importance. Men from the House of Lords rubbed shoulders with wealthy industrialists and their wives, along with a glittering array of Torys. But it was members from the Home Office that held Lucien's gaze. The perfect witnesses…

The music being played trailed off, the violin's strings screeching. Everyone in the room spun around to regard the new arrivals with blatant curiosity. Lucien gave a hard smile at his reflection in the mirror, the ever-impeccably turned out Viscount, looked as if he had been through a war. His evening blacks were mud-spattered, his cravat wilted and askew. His hair tumbled across his forehead and he'd torn off his gloves at some point. Mouths gaped open, hands pressed to breasts. But no one looked more gratifyingly stunned than Lord and Lady Pinchbeck and Neville Freyne.

"Lord Everdene?" Pinchbeck's jowls quivered as he left off speaking to the Home Secretary. "What is the meaning of this?"

"A bit of a shock to see me, Pinchbeck?" Lucien boomed in the voice that could hold all of parliament captive. "You are staring as if I've come back from the dead."

"Of course I am surprised. I understood that you were having an event of your own tonight. Is there some news from the continent? Some disaster you bring tidings of?"

"Were you expecting one?"

"See here. Whatever you have to say, spit it out."

"Permit me to return one of the kegs you had delivered to Raven's Court as decorations for my wife's charity event."

Simon swung the barrel down to the floor, setting it on end.

"The contents are untouched, as you must have surmised."

Pinchbeck waved one hand in dismissal. "Leave it in the stables. Whatever you are on about, it can wait until tomorrow. We are celebrating my daughter's betrothal. I'll not have the night spoiled."

"Betrothal?"

Alice blushed prettily and extended a hand with a large ring. "To Father's partner. Mr. Freyne."

"My condolences," Lucien said, then looked at Freyne who stood across the room, his eyes fixed on the barrel. "Planning to celebrate with fireworks, were you?"

The girl's worried voice cut in. "Lord Everdene, was there a problem with the barrels?"

"You might say so. Come and take a look inside." When Lucien signaled to Simon, his brother took out the pry bar thrust in his belt, using it to open the keg's lid.

"Alice, come here," her father said. "We will not indulge Everdene's nonsense—"

"The circumstances merit close inspection, Lady Alice," Lucien said smoothly. "Bring that candle from the table."

She grasped the nearest candlestick and came toward him. "My lord, I assure you, I was only trying to help your wife. I felt sorry for the way my mother behaved."

Lucien reached in to the barrel and brought up a handful of black powdery substance. He let it sift through his fingers.

The girl looked genuinely bewildered as she drew closer. "I don't understand…The barrels were empty when Neville and I chose them."

Five steps nearer. Six.

"Alice!" Freyne's voice. The man's face gleamed with sweat.

"Neville, I must make this right," Alice insisted drawing nearer. "Grace is my friend, and—"

"No!" White-faced, Freyne snatched the candle from her hand, blew it out.

Lucien saw the Home Secretary's keen eyes on the proceedings. "What the devil is going on here?"

"The keg was full of gunpowder—"

Guests gasped, shrank back.

"—as Mr. Freyne and the Lord Pinchbeck obviously knew. This, and two other kegs were placed as props for tableaux in the ballroom of my townhouse. They were delivered to Raven's Court courtesy of my wife's supposed friend, Lady Alice Pinchbeck. The others were so large, it seemed excessive to carry them here.

However, they will be available for Lord Russell and the members of his Home Office to examine at will. Mr. Freyne coerced a desperate man to set off an explosion tonight at the charity event my wife was hosting. His goal, to murder everyone gathered at Raven's Court."

"What the devil?" Russell strode up to examine the keg and its contents.

"You needn't fear," Simon said. "We emptied the powder in this keg and replaced it with coal dust before we brought it inside so it wouldn't explode. Unlike Freyne and Pinchbeck and whoever they are in league with, we are averse to spilling innocent blood. But when Nolan was holding a candlestick over this keg at Raven's Court, the powder was very much alive."

Alice stared at him, her face waxen with horror.

"Darragh Nolan, the man Freyne hired, told us everything," Lucien said.

"I've never heard of this Nolan person," Freyne sputtered. "You can't believe some Irish scum scrambling to keep a noose from around his neck!"

Lucien pinned the lying bastard with his glare. "Witnesses saw you engage his services at the Swan and Thistle, Freyne. You gave Nolan a tin soldier wrapped in my wife's handkerchief. The toy was sent to Raven's Court with a threatening note—which I still possess —and I would wager, if someone at the Home Office examined it, they would see similarities to your penmanship. As for the hand-kerchief, it was at the Nolan's home in the Seven Dials."

"What motive could these gentlemen possibly have for such a scheme?" the Home Secretary asked.

"The goal was to trigger another Peterloo. Convince parliament that Nolan and people from the streets were responsible for the attack," Lucien explained, then turned to his adversaries. "Pinchbeck, Freyne, you and your cohorts have been trying to incite riots for months so you could crush people who only wish for fair treat-ment, to feed their families."

Alice looked as sallow as the yellow gown she wore. Her hands knotted in her skirts. "What Lord Everdene says is true, isn't it? That is why Neville insisted I go back to Grace, offer her those specific kegs for her tableaux."

"Alice, be quiet!" Pinchbeck hissed.

"Neville instructed me to have them delivered. Have them put in place by specific footmen. Mother, I heard you attempting to convince Lady Aylcock and other friends not to go to the Harcourt's event. I thought you merely wanted to steal Lady Everdene's guests away. Did you know about this as well? Did you want to kill all of those people?"

"Alice!" her mother gasped.

All around them, disgust and horror flooded the faces of the guests.

Alice's voice broke. "You almost succeeded in it because of me."

Pinchbeck grabbed his daughter's arm, shook her with a violence that stunned the crowd. "Don't be a fool, girl!"

"Get your hands off of her!" Lucien lunged for the man, ripping Pinchbeck's hand away from Alice and thrusting the girl behind his broad shoulders. "By God, you'll not touch her again!"

Alice turned to Lucien, tears streaming down her cheeks. "I didn't know. Tell Grace…"

The Home Secretary met Lucien's gaze. "You'll present this proof you have, Everdene?"

"A full confession from Nolan and corroborating witnesses, not to mention Lady Alice's words here. The man they paid to set off the explosion was fired from Pinchbeck's factory. They knew he was desperate to feed his family. Offered him a choice. They would dismiss his wife and son from their factory jobs, have his family thrown out of their lodgings to starve in the streets or Nolan could die setting off this bomb and they'd pay enough to keep his children in comfort for the rest of their lives. If presented with such a choice, which man among you would choose differently?"

"You're excusing violence?" the Home Secretary huffed.

"No. I'm laying blame where the fault lies. I'm saying that there, but for an accident of birth, go any of us."

The Home Secretary gestured to some nearby men.

They came forward, taking Pinchbeck and Freyne by the arms. The two men stood rigid.

Lucien walked up to Freyne. "You were willing to kill a woman you supposedly once loved."

"She would have been the perfect hostess, get me into any drawing room in the land. An asset I refused to lose."

"So you were willing to condemn her to suffer a horrific death because you couldn't use her to gain power."

"She was *mine*," Freyne snarled.

Bile rose in Lucien's throat. "She was never some possession to be used or discarded for your own selfish purpose. She has the right to chart her own path."

"A woman?" Freyne scoffed.

"Yes. A woman. Workers in your factories. The slaves that pick your goddamned cotton. You believe the whole damned world is meant to be crushed under your heel. You destroyed the Nolans' lives, and God knows how many others. I would like nothing more than to kill you with my bare hands, but I won't. I will let the courts have you now. You'll pay if there is any justice in England." His jaw knotted with resolve. "I swear to *God*, I'll spend the rest of my life making damned sure there is."

CHAPTER 38

Raven's Court was silent by the time Lucien and Simon returned. Lucien was mind-numbingly weary, and was certain his brother felt the same after the race through London's wintery streets and the confrontation at Pinchbeck's. The guard at the door informed them that magistrates had escorted Darragh Nolan to Newgate, and Lady Everdene had settled Moira and the Nolan children into rooms until they could be taken to Everdene.

"A Mr. O'Malley arrived an hour ago," the footman continued. "Her ladyship tended his wounds, then settled him in one of the bedchambers."

Lucien's throat felt tight. O'Malley had saved the lives of every guest at Raven's Court. He owed the Irishman more than he could ever repay. Lucien vowed to sit down with the man and the leaders of his movement, and listen to what they had to say. Hadn't Grace urged him to do the same thing before this night's treachery?

But there would be time for that tomorrow. Tonight, he needed to find his wife and hold her as if he would never let her go.

Lucien and Simon mounted the stairs, talking in low murmurs, Simon veering off toward his bedchamber to find Penelope who had taken Kit there as well, refusing to let the boy out of her sight.

He heard a muffled voice from his own bedchamber, someone calling his name. Cassandra. Despite his eagerness to find Grace, something in his sister's voice drew him. Something small. Something lost.

He entered the bedchamber, finding her sitting on the floor, her skirts pooled around her, the wooden chest where Lucien kept his most precious mementos open beside her. His heart lurched. The blue tin box was open on her lap, her long, slender fingers holding the ragged bit of cloth that box had contained for almost twenty years.

He dragged a hand over his face. He'd been dreading this moment for decades. Knew it would be like hauling himself over hot coals. He couldn't do this now. He needed Grace in his arms, needed to assure himself she was safe…

But Cassandra raised her gaze to his and what he saw there rooted him to the spot.

"You know I never could wait for surprises," she said. "When you mentioned this box, before you rode out for Seven Dials, I had to know what was in it."

She lifted the ragged cloth, running her fingers over what remained of embroidered pansies. "It's the bit of the blanket I loved so much as a child." Her eyes glistened and Lucien felt the regrets of a lifetime roll over him.

I can't talk about this now…I'm too damned tired, still too shaken… The words were on the tip of his tongue, but she looked vulnerable in a way he'd never seen before. His throat caught.

"However did you come by it?" she asked. "No one even knew I still had the scrap."

Fierce Cassandra, suddenly tender and easily bruised. He'd wounded her so many times in the past. She deserved this truth now. "I found it, snagged on a shrub, the day after you tried to run away. I thought you were coming back, then, so I hid it from Father."

"I'd stashed it in my pocket. After the servants caught me, it was gone. I was sure I'd lost it forever." She set the box aside and rose to her feet, peering down at the bit of cloth. "It's not the first time you saved this for me. You were the one who suggested I cut a strip from my blanket before Father burned it."

"Because I'd never forgotten how you lay your blanket over me when we had the measles. And…mother embroidered it for you."

His lips curled and he wanted to tease even a hint of smile from her. "I was boiling hot, you know. And it made me itch."

Cassandra gave a watery chuckle. "Even when we tried to help each other, we never got it quite right, did we?"

He sobered. "I should have sent it to you in Italy once I realized you would not be coming home, but I found that I couldn't part with it."

"Why not?" she asked, her gaze searching his face.

"Because…it was the only piece of you I had left." Had he admitted that before? Even to himself?

She stared at the embroidery, her eyes shimmering in the firelight. "Oh, Lucien," she breathed, then finally looked up at him. "When did we lose each other?"

"*We* didn't," Lucien said. "It was father. *He* drove a wedge between us on purpose." And so the earl had, forcing them apart with his words, lies, actions, both praise and scorn. "I just didn't recognize what was happening until…"

"It was too late…?"

He nodded, surprised by the guilt that laced her voice as well. "I never stopped thinking about you," he confessed. "Wishing I'd done something different. If I could go back to that night father took you away, I would." The memory of what happened came crashing back, the screams, the crying, the desperate pleas. "I didn't know Father planned to send you to Thornsby. He was quite the expert at making people believe his lies. I thought I was saving you from—"

"From what?"

"I don't even know. I just thought I was doing the right thing. For you, for mother…I swear I had no idea what Father planned. By the time I discovered what had really happened, I was so ashamed of my part in it, I couldn't face myself in the mirror, let alone look you or Jane in the eye."

Silence fell between them, and he saw his own desolation echoed in Cassandra's eyes. Of anyone, she could understand the dark web they'd been trapped in.

What he didn't expect was her sudden show of support. "We were both victims of the earl's machinations. As such, we both took on the task of shielding our younger siblings. I, with Jane, and you with Simon."

He twisted the signet ring on his finger, speaking in hushed tones. "Do you know, I went to the docks with Mother and Simon, the day you arrived in London? But at the last minute, I made an excuse. Claimed some business for the Crown. And left to supposedly see an ambassador newly arrived."

"You *are* a very important man." There was a note in her voice that was almost teasing, the way they'd done once upon a time.

"But a coward, to be sure. I watched you and Jane from the window in the Custom's House. You were wearing a pale-blue frock and a scarlet cloak. Your bonnet had cream colored streamers, and it almost blew away. Simon caught it."

"Spying?"

Was that actually a smile on his sister's face? Deciding it was, he continued, "You deserved to enjoy your reunion. Being the last person you'd wish to see, I would only have cast a shadow over your homecoming. Considering your reaction when we did meet, I was right."

"Father did this. Set us against each other. Lied to us…" Her face darkened. "I hate him. I wish he would die."

Lucien winced at the fierceness in her voice. "Father said that the painting of Holofernes was a warning to me as well."

"That was before I saw…how far you were willing to go to make amends." She moved toward him. "Your vow not to live at Everdene Hall could have destroyed your marriage. And even then, I think you loved Grace."

"Who could help it?" Lucien said.

"You want to make things right between us?"

"Yes."

"Take Grace to Everdene Hall. Be *happy*, Lucien. Be the father we never had."

He swallowed hard, reaching for a life he could never have imagined. A sweetness that humbled him. Awed him. "I will," he vowed. "Please tell me you will stay at Everdene, too."

"I don't know. I have been angry for so long. What will be left of me after that is gone?"

He wanted to sooth her with a hug, but they had never been that sort…Instead, he squeezed her hand, the scrap of their childhood between them. He felt it slip through his fingers as she disappeared out his door.

GRACE FELT A POIGNANT STING AS SHE SETTLED THE NOLAN children in the nursery Lucien and his siblings had once shared. The four little beds lined up in military precision, the shelves of toys untouched for twenty years.

Tonight, a whirlwind of activity had transformed the room, Penelope, Cassandra and Jane joining Grace in wrestling filthy clothes off little bodies and scrubbing skin that hadn't seen a bathtub in months—if ever.

Finished at last, maids hauled off the tub and the children's clothes to be laundered, while her sisters-in-law retired to their own rooms.

Grace lingered, grateful for any distraction that kept her from obsessing over what was happening at the Pinchbecks' soiree. Sibby Rose and Scrap bounced from wonder to wonder like India rubber balls, awed by dolls in exquisite dresses, a Noah's ark and stuffed animals.

Grace could hardly blame them for having a hard time calming down after what they'd witnessed tonight. Her own nerves were stretched just as tight.

"Perhaps you could choose something from the shelf to help you sleep," Grace suggested, and Sibby Rose raced to pick up a doll, while Scrap hugged a stuffed dog.

She looked at Robert, but the boy scowled with affronted dignity.

"Don't need some baby toy t' go t' sleep," he declared and Grace felt a sudden wave of loneliness. He reminded her of Avery.

"Well, if you change your mind later..." She let her voice trail off.

"Only thing *I* need," Robert grumbled, "is one night free from bein' poked by pointy elbows an' daft buggers puttin' cold feet on me."

"Aren't you in luck, then?" Grace suppressed a smile as she tucked each little Nolan into their own bed and watched them fling their arms and legs wide. "Now I must go check to see if there is any word from Lord Everdene," she said, her heart racing. "I promise to come back as soon as I can," she said, gently untangling Scrap's fingers.

"Don't go," Sibby pleaded, and Scrap grabbed a handful of Grace's skirt.

"Better stay," Robert said, his voice wavering just a little. "For the wee'uns."

Grace hesitated, feeling torn. "Shall I leave the lamp burning? My brothers always liked that best."

Robert rose up on his elbow, looking at her with interest. "You have brothers?"

"Four. And I miss them terribly," she confessed, wondering when she'd see them again. She wanted nothing more than to go downstairs, wait for Lucien's return. But she took a deep breath and turned back to the children. "Shall I tell you the story of when they put a toad in my stepmother's sugar bowl?" she asked Robert.

He nodded, and the other two scurried from their beds into his, Sibby saying, "It's how our ma tells us stories." They snuggled in on either side of their big brother, all three watching her as she began.

"Once upon a time there was a toad named Trevor..." She didn't even make it to the ladies' shrieks, when all three Nolan children drifted off to sleep.

***

GRACE TIPTOED OUT OF THE ROOM, THINKING OF LUCIEN, SIMON, Jane and Cassandra, innocent and vulnerable as her own brothers, but at the mercy of the cruel Earl of Ravenscroft.

They'd survived so much—the Harcourt siblings—yet there was so much healing to be done. Especially between Cassandra and Lucien.

"Please God, give them the chance...," she whispered, picturing Lucien in Pinchbeck's townhouse. Simon is with him, she told herself. Other men were as well. But Pinchbeck and Freyne had shown themselves ruthless enough to stoop to any evil.

Just one well-aimed pistol shot...She bit her lip, aware just how fragile life was.

She pressed her fingertips to her lips, tears trickling from her eyes when she heard the low rumble of a voice behind her. "Grace."

She stifled a cry with her hand, spun and saw Lucien hastening toward her. In a heartbeat she was in his arms. "You're back…safe. Oh, thank God!" she whispered. "I kept imagining the most awful things. Those men would stop at nothing to silence you."

"They would hardly shoot me in the middle of a soiree, my love," he murmured into her hair. "It would have been considered very bad ton."

Was he smiling? She could feel it against the side of her face.

"It is over," he soothed.

She felt tears burning in her eyes, the stress of the night, the fear finally overwhelming her.

"We managed to set off an explosion of a different sort at Pinchbeck's soiree. Freyne and Pinchbeck are in custody We have witnesses to testify against them. Lord Russell was there from the Home Office. Moreover, your friend, Alice put the final nail into the case, in front of half of London, telling how Freyne had used her to get the kegs into the ballroom. She knew nothing of the explosives."

"Poor Alice. How could he have done such a thing to her?"

"They were announcing their betrothal tonight. But that is a conversation best left for later." Lucien hesitated, looking at the nursery door. "Who have you tucked in the nursery?"

"Sibby Rose and her brothers." Grace felt a momentary shyness. "I hope it is all right that I put them here. Penelope is keeping little Kit with her and after all the Nolan children have been through, I thought…such a cheery room might comfort them."

He drew back, cupping her face in his broad palms. "It's perfect. But then, you always do know how to make people feel safe. It is a gift, Grace. Greater than you will ever know. Will I wake them?"

"No."

He opened the door and slipped inside. "But why are they all in one bed?"

"At first, they were thrilled to have their own beds, but then… when I was telling them a story, they cuddled together like puppies. I think they sleep better, holding on to each other."

A child softly moaned, and Robert thrashed a bit. One long,

scabbed leg thrust out from under the coverlet, pale white in the light of the candle she'd left burning. Lucien released her and crossed to the child's side. Grace's throat felt tight at the poignant expression on his face as he lifted Robert's small leg back onto the mattress.

"I spoke to Cassandra before I came to find you," he said, smoothing the blanket over the boy. "I think we have made peace at last."

"Truly?"

"Do you remember the tin box? The blue one you saw?"

She nodded.

"I will tell you about it sometime. But for now..." His hand curled around her fingers, so warm and strong as he led her from the room. "What matters is that I can keep my promise to you," he said. "We can go home to Everdene Hall. Our child can grow up running the same green fields we did. You can be close to your brothers as you hoped."

"Oh, Lucien!" She blinked back tears, her happiness almost too great to hold.

He drew her down the stairs to their own bedchamber, the room where they'd shared so much passion. Once the door was closed, he faced her. She needed to reassure herself that he was safe, that he was well, that he was hers. She ran her fingertips over his face, the bristles of his beard darkening his strong jaw, his mask of cool restraint gone. "You're sure you're not hurt?"

"I'm fine."

"Well, I'm not. I worried about you every second you were gone. It's bad enough that Pinchbeck was involved. I can't believe that Neville was part of this."

"I can't even imagine how horrible Alice must feel. Why would he do this? And single you out? It's all so very strange."

"Not so strange. If he was to succeed in his plan to start a war against the reformers, he needed to convince his peers that the danger was real. And what better target than the man who stole the woman he wanted?"

"But he didn't want me. He was the one who jilted me."

"He'd secured the cotton resources with his American wife. After she conveniently died, he saw you as the perfect match. With

Lady Barbara Elliot's daughter on his arm, he would have access to the most powerful men in the land."

"Where I would have decried everything he stands for! Enslaved people and children in his factories."

Pride shone in Lucien's smile. "If he believed for an instant he doused the fire in my fierce crusader just because she wears a bonnet, he was a fool."

"I'm not sure how you managed not to throttle the man right there, and save the Crown the trouble of hanging him!"

"The thought crossed my mind. But I had something far more pressing to do," he insisted, his voice rough with emotion. "Get home to the woman I love." He pressed his cheek to hers, and she felt a tremor go through him. "The day you came back into my life was the day I began to awaken. I didn't want to. I fought it. I'd spent so much of my life concealing who I was, any tenderness or weakness. Even when I began to love you, I resisted the truth."

"What truth?" she asked softly.

"In my haste to put you between my shoulder and my shield, protect you from any pain or danger, I didn't realize that *I* was the one locked in a tower of my own making and you held the key. You were—*are* my north star." He took her hand in his, looked down at her, his heart in his eyes. "I'm not a man who trusts easily. But I love you, Grace. Until my last breath, I will be yours. And you…my beautiful, brave love. Will you be my countess of stars? The light that leads me home."

EPILOGUE

verdene Hall, all decked out for Christmas, devolved into utter chaos. From the moment Grace's younger brothers rushed in like a hurricane, the air seemed to sizzle with excitement. The three lads nearly bowled their sister over in their enthusiasm, all talking at once. Lucien couldn't understand a word they said—and God knew, he couldn't get anywhere near his wife—but he saw the dull metal figure in her hand as she returned Lord Admiral Nelson to little Bennet. Saw Avery and Ethan puff up with pride as Grace marveled at how they had grown.

Tears sparkled on her lovely cheeks, her face positively aglow. God, she was so beautiful, Lucien marveled, his throat uncomfortably tight.

She looked at him over the children's heads. "Thank you," she mouthed.

He put his hand to his chest, then held it out to her…Moments later, Arkwright—damn him—pushed his way to the center of the cluster of children and placed the last thing this evening needed into Bennet Elliot's arms: A wriggling, face-licking spaniel puppy, doubtless bent on destruction. "This is for Grace," Arkwright told him, with a devilish look in Lucien's direction. "But we'll need you to help take care of the wee fellow whenever you're here."

Lucien started forward, intending to have a sharp word with his friend. Maybe send the animal out to the stable for the duration of the party along with Arkwright's boots to chew for good measure. But Bennet's joy seemed to be bubbling over, filling the manor house that had been grim and empty for so many years.

Lucien looked around, taking it all in. Tables were laden with gifts for the family servants and those who worked on the estate. Lengths of cloth for dresses, shirts and breeches, papers of hair pins, pots and tools waited for adults to claim them. For the children: dolls in pretty dresses, clockwork toys, more tin soldiers and the like. Mountains of bright oranges waited to be peeled, releasing their tart scent to mingle with the gingernuts' spicy fragrance and the taste of boiled sweets.

Leaving Grace to enjoy the reunion, Lucien mingled with the other guests, his gaze tracing back to her again and again as the night progressed. She took his breath away, with her kindness, her warmth as she began distributing the largess to the children with the help of Jane, and Pen.

His mother came to stand beside him. "It is lovely, isn't it? All of us together."

"Yes. Yes it is."

"It's something I feared I would never see."

He smiled down at her. "This has been a year of surprises for all of us."

"Mr. Arkwright tells me that you intend to stand in parliament and speak for the factory workers. Is it true?"

"Yes," he said.

"Your father will be furious beyond imagining if you do this thing. But you will triumph in the end."

"I hope so."

"I am sure of it. You were always so strong. I fear that gift cost you more than you'll ever know." She looked so sad it made Lucien's chest ache.

"I don't understand."

Guilt flooded his mother's eyes. "I knew you would survive no matter what challenges you faced and your father would never release his hold on you. So I let you deal with his tempers, his ruthless schemes when I could not. I threw all my effort into protecting the others, trying to save who I could from your father's machinations."

He heard the echo of his own words to Grace in that square where they'd first met Sibby Rose and Scrap. *You cannot save them all...*

"You blame yourself for what happened to me and to your sisters," his mother said, "but *I* am the one who was fault. *I* was supposed to protect *you*. I should have found a way..."

Her words curled around his heart. Suddenly fresh memories flooded him. Standing a little ways apart, always, watching the others cluster around their mother, laughing and frolicking and free. Knowing, somehow, he was not. It hurt, to hear the truth put into words. And yet he understood.

"I was the one most able to fight back," he said. "I had the best chance."

Tears streamed down her cheeks, and Lucien felt his own eyes burn.

"You think I am tentative around you because of what you did so long ago. That's not the reason. Every time I looked into your eyes, I could see the cost of what I had done...How isolated you have been. When I see you, I know that *I* am the one who failed you, my dear, brave son. I am so sorry."

Had he been waiting his whole life to hear those words? From the moment he'd been a boy, looking over his shoulder as his father pulled him away from the others? "I would not change what happened, except...I thought...there was something about me, something that made me hard...no, impossible to love."

"You cannot believe that any longer. Not when you look into your wife's eyes. And I pray, my darling boy, that you know your place in my heart as well."

"Perhaps we could make a fresh start," Lucien said. "Grace says that is what you must do when you make mistakes. Forgive yourself and begin again."

"Yes. Just so. And when your own child comes, I know you will protect that babe as I was not able to protect you. I know you will love with every fiber of your heart. As I love you."

"I will."

"I only hope someday all my children will heal."

He followed her gaze across the room to where Cassandra stood in a corner with Jamie MacLeod, arguing over God knew what. The Scotsman face's was contorted with anger, his eyes blazing. Cassandra glared back, defiant. Something was flaring between the two. Lucien had noticed it since the night of the charity event in London. God knew, he felt for them both, remembering his own tumultuous passage a few weeks past. He was about to go over and see what was amiss when Cassandra spun away and stormed out. MacLeod slammed his fist into the wall but did not go after her. Before Lucien could do so, Lord Elliot approached.

"May I have a moment?" the older man asked, his face furrowed with concern.

Lucien bit back a groan. He'd not forgiven Grace's father or stepmother for their treatment of her. "Of course."

"Grace told me what happened the night of her charity event," Lord Elliot said, his glasses askew. "You saved the lives of everyone at Raven's Court, then chose to bring the family of the man who intended to kill you to Everdene."

"Yes. And I hired a barrister to take Nolan's case."

"You may very well destroy your political career, championing such people. Your father—"

"I am not my father. I have no intention of shaping my policy to satisfy him."

"I know that now. When you came to court my daughter, I feared the Harcourt ruthlessness." Elliot looked across the room at his daughter, tenderness suffusing his face. "But anyone with eyes can see how happy Grace is now. I regret..."

Elliot's words trailed off. Much as Lucien wanted to blame the man for driving Grace to such desperate measures, she would not be his wife tonight had her father not tried to force her hand elsewhere.

"We both have regrets," Lucien said, "but whatever happened in the past led us here." Lucien offered the old man his hand.

Elliot shook it just as his wife called him over. "You *must* come see this darling puppy, Vernon," Helen said, her red plaid gown pooling about her as she sat on the ground next to Bennet and the squirming dog. "Be gentle. He's very tiny."

"Can't we take him home?" Bennett begged.

Arkwright stood over them, looking at Lucien. "This one is

Grace's. But I have it on good authority there's another just like him, waiting for someone to take care of him."

Bennett looked at Helen, his eyes going wide. "Could we...?"

"I'm afraid puppies and toads do not mix. A pup is likely to eat it."

"I promise no more toads in the house!" The other two boys looked at her, both nodding.

Helen glanced at her husband, her brows raised, waiting for his input.

"Let's hope the dog is better received than the toad," he muttered under his breath. Then, much louder, said, "Why not! It's Christmas."

The boys cheered. Elliot turned back to Lucien, a look of concern in his eye. "I applaud you for the stand you're taking," he said. "Just...have a care. Freyne and Pinchbeck are not alone in their willingness to do anything to maintain the gentry's hold on power. And your father is a most formidable enemy."

As if Lucien didn't know it. He would be even more vigilant now. But that was for later. Tonight, he wanted to revel in this first Christmas with Grace.

Lucien strolled toward her as she stood near the Nolan children, the sight of them with their new toys cheering him. Sibby and Scrap gathered around Bennet's puppy, while Robert Nolan took lessons in swordsmanship from Avery and Ethan. Lucien wondered at the wisdom of arming the boys in a crowd.

Yet he couldn't help but feel pleased at the transformation in the Nolan children. Two weeks at Everdene had worked miracles. They were turned out in new clothes, their cheeks pinkened from time running about in the wintery country air. Moira hung back with the village wives who had taken her under their wing. But even as Jane and his mother distributed yard goods and pretty combs to the women, she still wore that sorrowful, tired expression. Lucien didn't dare tell Moira yet, but the discussions regarding Darragh Nolan's case were taking encouraging turns as he uncovered threats Freyne had made and called in favors from the most powerful men in the kingdom.

He smiled as he heard Sibby Rose pipe up.

"We got a house for Christmas," she told Bennet as she stroked the spaniel's silky ears. "You should see it! Me an' Scrap sneaked outside at night an' you never saw so many stars in the sky!"

"My mama is a star," Bennet said softly.

Lucien remembered how Grace had comforted her grieving brothers, pointing up to the heavens.

He felt a pang, thinking of his own sister. Cassandra had not returned after her quarrel with MacLeod. Men now surrounding the stablemaster were enthusing about the Harcourt horses, but for the first time in Lucien's memory, the Scotsman didn't seem to give a damn about the equine bloodline he and Simon had fought so hard to create. If anything, MacLeod looked grimmer than Lucien had ever seen him, the Scotsman glaring again and again at the door through which Cassandra had disappeared.

Lucien understood his sister's reasons for leaving all too well. He'd fled from this kind of family celebration himself until Grace had come into his life.

He stepped up behind her, the blue silk of her skirts brushing against him as he whispered near her ear, "Might I steal my wife away from her adoring throng for just a moment?" He could feel the shiver of awareness that went through her as his breath warmed her neck.

"Always..." She turned back toward him, her face lighting up. "And for much longer than a moment!"

Tonight, he had a special gift to deliver to the woman who had made this day possible. He drew her beneath a kissing ball streaming with ribbons, and she turned her face to him. He wanted nothing more than to kiss her, but his gaze caught on a white bit of fluff from her hair. "Is this supposed to mimic snowfall?" he asked, plucking it off, then showing her.

"Oh, no!" She laughed. "The puppy stole a toy horse from the present table, and I fear the wee rogue was flinging the stuffing in the air."

"Of course, you came to the rescue."

"And mended the tear without anyone being the wiser," she said with a mischievous grin. "Please tell me that's the only stowaway!" She bent her head down for him to examine the glossy brown locks in their sweet chignon.

"You could be covered in it and you'd still be beautiful, you know. Disheveled suits you," he said.

She looked up at him, smiling. "It seems to me that you're stalling. What did you want to steal me away for?"

"I have a gift for you."

"This is gift enough." She waved her hand around the room filled with family and laughter and love. "Everyone I love, here. Especially you."

"Give me your hand," he commanded.

She held them both out with delighted anticipation. He caught her left hand in his then tugged off the betrothal ring.

"Lucien!" she cried in protest as he thrust the ring in his pocket. "Whatever are you doing?"

"I was a pompous arse when I selected that," he said. "I wanted you to wear something imposing. Something that screamed the Harcourt name, told every man in England that you were mine." He stared down at her finger, gliding his thumb over the slender gold band that remained. His voice softened. "I know better now."

He drew a small jeweler's box from the pocket of his coat, then opened it.

Grace stared at the ring pillowed on black velvet, and he loved the gasp that came from her pink lips as she took in the simple pearl glowing soft in the light, a sapphire on each side.

He slipped the ring from its case, then slid it onto her fourth finger. "I had this made just for you," he said.

"It's exquisite." Her face shone with such happiness his heart squeezed. "Like a little moon with stars on each side."

"Exactly what I thought when I described it to the jeweler."

"And here I thought it might be something about grit turning to pearl after being hauled from a lake." Her eyes sparkled as bright as the cut stones. He kissed her knuckles. "I suppose grit turning to pearl is…a fair description of our love. Even then you had begun to chip away the hard shell I wore," he said. Somehow, he realized, Grace had created a love so beautiful, so surprising…that it scarce seemed real. He turned her face up to his, not caring that half the people in the ballroom were staring at them. "The sapphires I chose have meaning as well," he said. "One is for you, my bright star. One for our babe."

"A babe!" The nearby jolting squeal came from Helen Elliot. Puppy forgotten, she jumped up, clasping her hands in delight.

Lord Elliot stood beside her, his voice was rough with emotion as he looked at his daughter. "Oh, my dearest…"

Lucien slid his arm about his wife's waist, and turned to the assembled guests. "It's true," he announced, his voice carrying across the room. "Come May, I will be a father."

Applause broke out, and soon they were crowded by well-wishers. Lucien accepted congratulations, his chest swelling with pride and happiness until suddenly he was aware of the three Bennet boys and the Nolan children pointing and whispering and eyeing him askance.

"You heard our news?" Lucien asked, his arm still about his wife.

"Aye." Robert Nolan's eyebrows arched to his hairline. "But ye a da? Gor'! Scrap likes ye well enough, but ye don't seem very good at babies an' such."

Bennet, puppy in his arms, leaned toward Sibby Rose, with a solemn nod. "Scared my brother so bad Avery bit him once."

"Wasn't scared!" Avery protested.

"Well I was!" Lucien said. "I thought I'd found an alligator under my bed." The two glared at each other in mock outrage. When Avery's mouth stretched into a grin, Lucien laughed. His sides ached with it, joy he'd lost for decades spilling forth…joy he could barely remember feeling before Grace. For a moment, the children gaped at him, then they dissolved into giggles as well.

The villagers stared, his family stunned. But it was Grace who filled Lucien's vision, filled his heart. "You're right," Lucien told the children. "I do have a lot to learn about being a father. Luckily I have Grace to teach me."

Later, Lucien drew her to the window, where the stars spread across the sky.

"You seem to be handling the gathering exceptionally well," she said.

He grinned. "I've little choice. If I wish to be with my wife, it seems I will always be awash in children." He curved one large hand over her belly.

Something moved out in the moonlight, a lone man stalking

toward the stables. Jamie MacLeod. Lucien gestured to the fast-disappearing man.

"Before you, I would have been one step behind him," Lucien said. "Putting as much distance as I could between myself and all of this." He hesitated, needing to say it all. "It was too painful a reminder that I was alone and, I believed, always would be."

"You will never be alone as long as I have breath. In fact, there may be times you crave a bit of solitude. That is why I arranged a special gift for you when we retire to our bedchamber."

"You did?"

Imps of mischief danced in her eyes. "I felt you would need sustenance after the chaos of tonight, so I had the cook make a special treat. A tray of pink iced cakes…"

He laughed again, gratitude welling up inside him, his blood heating at the memory of that night in Everdene Hall's kitchen, when he'd kissed the sweetness from her skin. Just the first taste of the life that could be…He felt his passion rise. "The day I dove into that lake was the luckiest day of my life, my Lady Grace."

And she was. *His*. Full of life, laughter and love. Full of surprises. He'd move heaven and earth to give her what she deserved.

A future, brighter than stars.

ABOUT THE AUTHOR

When Kimberly Cates was in third grade she informed her teacher that she didn't need to learn multiplication tables. She was going to be a writer when she grew up. Kimberly filled countless spiral notebooks with stories until, at age twenty-five, she received a birthday gift that changed her life: an electric typewriter. Kimberly wrote her first historical romance, sold it to Berkley Jove, and embarked on a thirty-year career as an author. Called "a master of the genre" by Romantic Times, her thirty-three bestselling, award-winning novels are noted for their endearing characters, emotional impact and their ability to transport the reader to the mists and magic of the British Isles.

Kimberly Cates

Kimberly has also penned historical romances as Kimberleigh Caitlin and contemporary romances under the pseudonyms Kimberly Cates and Kim Cates.

f X ⓟ

Fly Away Home

Historical Fiction:

The Queen's Dwarf by Ella March Chase

The Virgin Queen's Daughter by Ella March Chase

Three Maids for a Crown, a story of the Grey sisters by Ella March Chase

www.ingramcontent.com/pod-product-compliance
Lightning Source LLC
Chambersburg PA
CBHW021225060726

47590CB00005B/1641